SEVEN DAYS
IN JUNE

SEVEN DAYS IN JUNE

A Novel

TIA WILLIAMS

GRAND CENTRAL
PUBLISHING

NEW YORK   BOSTON

Copyright © 2021 by Tia Williams

Cover design by Sarah Congdon. Cover photograph by Victor Torres/Stocksy. Cover copyright © 2021 by Hachette Book Group, Inc.

Grand Central Publishing
Hachette Book Group
1290 Avenue of the Americas, New York, NY 10104
grandcentralpublishing.com
twitter.com/grandcentralpub

First Edition: June 2021

Grand Central Publishing is a division of Hachette Book Group, Inc. The Grand Central Publishing name and logo is a trademark of Hachette Book Group, Inc.

The publisher is not responsible for websites (or their content) that are not owned by the publisher.

The Hachette Speakers Bureau provides a wide range of authors for speaking events. To find out more, go to www.hachettespeakersbureau.com or call (866) 376-6591.

Library of Congress Cataloging-in-Publication Data

Names: Williams, Tia, 1975- author.
Title: Seven days in June : a novel / Tia Williams.
Description: First edition. | New York : Grand Central Publishing, 2021.
Identifiers: LCCN 2020054050 | ISBN 9781538719107 (hardcover) |
    ISBN 9781538719114 (ebook)
Classification: LCC PS3623.I566 S48 2021 | DDC 813/.6—dc23
LC record available at https://lccn.loc.gov/2020054050

ISBNs: 978-1-5387-1910-7 (hardcover), 978-1-5387-1911-4 (ebook)

Printed in the United States of America

LSC-C

Printing 1, 2021

For CC and FF, my loves.

SEVEN DAYS
IN JUNE

Prologue

IN THE YEAR OF OUR LORD 2019, THIRTY-TWO-YEAR-OLD EVA MERCY NEARLY choked to death on a piece of gum. She'd been attempting to masturbate when the gum lodged in her throat, cutting off her air supply. As she slowly blacked out, she kept imagining her daughter, Audre, finding her flailing about in Christmas jammies while clutching a tube of strawberry lube and a dildo called the Quarterback (which vibrated at a much higher frequency than advertised—*gum-choking* frequency). The obituary headline would be "Death by Dildo." Hell of a legacy to leave her orphaned twelve-year-old.

Eva didn't die, though. She eventually coughed up the gum. Shaken, she buried the Quarterback in a drawer full of hip-hop concert tees, slipped on her ancient cameo ring, and padded down the hall to wake up Audre for her BFF's Hamptons birthday party. She had no time to dwell on her brush with mortality.

While she'd admit to being a damn good mom and a capable novelist, Eva's true talent was her ability to push weird shit aside and get on with life. This time, she did it a little too well and missed the obvious.

When Eva Mercy was little, her mom had told her that Creole women see signs. This was back when Eva's only understanding of "Creole" was that it was vaguely connected to Louisiana and Black people with French last names. It wasn't until junior high that she realized her mom was—what's a fair word?—*eccentric* and curated "signs" to justify her whims. (*Mariah Carey released an album called* Charmbracelet? *Let's blow rent on cubic zirconia charms at Zales!*) Point is, Eva was wired to believe that the universe sent her messages.

So it should've occurred to her to expect a life-altering drama after Tridentgate. After all, she'd had a near-death experience before.

And that time—like this one—she woke up to her world forever changed.

SUNDAY

Chapter 1

BITE ME

"A TOAST TO OUR SEX GODDESS, EVA MERCY!" HOLLERED A CHERUB OF a woman, raising her champagne glass. Eva, whose throat was still raspy from yesterday's gum incident, coughed back a snort at "sex goddess."

The forty women crammed around long dining tables cheered loudly. They were bombed. The book club, composed of rowdy, upper-middle-class white women on the business end of their fifties, had traveled from Dayton, Ohio, all the way to Manhattan to celebrate Eva with a brunch. The occasion was the fifteenth anniversary of her bestselling (well, formerly bestselling) erotica series, *Cursed*.

Lacey, president of the chapter, adjusted her purple witch hat and turned to Eva, who was at the head of the table. "Today," she bellowed, "we celebrate the magical day we met our bronze-eyed vampire, Sebastian—and his true love, the badass unwicked witch, Gia!"

The tables erupted in squeals. Eva was relieved that Times Square's deliriously cheesy S&M-themed restaurant, A Place of Yes, had provided a private room. And oh, what a room. The ceiling was awash in red velvet, and a web of bondage ropes and riding crops decorated the walls. Goth candelabras dangled dangerously low over the black lacquered tables.

The Menu of Pain/Pleasure was *the* tourist attraction. Depending upon your selection, waitstaff in bondage gear would lightly flog you or do a lap dance or whatever. If you so desired.

Eva did not desire. But she was a good sport, and the Real Housewives of Dayton had traveled such a long way. These were her people— the rabid fandom who kept her afloat. Especially recently, as the vampire phenomenon (and her book sales) had cooled off.

So Eva chose "Cuffs + Cookies" off the menu. And now she was seated on a gothic throne, her hands cuffed behind the chair while a bored waitress in a pleather corset fed her snickerdoodles.

It was 2:45 p.m.

She should've been mortified. But she was no stranger to this scene. After all, Eva did write supermarket-checkout porn. While most authors had speaking engagements at bookstores, universities, and chic private homes, Eva's events were, well, raunchier. She'd done signings at sex shops, burlesque clubs, and tantric workshops. She'd even sold books at the 2008 Feminists in Adult Film (FAFFIES) after-party.

This was the gig. She smiled indulgently while her readers swooned over the two horny, dysfunctional permanently nineteen-year-old basket cases she'd invented when she herself was a horny, dysfunctional nineteen-year-old basket case.

Eva had never set out for her name to be synonymous with witches, vampires, and orgasms. As a double major in creative writing and advanced melancholia, Eva had accidentally stumbled upon this life. It was sophomore year, winter break. She had nowhere to go. So she holed up in her dorm room, pouring her teen angst and horror-fan day-dreams into a violent lustfest—which her roommate secretly submitted to *Jumpscare* magazine's New Fiction contest. She got first prize and a literary agent. Three months later, Eva was a college dropout with a six-figure multiple-book deal.

Ironic that she made a living writing about sexy sex. Eva couldn't remember the last time she got naked with anyone, undead or otherwise.

Between authoring, touring, single-mothering a tween tornado, and fighting through a chronic illness that ranged from manageable to utterly debilitating, she was too depleted to romance a real-life penis.

Which was fine. When Eva had an itch, she scratched it in her books. Like a boxer abstaining before the big match, she used her unconsummated lust to give Sebastian and Gia's story a wild edge. It was fiction ammunition.

But in the social-media era, nobody wanted to picture their favorite erotica author zonked on painkillers, drooling on her couch by 9:25 every night. So in public, Eva looked the part. She had her own tomboy-chic take on sexy. Today, it was a gray T-shirt minidress, Adidas, vintage gold hoops, and smudged black liner. With her signature sexy secretary glasses and collarbone-length curls, she could almost convince anyone she was a man-killer.

Eva was brilliant at faking things.

"...and bless you," continued Lacey, "for instilling our faith in passion, even though Gia and Sebastian are bound by an ancient curse to wake up on opposite sides of the world the moment after orgasm. You gave us a community. An OBSESH. Can't wait for *Cursed, Book Fifteen!*"

Amid applause, Eva smiled brightly and attempted to rise. Unfortunately, she forgot she was handcuffed to the chair, and she was abruptly yanked back down. Everyone gasped as Eva plummeted to the floor. Her dominatrix-waitress sprang to action two seconds too late, uncuffing her from the overturned chair.

"Whoa, too much merlot," giggled Eva, popping back up. It was a lie; she couldn't drink alcohol with her health issues. Two sips would land her in the ER.

Eva raised her glass of seltzer up at the sea of happily wasted boomers. Most of them, like Lacey, were wearing Gia's signature purple witch hat. A handful had a blingy *S* pendant pinned to their Chico's blouses. It was Sebastian's *S*, meant to emulate the vampire's scrawled signature ($29.99 at evamercymercyme.com).

Eva had the same *S* branded on her forearm. A regrettable decision made years ago on a blurry night by a blurry girl.

"I can't thank you enough," she gushed. "Really, your support keeps the *Cursed* world turning. I hope book fifteen lives up to your expectations."

If I ever write it. The manuscript was due in a week, and paralyzed with writer's block, she'd barely cobbled together five chapters.

Swiftly, she changed the subject. "So, does anyone read *Variety*?"

This was a *Redbook* and *Martha Stewart Living* crowd, so no.

"Exciting news broke yesterday." Eva sat down her glass and clasped her black-manicured fingers under her chin. "Our wish was granted. *Cursed* has been optioned for film rights!"

There were shrieks. Someone threw a witch hat in the air. A flushed blonde whipped out her iPhone and recorded Eva's speech so she could post it to *Cursed*'s Facebook fan page later. Along with several Tumblr and Twitter fan accounts, Facebook was a deeply important book-promo platform for Eva, where her readers shared fan art, gossiped, wrote obscene fan fiction, and debated casting decisions for the movie they'd fantasized about for years.

"I landed a producer"—*a Black female producer, thank you, Jesus*—"who really gets our world. Her last film was a steamy Sundance short about a real estate agent seducing a werewolf! We're interviewing directors now."

"Sebastian on film! Imagine?" swooned a faux redhead. "We just need a Black actor with bronze eyes. One who's a good biter."

"Eva, how do I ask my husband to bite me?" whined a Meryl Streep look-alike. This always happened, the sex talk.

"Arousal through biting is a thing, you know. It's called odaxelagnia," Eva divulged. "Just tell him you want it. Whisper it in his ear."

"*Odaxelagnia me*," slurred Meryl.

"Catchy," Eva said with a wink.

"I'm stoked to see big-screen Gia," said a husky-voiced brunette.

"She's such a fearless warrior. Sebastian's supposed to be the scary one, but she's killed armies of vampire hunters to protect him."

"Right? The force of teen-girl passion could power nations." With a twinkle in her eye, Eva launched into the mini-monologue she'd perfected ages ago. This part was still fun. "We're taught that men are all animal impulse and id. But girls get there first."

"And then society stomps it out," said the brunette.

"Word." Eva knew the pain was close. Before an episode, her mask slipped and the Black popped out.

"Look at history," Eva continued, rubbing a temple. "Roxanne Shanté out-rapping grown men at fourteen. Serena winning the US Open at seventeen. Mary Shelley writing *Frankenstein* at eighteen. Josephine Baker conquering Paris at nineteen. Zelda Fitzgerald's high school diary was so fire that her future husband stole *entire passages* to write *The Great Gatsby*. The eighteenth-century poet Phillis Wheatley published her first piece at fourteen, while enslaved. Joan of Arc. Greta Thunberg. Teen girls rearrange the fucking world."

An electrified hush fell over the group. But Eva was sinking. The pounding in her temples was sharpening by the millisecond. Sugar triggered her condition, and she'd been force-fed all those cookies. She knew better—but she'd been cuffed.

Absentmindedly, Eva snapped the rubber band she always wore around her right wrist. It was a pain distraction. An old trick.

"Remember when Kate Winslet escapes the *Titanic*?" asked the brunette. *"And then jumps back on* to be with Leo? That's teen-girl passion."

"I'd do that today to get to Leo," admitted Lacey, "and I'm forty-one." She was fifty-five.

"Just like Gia," gasped a petite woman with a clip-on bun. "In every book, she fights her way back to Sebastian—despite knowing that when they have sex, they're cursed to lose each other again."

"It's a metaphor," said Eva, her vision blurring. "No matter how perilous the journey, it's never over for true soul mates. Who *doesn't* want a connection that burns forever, despite distance, time, and curses?"

She didn't. The thought of perilous love made her nauseous.

"Confession," whispered a flushed blonde on her fourth glass of rosé. "My son plays Ohio State basketball, and I get so horny during games. To me, all those beautiful Black players are Sebastian."

Speechless, Eva gulped down her seltzer.

This'll be my legacy, she thought. *I have friends organizing protest rallies and writing Pulitzer Prize–winning* New Yorker *essays on race in America. My own daughter's so militant that she begged a cop to arrest her at the Middle School March on Midtown. But my contribution to these troubled times will be inciting white women of a certain age to sexually profile Black student athletes who'd really just like to make it to the NBA in peace.*

Then Eva's head was seized by a thunderous hammering. She clutched the edge of her seat with trembling fingers, bracing herself for each blow. The world went fuzzy. Features were melting off faces like Dalí's clocks; the competing perfumes in the room made her stomach lurch, and then the hammer slammed into her face harder and faster, aiming to maim, and she heard everything at a punishing decibel—the AC, clanging silverware, and merciful Christ, did someone open a candy wrapper in Connecticut?

They always escalated so fast, the ruthlessly violent migraines that had tortured her since childhood and baffled the most decorated specialists on the East Coast.

Eva's eyelids started to droop. In a well-practiced fake-out, she raised her brows to look alert, shooting a dazzling smile at her audience. Looking at those bawdy broads, she felt the low-grade envy she always felt in a group. They were normal. They could do things.

Regular-ass things. Like diving headfirst into a pool. Holding up their end of a conversation for more than twenty minutes. Burning scented candles. Getting tipsy. Surviving an F-train ride while a subway saxophonist blared "Ain't Nobody" for nine stops. Enjoying sex in ambitious positions. Laughing too heartily. Crying too mightily. Breathing too deeply. Walking too swiftly.

Living, period. She'd bet these women could do most of these things without shredding agony smiting them like punishment from an angry god. What was it like, the luxury of not hurting?

I'm an alien, Eva thought. She'd always felt as if she were impersonating a human, and she accepted it. But she'd never stop fantasizing about being unsick.

"Uhhh...excuse me for a sec," Eva managed. "J-just need to call my daughter."

Calmly clutching her tote, she swept through the red velvet door of the private room. Weaving through tables of suburban theatergoers gushing over *Hamilton*, she spotted the ladies' lounge behind the hostess area. She rushed in, burst into a handicapped stall with a sink, and vomited into the toilet.

For moments afterward, Eva stood there, breathing deeply through the pain, the way her team of neurologists, acupuncturists, and Eastern healers had taught her. Then she vomited again.

Swaying, she grasped the sink rim for balance. Her eyeliner was a mess now. This was why she wore it smudged. She never knew when an episode would strike—so if her makeup aesthetic was Rihanna-at-3:00-a.m., then she could pretend it was intentional.

Eva pulled her box of disposable painkiller injections out of her bag. Yanking up her dress, she exposed her scar-addled thigh, jabbed in a needle, and tossed it in the trash. For good measure, she grabbed an Altoids tin and chose a medical-marijuana gummy bear (prescribed by NYC's top pain specialist, thank you very much). She chomped off an ear. *Fuck it*, she thought and tossed the whole thing in her mouth. This would take the edge off until nighttime, so she could get through mommy-daughter after-school rituals and then crash.

Gingerly, Eva leaned back against the tiled wall. Her lids shuttered closed.

Sickness wasn't sexy. And her disability was invisible—she wasn't missing a limb or in a full-body cast. Her level of suffering seemed impossible for others to fathom. After all, everyone got headaches sometimes, like during coffee withdrawal or the flu. So she hid it. All people knew was that Eva canceled plans a lot ("Busy writing!"). And was prone to fainting, like at Denise and Todd's wedding ("Too much prosecco!"). Or forgot words midsentence ("Sorry, just distracted"). Or disappeared for weeks at a time ("Writing retreat!"—definitely not an in-patient stay in Mount Sinai's pain ward).

White lies were easier than the truth.

Case in point: what would the Orgasmic Ohioans think if they knew she wanted to strangle Sebastian and Gia? To banish them to wherever those *Twilight* fuckers went?

She loved her books at first. She wrote to tickle herself, the ideas sparking like wildfire. Then she wrote for her readers. Now she lifted entire plot points from the comments sections of *Cursed* fansites—the depth of author-cheating.

She just couldn't peddle "tortured romance" anymore. Years ago, she'd thought love wasn't real unless it drew blood. She, Sebastian, and Gia were all teens once, sharing the same twisted brain. Sebastian and Gia didn't grow up. But Eva did.

She wanted *Cursed* to die, but the series provided a stable, secure life for Audre. Eva had fought dragons to spare her baby from the childhood she'd had. And she'd won. She just wished she could find her spark again. The movie might help her rescue it.

Not only that, but deep down, Eva hoped it'd give her a fresh start. With her cut from the deal, she could finally afford to take a break from writing *Cursed* and work on her dream book, the one that'd been buzzing under her skin forever. She was so much more than her silly, raunchy romance (at least, she hoped she was). It was time for her to prove it to herself.

Feeling a bit better, Eva rinsed her mouth out with her travel-size mouthwash. Almost unconsciously, she raised her left middle finger, where she always wore her vintage cameo ring (she felt naked without it), to her nose and inhaled. It was an old habit—the barely there scent of some long-ago woman's perfume always soothed her.

Finally, in a quiet moment, she decided to check her phone.

Today, 12:45 PM
Queen Cece
MA'AM. Where are you? As your editor, I HOPE you're writing. As your best friend, I DEMAND you take a break. HUGE NEWS. Text back.

Today, 1:11 PM
Sidney the Producer
Been trying to get you for 3 hours! I think I found our director! Call me.

Today, 2:40 PM
My Baby
did u get me the feathers 4 my #feministicon art project I need it 4 grandma's portrait specifically her hair it was so fluffy thx mama enjoy ur cringey sex luncheon xo

Today, 3:04 PM
Jackie, the Weirdly Hypochondriac Sitter I Only Use 4 Emergencies
Audre's home from the Debate Team pizza lunch. But she brought 20 kids with her. I noted on my ChildCare.com profile that I don't do large groups. (Agoraphobia, germaphobia, claustrophobia).

"Jesus, Audre," she moaned.

Light-headed from her gummy-and-injection cocktail, she scheduled an Uber, offered her apologies to the Ohio Players, and was Brooklyn-bound in six minutes.

Chapter 2

SINGLE-MOM SUPERHERO

"Jackie! Where's Audre?"

Breathless, Eva stood in the doorway of her apartment. She took a cursory sweep of the bright, eclectic space. Her Indonesian (via HomeGoods) throw pillows and rugs were in their rightful place. Not a book was askew in the wall-to-wall library behind the purple armoire she'd bought when Prince died. Her Pinterest-inspired Park Slope home was exactly how she'd left it.

Park Slope was a hippie-dippie Brooklyn hood, thoroughly gentrified with wealthy liberal families. Most of the parents had kids when they were in their late thirties, after having conquered careers in new media, advertising, publishing, or in one celebrated case, *Frozen* songwriting. Mostly white, the hood *felt* diverse because of its sprinkling of same-sex parents and biracial kids (in predominantly Asian-Jewish, Black-Jewish, or Asian-Black combos).

Eva and Audre stood out because (a) Eva was a decade younger than the other moms; (b) she was single; and (c) Audre had a Black mom and a Black father, as opposed to her dad being Jewish or Vietnamese. Or a woman.

"Oh, hey." Jackie, the babysitter, was chilling on the couch with her feet propped on a boho ottoman.

"Jackie, I was *working*! I ran here from Times Square!"

"On foot?" Jackie, a divinity student at Columbia, was very literal.

Eva stared at her.

"Audre's in her room with the kids. On Snapchat."

Eva squeezed her eyes shut and fisted her hands. *"Audre Zora Toni Mercy-Moore!"*

She heard murmurs bubbling from Audre's bedroom, down the short hallway. Then a crash. Giggles. Finally, Audre cracked the door and slipped out, grinning guiltily.

At twelve, Audre was Eva's height, with her dimples, curls, and rich hazelnut complexion. But she took her style cues from Willow Smith and Yara Shahidi, hence the two space buns atop her head, tie-dye crop top, cutoffs, and Filas. With her mile-long lashes and gawky frame, she looked like Bambi at her first Coachella.

Audre galloped over to her mother, giving her a hearty hug.

"Mommy! Are those my jeans? You look so cuuute." Pronounced *kyuuu*, no *t*.

Eva disentangled herself from Audre's grasp. "Did I say you could bring the entire debate team home?"

"But... we're just..."

"You think I don't know what you're doing?" Eva lowered her voice. "Did you charge them?"

Audre sputtered.

"Did. You. Charge. Them."

"IT'S AN EXCHANGE OF GOODS, MOM! I provide counseling services and they pay me! Everyone at Cheshire Prep is addicted to my Snapchat therapy sessions. The one when I cured Delilah's fear of flying coach? I'm a legend."

"You're a child. When you're sleepy, you still pronounce 'breakfast' *breckfix*."

Audre groaned. "Look, when I'm a celebrity therapist making several mil a year, we'll giggle about this over bubble tea."

"I told you to stop this therapy business," hissed Eva. "I don't send you to that fancy private school to hustle white children out of their lunch money."

"Reparations," said Jackie from the couch.

Eva jumped, forgetting that the babysitter was still there. Sensing her dismissal, Jackie scurried out the door while Audre murdered her with her eyeballs.

She whipped her head around to her mother and said, "I'm too old for a babysitter! And Jackie is the *entire worst*, with her judgmental eyes and Crocs with socks."

"Audre," started Eva, rubbing a temple. "What do I always say?"

"Resist, persist, insist," she recited.

"What else?"

"I've never been sleepier than I am at this moment."

"WHAT ELSE?"

Audre sighed, defeated. "I trust you, you trust me."

"Right. When you break my rules, I can't trust you. You're grounded. No devices for two weeks."

Audre shrieked. The noise reverberated in Eva's head for thirty seconds.

"NO PHONE? What am I gonna do?"

"Who knows? Read *Goosebumps* and write poems to Usher, like I did at your age."

Eva stormed down the hall and entered Audre's room. Twenty girls were crammed on the bunk beds and floor, a blur of spring-break-tanned skin and crop tops.

"Hi, girls! You know you're always welcome here if Audre asks my permission. But she didn't, so...time to go." Eva beamed, careful not to disrupt her standing as "cool mom," which wasn't supposed to matter but did.

"We'll host a sleepover soon," promised Eva. "It'll be lit!"

"*Tell me you didn't just say 'lit,'*" wailed Audre from the living room.

One by one, the girls filed out of the bedroom. Audre stood slumped next to the front door, a droopy weeping willow of misery. She pulled a wad of cash out of her back pocket, and as the girls left, Audre handed each one her rightful twenty dollars. A few of the girls hugged her. It was like a funeral procession.

"Whoa!" Eva noticed a blond boy attempting to sneak out with the crowd. He rose to his full height—a full three heads taller than Eva.

"Who are you?"

"Omigod, Mom. That's Coco-Jean's stepbrother."

"You're Coco-Jean's stepbrother? Why are you so tall?"

"I'm sixteen."

"You're in high school?" Eva glared at Audre, who sprinted down the hall and flung herself on her bottom bunk.

"Yeah, but I'm chill. I'm in the honors program at Dalton."

"Oh, I'm bathed in relief. Why are you hanging out with twelve-year-olds?"

"Audre's, like, a really gifted mental health specialist. She's helping me manage the anxiety I feel due to my gluten allergy."

"Quick question. Did my daughter diagnose this gluten allergy?"

"He breaks out whenever he eats focaccia or crostini!" Audre yelled from her bedroom. "What would *you* call that?"

"Listen, you seem like a nice"—*gullible*—"kid, but you being here in my home without my knowledge is a hard no."

"I can't believe I missed my hip-hop violin lesson for this," he grumbled, storming out.

Eva leaned against the door for a moment, trying to decide how deeply she was going to freak out. In these moments, she wished she had the kind of mom she could call for advice.

She had an ex-husband, but she couldn't call him for advice, either. Troy Moore, a Pixar animator, had two settings: cheerful and really cheerful. Complicated emotions upset his worldview. It was why Eva had fallen for him. He'd been a ray of light, back when everything in Eva's world had been dark.

She had literally tripped over him in the lobby of Mount Sinai Hospital. Troy had been a volunteer, sketching portraits for patients. She'd realized she liked him when she scrambled to hide the IV bruises on her arms (as a result of her weeklong stay upstairs). After six weeks of rom-com-cute dates, they wed in city hall. Audre was born seven months later. But by then, they'd unraveled. The girl Troy had fallen for, the one who could sustain bubbly spontaneity on dates and lusty sleepovers, was different at home. Dazed from pain and pills. And soon her illness overwhelmed Troy's life—killing patience, choking love.

Troy belonged to the Church of Just Think Good Thoughts. Despite watching Eva suffer—the nights she'd repeatedly smash her forehead against the headboard in her sleep, or the time she fainted into a *2 Fast, 2 Furious* display at Blockbuster—he believed the real issue was her outlook. Couldn't she meditate it away? Send positive energy into the universe? (This always baffled Eva. The universe *where*? Could he provide cross streets? Would someone greet the positive energy when it landed, and would the greeter be Lena Horne's Glinda in *The Wiz* like she imagined?)

Once, after a late night at Pixar, Troy climbed into bed next to his fetal-positioned wife. She'd just given herself a Toradol injection in the thigh, and a little blood had leaked through her Band-Aid onto their dove-gray sheets. Moving was excruciating, so Eva just lay in it. Through slitted eyes, she saw revulsion, and just beneath it, martyrdom.

She was gross. Cute girls weren't supposed to be gross. Quietly, Troy snuck out and slept on the couch—and never returned to their bed. In their one couples'-counseling session, he admitted the truth.

"I wanted a wife," he wept. "Not a patient."

Troy was too polite to end it. So Eva liberated him. Audre was nineteen months old; she was twenty-two.

Troy went on to be blissfully happy with his second wife, a yogi named Athena Marigold. They used words like "paleo" and "artisanal" and lived in Santa Monica, where Audre spent her summers. Next Sunday, she was flying out to "Dadifornia" (the name Audre gave her West Coast trips), where Troy excelled as a carefree summertime dad.

But tricky stuff? An *almost man* sneaking into his baby's room? Not his territory.

Eva staggered to her couch. She'd never been able to think clearly with jeans on, so she wriggled out of them. Sitting there in Wonder Woman panties, she googled TWEEN DISCIPLINE TIPS on her phone. The top article suggested a "behavior contract." She had neither the legal prowess nor the energy to draw up a contract! Huffing, she tossed her phone aside and clicked on the Apple TV. When life got too challenging, she watched *Insecure*.

"Mommy?"

She looked up, and there was Audre, framed by a 120-year-old arched entryway. Her face was puffy and tear streaked. She'd added a black shawl and oversized Ray-Bans to her outfit.

Eva tried to look stern. Tough work without pants.

"Audre, what are you wearing?"

"This is my Upscale Sadness outfit."

"Nailed it," Eva admitted.

Audre cleared her throat. "Therapy is my calling. But I should've closed my practice when you told me to. I'm sorry for that and for having Coco-Jean's brother over. Though it's heterotypical of you to assume that just 'cause he's a boy we're being…weird."

Heterotypical. Brooklyn private schools produced ultra-progressive students. They protested abortion bans and marched for gun control. Last month, Audre's seventh-grade class carried buckets of water two miles across Prospect Park to empathize with the plight of sub-Saharan women.

The upside? A top-notch liberal education. The downside? Kids who struggled to divide decimals or name a state capital.

"Honey, can you give me a sec?" Eva sighed, shutting her eyes. "I just need to think."

Audre knew that "think" meant "rest her head," and she sulked back into her room. Watching her through one open eye, Eva felt a wistful pang. Audre had been the dreamiest, most delightful kid. Now she was an eye roll shaped like a human. Thirteen was coming, and who knew what horrors it'd bring? She'd sneak out, or learn to lie, or discover weed. Not Eva's, though, which was well hidden in her dildo drawer.

Just then, her phone buzzed. It was Cece Sinclair, Eva's best friend and Parker + Rowe Publishing's most celebrated book editor.

Eva answered with a tortured "Whaaaaat?"

"You're alive!"

"According to my Fitbit, I've been deceased for weeks."

"You're in there. I hear Issa Rae through the phone. I'm outside—I'll let myself in."

Cece swept through the door seconds later. She was overwhelming in every way—six feet tall, creamy cocoa skin, bleached-blond coils. A product of Spelman, Vineyard summers, and white-gloved cotillions with Talented Tenth debs, she dressed exclusively in vintage Halston and always appeared to have leapt off a 1978 *Vogue* cover. Or at least to be someone who knew Pat Cleveland.

She did, actually. Cece knew everyone. At forty-five, she'd long been one of the industry's most notorious editors, but her unofficial title was Social Queen of Black Literati. She collected authors, nurtured them, and whispered plot advice over cocktails—and her membership-only book/art/film-world parties were legendary. Eva had quickly discovered all of this after she'd won the short-story contest and Cece had become her editor.

During their introductory lunch on the Princeton campus, Cece took one look at the teen's "haunted doe eyes and chaotic coffee-shop-poetess curls" (a description she oft repeated), and her soul screamed, *Project!*

Before Eva knew it, she had a doting big sister. Cece helped her move to Brooklyn, quit her vices, and learn the art of curl maintenance—and introduced her to a social circle of happening young writers.

Cece was bossy as hell, but she'd earned it. There'd be no Eva without her.

Humming, the glamazon disappeared into the kitchen, emerging seconds later with a glass of pinot grigio and the ice pack Eva kept in the freezer. Sitting beside her, Cece slipped the frosty pack atop Eva's head with a flourish, as if it were a crown.

Cece was one of the few people who really knew about Eva's condition, and she helped out however she could.

"I'm here," she announced grandly, "to discuss the State of the Black Author panel."

"The Brooklyn Museum event you're moderating tomorrow night? Belinda's a panelist, right?" Celebrated poet Belinda Love was their close friend.

"Auntie Cece!" Audre appeared again, wearing her third costume change: a neon unicorn onesie.

"Audre-Bear! I've been meaning to text you for stress-management advice. My kitchen renovation is taking such a toll."

Audre plopped down on Cece's lap. "Try chocolate meditation. You stick a Hershey's Kiss in your mouth and sit quietly, letting it melt. No chewing. It's about mindfulness."

"I've no doubt, doll, but is there a sugar-free option?"

"Cece, focus," wailed Eva, smushing the ice pack against her temple. "The panel?"

"Oh. An author dropped out. She got salmonella from a food truck in British Columbia."

Audre frowned. "Colombia has a British section?"

Brooklyn schools strike again, thought Eva. *No concept of geography, but she's mastered mindfulness.*

"British Columbia's in Canada, babe," Eva said.

"Interesting. I could've looked it up if I had a phone." Sulkily, Audre rose and disappeared back into her room.

"Long story short," continued Cece, "I offered you as a replacement.

You're on the panel!" She shimmied her shoulders, pleased with her sorcery. "Every relevant media outlet is invited. It'll be livestreamed. This is *the* career boost you need."

The blood drained from Eva's face. "Me? No. I can't . . . I'm not qualified to pontificate on race in America. You *know* how intense it'll get. Every Black book event since the election has turned into a woke-off."

"You named your child after a noted civil rights warrior. Are you not woke?"

"I'm woke *recreationally*. Belinda and the other panelists are woke *professionally*. They have NAACP Awards and are on the talk-show circuit! Who was the panelist with food poisoning?"

Cece paused. "Zadie Smith."

With a defeated grimace, Eva slid the ice pack over her eyes. "Cece, this is a *New York Times*–sponsored panel at the Brooklyn Museum. I'm not a serious author. I'm a last-minute airport purchase."

Cece's brow furrowed. "Let's be absolutely real. You tried for ages to get a film deal. You've finally got a producer, and now quality directors aren't biting, because *Cursed* is too genre. Show Hollywood your power! This'll be PR gold. Well, this plus the 2019 Black Literary Excellence Award you'll win on Sunday."

"You think I'll win?"

"There's a vampire-witch-mermaid threesome scene in *Cursed Fourteen*," noted Cece. "You'll win for the audacity alone."

Eva groaned into a throw pillow. "I'm not up to this."

"You're nervous about sharing a stage with Belinda? The daughter of a *hairdresser*?"

Eva glared at her. "Beyoncé's the daughter of a hairdresser."

"Fine. Go explain to Audre why you're scared to try new things."

She threw up her hands. Of course Cece got her with the Audre stuff. Every time Eva made a move, she considered how it'd look to her daughter.

Eva's parenting wasn't mommy-blog approved. They often had pizza for dinner and fell asleep watching *Succession*, and since childcare was a luxury, Audre attended too many grown-up events. Plus, on bad head days, Eva allowed Audre unlimited TikTok time after homework so she could crash for a bit.

But Eva let herself off the hook for those things. When it came to mothering, what mattered to her was setting a powerful example. When Audre audited her memories, Eva wanted her to remember a ballsy woman who invented her life from scratch. No man, no help, no problem.

The Single-Mom Superhero myth, thought Eva, *and it's a trap.*

Eva dug the heels of her hands into her eye sockets. "What am I gonna wear?"

Cece grinned.

"I already have a Gucci number on hold for you. You're adorable, but you dress like you host a hip-hop podcast," she said with a sigh. "It'll be an adventure! Writers need stimulation. The thrill of your day can't be memorizing your positive Amazon reviews."

"I don't do that anymore," Eva grumbled.

"Speaking of stimulation, will you please revisit Tinder? When's the last time you met someone you didn't ghost after three dates?"

"I'm doing them a favor by ghosting." Eva pointed to her Wonder Woman panties. "Would you wanna fuck this?"

"There's a fetish for everything," said Cece generously.

Eva chuckled. "When I feel lonely, I scroll through Tinder and remind myself what I'm missing. Which is dudes with coconut-oiled beards all posing next to the same graffitied wall in Dumbo with profiles written entirely in emojis. And I remember that I'm not lonely. I'm *alone*. When I'm comatose from writing and mothering, when I'm hurting too badly to cook, talk, or smile, I curl up with 'alone' like a security blanket. Alone doesn't care that I don't shave my legs in the winter. Alone never gets disappointed by me." Eva sighed. "It's the best relationship I've ever been in."

"Are you speaking metaphorically," asked Cece, "or are you dating a man named Alone?"

"You can't be serious."

"My doorman is a SoundCloud rapper named Sincere. One never knows."

"I like being single," Eva continued quietly. "I don't want anyone to have to really see me."

They sat in silence, Eva idly snapping the rubber band on her wrist.

"I'm scared," she admitted finally.

"Good." Cece kissed her cheek. "I've seen what you come up with when you're scared."

Chapter 3

ROMANTIC COMEDY

2004

"Sweetie, you up?"

Lizette's Louisiana drawl was both syrupy and whisper light. No one's mom sounded like that.

"You awake? Genevieve? My Evie Sweetie? My Eva Diva? You up?"

Well, Genevieve, a.k.a. Eva Diva, was up now. The covers were pulled up to her eyebrows, and she was in the fetal position on the ancient, springy twin mattress. Exactly four days ago, when Genevieve Mercier and her mom drove from Cincinnati to Washington, DC, they'd dragged the mattress up the five-story walk-up and flung it on the patchy carpet of the bedroom floor. And there it had stayed. Genevieve and Lizette were both the same brand of scrawny and couldn't afford movers, so after struggling to carry Genevieve's mattress and her mom's mattress, plus a small kitchen table and two folding chairs, up all those stairs—in the blazing June heat, no less—the nomadic mother-daughter duo had decided they needed no more decor.

Genevieve opened one eye and scanned the itty-bitty space. She was seventeen, and this was a new bedroom, but it could've been any of the ones she'd occupied in any of the cities she'd lived in at fifteen, twelve, or eleven. It was nondescript, with disposable details, except for one thing that was unmistakably hers: a plaid suitcase erupting with clothes, pill bottles, and books. She squinted at the dollar-store alarm clock on the bare windowsill. It was 6:05 a.m. Right on time.

Lizette always came home just as Genevieve was waking up for school. Her mom was a purely nocturnal animal. It was like their personalities were too outsized to exist at the same time—so the mother claimed night, and the daughter got day.

Daytime was for responsible people, and Lizette was a delicate, distracted woman, too wispy to negotiate the details of grown-up living. Like cooking. Paying taxes. Cleaning. (One time, Genevieve watched her mom vacuum for an hour before realizing it wasn't plugged in.) Lizette's beauty kept them afloat, which was hard work, Genevieve knew—so she handled everything else. She forged Lizette's signature at banks. She monitored the pills in Lizette's Valium bottles. She toasted Lizette's Hot Pockets. She roller-set Lizette's hair before she went out on her "money dates" (*You're for sale—just fucking say it...*).

They'd moved several times since Genevieve was a toddler. Each time was for a different man who promised Lizette a dazzling life. They always set her up with a place to live, all expenses paid. And it used to be such an adventure. Genevieve had spent first grade living in a designer cottage in Laurel Canyon—rented for them by a famous pop producer who bought her a parrot named Alanis. The year before, an oil big shot had set them up in a Saint Moritz chalet, where their cook taught her how to ask for *Birchermüesli* in impeccable Swiss German. But as Lizette graduated from her "hot young thing" years, the dazzle dulled. Slowly, and then suddenly, the cities got seedier, the apartments got shabbier, and the men got meaner.

This latest guy wasn't paying for the apartment. But he did give Lizette a job as a hostess in his cocktail lounge, the Foxxx Trap. And he was paying her double time. For what, Genevieve didn't want to know.

Lizette crawled under the covers, still wearing her Bebe freakum dress, and snuggled up to her daughter. She gave Genevieve a lipsticked peck on the cheek and clasped her hand. With a resigned sigh, Genevieve sank into her mom's lushly perfumed embrace. Lizette always wore White Diamonds by Elizabeth Taylor, and Genevieve found the scent overwhelmingly glamorous but also soothing.

That was her mom in a nutshell. White Diamonds.

And Black drama.

"Assess your pain level, Spawn of My Loins," Lizette ordered in her outrageous southwestern-Louisiana accent.

Genevieve raised her head up from the pillow, giving it a little shake. She did this every morning to see how bad it was and determine how many painkillers she'd need to take to start the day. Luckily, she wasn't in agony. It was just a slow, steady pounding on a door. She could still breathe between thuds.

"I'll live," she reported.

"Good, then gimme a story."

"I'm sleeping!"

"You ain't. Come on, you know I can't sleep without a story."

"Can't we go back to when you used to do the stories?"

"I would, but you abolished my storytelling five years ago, you little shit," she cooed, her breath bourbon-scented.

Years before, Lizette would come home in the mornings and regale Genevieve with tales before she got up for elementary school. Their favorite ones involved long-ago scandals from Lizette's Louisiana hometown, Belle Fleur. And though Genevieve had never been there, she knew the place by heart.

Belle Fleur was a tiny bayou where there were only about eight last names, Black was the race, Creole was the culture, and everyone could trace their bloodline to the same eighteenth-century pair: a French plantation owner and an enslaved African woman. Along the way, their descendants mixed with Haitian Revolution rebels, Indigenous peoples, and Spaniards to produce a rich, insular, filé-flavored culture both highly religious and deeply superstitious. And colorful in the extreme.

The most colorful, though, were Lizette's mother and grandmother. Their reputations were as wild and dramatic as their names—Clotilde and Delphine. Their lives had been affected by murder and madness and mysterious rage. Explosive secrets and a conspicuous absence of fathers. It was as if Genevieve's entire matriarchal lineage had spontaneously regenerated from alien pods.

As a little girl, Genevieve assumed that these were tall tales, half-truths. But her grandma and great-grandma sounded fabulous, just the same.

Lizette wasn't sentimental. The only moment that mattered to her was the one she was in. But she did keep a thin, fraying scrapbook, which Genevieve had discovered in a cardboard moving box as a kid. On the last page, there were two four-by-six black-and-white photos with "Delphine" and "Clotilde" scrawled under them in Lizette's Catholic-school cursive. Genevieve stared and stared into their faces until her eyes unfocused, the photos blending into each other. It was like time hiccupped. And she knew Lizette's stories were real.

Delphine and Clotilde looked haunted, intense, wild. They looked like women who were born with the wrong mind at the wrong time. They looked like her mom. They looked like her.

And suddenly, the women didn't seem fabulous. They seemed dark, dangerous, and self-destructive. And it was too familiar.

There were corners of Genevieve's brain that terrified her. She was friendless and restless, and pain ruled everything. On her best days, she felt as if she were clinging to sanity by her fingernails. If her great-grandma, grandma, and mom were nuts (and yeah, her mom definitely was), then she was right on their heels.

Genevieve wanted to be normal. So she decided to tell the tales instead. Since it was usually too early in the morning to think of anything original, she'd just plug Lizette into movie plots.

"There was once," she started, "a down-on-her-luck cutie named Lizette. She wore thigh-high boots and a platinum bob wig and worked…um, on Hollywood Boulevard. In human resources. One night, she meets a dashing, wealthy businessman. He doesn't care that she can't eat lobster correctly..."

"*Pretty Woman*," sighed Lizette. "Richard Gere's Black—I feel it."

"You think everybody's Black until proven otherwise."

"I won't know peace till I see his genealogy report."

Lizette felt that since Belle Fleur was full of Black folks who looked white, numbers suggested that many whites could be Black. It was all a fine line in the South, she'd say. Given that those sinning, raping plantation owners had both white babies and Black babies, everyone was six degrees from being one or the other. Which was what scared southern white people the most.

Lizette let go of Genevieve's hand and launched into a catlike stretch. "I'm gonna have a *time* falling asleep. Honey, can you brew me up some Lipton's?"

Genevieve nodded robotically. It was 6:17, and she should've been asleep. But this was her job. She was in charge of daytime. So she disentangled herself from Lizette and shuffled down the short hallway to the kitchen.

The hallway was dark, but the kitchen light was on. This was odd. Lizette was maniacal about keeping lights out unless absolutely necessary. To keep the light bill reasonable, and also for mood lighting.

She froze, a creeping feeling rising in her chest.

Nooo. Not today, of all days.

She'd begged her mom not to invite her boyfriends over. And Lizette always assured her that she'd stop, that their home would be a no-man zone. But by the end of a long, liquor-soaked night, Lizette never remembered her promises. Or why she'd made them in the first place.

She smelled him before she saw him. Hennessy and Newports. There he was, a small round man who looked about sixty, slumped over their tiny Salvation Army kitchen table, snoring jaggedly. He was wearing a cheap suit—shiny at the elbows and knees—and a lush, curly black toupee that was as crooked as it was shameless.

Genevieve took a hesitant step into the kitchen, the linoleum floor crackling a bit. Bending down to his level, she snapped her fingers in front of his face. Nothing.

Good, she thought. Passed out, he was harmless.

Holding her breath, she tiptoed past him to the cabinet over the sink. As she reached in for the Lipton, she knocked over a box of Bisquick. It hit the counter with a dull thud, emitting a cloud of pancake powder.

"Genevieve," he slurred. His voice was higher pitched than it should've been. And two-packs-a-day raspy. "Wassup, Genevieve? 'S your name, right?"

"Yeah," she said, turning around to face him. "We met yesterday."

He smiled at her with discolored teeth. "I remember."

"I bet you do," she muttered. She leaned back against the counter, defensively folding her arms across her chest. Chuckling, he shimmied out of his suit jacket and then thrust it in Genevieve's direction.

"Hang this up somewhere, baby." It sounded like *Haydisumwheah bebeh.*

She eyed the jacket with extreme disgust. "We don't have hangers."

With a barking laugh, he shrugged and tossed the jacket on the floor. And then he leaned back in his chair and adjusted each pant leg with painstakingly slow precision. He leered at her while he did it, checking her out from the top of her poufy high ponytail to her socks.

Genevieve was wearing an oversized men's Hanes tee and sweats; he definitely wasn't catching any of her actual body. It didn't matter, though. His type just wanted to intimidate. Assert dominance.

She wanted to call out for her mom, who she knew was already asleep. But Lizette wouldn't have helped, anyway. The last time she'd told her mom about a run-in with one of her boyfriends, a shadow of...something...had passed behind Lizette's eyes, and then she'd dismissed it.

"Oh, girl, he's past the point of God's forgiveness," she'd said, all breezy with her movie-star smile. "You like to be clothed and fed?"

Genevieve had nodded, teary-eyed but almost numb.

"Well then. Be nice. Be good," she warned, still smiling. "Besides, you're too clever to be prey."

Unlike me was Lizette's implication. When it came to men, her mom was, indeed, not clever. Every time one of her terribly dysfunctional relationships imploded, she was confused and stunned. And then with fresh hope, she'd fling herself at another jackass. Hope was Lizette's greatest downfall. She was like a kid at one of those toy claw machines at Chuck E. Cheese. The claw never actually picks up a toy, no matter how strategically you aim—the game is obviously rigged. But you try every time, because the hope of it finally working, just this once, is such a thrill.

"You're pretty," the guy said, the whites of his eyes gone splotchy red. "Just like your mom. Lucky you."

"Yeah," she said dryly. "It's worked out so well for me."

Genevieve eyed this fool—his insane hairpiece, his wedding ring—and, not for the first time, wished she were a boy. If she were a boy, she'd knock him into his next life for the tone alone. And again for being married. And then again for letting her mom drink on the job because he knew that was the only way she'd agree to offer off-menu, high-priced services to VIP customers.

Be nice. Be good.

"But are you?" he asked.

"Am I what?"

He stroked the shiny fabric on his meaty thigh. "Are you just like your mom?"

"In...what way exactly?" Genevieve was buying time, trying to figure out how she'd defend herself if it came to it. "You mean, like, in terms of hobbies and interests? Astrological signs? Favorite Ying Yang Twin?"

He bark-laughed again and shook his finger at her. "You're a smart-ass."

He hoisted himself out of the foldout chair, ambled toward Genevieve, and stopped about a foot from where she was standing. Despite her thrumming sense of unease, she tried to look tough.

"How old are you?" he asked.

"Seventeen."

"You look younger," he said, moving a bit closer to her.

Jesus, he's one of those, thought Genevieve, her mind racing. He had one hundred pounds on her, but he was also drunk and sluggish—and she was fast. Desperately, her eyes darted around the tiny kitchen. There was nothing hard she could hit him with, like a pan or a teakettle. There was nothing but Honey Bunches of Oats, plastic forks, and Capri Suns.

My pocketknife's all the way in the bedroom.

She wanted to hurt him before he hurt her. But then there was that old hesitation. Her mom needed this guy. He'd found them this shitty apartment. He'd given her mom a job. He was supporting them. She and her mom were a team.

Be nice. Be good.

"How old are you?" she asked, stalling even more.

"Fifty-eight." He leaned a bit closer, unsteady on his feet. His after-hours club stench was pungent. "But I got stamina."

Grinning, he slapped his clammy palm down on her forearm. And then the Lizette-wired part of her brain clicked off. She went completely still. Eyes narrowed. Senses sharpened.

"Wanna hear a joke?" she asked abruptly, with a sweet smile.

"A joke?" He was caught off guard. "Oh. Okay, I like jokes."

"What did Satan say when he lost his hair?"

"I don't know. What?"

She chuckled a bit to herself. "How bad do you wanna know?"

"Stop playing. Tell me!"

She glanced up at the rug atop his head. "There'll be hell toupee."

His mouth dropped open grotesquely. "W-what? Oh, you little *cunt*."

He lunged at her. Genevieve dodged to her left, eluding his grasp. Knocked off-balance, he toppled drunkenly and then crashed to the floor, a cumbersome, slow-moving vat of lard. Momentarily paralyzed with shock, she just stood there, breathing heavily—and then he grabbed her ankle and yanked her to the ground. She fell down hard. Her head exploded into a thousand shards of razor-sharp glass.

"*Fuck! You!*" she wailed, clutching her face. And then, purely out of pain reflex, she reared back and power-kicked him in the ribs.

While he roared, she scrambled out of the kitchen on her hands and knees and then sprinted into the bathroom. She slammed the door, locking it with badly shaking hands. Grasping her face with one hand, her head thundering, she grabbed a bottle of Percocet from the sink drawer, climbed into the tub, and snatched the shower curtain shut. And only then did she breathe.

Through the cheap hollow-core bathroom door, Genevieve heard the guy screaming Lizette's name. And then there was the gossamer pitter-pat of Lizette's feet as she ran down the hall to the kitchen, hollering bewildered nonsense.

From experience, Genevieve knew to wait this out in the bathroom. She popped two pills into her mouth and chewed them dry. (They were prescribed by her Cincinnati doctor—who, like the countless frustrated docs before him, solved her unsolvable problem with opioids.) As Lizette and her man starred in their own chitlin circuit revival in the kitchen, she curled up on her side, waiting for relief.

Lizette had stopped the hysterics. Now she was cooing. Then Genevieve heard footsteps heading toward the master bedroom—Lizette's Tinker Bell toes barely touching the ground, his steps heavy, labored. Genevieve knew this was her mom's way of protecting her: luring him away and locking the door. Of course, it never occurred to Lizette to kick him out. Break up with him. Call the police. Be single for a minute, for that matter. Get her own job. Finance her own life. Save the day herself instead of depending on horrible men to do it for her.

Are you just like your mom?

Genevieve curled up tighter on her side, trying to make herself smaller. She was exhausted. All she wanted was to escape this repetitive, redundant hell.

Her eyes shut. She had only a few more minutes to pull herself together. She had to get ready.

Today was her first day at her new school.

MONDAY

Chapter 4

MANTRA

"You gotta let me talk to Ty, Principal Scott."

The beleaguered woman leaned forward on her paper-strewn desk. "Mr. Hall, last time you 'talked' to Ty, I found him sitting in a fifth-floor window with his feet dangling down the side of the building."

"His writing was flat. He needed a perspective change."

"He's thirteen. You encouraged a child to engage in potentially fatal behavior."

"Ty spent last year in a maximum-security juvenile detention center. You think that window was the most colorful moment of his life?" He smiled pleasantly, belying the panic he really felt.

Shane Hall wasn't where he was supposed to be. According to the itinerary issued by his publisher's publicity department, he was due at the airport five minutes ago. But Ty was his favorite student. And healthy, functional people didn't leave town without saying goodbye.

At thirty-two, Shane was new to being healthy and functional. When he woke up twenty-six months and fourteen days ago, clean for the first time since he was under five feet tall, he realized that he finally knew how to stay sober. But he wasn't sure how to be a responsible adult. The program encouraged therapy, but *fuck no*. He was a writer—why would he give his shit away for free? Instead, he ran five miles a day. Drank

37

his weight in water. Added chia seeds in things. Avoided red meat. And sugar. And hookers.

Patiently, he waited for the day it'd all make him feel normal.

The only thing Shane could ever do well was write, but he'd only ever done it drunk. He'd become a critic's darling while drunk. He'd gotten rich while drunk. He'd churned out four "hypnotic, ecstatic elegies to shattered youth"—according to the *New York Times*—while drunk. He'd won the National Book Award while drunk. He'd never composed even one sentence sober, and frankly, he was scared to try. So the writing was on hold for now. He began doing what every nonpracticing writer does—he taught. Because his name opened doors (and attracted donors) at high-paying private schools, he became in demand on the "visiting-author fellowship" circuit.

Shane taught creative writing to elite little shits in Dallas, Portland, Hartford, Richmond, San Francisco—and now Providence, Rhode Island. He was usually hired for a semester only. Just enough time to shake them up, poke holes in their privileged worldviews before they slid back into complacency. Fine, but these weren't the real reasons he booked teaching tours.

Whenever Shane landed in a new city, he asked his Uber driver where the worst neighborhood was. He'd go and find the most underserved school in the area—the kind of school that made seven-year-olds line up in the cold at 7:15 a.m. for a security check that took almost an hour to pass through, making them late to class, only to then expel them for tardiness. The kind of school that turned a blind eye to school security officers who maced kids for "obscene language." The kind of school that allowed traumatized, abused, underfed, uncared-for, often homeless children to be carted off to kiddie prisons for made-up infractions.

They'd receive their *real* education at juvie. And by eighteen, they'd realize that the thing they were most qualified to be was an inmate.

Shane would find a school like this in each city and then practically throw himself at the principal, offering after-school tutoring, mentoring, anything. Shane had a restless urge to help these kids. Actually, he wasn't sure who was helping whom more.

Shane stood on the other side of Principal Scott's desk, taking in the dank closet-sized office. And for some reason, his eyes lingered on a yellowing poster plastered to the puke-green painted wall:

Forbidden Items: Electronics, Sunglasses, Clothing In Gang Colors.

"Gang colors" was written in red ink, presumably to target any Bloods with big ideas—the cluelessness of which embarrassed Shane. Was that Principal Scott's idea? He was sure that twenty years ago, she'd taken the gig thinking she could save the youth, like Morgan Freeman in *Lean on Me*. But today, she was extremely over it—and sporting a violet bruise on her cheekbone where a student had hurled a pencil sharpener at her. Shane had seen it happen.

"Mr. Hall," she said wearily. "Would you have pulled the window stunt with one of your private-school students?"

"No, 'cause I don't give a fuck about them." He froze, realizing what he'd said. Christ, he had to be better about blurting out whatever he was thinking. "I mean...I care. I'm just not as invested. Those kids are legacy at Ivy schools; they're good. They're using me for recommendation letters and selfies."

"You take selfies with your students?"

Was that unethical? Shane didn't understand social media; he honestly didn't know. In terms of civilized behavior, he had so many blind spots. Shane wasn't far removed from the man he'd been when he passed out on Gayle King's shoulder as Jesse Williams announced that he'd won the 2009 NAACP Award for Outstanding Fiction.

His fans thought he was mysterious—living off the grid, no signings or readings or appearances, because he was a no-fucks-given bad boy. But really, Shane was just a mess. He just didn't want to be a mess with an audience. So as soon as he could afford to be a nomad, fucking up his life privately from hidden corners of the globe, he did exactly that.

In Tobago, he shared his beach shack with a roommate who wasn't shocked by his sketchy table manners or infant-esque sleep patterns, because his roommate was a turtle. Shane enjoyed sharing his most demented confessions with that bartender in Cartagena, because she spoke four languages and none of them were English.

While Shane Hall had had tremendous success thanks to his writing, the writing happened to come from a person who was never supposed to be famous.

Which, in the highly conventional literary world, had only made him more so.

Glancing at his watch, he realized he was dangerously close to missing his flight. Assessing his options, Shane furrowed his brow. And then scratched at his biceps, just under his short-sleeve tee. He tugged at his bottom lip a little, distracted. Nervous tics, all. But Shane felt a faint energy shift in the room. Principal Scott's gaze had gone from weary to...watchful.

Shane was a fidgety person (a new thing he realized, now that he *felt* everything). But calling attention to his mouth, his arm, his anything wasn't fair. He knew that he pulled a strong reaction from women. He'd first realized this when he wasn't much older than Ty. Back then, Shane hadn't really known why he elicited this response, and he hadn't cared. He'd just been grateful to have a card to pull, something to use when he was desperate, hungry, and alone.

You think I look like an angel? Good, maybe you'll leave me here with the register while you get my favorite soda in the back. You think I'm a thug? Good, maybe you'll hire me to rob your ex's crib. You think I'm fuckable? Good, maybe you'll give me a place to stay for a month.

Shane neutralized himself. Healthy, functional people didn't take shortcuts.

"I'll buy your lunch for a month," he blurted out.

"Excuse me?"

So much for no shortcuts.

"You got Venmo? I don't carry cash—I have poor impulse control."

Half-heartedly chuckling, she said, "Go 'head. He's in detent..."

Shane was halfway down the hall before she could finish the word.

Shane found Ty slumped over a desk in an empty classroom. Trance-like, he was doodling on the cover of his composition notebook. He'd scribbled on it so much that he could no longer see the designs. But if he ran his fingers over it, he could feel the grooves from the ball-point pen. Shane had been watching him do this for weeks. It must comfort him, somehow.

Ty was enormous for his age—about three hundred pounds—and at six foot four, he was two inches taller than Shane. The boy had a morose self-consciousness that quickly turned to rage if he felt embarrassed or threatened. But he trusted Shane. Shane didn't roast him for wearing the same massive sweatpants and hoodie every day. And Shane knew that he lived with his aunt in a Portuguese-gang-run trap house (and that his mom and sister were last seen soliciting, together, in Hartford Park), but never mentioned it. Shane talked to Ty like they were the same.

Shane stood across from him, leaning against the teacher's desk, and told Ty he had to leave Providence.

Ty didn't look up. "Where you going."

"To Brooklyn. The Littie Awards are there, this Sunday," he explained. "I'm a presenter. Which is weird, 'cause I don't go to awards shows."

"Why."

"Ever heard of Gayle King?"

"Who?"

"Never mind," mumbled Shane. "I don't go 'cause they're meaning-less. In 2013 the National Book Critics Circle gave Best Fiction to Chimamanda Ngozi Adichie instead of me. Do I think she's a superior writer? Nah. But it's all subjective."

The corner of Ty's mouth curved. "You mad."

"Hell yes, I'm mad," said Shane. "'Cause I care. It took fortunes made and lost, one tarot-card reader, and too much AA for me to be evolved enough to say those words. *I care about things.*"

Ty knew he was being led somewhere. "You say that to say what."

"Ty, why do all your questions sound like statements?"

"The fuck that means."

"Look, I'm admitting that I care about awards. What do you care about?"

"Nothing. I ain't *soft*, nigga."

"Ain't no niggas in here."

Ty was confused. "You Dominican?"

"What? No. And Dominicans are niggas. Google 'African diaspora' and learn something. Jesus." Shane shook his head. Time was ticking. "Listen, caring about things don't make you soft. It makes you alive."

Ty shrugged.

Shane eyed Ty for a moment, his expression serious. Ty looked back, challenging him.

"Tyree."

"Yeah."

"You need to listen to me."

"Yeah."

"This school is not designed for you to excel. It's raising you up for prison. Your every move is criminalized, by design. In most schools, kids don't get expelled for saying 'fuck' or get tased for tardiness or incarcerated for missing one detention. In most schools, eighth-grade boys aren't terrorized this way. They're allowed to be kids, nothing on their minds but pussy and Roblox."

Ty's eyes focused on his notebook. He was painfully aware that Shane was referring to him. He'd been sent to juvie for missing a detention.

"You're mad about it? You wanna fight? You're not wrong. They'll tell you you're an animal, but you're not. *You're a sane person reacting to an insane situation.* And I know, 'cause I been you. It took me getting locked up three times by twelfth grade to learn the lesson that you're gonna learn today."

Shane paused, realizing he was talking so fast, his words were running into each other. "I fought, too. Just like you."

Well, not exactly. Like Ty, "violent and unpredictable" had been stamped in Shane's student file since grade school. Unlike Ty, Shane's violence wasn't about rage. He didn't even fight to win. It was about hurting himself, soothing his self-destructive streak—to tear his skin, shatter his bones, gag blood. And that was what kept him shuttling from foster homes to group homes to finally nothing, because no one wanted to adopt a hollow-eyed, passed-over preteen Black boy with disturbing compulsions and an unsettling...beauty...that was weird on a kid so tragic.

"No one's coming to save you. You have to do it." Shane lowered his voice, wanting Ty to work hard to hear this. "*Do not* react to the school security officers. *Do not* fight. Stay low, work hard, graduate, and get the full entire fuck out of this city. And don't come back until you're in a position to help a kid like you. You understand me?"

Silence.

"Ty." Shane stepped forward, smashing his fist down on Ty's desk. The boy jumped. "You understand me?"

Ty nodded, shell-shocked. Shane was like his fun faux uncle. He'd never seen him be so serious. Hesitantly, he said, "I get so heated. I can't stay low."

"Yeah, you can." Shane's shoulders relaxed a bit. "Have faith."

"Oh. Church."

"I mean, if that works for you. But I meant faith in yourself. What do you like?"

Ty shrugged broadly. "I guess...planets."

"Why?"

"I like...that there's more out there. I don't know. I like thinking about other worlds." He was at a loss to describe something he'd never even thought about. "I...I used to draw the planets when I was a li'l nigga. Stupid shit."

"Nice." Shane pulled a Trident pack out of his pocket and popped two pieces into his mouth. Then he tossed one to Ty, who caught it with one hand. "There's eight planets, right? I don't remember all their names. Do you?"

"Mercury, Venus, Earth, Mars, Jupiter, Saturn, Uranus, Neptune."

Shane folded his arms across his chest. "When you wanna fight, recite them in your head. It's called a mantra. A mantra's like a magic spell for your brain, telling it to chill."

"That's dumb."

"Is it? You like *Game of Thrones*, right?"

"No."

"You taught yourself Dothraki. I've seen the inside of that notebook."

Ty shrugged again, his chin disappearing into his neck.

"What does Arya do? When she's in danger? She recites the names of people she wants to exact revenge upon. It's her mantra, and it keeps her alive. The planets will be your mantra."

Ty could barely hide his delight and mortification at being compared to Arya Stark, and his head sank farther into his neck, rolls of skin puddling up beneath his cheeks.

"You got a mantra?" Ty actually delivered this question as a question.

"Yeah."

"What is it?"

"Mine," said Shane simply. He did have one. It was a gift from a girl when he was a boy. And back when he really needed it to, it had worked.

He checked his watch. It was time to go to New York.

"You need activities," said Shane. "Your science teacher told me you like astronomy. So I set you up with an internship at the Providence Planetarium. Also, every Friday at three thirty, you'll be a science tutor for struggling students. And don't forget, *Mercury, Venus, Earth, Mars, Jupiter, Saturn, Uranus, Neptune.*"

"Wait. You already knew I liked planets?"

Shane grinned and gave Ty a hearty pound.

"And you said you couldn't name them all, but you just did!"

"Of course I know the planets," said Shane, patting his jeans pockets, making sure he had his wallet. "I tricked you."

Ty's mouth opened.

"It's your mantra, not mine. *You* had to say it out loud to give it power."

"I'm clueless," whispered Ty, in awe.

Shane chuckled a little. He'd miss Ty so much. He wanted to hug him, but his file said that he didn't like being touched. Shane understood; neither did he.

He was headed for the door, when Ty's voice stopped him.

"Do you...Maybe you need help? In New York?"

Shane turned to face him. "Help?"

"Can I go with you?" Ty's voice was a shy mumble. "I could be your assistant."

Shane's shoulders slumped a little. "If you need me, I'll come back. Anytime. For any reason. I promise."

Ty blinked several times and slumped down in his chair.

"You won't even have time to miss me, dog. I'll text you relentlessly."

The boy nodded.

"I gotta go. Be good. Just...be good," said Shane, and then he all but sprinted out the door. He'd run out of words to say. And he was late. And there was a lump in his throat and a tingle behind his eyes. He wasn't going to cry, though. He hadn't since he was seventeen.

Shane slid into the driver's seat of the rented Audi, blasted the AC, and sped down Route 1 toward Green Airport. He loved that kid too much. He didn't know how to mentor without loving. Maybe doing this wasn't healthy.

He knew Ty probably wouldn't make it to his planetarium internship.

He might not make it, period. Shane couldn't control that, but he would stay in touch. He always did. He had a Ty or a Diamond or a Marisol or a Rashaad in every city. He'd keep them all alive by sheer force of will.

The new Shane didn't love and then vanish.

That was what he'd done to her. Which was the real reason he was going to New York.

Shane didn't want—or deserve—anything from her. And he hated the idea of disrupting her life or dredging up the past. But he had to explain what he couldn't before. Then he'd go.

To his credit, he knew this was a terrible idea. To his discredit, he was doing it anyway.

He had to. Shane couldn't pretend to embrace his new life when he was still on the run from his old one.

She was a fire he'd started ages ago—and for too long, he'd just let it smolder. It was time to put it out.

Chapter 5

FUN BLACK SHIT

THE STATE OF THE BLACK AUTHOR EVENT WAS A *SCENE*. THE PANEL WAS BEING held at the Brooklyn Museum's spacious Cantor Auditorium, and it was staged perfectly. To find the space, you had to wind your way through a warren of rooms showcasing the hottest exhibit in town, *Nobody Promised You Tomorrow: Art 50 Years After Stonewall*. Every clued-in hipster was pretending to have seen it. By the time the crowd had taken in all the gorgeously curated protest art, everyone had entered the auditorium, hyped for a fiery conversation.

The space was stark, industrial modern, with two hundred or so seats and a massive window looking out onto the Caribbean-flavored Eastern Parkway. The crowd was ablaze with color. It was the first hot week of the year, and the sundresses, statement lipstick, and natural dos were in full bloom. Milling about were a mixed bag of high and low literati: Old Guard writers (whose heyday was circa the '70s and '80s); millennial essayists, novelists, and culture journalists; a handful of deeply feared, bespectacled book bloggers; and coeds from Columbia and NYU—whose slogan tees and fashion Birkenstocks screamed "feminist-studies major." Weaving throughout were digital reporters and their photographers, scanning HELLO MY NAME IS tags to see who was interview-worthy.

Eva was nursing a seltzer with a sprig of basil. She was also concentrating on looking like a person who wasn't staving off a panic attack. Though she'd killed some time chitchatting with the few publishing vets she knew, she'd quickly realized that to the majority of the crowd, Eva Mercy was unknown—or, at best, recognized as a "name" in a genre that inspires a very silly fan base. And in a few minutes, she'd have to talk knowledgeably about serious things in front of them.

Chill, woman, she told herself, twirling her vintage cameo ring around her finger. It was her lucky talisman, and she was counting on it to pull her through tonight. The ring always calmed her. It was stained, nicked, and possibly a century old. Eva had no idea what Victorian-era woman it had originally belonged to, but decades before, she'd discovered it in her mom's jewelry box. No doubt it had been gifted to her by some guy. But Lizette hated vintage jewelry— she demanded brand-new diamonds, honey—so she never wore it. Eva cherished old things, though. One day, when she was lonely and pimply and thirteen, Eva stole it from her bedroom. Lizette never noticed. Her mom never noticed anything.

"Sis!"

Hearing the familiar voice, Eva spun around with a relieved smile. It was Belinda Love, the Pulitzer Prize–winning poetess who was one of Eva's co-panelists. In Belinda's poetry collections, she hopped into the brains of Black historical figures and wrote lyrical poetry about modern life from their specific points of view. Her Langston Hughes piece, "Everything Ain't a Hashtag," was iconic.

She'd fallen in instant love with Belinda years ago, when they were seated together at one of Cece's exclusive parties. Raised by humble hairdresser parents in Silver Spring, Maryland, Belinda had attended Sidwell Friends School on scholarship during the Chelsea Clinton years and had been a dialect consultant for ten years' worth of films featuring enslaved or Jim Crow–era Black people (suffice it to say, she was rarely out of work). As prestigious as her résumé was, her vibe was a charming, accessible blend of earth mama and around-the-way girl. She enjoyed Reiki healing and shamanic readings—but also raunchy memes and seducing young men who worked in the service industry. She'd just broken up with a Chilean stunner she'd met while he was passing out flyers in front of a MetroPCS store.

"Heyyy, Belinda." Eva hugged her gently so as not to disturb her cluster of street-fair necklaces. Belinda's signature box braids spilled out of her tribal-print headwrap, falling to her peach-shaped ass. She looked like a sexy doula.

"Come on, dress! Come on, body!"

"Honestly, I can't move," Eva whispered. She was wearing a black sleeveless Gucci sheath dress with major plunge and scarlet stiletto booties. Her boobs were hiked up to her chin, and her hair was blown out poker-straight.

"You. Did. Not. Come. To. Play. This. Monday. Evening." Belinda executed a body roll between each word.

Eva fidgeted with her hem. "I feel like the office vixen on a network drama about sultry lawyers."

"Worked for Meghan Markle. Come on, let's mingle."

Belinda linked arms with Eva, and they strolled through the crowd, chatting.

"Girl," started Eva, "I have someone I wanna set you up with. He's *cute* cute. Check his IG, @oralpro."

Belinda's mouth dropped open. "What kind of blessing...?"

"Relax, he's an orthodontist. He did beautiful work on Audre."

"Pass. I'm already checking for the hot produce guy at my Trader Joe's. I was there earlier, shopping for my vegan-bakery course. It's taught by the woman who pioneered vaginal-yeast brioche."

"Vaginal-yeast brioche," repeated Eva.

"She's famous for it."

"There's more than zero people famous for making vaginal-yeast brioche?"

"Anyway, stop trying to set me up. You just want to mine my sex life for book inspo. Why don't *you* date @oralpro? Get out there! Stop wasting your good legs and youthful complexion."

"Know why I have nice skin?" Eva winked. "No man stressing me out."

Just then Cece appeared out of nowhere, popping her head between them. "Ask her about *Alone*," she announced. Then she grabbed Eva's watered-down seltzer, replaced it with a fresh one, and disappeared back into the crowd.

Belinda gasped. "How does she just *materialize* like that? And what's she talking about?"

Before Eva could answer, a young girl rocking a dyed-blond 'fro and a tube top launched herself into Belinda's arms.

"Your poetry is the only thing getting me through my NYU finals! Sign my book?" She thrust a tattered copy at Belinda.

"Of course!" She signed the title page and gestured at Eva with her elbow. "This is Eva Mercy. You must've heard of *Cursed*?"

"My stepmom reads that series," she said before quickly snapping a selfie with Belinda. "But I avoid texts depicting explicit cisheteropatriarchal sex. Sorry."

The girl threw up a Black Power fist and bounced. In seconds, Cece materialized again, glaring at her.

"Who let that bleached peasant in here?" Cece was the queen of policing women who had her hairdo. Which was half of Brooklyn. "Is she wearing Walmart denim?"

"Have you ever been in a Walmart?" asked Eva.

"Physically, yes. Spiritually, no." She spun on her heel. "To the stage! It's showtime."

Belinda grabbed Eva's hand, and they trailed Cece through the crowd, like ducklings.

The stage was intimate: a row of four club chairs for Cece, Eva, Belinda, and Khalil. Khalil didn't appear until after Cece's introduction, due to a misunderstanding with his Uber driver. The misunderstanding was that he stole someone else's Uber and the driver kicked him out.

He was a thirty-seven-year-old cultural studies PhD who favored pastel Ralph Lauren chinos and bow ties. He was famous for writing tomes on systemic racism—and he lived with a sixty-something Swedish heiress, who financed the Ralph Lauren pants and ties.

The summer of Eva's divorce, when Khalil was a *Vibe* columnist, he unsuccessfully pursued her over the course of several Clinton Hill rooftop cookouts. The word "mansplainer" hadn't been invented yet but would've been useful.

The packed house was fully engaged in the lively discussion of the panelists—nodding, giggling, and recording IG Lives on their phones. Eva was sitting up pin straight, stilettoed feet crossed at a ladylike angle.

And she was killing it.

Yes, the first couple of times she spoke, a few people eyed her with a *who is this again?* expression, but slowly she won them over. So much so that she was wondering what she'd been worried about.

As she, Belinda, and Khalil answered Cece's leading discussion questions, their roles became clear: Belinda was the Tell-It-Like-It-Is Sistafriend, Khalil was the Smug Blowhard, and Eva was Hopelessly Drunk on Unexpected Success.

"And here's what's really good," continued Belinda. "The publishing industry has a hard time processing Black characters unless we're suffering."

Nods and murmurs from the audience.

"We're expected to write about trauma, oppression, or slavery, because those are easily marketable Black tropes. Publishers struggle to see us as having the same banal, funny, whimsical experiences that every human has—"

"Because it'd imply that we *are* human," interrupted Khalil. "AMERICAN SOCIETY DEPENDS ON THE NEED TO DEHUMANIZE, DEGRADE, AND DENY THE BLACK MAN."

Belinda ignored him. "My first novel was about an architect and a chef who witness a murder on a side street during the '03 blackout—and have hot sex while solving the mystery. It was rejected everywhere. I kept hearing, 'Cute story, but can we hear more about their struggles as Blacks in mostly white professions?'" Belinda sighed. "Like, damn, there's no room for fun Black shit? Why can't I make millions off *Girl on the Train* or *Fifty Shades*?"

"*Fifty Shades* was okay," sniffed Cece. "I do wish Ana would've shaved her legs. But yes. White authors have the freedom to tell a good story for the sake of a good story."

"Imagine if one of us tried to get *Girl on the Train* published," said Eva. "*For Colored Girls on the Train When Suicide Isn't Enough.*"

The crowd erupted in laughter, and Eva beamed like she'd just arrived at the gates of heaven. Sunshine burst from her ears, and her pupils turned into emoji hearts.

"Growing up, I was obsessed with horror and fantasy," she said. "But Black characters were invisible in those stories. Why couldn't I go to Narnia or Hogwarts? When I wrote about a Black witch and vampire, the industry was shocked. Like, can paranormal creatures even *be* nonwhite? Despite there being a rich Black vampire tradition—I mean, hello, *Blade*, *Blacula*, Louisiana *fifollet* folklore. And don't get me started on Black witches like Bonnie in *Vampire Diaries* or Naomie Harris in *Pirates of the Caribbean*..." She paused, realizing she was geeking out and losing her audience.

"Anyway, only a handful of us succeed in this genre, because it can be a stretch to envision a world, even a fantasy one, where all the power players are brown. Comics are the same way. Anybody here been to Comic-Con?"

Only one person, way in the back, raised their hand. She squinted through her glasses to spot the person's face and saw a forty-something man wearing twinkly eye shadow and Gia's purple witch hat. A *Cursed* fan. Aside from wine moms, queer male Gen Xers were her most vocal readers—and were loyally devoted to *Cursed*'s social-media fan accounts. Which flattered Eva to death.

But the witch hat? Here? When she was trying to look like a Serious Author?

"I rebuke comic culture," spat Khalil. "Even *Blank Panther*. The real hero is Erik Killmonger. But of course, Hollywood STRATEGICALLY EMASCULATES THE DIVINE ASIATIC BLACK MAN TO APPEASE EUROCENTRIC AUDIENCES."

"Do you get your material from a hotep word generator?" Belinda asked him, off mic.

"Fuck immediately off, Belinda," he hissed, and then continued. "Look, I feel like I'm misusing my gift if I don't speak to Black-male marginalization. The DUALITY of the simultaneous CONSUMPTION and DESTRUCTION of Black men."

Belinda let out an exasperated snort. "I just think it's really tired and ashy, the way you highlight the plight of Black men only. Do Black women exist in your world?"

"Khalil, your misogynoir is showing," said Eva, to more audience chuckles. She was *slaying*.

"My only point is, if Black *people* aren't writing with the intent to DISMANTLE WHITE SUPREMACIST HOOLIGANERY, then we're wasting our voices." He straightened his bow tie. "That said, books like Eva's are important, too. Fluff provides an escape."

"Fluff?" Eva was offended.

"Maybe I should've said easy reading," said Khalil.

"Maybe we should move on," intercepted Cece, who suddenly paused. She peered into the audience and then drew a wheezy gasp, clutching her Pilates-tightened tummy. Since it was impossible to shock this woman, Eva knew something cataclysmic had happened. Had a masked gunman snuck in? Had Zadie Smith shown up after all?

The panelists looked in Cece's line of vision. There was a tall male-shaped figure leaning in a doorway in the shadowy back corner of the auditorium.

With a recognizable face.

"*Shane...*," started Cece.

"*Hall*," finished Belinda.

The audience began peering over their shoulders, eyes darting around the room. A flurry of exclamations floated from the seats. "What? WHERE? Stop!"

Eva said nothing.

When a horror-movie character sees a ghost, she emits a bloodcurdling shriek. Claws at her cheeks. Runs for her life. Eva was trapped onstage in broad view of New York's literary community, so she did none of those things. Instead, her hands went completely slack, and her microphone slipped to the floor with a heavy thunk.

No one noticed, because everyone was focused on *him*.

"Shane," Cece bellowed, "is that you?"

He peered around the doorway, wearing a sheepish grimace.

"No," he said.

"*Yes!*" someone yelled.

"Get up here," ordered Cece.

He shook his head, with a *please don't make me do this* desperation in his eyes.

"Excuse me? I discovered you cleaning rooms at the Beverly Wilshire, kid—you better get up here. And you owe it to everyone in the room who has contributed to your popularity despite the careless way you've treated us."

Shane looked behind him, as if assessing whether he could make a run for it. Begrudgingly, he headed to the stage.

Eva rarely saw things in crisp focus. Even with her glasses. Her head always made the world a shade fuzzy. But as Shane walked down the aisle toward the panelists—toward her—every detail in the room became razor sharp. She was agonizingly aware of everything and every part of herself.

This couldn't be real. She knew it was, though, because her physical reaction was operatic. Her breath went shallow. Her pulse was thundering. She began to tremble all over, caught in the cross fire of a zillion powerful, conflicting emotions. Eva wasn't particularly religious, but she'd always felt there was...something...out there, watching over her. For many reasons, but mostly because she had never run into Shane Hall. Ever. After all this time, it was definitely astonishing, given that they were both Black authors of the same age, who'd become successful in the same era. If that wasn't divine intervention, she didn't know what was.

But now he was here, flesh and blood. It was the moment she'd always feared. But below that, in the tucked-away pockets of her subconscious—wasn't it also the moment she'd always anticipated? Planned for? Even dreamed of?

Maybe. But not like this. Not in public. Not unprepared.

The deafening applause sent the gentle throb in her temples to daggers and reminded Eva where she was. The room was in an uproar. Shane was a literary star. He'd written only four novels—*Eight*, *See Saw*, *Eat in the Kitchen*, and *Lock the Door on Your Way In*. But they were canon. The setting was always the same nameless neighborhood crippled by devastating poverty.

His characters were whimsical, vivid, practically mythologized humans. And through ecstatic attention to detail, emotion, and nuance, he artfully manipulated readers into becoming so invested in his characters' every thought that fifty pages would go by before they realized that there was no plot. None. Just a girl named Eight, who lost her keys. But they'd weep from the beauty of it. Eight could've seen a dude shot dead in the street while she was locked out, but readers would've cared only about *her*.

Shane tricked his readers into seeing humanity, not circumstance. You walked away from his books dazed, wondering how he'd managed to rip out your heart before you realized what was happening.

Every five years or so he'd drop a book; give a few choppy, unrevealing interviews; sulk through an MSNBC segment; sweep awards season (unless he was up against Junot Díaz); land a massive grant to go off somewhere and write more classic shit; and then disappear again.

Of course, he never fully disappeared. There were sightings. He'd visited the opening reception of a Kara Walker exhibit in Amsterdam three springs ago, but when it was time to read the foreword he'd written for the show, he'd vanished (so had Kara's curvy publicist, Claudia). In 2008, he'd gone to the White House Correspondents' Dinner but spent the whole time drying dishes with the busboys in the kitchen. He'd definitely attended J. Cole's nuptials in North Carolina, because he'd told a guest that the only thing he liked about the South was Bojangles—which was instantly all over Twitter.

Years ago, an *LA Times* editor had started a rumor that Shane was a hoax. And someone else was writing his books. Because he didn't behave like an A-list author and, frankly, he didn't look like one. He was all jawline, pouty mouth, and unreal eyelashes—a face that had made him special before he had proved it.

Shane Hall was intimidatingly handsome. And yet on the rare occasion he smiled, it was so radiant, so warm. Like peering into a goddamn sunbeam. The effect was disorienting. You wanted to either pinch his cheeks or beg him for a hard fuck on a soft surface. You just needed whatever he had.

Eva knew this better than anyone.

At least, she used to know. She hadn't seen him since twelfth grade.

Chapter 6

WITCH TRUMPS MONSTER

"He came back."

Eva didn't realize she'd said this out loud until Khalil and Belinda both whipped their heads in her direction.

"What?" asked Khalil.

"Came back where? Do you know him?" Belinda whispered, a hand covering her mic. The audience was all aflutter. And it was taking Shane forever to get to the stage, because there were hands to shake and things to sign (event programs, books, one flirty girl's forearm . . .).

"I just meant I can't believe he's making a public appearance," Eva sputtered. "You've met him, right?"

"Yeah, we both had Fulbrights in 2006. We spent a summer writing at the University of London," whispered Belinda. "But I barely saw him. Put it this way: there's a pub on every corner in East London."

"Overrated," pronounced Khalil. "I was supposed to interview him for *Vibe* once. He kept me waiting in a West Hollywood Starbucks for four hours, then showed up, rambled about a turtle for ten minutes, and ghosted. The story got killed, of course. *Clown.* This is why Negroes can't have nice things."

"The hate is strong in this one," Belinda said with snark.

He glared at her. "I've grown weary of you."

Eva was no longer listening. Because there was Shane. Onstage with them, swept up into Cece's possessive embrace, to the tune of a thousand iPhone snaps. Then Cece let him go, and the panelists stood up (Eva unsteady in her skyscraper heels and agita). Shane gave Khalil a pound and Belinda a hug, and then it was just him and Eva.

She was shaking uncontrollably. There was no way she could hug him. Or even step an inch closer to him. Instead, she offered her hand—it jutted out from her arm, a strange appendage—and he shook it.

"I'm Shane," he said, her hand still in his. "I love your work."

"Th-thanks. I'm...Eva." Eva sounded unsure of her own name. He squeezed her hand a little, a private gesture, telling her to relax. She immediately yanked it out of his grasp.

A *New York Times* intern sprinted out of the wings with an extra chair, scooted it between Cece and Belinda, and handed Shane a mic. Everyone sat down. Khalil was fuming.

"Well," started Cece, "this person needs no introduction, I'm sure. Let's give Shane Hall a warm welcome, shall we? Shane, you can join us for a couple minutes, can't you?"

Cece graced him with a blinding proud-mama smile. Like the way Diana used to look at Michael: *I'm fucking brilliant; I discovered this unicorn.*

"I mean, do I have to?" said Shane, with an amused chuckle in his voice. He grew up in Southeast Washington, DC, and the inflections still lived in his vaguely Southern-sounding, slow accent. That *Ah meeaaan* took him ten years to get out.

"You have no choice. Payback for allowing that Random House editor to steal you from me." Cece gestured toward Eva and company.

"But I...um...I'm not the best public speaker. I really just came to watch. This is awkward." He looked out into the crowd apologetically. "But when Cece Sinclair tells you to do something, you do it. I ain't crazy."

"Unconfirmed," mumbled Khalil.

Before Shane could address this shade, a young woman raised her hand. She was wearing a snapback that said MAKE AMERICA NEW YORK. Her face was beet red.

"Mr. H-Hall," she stammered. "Not to be rude, but I love you."

He smiled. "Rude would be 'I hate you.'"

She laughed way too hard. "I can't believe you're here. Just had to tell you, *Eight* is the reason I write. Eight, the character, is *me*. You never see angsty, depressed Black girls in pop culture. There's no Black *Prozac Nation* or *Girl, Interrupted*. I love that she narrates every book."

"Thank you." He shifted a little in his seat. "I like her, too."

"Is Eight based on a real person? You describe her so intimately. It's like I'm peeking in on something I shouldn't see."

"Do you think Eight's real?"

"Definitely," she said, nodding.

"Then she is."

"That's not an answer."

"I know." He grinned.

And then Eva had to do it. Finally, she had the nerve to look over at him—and regretted it instantly.

Age had made the skin around his eyes crinklier. Eva had forgotten about the scar snaking across his nose. He had scars everywhere. Once, while he was sleeping, she'd counted them all. Traced them with her mouth. And then named them, like constellations.

Perfect jeans; rugged boots; expensive watch; sinewy, lanky build; two-day stubble; simple white tee. Could've been Hanes or Helmut Lang. Fuck him—it was exactly what she wished she were wearing.

How am I gonna survive this?

A blond journalist Eva recognized from *Publishers Weekly* raised her hand. Cece nodded in her direction.

"Speaking of Eight," started the blonde, "you've gotten some flak for writing exclusively from a female point of view. Is that fair? As a man, do you feel qualified to speak from a feminine place?"

At this point, Eva, Belinda, and Khalil were effectively back-burnered.

Shane chewed his bottom lip and stared into his mic, like it held the answers to every mystery. "I guess...I don't think a lot about whether or not I'm qualified to do things. I just do them."

"But it's a ballsy move, as a man, to explore young female angst in such an intimate way."

"I don't think I'm exploring female angst. I'm just...writing a character? Who has angst." He rubbed his hands on his jeans, looking deeply uncomfortable. "Novelists should stretch beyond their experience, right? If I can't adequately manage a female voice, then I'm probably in the wrong profession and should revise my LinkedIn."

"Oh! Do you have LinkedIn?"

"No," he said, his eyes playful. To Cece, he whispered, "Told you I was bad at this."

And in that moment, whatever was holding Eva together snapped. Suddenly she was volcanically offended by his existence. She'd worked herself into a frenzy prepping for this event, running lines with Audre, and squeezing into this dress, but Shane was allowed to be exactly himself. His whole career, he'd done whatever the hell he'd wanted—evading interviewers, dropping off the face of the planet, sleepwalking through events Eva would kill to be invited to—and generally been awarded for bad behavior in a way that, in the history of creative pursuits, no female artist had ever been indulged. Women didn't get to be bad boys.

"I don't think; I just do."

Shane made it all look so easy. Everything Eva did was so effortful. And the worst part? This was supposed to be her moment to prove that she was a legitimate author, a force to be reckoned with. And it was shot to hell the second the One Who Mattered showed up. Was this even her real life, or a Mona Scott-Young production?

For all these reasons—as well as the older, darker ones—she had to say something.

"I hear what the reporter's saying," started Eva, slowly, to quell the tremble in her voice. "You're co-opting an experience you know nothing about. Eight's troubled. She self-harms. She's suicidal. And you idealize it, making her this adorable, sad chick. Depression isn't a 'catastrophe of a girl' weeping a single, pretty tear while gazing out of rain-streaked windows and dropping one-liners. Depression is tragic. Eight is tragic. And a male writer romanticizing female mental illness is inappropriate."

"You're right," Shane said. He scratched his jaw slowly, thinking, and then dragged his eyes over to Eva. For the first time, she met his gaze. Which was a mistake.

The air had gotten thick. They both blinked. Once, twice, and then continued to stare at one another. Not stare. Gawk. With such single-minded focus that the crowd was forgotten. The event was forgotten.

Belinda and Khalil sat between them, looking back and forth like they were in the stands at Wimbledon. Cece's eyes grew to anime proportions. What were they witnessing?

"It's true. I'm not a woman," started Shane.

"Exactly."

"And you're not a vampire. Or a man."

"Bloop," muttered Belinda.

"And yet Sebastian? He's one of the most vivid, true portrayals of masculinity I've ever read. Especially in the third and fifth books. Sebastian literally and figuratively sucks the life out of everything around him. And he'll drain Gia one day, too—he *knows* he will—but he can't stop himself from loving her. Maybe it's 'cause he knows that in the end, she'll survive him. He knows Gia's tougher than him. By virtue of being a woman, she's stronger. Girls are given the weight of the world, but nowhere to put it down. The power and magic born in that struggle? It's so terrifying to men that we invented reasons to burn y'all at the stake, just to keep our dicks hard." He paused. "You made Gia's magic broom ten times stronger than Sebastian's fangs. Witch trumps monster. Tells me everything I need to know about why men are scared of women."

Eva was too stunned to breathe. Against her better judgment, her eyes locked with Shane's again. Whatever he saw there made him hesitate for a moment. But then he kept going.

"You're not a man," he continued, "but you write the fuck out of ambivalent masculinity. You're not a man and it doesn't matter, because you write with sharpened senses and notice the unnoticed, and your creative intuition's so powerful you can rock any narrative to sleep. You *see*. And you *write*. With Eight, I do the same thing." He eyed her with an unmistakable familiarity. "I'm just not as good as you."

Belinda leaned over to Khalil and whispered, "You wanna reopen the *fluff* conversation, or you good?"

Eva's jaw went a little slack. Light-headed, she nodded in slow motion. She would not let him see how thunderstruck she was. And she refused to let him have the last word.

"Well," she managed. "That was quite the interpretation."

"It was quite the read," he said, his voice low.

"Yours . . . too."

"Appreciate it."

Then Eva finally tore her eyes away from Shane. And only then did he seem to remember that he was in public, and let out a small breath.

The audience was loud in its utter silence. No one spoke; everyone was transfixed. In over a decade of authordom, Shane Hall had barely spoken five (comprehensible) sentences to the public. And suddenly, he was here, in person, delivering a clear-eyed, feminist monologue. About Eva Mercy? It was so thrillingly random. And curiously, unmistakably charged. Hardly anyone in the audience had read the *Cursed* series before tonight, and now they couldn't get on their Amazon apps fast enough.

Eva forgot about the audience. It was just her up there, trapped in the spaces between Shane's words—the things he didn't say.

Eva nervously twisted her cameo ring around her finger.

He's read my entire series, she thought, frantically fidgeting with her ring. *Every word.*

Just then, the single *Cursed* fan in the audience burst into applause, his purple witch hat wiggling. Then he exclaimed, "You're a fellow fangirl! Do you have Sebastian's *S* pin?"

"Nah, it's been sold out every time I've logged on to EvaMercy-MercyMe.com."

Eva's face was on fire. *He's tried to buy the pin? He knows my website?*

"One more question, then we'll let Mr. Hall go," said Cece, breaking the spell with a dainty cough. She had to do this because Khalil was so upset about losing the audience's attention he was practically spurting cartoon steam out of his ears.

A twenty-something ginger stood up. He looked like Prince Harry, if Prince Harry lived in Red Hook.

"Hi, I'm Rich from *Slate*. Brenda, Khalil, and Shane, your work is powerful. Eva, I wasn't familiar with you before this evening, but that was quite a testimony from Shane."

Eva smiled weakly, like a woman on her deathbed trying to be brave for her loved ones.

"Can you detail some of the explicit racism you face as Black authors? Shane?"

"Me? Uh...no."

"No?"

Shane repeated, "No."

"Is that not why we're here?" said Khalil.

"It's why you're here," said Shane.

Okay, but why are YOU here? Eva's brain screamed. Temples throbbing, she unconsciously snapped her trusty rubber band against the flesh of her right wrist.

As if hearing her thoughts telepathically, Shane shot her a quick glance. When he saw the rubber band, his expression went cloudy, concerned. He paused, as if forgetting what to say next. It was a look she remembered vividly. Eva dropped her hand to her side.

"You want the truth, Rich?" asked Shane.

"Please," said Rich, his eyes lighting up in the way that so many liberal white people's had since the election. Like they were aching to be told how bad it was, how bad they were, their guilt turning them into masochists. Rich's thumb hovered over the voice-recorder app on his phone. "In this climate, it's important to share testimonies. Let's hold America accountable. Let's take her crimes seriously."

Shane thumbed his bottom lip, thinking.

"I don't take America seriously, though," he said with the blithe ease of a person who'd never needed to care about political correctness. Or correctness in general. (The Random House publicity department would have an apologetic press release drafted by 8:00 a.m. the next morning.)

On the surface, he looked at ease. No one but Eva noticed that since their exchange, his hand had been gripping his mic so tightly, his finger-tips were turning white. It was the only thing that gave him away.

That, and his mic was shaking.

"Look, this quote-unquote current sociopolitical climate? It's always been my climate. I've been up against Trumps and Pences and Lindsey Grahams since forever. The first one was the guard I was trapped alone in a cell with at eight years old. No laws, no cameras, no mercy. What happened in that hour made me the kind of person who doesn't feel obligated to workshop racism with white people." He shrugged. "The burden isn't on me to explain it, Rich. The burden's on y'all to fix it. Good luck."

Shane spoke with such blandness, it wasn't clear whether he cared in the extreme or not at all. Whatever the case, he'd delivered one hell of a sound bite. After refusing to shed light on The Struggle, he did exactly that, and his one brief personal anecdote resonated more than an hour of Khalil's dick-first rants.

"Understood," said Rich.

Squinting a little, Shane peered at the name tag on Rich's shirt. An impish look spread across his face, and he smoothly changed the subject. "I do, however, feel like discussing carrot tagliatelle."

Rich gasped. "You...you read my..."

"You're *Rich Morgan*, right? You cover food on *Slate* sometimes? That piece was revelatory. I didn't know you could make noodles out of vegetables."

"I suggest the five-blade spiralizer from Amazon Prime," enthused Belinda.

"I got mine at a *lovely* kitchen-and-home shop in Lake Como," said Cece.

Eva shut her eyes, wondering if someone had slipped acid in her seltzer. This conversation was ridiculous. Shane had single-handedly changed the mood in a room, in milliseconds. When had he become so unguarded? So chatty? She'd never heard him say more than a grunt to anyone but her.

"I'm ordering that shit," said Shane. "I'm new to eating healthy. Like, I'm still on avocado toast. Rich, thanks for your service."

Rich beamed and floated down to his seat.

Khalil was disgusted. "Help me understand this. You *won't* talk about racism, but you *will* open a discourse on hipster pasta?"

Shane shrugged. "Health is wealth."

Cece waved her arm across the stage with a flourish. "Shane Hall, ladies and gentlemen!"

And then Shane handed Cece his mic, wiped his damp palms on his jeans, did *not* look in Eva's direction, and returned to the wildly applauding audience.

There was twenty minutes left of the discussion, but the panel was effectively over. Shane had stolen it out from under them.

And Eva was a wreck.

Chapter 7

YOU FIRST

THIRTY MINUTES LATER, THE ATTENDEES WERE STILL CROWDING AROUND THE panelists—chatting them up, asking Belinda and Khalil to sign the beat-up paperbacks they'd carried in their bags. No one had brought any *Cursed* books for Eva to sign, but she was suddenly hit with an influx of people itching to hear more about her "feminist fantasy" series. Meanwhile, the delightful *Cursed* fan in the hat was acting as Eva's one-man street team, hopping from group to group, spreading the gospel according to Sebastian and Gia.

It was everything Eva had hoped would happen. She was suddenly on the radar of a whole new demo of the book-buying population. *Literary types.* And they would tweet and Snap and Instagram about her, and buzz would grow, and (fingers crossed) she'd ascend from popular niche author to a major voice in the book world. A thought leader! Someone whose interspecies sex movie you'd pay to see!

But at that moment, she couldn't feel it.

Both Belinda and Cece had tried several times to corner her, with a ravenous, gossipy gleam in their eyes. But Eva had conveniently found herself entangled in a new conversation each time. She couldn't face them. Not yet. Where would she even start?

Heart pounding, she glanced over at Shane from across the room.

Visibly uncomfortable with the crowd of fans surrounding him, he'd somehow escaped to a back corner. (The Shane of 2019 was more comfortable around people than the Shane of 2004, but still no social butterfly.) He was pretending to talk on his phone. Eva knew he was pretending, because he had the phone to his ear but wasn't saying anything. And she knew this because she was staring.

And he'd been stealing glances at her, too. Here and there, and then as though he couldn't help himself...a lot. It was making her dizzy. Everything was making her dizzy. The dull throb in her temples. The impossible heels. The sexpot dress. It had gotten tighter somehow, sucking at her like Saran Wrap. She kept shifting it around her hips. It was a sample-size 2, which was really a 0, and Eva was a size 4 but a PMS 6. Between all of that and her past so rudely colliding with her present, she hadn't breathed in hours.

Her phone dinged with an incoming flurry of texts from Audre, berating her for forgetting to shop for her "feminist icon" art final:

Today, 7:35 PM
My Baby
mommy u forgot to get me the supplies for my portrait of grandma lizette! It's due friday! I can't finish till i have feathers for her hair but no its cool keep compromising my artistic creativity ttyl xoxo

For once, she chose to ignore her daughter. She was also pushing aside the shame she felt about raising Audre to believe that her grandmother was a feminist icon. Revisionist history at best. Outright lie at worst.

Her phone dinged again, a new post notification from the top *Cursed* Facebook fan group. The moderator was a high-energy Vermont housewife whose wealthy Christmas-tree-distributor husband had funded her visits to every tour stop Eva had ever had. @GagaForGia was her biggest fan. And the most resourceful.

The *Cursed* Crew Group

Gossip incoming from some author thing at the Brooklyn Museum. Our own Eva (plus randos) spoke on a panel about racism or something. Sources say that ONE OF US was on stage! He's a Famous Author™ named Shane Hall? And he RAVED about *Cursed*. Also, you know how Eva has Sebastian's signature branded on her wrist? The zig-zag "S"?

This Shane guy has a "G" signature branded on his wrist. SAME PLACE, SAME ZIG-ZAG SCRIPT. G is for Gia, obviously. He's obsesseddd.

But the plot thickens, friends. We all know that Gia doesn't write using the Phoenician alphabet. And her signature is never even mentioned in *Cursed*.

And there's more. Shane Hall has BRONZE EYES. Like Sebastian.

As always, leave your Book 15 plot predictions in the comments. And #staycursed.

Eva's stomach hit the ground.

In a mere forty-five minutes, her deeply private life had become a public soap opera.

Eva had no idea why Shane had roared into her life on a Monday evening, but she knew one thing: he had to go. Not just now, but *right* now.

The urgency wasn't really about Shane at all. Eva was scared of who she'd been with him: out of control. Irresponsible. One big, raging impulse. It had taken everything she had to bury that troubled teenager. And now he was here, digging that girl up.

Two years after Shane, she had landed in New York with a new book, new money, and a new name. Genevieve Mercier had seamlessly become Eva Mercy. And Eva Mercy had devoted herself to building a life that was as safe as a Disney movie. She'd married the most uncomplicated man in the land and then had the friendliest divorce. She lived in the most family-oriented hood in Brooklyn. The *Cursed* series was smut, sure, but her refusal to try writing something new? Peak safety.

But. She did think of him sometimes. Lying alone in a hospital bed at 2:00 a.m., or during bouts of writer's block. He'd appear on the fringes of her thoughts—no face, just a feeling. His warm, minty-vanilla scent. The rough softness of his skin, like velvet caressed against the grain.

They'd stayed out of each other's way for fifteen years. Eva had to find out why he was here now. She was also prepared to offer her own Amex points to help book his outgoing flight. She needed Shane gone.

Eva felt his eyes on her again. With a vague tilt of his chin, he beckoned her to his corner of the room. Frowning, she gestured for him to come to her instead. This situation was stressful enough without having to hobble across the room on stilts.

Shane nodded. Hesitated. Then he shoved his fists in his pockets and headed over to her.

Eva slipped her phone into her clutch. When she looked back up, there was Shane. Right in front of her.

The room had been clanging with chatter. But to Eva, it suddenly simmered down to a muted hum. God, had he gotten taller? He was so at ease in his bones now. So broad-shouldered, so…much. Too much.

She reminded herself to breathe. She wasn't going to do this now. Take him in like this, in public. After their little performance onstage, they had an audience.

"Hello, stranger," she said, and full-body cringed.

"Hi."

Shane's eyes locked in on hers. Her stomach seized.

You're fine. Just say what you need to say and get out fast. Do it now…

"Can you meet…"

"Do you wanna…"

"Sorry, you go."

"No, you."

Eva refocused, threw her shoulders back, and started again. This was excruciating.

"Can you meet me at the Kosciusko Café, just down Eastern Parkway? Tomorrow morning, ten a.m.?"

Shane rarely did what he was told. But to this, he nodded vigorously.

"Yeah, let's do that."

"Good," said Eva, and then she began stress-babbling. "I'd ... uh ... meet up now, but I ... I need to pick up something for my daughter's art project. Feathers. Hashtag mom life! Also, I gotta get out of this dress."

Then she thrust a wad of paper into his hand. It was her number, scrawled on a Hale and Hearty receipt from her purse. "In case you need it ..."

Shane tucked it into his jeans pocket and then paused a beat. "Hey. I didn't know you'd be here."

"Not now."

"Honestly, you weren't listed on the invite. I'd never just show up ..."

"Not now."

Eva was supposed to walk away then. But she couldn't move. She just stood there, temples thumping, heart thudding. People were pouring out of the auditorium, making plans for the rest of the night, snapping pics. Giggling. Everything normal. And Shane and Eva were in the middle of it. Being anything but.

Acting on an impulsiveness Eva had thought she'd lost forever, she boldly leaned closer to Shane, narrowing the space between them. They were close. Too close.

"One thing," she whispered, her lips by his jaw. She didn't want anyone to overhear. "Before I forget."

"What's that?"

"Stop writing about me."

Only Eva could've noticed the change in his expression. She saw the flinch. The slow, satisfied curl of his lip. His bronzy-amber eyes flashing. It was like he'd been waiting years to hear those words. Like the girl whose pigtails he'd been yanking during recess all year had finally shoved him back. He looked *gratified*.

In a voice both raspy and low, and so, so familiar, Shane said, "You first."

Chapter 8

THUS WITH A KISS I DIE

2004

GENEVIEVE'S TEMPLES WERE THROBBING LIKE CRAZY. THE TUSSLE WITH Lizette's pedo boyfriend earlier that morning had wrecked her head. And the sunlight beaming brightly on the schoolyard wasn't helping.

It was the first Monday in June, and her first day at this Washington, DC, high school.

Admittedly, being new at the tail end of senior year was awkward. But Genevieve was a pro at not fitting in. At her previous four high schools, she'd been either catnip for generic mean girls or ignored. But each night, with clockwork regularity, she'd whip out her steno pad and fix it. She'd rewrite the day in her favor. Turn herself into a superhero. Get them all back in fiction.

It's my own fault. Who'd want to be friends with me?

Her face was usually contorted into a pain-induced grimace. In terms of conversation, she had two settings: searingly blunt or deeply sarcastic. She didn't giggle. Genevieve didn't mean to be off-putting, but just like today, she'd usually lived five lives by the time she got to school. She hadn't yet learned how to put on a mask of being fine, despite her personal disasters.

And so far, twelfth grade had been a disaster. She'd always managed to maintain a 4.0. But this year, her migraines had blossomed into gothic territory. Hurting too badly to focus on school, she'd started skipping, spending multiple days in bed—either in paralyzing agony, high from painkillers, or a nauseating combination of both. Her As had become D minuses, causing Princeton to rescind her admission. Princeton was supposed to save her. What would save her now?

In the tub that morning, Genevieve had had an epiphany. It was time for a friend. She wanted to know someone's secrets. And she needed someone to know hers.

Washington, DC, would be a fresh start. She'd just pick someone and dive in. How hard could it be? Horrible people had friends. O. J. Simpson had friends.

Her last school, back in Cincinnati, had been tough. But West Truman High was way tougher. The schoolyard was erupting with kids in utter chaos, with no teachers in sight. The crowd was G-Unit-video fresh in throwback jerseys, Timbs, and candy-colored weaves. Percussion-frenzied go-go beats were blasting from a boom box, and half the school had on Madness tees.

In contrast, Genevieve's look was "Tomboy" meets "I Don't Give a Shit." She was wearing an ancient Nas *Illmatic* concert tee, sweatpants she'd cut into shorts, and Air Force 1s. Her curly coils were piled into a massive pony atop her head. As usual, she hid her scrawny frame in an oversized men's work shirt.

She stationed herself by the bleachers, in a cigarette graveyard. Operation Friend looked bleak. The schoolyard crowd seemed impenetrably cliquey. There were some lone students scattered on the bleachers, though. Squinting in the sun, she surveyed the rows for a friendly face.

He was sitting in the top row of the bleachers, leaning against the heavily tagged brick wall. White tee and Timbs. A book was balanced on his lap, and he was reading it with his brow furrowed in concentration, chewing his lip. He looked like he was living the words.

That's how I read, too, she thought.

Then he turned a page, and she caught a glimpse of his gold-flecked chestnut eyes. The sun caught them, and they shone bronze. Was it a trick of the light? This boy radiated such peacefulness. An angel among mortals.

Genevieve trusted beautiful boys. She was safe with them, because they wanted prom queens, not her. Boys in her league were the ones to worry about.

She headed up the rickety bleachers. That was when she noticed the fraying cast on his left arm. No signatures. She got a bit closer and saw a fresh scab slashed across his nose. A step closer, and she saw that his knuckles (on both hands) were bruised purple and green. And his pupils were really, *really* dilated.

Okay, he was looking less angelic. But now that she was standing in front of him, it was too late to turn back. He peered up at her with mild curiosity and then went back to his book. James Baldwin's *Another Country*.

"Hey," she said. "Can I sit here?"

Silence.

Before she lost her nerve, she plopped down next to him.

"I'm Genevieve Mercier." She pronounced it *John-vee-EV Mare-see-AY*.

He frowned at her.

"It's French."

He gave her a look like *no shit*.

"Is it cool that I'm sitting here?"

"No."

"Are you an asshole?"

"*Oui.*"

Social experiment, failed. Genevieve knew better than to equate beauty with perfection. She lived with a former Miss Louisiana who looked pristine but had once dusted their entire apartment with a Neutrogena face wipe.

She still had fifteen minutes until the bell would ring—and in the meantime, the sun was slaughtering her head. Clumsily, she rifled through her backpack and pulled out a palm-sized roller vial of lavender-peppermint essential oil and rubbed it over her temples. It tingled pleasantly.

Then Genevieve noticed he was watching her, his book abandoned.

"I get migraines," she explained. "It's so bad, I barely ever move my head. For example, if I want to look to the right, I have to move my whole body. Like this."

She swiveled from her waist to face him. His expression was cloudy with distrust and confusion.

"Is this a setup? Is someone about to jump me?" His voice was drowsy and bored. "You a dealer? My bad if I owe you money."

"I look like a dealer to you?"

"I've had girl dealers." He shrugged. "I'm a feminist."

"I wouldn't set you up to get jumped. I'd do it myself."

He checked her petite frame. "You're the size of a Jolly Rancher."

"I have a Napoleon complex."

"Girls can't have that."

"Okay, *feminist.*" Genevieve rolled her eyes, causing a small tornado in her temples. Two girls walked by, glanced up at them, and giggled before scurrying away.

He scowled at her. "Why are you here?"

"I'm trying to make friends," said Genevieve.

"I don't have friends."

"Can't imagine why."

"I don't know what to say to people." He stuck the eraser end of a pencil into his cast and, in slo-mo, dragged it back and forth. "What do normal people talk about? Prom? Murder Inc.?"

"Fuck if I know," she admitted. "It's all good, though! We can sit in silence."

"Knock yourself out." He returned to his book.

So he wasn't super welcoming. But at least now she knew someone at this big, intimidating school. At a loss for what to do now, she shielded her eyes from the sun with her hand and rubbed more oil into her temples.

Genevieve sensed the guy watching her. She was about to explain to him the tension-relieving benefits of lavender, when he pulled Ray-Bans out of his jeans pocket and handed them to her. She put them on, stunned by his generosity. Then he exhaled (with resignation?), shut the book, and leaned back against the brick wall, eyes closed.

Genevieve couldn't help but stare. She'd never seen a face like his. Her stomach fluttered a bit, and she bit her lip. *No.* She couldn't get a crush. She didn't trust herself; she always went too far.

But looking at him wouldn't hurt. She studied his dreamy, far-out expression, wondering what he was on.

"Morphine?" she asked. "Ketamine?"

He opened one eye. "You sure you're not a dealer?"

"I have legal prescriptions. I'm basically an apothecary." She paused. "'Oh true apothecary. Thy drugs are quick.'"

"'Thus with a kiss I die,'" he replied reflexively. "Keats?"

"Shakespeare!" exclaimed Genevieve. "Remember which play?"

"*Romeo and Juliet*," he grumbled.

"You a writer? Or just an AP English ho?"

He shrugged.

"I write, too. You any good?"

Same shrug.

She smirked. "I'm better."

And then he chuckled. And it was an unlikely, surprising thing, like being trampled by a unicorn stampede in Narnia. Jesus, he was a lot. She needed a distraction.

"I'm…hungry," she blurted out awkwardly. "You want a peach? I have two."

He shook his head. Genevieve unzipped her backpack, unearthing a peach and a delicate, razor-sharp pocketknife. Propping her elbows on her knees, she clicked open the blade and angled it along the seam of the peach. It was always so satisfying, feeling the tautness of the skin under the blade. The tension. With a gentle press, the skin burst and juice dribbled out. She caught it with her tongue. Then she cut off a piece, using her thumb as an anchor, and popped it into her mouth.

Chomping, Genevieve glanced at her new friend. He looked like he'd just seen his first natural rainbow.

"That's how you eat peaches?"

"I like knives."

He blinked. Once. Twice. Then rapidly shook his head, as if descrambling his brain.

"Nah, man," he said. "You gotta go. I'm trying to stay out of trouble."

"Trouble? But..."

"You're dangerous. And I'm worse. I'd be hazardous to your health."

"I'm already a health hazard." Genevieve ripped off the sunglasses for emphasis. "We're friends now! You said you don't know how to talk to people, but you're talking to me!"

"I said I can't talk to *normal* people." He eyed her. "You're not normal."

She wasn't sure, but it felt like a compliment. She felt understood. This was new. There was that stomach flutter again.

"How do you know I'm not normal? We just met."

"What are you, then?"

Genevieve rested her chin in her hands, her elbows on her thighs. She didn't know how to answer. What *was* she?

She was tired. Tired of being sick, tired of her mouth getting her into trouble, tired of moving, tired of fighting off the kind of men who thought mothers and daughters were a package deal, and tired of hating who she was.

Maybe she shouldn't tell him the truth. It was too ugly. But maybe honesty was what it took to make a real friend.

Be nice. Be good.

"I'm not nice," she admitted quietly. "Not good."

He nodded slowly. Then he scratched his jaw, peering down at his Timbs.

"Neither am I."

That was how it started. That small confession. Genevieve had never told anyone she wasn't okay, and it sounded like he hadn't, either. She turned her face toward him to speak. And froze. Because his eyes were already on her.

Something crackled between them, an understanding, a mutual pull—and it was so extraordinary, so involuntary, Genevieve actually gasped. Stunned, she parted her lips a little. And then she couldn't breathe at all, because slowly he dragged his drowsy, drugged-out gaze from her eyes to her mouth and then back up to her eyes. A sure, satisfied smile crept across his face. Hesitantly, she smiled back.

Then it was over. He went back to his book, like that incredibly intimate look hadn't even happened. And Genevieve's world was knocked off its axis. But of one thing she was certain.

I'm supposed to know him, she thought.

"Soooo," she breathed, "what's your name?"

"I told you, I don't have friends. Let me brood in peace."

"Don't fight it. What's with the cast?"

He sighed. "I keep breaking my arm."

"Damn. Calcium deficiency?"

"No. I do it on purpose."

Genevieve gawked at him. The bell rang. A baritone voice shouted something over the loudspeakers, and the bustling student population filed into the redbrick building. Neither one of them moved.

"You don't break your own bones," she whispered. "You're just antisocial and trying to freak me out so I'll go away."

"Is it working?"

"No." Genevieve was thunderstruck. "What's wrong with you?"

He sighed. "A lot."

"I can't imagine doing something so sick."

"No?"

She followed his eyes, which had traveled down to her right arm. Her men's shirt had slid off her shoulder. And the rows of shallow, horizontal slices on her upper arm were visible. A few were covered with Band-Aids, the rest were scabs, and some had grown into scars. Genevieve wore her big shirt daily to hide this—but it had slipped at school a few times. She'd always been prepared to say it was eczema. No one had ever asked.

She yanked her sleeve back up on her shoulder.

"You don't know what my life's like," she spat.

"Try me," he said, his galaxy eyes eating her alive.

A wild current charged through her, something primal, dirty, desperate, confusing. Was this being seen for what she really was? Being witnessed? It was heady and terrifying. Genevieve had hoped for someone to share secrets with. But she hadn't bet on someone beating her, crazy for crazy. And she hadn't bet on the person being a boy, a boy who looked like that, who looked at her like that.

Somehow, he'd snaked into her head and sunk his fangs into her brain, poisoning her with hope. A cruel trick.

Genevieve lurched forward and grabbed his tee in her fist, yanking him down to her level.

"Stop looking at me like your dick's in my mouth," she said, seething, still clutching the peach in her left hand. "You like me now? Think you're original? Boys love to torture the weird girl, the freak. But guess what? I'm already in pieces, so—"

With feral quickness, he plucked her fist from his shirt and pinned her arm behind her back. Genevieve arched, drawing a breath. A delicious tremble tore through her.

He held her like that for a beat and then brought his mouth to her ear. "Don't."

"D-don't what?"

"Call yourself a freak."

He let her go. Then he grabbed the peach out of her hand and took a deliberately indulgent, wet bite. He wiped the back of his mouth with his hand.

"I'm Shane," he said, a spark of triumph in his eye. And walked away.

* * *

79

Genevieve found her classroom. Peering through the doorway, she saw chaos. A couple of kids were in a cypher, one girl was unbraiding her hair, and a boy was banging his desk on the floor. Four kids were napping in their chairs; another, on the floor. At the chalkboard, the teacher was explaining photosynthesis, which Genevieve had learned in private school in fifth grade.

In a far corner, tipped back way too far in his chair, was Shane.

She wasn't ready to see him after whatever monumental thing they'd just experienced. She'd staggered away from the bleachers, feeling like she'd toppled into a tornado.

She wiggled the nicked vintage cameo ring she'd once stolen from Lizette's jewelry box. It usually calmed her. But not now.

With a deep breath, she entered the room. The class gradually quieted to watchful silence. Thirty pairs of eyes followed Genevieve to an empty desk in the front. She sat down.

Reacting to the sudden stillness, the teacher turned around.

"Who are you?"

"Genevieve Mercier. Sorry, I got...lost."

"We're all lost." Mr. Weismuller was whippet thin with a sallow complexion. He looked like he had mono. "Class, welcome Genevieve."

"The fuck's that *name*, though?" a girl shouted.

"Young, why her name sound like Pepé Le Pew?"

Genevieve sank lower in her chair. Mr. Weismuller turned to face the chalkboard.

"This bitch think she Aaliyah 'cause she got a half a cup of hair."

"That ain't hers," said a tall girl in Apple Bottom jeans, sitting behind Genevieve.

She turned around to face her. From his corner in the back, Shane caught her eye. And shook his head. A warning that Genevieve ignored.

"What'd you say?"

"I said that hair ain't yours, ho. And what?"

"Yeah, and what?" said a slight boy who materialized next to Apple

Bottom, presumably her boyfriend. The whole class was watching Genevieve. She was surrounded. The only person she knew was four rows back. She wasn't going to win.

"Nothing," she muttered.

"I thought not," said Apple Bottom, and the class resumed cutting up. Behind her, Genevieve heard The Boyfriend whisper "Yeah, do that shit" to Apple Bottom.

There was an electric calm. Suddenly, Genevieve's neck snapped back, hard, and her head felt eerily weightless. She turned around, and Apple Bottom was grasping three-fourths of Genevieve's ponytail in one hand and scissors in the other. The Boyfriend cackled.

"I'm getting Principal Miller," Mr. Weismuller said with a robotic lack of urgency and left the room.

Genevieve felt behind her neck, where her hair no longer was. A red fury raged through her, and she pushed Apple Bottom's desk violently, knocking her backward. Apple Bottom shrieked, unhurt but tangled under a chair.

"Kill this new bitch," screamed The Boyfriend to no one.

"No," said Shane, standing up. "You. Fight me."

Everybody looked at The Boyfriend. It was clear he didn't want to do this.

One girl went, "Nope. When Shane starts with his shit, I'm out. Y'all ain't gonna fuck around and get me suspended right before graduation." She grabbed her backpack and left.

"Fight me, nigga," Shane repeated. They were nose-to-nose now. The crowd formed a wide circle around them.

The Boyfriend threw a weak punch, knocking Shane across the nose. Shane folded his arm across his chest. He hit Shane harder. Then Shane whispered something in his ear, causing him to really rear back and crack Shane on the temple. Then the class was shouting *Fuck him up, fuck him up,* and The Boyfriend shoved Shane to the ground, fists flying. Shane's nose and lip were bleeding, but he didn't fight back.

"Stop!" Genevieve yelled. "Jesus Christ, Shane, it's just hair!"

Abruptly, Shane heaved the kid off him and stood up. His breathing was jagged, erratic. And then he lifted up his hurt arm, the one in the cast, and whacked The Boyfriend across the cheekbone, hard, with a sickening thwack. The Boyfriend dropped.

Shane clutched his ravaged arm to his chest, the bone rebroken. He stood there, trembling, gritting his teeth, radiance draining from his skin. Then he shot Genevieve a bloody smile and crumpled to the ground. It was the most terrifying, graceful thing she'd ever seen.

"Someone get help. He's . . ."

The last thing Genevieve saw was Apple Bottom's fist inches from her nose, and then a zillion bright lights.

Six hours later, Genevieve and Shane lay in cots next to each other in a curtain-enclosed space at United Medical Center's emergency room. They'd been there all day with the school guidance counselor, Ms. Guzman, perched between them in a foldout chair. The Boyfriend was discharged and went home with his grandmother, sporting a fractured cheekbone. Apple Bottom left with her aunt and a bruised shoulder. Shane's arm was reset with a new cast, and between his upper lip and left eyebrow, he had a total of fourteen stitches. Genevieve got off easiest, with a ghastly black eye and an even ghastlier bob.

She and Shane were suspended, but as seventeen-year-old minors, they couldn't legally be discharged until a parent or guardian picked them up. Ms. Guzman couldn't reach Lizette, which was no surprise.

Ms. Guzman couldn't find Shane's guardian, either. Apparently, he lived in a foster-kid shelter, and no administrators were reachable.

Now they were just lying there. Waiting. While Ms. Guzman dipped outside for her thirty-seventh smoke break.

Genevieve was in agony. That punch had rattled her brain. The ER docs had treated her bruised eye, but despite her increasingly panicked pleas, they'd given her only Advil for her head. At her pain level, this was as helpful as an M&M.

Shaking badly, she'd curled into a ball, clawing into her forearm with her nails as a distraction.

"Genevieve?" Shane whispered from his cot.

"*John-vee-EV*," she groaned, through gritted teeth.

"You good?"

"*No.*"

She watched him peer out into the hallway and then shut the curtain. He dug in his jeans pocket, yanked out a baggie of pills, and grabbed a Dixie cup of water. He handed both to her.

"Will OxyContin help?"

"Grind it up," she rasped.

Shane pulled an ATM card (name unknown) from his magic pocket and cut the pills into four lines of chunky powder on a metal medical tray. Gently, he held the tray under her nose, steadying the back of her head with his good hand, and Genevieve sniffed each line. It went down rough but worked fast—the hurt dulling, her face slackening, muscles going gooey. *So good.* Oxy didn't kill the pain, just made it so it didn't matter.

He smoothed her ruined curls from her face. She tucked his hand under her cheek. It belonged there.

"You're my bestbestbest friend," she sighed, groggily and goofily.

"Better learn how to pronounce your name, then."

"Don't care what you call me," she slurred. "Just call me."

Shane smiled. "Let's go."

"Where?"

"I know a place. But no one gives a shit where I am. You got parents who do?"

Genevieve thought about Lizette at home, waiting for her daughter to wake her up for her gross job at her disgusting boyfriend's lounge.

Her answer was obvious.

They walked down the hallway, cool, calm. But the second they hit the exit doors, they linked hands and ran. Wherever Shane was going, she was going, too.

TUESDAY

Chapter 9

A VERBAL BLUSH

SHANE SHOWED UP TWENTY-FIVE MINUTES EARLY TO KOSCIUSKO CAFÉ, WHICH wasn't a café at all. It was an untrendy sixty-year-old diner left over from the days when Crown Heights was still a Polish neighborhood. The decor was frozen in 1964: Formica tables, intense fluorescent track lighting, shiny red vinyl booths, and ceiling fans instead of AC. According to Shane's cursory glance at Yelp, lasagna was their thing. But he was too anxious to eat.

He was too anxious to do anything but seat himself in a booth by a window. And wait. And calm his thundering heart by watching airport-reunion videos on YouTube. (Besides running, this was his clean coping mechanism.)

At 10:02, Eva stormed in. She stomped to the hostess stand, looking notably different from last night's sleek glamazon thing. She was simple in wild curls, clingy tank, boyfriend jeans, Jordans. Unfairly sexy glasses. This morning, she was even more dangerous—if that was possible.

And Shane devolved from a composed adult to a besotted adolescent.

Genevieve. That's really her, all grown up. Eva. But also definitely Genevieve.

Shane's thoughts were a jumble. As usual, he hadn't really thought last night through. He'd never dreamed Genevieve would be at the event. His only goal had been to connect with Cece and nonchalantly ask her for Genevieve's contact info. And if Cece had asked why? Well, he wasn't sure what he would've said.

If he'd thought too much about any of this, he wouldn't have come.

Shane watched Genevieve (*Eva*—he had to get used to her new name) whisper something to the hostess. She hadn't seen him yet, though, and he stole this small, secret moment to drink her in. To try to reconcile the girl with the woman.

As a girl, she'd been all angles, sharp lines, a wiry spark plug of unpredictability. A little scary. A lot breathtaking. Her expressions were in HD—she broadcast everything on her face. And then there was the dimple, that fucking adorable dimple in her right cheek. It popped when she smiled; it popped when she talked; it popped when she breathed. There was a matching one on the left, too, but it was less prominent. As if once God had so masterfully conceived the right one, he was like, *I'm exhausted; this'll do.*

The girl had been irresistible. This woman was something else entirely. Her sharpness had softened. She stood straighter and spoke with clever confidence. She was a badass writer, had been a publishing success story since nineteen, and wore it so well. Her teenage fury had morphed into something else: power.

The hostess pointed to Shane, and Eva strode over to him. Looking stern and gorgeous.

And he knew that he was fucked.

She slid into the seat across from him, plopping down a tote bag that read WELL-READ BLACK GIRL. And then they were finally alone.

Eva, whose written words were bold enough to inspire PTA moms to dream of hopping on a broomstick (or a hot Black dude) and escaping their lives, said, "So. Uh. Hi."

Shane, whose written words were lyrical enough to make the stuffy Pulitzer Prize board want to roll up, stream *Damn*, and ruminate on the paradoxical mysteries of man, managed, "Glasses. Nice."

"Oh. Really? Uh...th-thank you," she said. "I...found out I was nearsighted after I started writing, so I got LASIK. And I had twenty-twenty vision for ages, but then a couple of years ago, in 2017...no, 2015...my eyesight started deteriorating. And my very helpful Hasidic ophthalmologist, Dr. Steinberg, said I'd developed an astigmatism. So, glasses. I wear them now."

Shane tried and failed not to smile at this. Her words were a verbal blush.

"The word 'astigmatism' feels wrong," he said. "Like, it should be 'I have *a stigmatism.*'"

"'Opossum,' too. I always think it's *a possum.*"

"So, this isn't awkward at all."

"Super normal," Eva said, downing her entire glass of water.

"I...I'm kinda speechless," he stammered, still awestruck. "You look the same but so different."

"Cece made me wear that dress last night. And straight hair." Nervously, she fluffed her bangs. "This is what I really look like."

"I know what you really look like," he said simply.

Eva shifted slightly in her seat and picked up the laminated menu on her plate.

"You look different, too," she started.

"How?"

"Your eyes are open."

"I'm sober."

"I'm...stunned."

"Me too."

"How long?"

"Two years and two months."

"Is it sticking?"

"I'll let you know in another couple years."

"No, you got this."

A hot flush radiated across his chest, but he ignored it. "So. You had to make me evil, huh? A vampire?"

"If the fangs fit," she shot back. "Did you have to make me an adorable runaway with a heart of gold?"

"I didn't make you that. You were that."

Eva grabbed a half-moon of seven-grain bread from the basket and began anxiously tearing at it. Whatever she was feeling, he didn't want her to be alone in it. In a sign of solidarity, he grabbed a roll, too.

Just in time, a waitress appeared to take their drink orders. She was a sixty-something minx with a fuchsia lace headband and an eastern-European accent.

"Just water," said Eva primly. "No, I'll have a chocolate milkshake."

"Two ztrawz?" said the waitress. She winked at Eva and then looked Shane up and down. "Well, aren't you a chocolate doughnut?"

"One straw," said Eva.

Shane scanned the menu, stopping on the natural juices, ever mindful of his new healthy lifestyle. "I guess I'll have the Mint-Kale Clean Green Mean juice?"

"You zound like you don't really vant that," the waitress remarked, and bounced.

"So," began Eva. "You've read my whole series."

"Every line." He popped a piece of bread into his mouth. "You've read mine, too."

"With a highlighter."

"I meant what I said in there," he said. "I'm your biggest fan. I'm an English teacher now, and while my students are reading Hawthorne in class, I read you."

"*You* teach?" Eva's skepticism was palpable. "What school would allow you anywhere near their student population?"

"I've changed." His confident smile made it believable. "I think this is what writers call a character arc."

"I see." Eva cocked her head. "Speaking of writers. Your little speech about *Cursed*? It was...like...What were you..."

Shane cringed. He never would've thought that there'd be a time when they didn't know how to talk to each other. Years ago, they'd had a purely instinctual rhythm. A wordless connection so raw that minutes after meeting, they pounced. But rational-minded adults didn't take such liberties.

Of course, Shane was, historically, not great at being an adult.

"Just talk to me," he said. "Whatever it is, I can take it."

"Fine." She shoved her glasses up her nose, inelegantly and irresistibly. "Your speech about *Cursed*? It was a lot. You can't just jump from 2004 to 2019, shock me to death, and then hit me with a . . . rapturous, doctorate-level thesis of my supernatural erotica. Those books are my babies, and even I know they're not that good. Hearing you talk like that? *You?* After fifteen years? I couldn't breathe." She huffed, exasperated. "Why'd you come on stage last night?"

"Cece made me."

"You could've said no."

"True. And you could've worn jeans."

"Okay, fair point. Cece owns us all."

"Honestly? I was shook." Shane reached for more bread. "I wasn't expecting to see you. Next thing I know, we're up there together, and you bring up *Eight*, and I just . . . blacked out and said too much."

"We weren't really talking about our books, Shane. Everyone knew."

"I know. *Fuck.* I got a certificate for best communicator in AA. How'd I get here?"

"Good question," she said pointedly.

With impressive timing, the waitress swept by the table with Shane's radioactive-green mint-kale juice and Eva's milkshake.

Shane took a gulp and instantly regretted it. The mint was awful. It tasted like a Listerine smoothie. He swallowed, cheeks puffed out, miserable. Generously, Eva slid her milkshake toward him.

"Thanks," he said, taking a swig. He hated being healthy. "I'm here to present at the Littie Awards on Sunday."

"Nope. You don't do awards ceremonies. Or panels. And you're never in Brooklyn. You've been very careful to avoid me."

"I've been avoiding life in general."

Eva rolled her eyes extravagantly.

"It's true!" insisted Shane. "Meanwhile, you mastered it. You made it to Princeton. Got married, had a beautiful girl."

"How do you know anything about me? You're not on social media."

"Nah, people are strange enough in real life. I don't need to view their psychosis through a zany filter," he said, scowling. "But yeah, in some masochistic moments, I've looked you up. You and Audre are like a mother-daughter Thelma and Louise, with your museums and road trips and rallies. Travis Scott at Radio City."

Eva preened, deservedly smug. "Audre's a great kid. She got the best of me and her dad."

"What's he like?" Shane knew he was going too far.

"Travis Scott?"

"Audre's dad."

Eva sat back in the booth, hard. She grimaced and massaged a temple with her knuckles. "He's *stable*."

Shane went further. "Where is he?"

"You tell me. Where do men go when they're done?" Eva's eyes blazed. "He's none of your business. You don't know me anymore."

"I know too much," he said, his words weighted with old pain. The kind that makes a home on the fringes of your thoughts forever.

"You don't," she sighed. "I'm not who I was. And when I look back, I'm horrified."

"You were just trying to survive," said Shane. "When you're drowning, you'll do anything to get air."

Eva studied her black mani, her expression maddeningly blank. And then Shane's brain ordered him to utter the dumbest sentence ever.

"I've been meaning to call you."

Hearing himself say this, Shane knew he deserved Eva's incredulous, outraged brow raise. She looked equally likely to flip the table or die laughing.

"Riveting," she said. "I've been meaning to try lash extensions."

Shane tried again. "I couldn't call you, because I was too fucked to make rational decisions. Things were bad for me for years."

"Please," she scoffed, "you're one of the most celebrated writers of our generation."

"And one of the drunkest," he said. "Look, fame doesn't save you. It just means that fans try to hack your Pornhub account to get your credit card info, track your whereabouts, and show up at your New Zealand Airbnb in revealing clubwear."

"Revealing clubwear? I'm struggling to understand your demo."

"You got grown men out here in witch hats. The nerve of you."

"And why don't you just stream Pornhub, like a civilized person?"

Shane looked offended. "Viruses."

"Ah."

"Anyway," he said, cracking his knuckles, "part of AA is making amends. I wanted to be permanently clean before I ever contacted you again. Now I'm ready."

"Oh, so you contact me when *you're* ready? You're *arrogant* enough to think I want to talk to you?"

Shane looked her squarely in the eye. "Yeah. I am."

"Fuck you." Eva grabbed her bag and stood up.

"Don't go," he blurted out, halting her with his pleading eyes. "Please. I know what I did was unforgivable. I broke our promise. And now I can explain why."

"No you don't. I'm good!" She wasn't good. She was trembling and it killed him, knowing her anguish was his fault.

It always was, he thought.

"We have unfinished business," he said. "You know we do. We've made careers off it."

Eva sat back down. The tension rippled between them, charging the air and stretching for seconds that felt like hours. Shane was praying she'd speak—but she just sat there, fuming and staring down at the table. Slowly, she began ripping her napkin into pieces, her mouth set in a tight, narrow line.

When she finally looked at him, her glare was a conflagration.

"*We* didn't make careers. *I* made a career," she whisper-yelled. "You drunk-wrote four classics? I have to write a shitty book a year to survive. You can't be bothered to tour? I have to constantly promote. You're philosophically opposed to social media? I have to post all day to stay relevant. You're lucky I don't take a selfie with you for likes!"

"In this lighting?"

In AA, Shane would diffuse tension with a joke. Luckily for him, Eva was too lost in her rant to hear it.

"And I've never even been to New Zealand! I spend all my time churning out *Cursed*! I owe Cece another one, and I don't have a single idea, and now I'm gonna go broke, and even worse? I keep back-burnering my dream book!"

"What's your dream book?"

"Doesn't matter," she snapped. "The point is, I work my ass off. While you, with minimal effort, have become a legend."

"I'm only a legend 'cause I'm mysterious."

"You're a legend 'cause you write about *me*." She grabbed her milkshake back, spilling a bit on her hand. Distractedly, she sucked it off.

Shane's brain left their conversation for a few agonizing moments.

"You capitalized off of my trauma," she raged. "A time when I was in crisis. Not lovable. Not Eight."

Shane stared at her, eviscerated. *Not lovable.* Eva had no idea the effect she'd had on him. How he saw her. How could she not know?

"Eight's lovable because you were." His voice was firm, definite. "You can't imagine what you were like then."

"I know what I was like."

"You don't." Shane went dead serious. "You burst into my solitude, demanding to be seen. You were overwhelming. Just wild and weird and brilliant, and I never had a choice. I liked everything about you. Even the scary parts. I wanted to drown in your fucking bathwater."

Eva opened her mouth to speak. He shook his head, silencing her.

"I idealize you in fiction because I idealized you in real life," he continued. "It *is* male-gazing, you're right. And I'm sorry. But I can only write my shit my way."

"It's *my* shit!" Eva pounded a fist on the table. At the next table over, a family looked up from their menus.

"You get to decide who owns what?" asked Shane, voice rising. "I've written four novels. You've written fourteen! A whole series, in which you put a Creole hex on me."

She burst out in a mirthless laugh. "If I could hex you, you think I'd stop at roasting you in books?"

"If I'm a vampire, at least let me do cool shit! I spend the whole series cowering in castles, while my cross-between-Serena-Williams-and-Wonder-Woman witch soul mate gets to fight for truth and justice. The only thing Sebastian's good at is—"

"Stop!" she interrupted. "Those scenes pay my mortgage."

Shane said nothing and quietly took a swig of water. His devilish grin showed behind the glass.

"I will throw this milkshake at you right now—think I won't?"

"I'm not doing anything!"

"Look," said Eva, cheeks aflame. "No one was supposed to read *Cursed*. I wrote it for myself, to get over you. I cast myself as a super-hero to give me strength I didn't feel. And made you a useless fuckboy, because I'm petty. But it turned into a career, and I'm *stuck* with us."

"Are you, though? Vampires die all the time. What about stakes and sunlight and shit?"

"My vamps," she started haughtily, "can only die from silver scalpels marinated in garlic paste from a very particular vine during the summer solstice on a leap year."

"Exactly." A smirk played at the corners of Shane's mouth. "Ever wonder why you made it so hard to kill me?"

"Because I have private school to pay for! Why do you keep writing about me?"

"Isn't it obvious?"

"Apparently not."

"I'm not just writing about you," said Shane. "I'm writing to you."

His words hung in the air a moment—bold and impossible to misconstrue. He hesitated, wondering how she'd react. Telling the truth was something he always did, with no regard for how he was received. But Eva's thoughts mattered.

"I wrote my books like you were the only one who'd ever read them," he continued carefully. "My books did what I couldn't."

Eva's breath slowed. "Which was what?"

"Talk to you," he said. "And when I read yours, I knew you were reading mine. You put in so many clues. I mean, Gia has to strike her enemies *eight times* with her broom to kill them." A shadow of a smile passed over his face. "Even when you were ripping me to shreds, it felt good. Like we still had our secrets."

Eva's mouth parted slightly, her brows knitting together. And Shane started lightly scratching his biceps, the stubble of his jawline. Neither of them was emotionally prepared for this confession.

When he felt Eva watching him, Shane stilled. Boldly, he met her gaze and got caught there, a breath too long. A charge passed between them, flickered, and faded.

There's an alternate universe where I never left, he thought.

"Can I be honest?" asked Eva.

"Please."

"I cried for two weeks when I found out I was having a daughter." Her voice was barely audible. "I was terrified she'd be like me. My only goal is making sure Audre's world is unicorns and rainbows. And it is. When she's sad, she reads Shonda Rhimes's *Year of Yes*, listens to the *Hamilton* soundtrack, and moves on. She doesn't hurt like I do. *Did.*" Eva corrected herself. "My mother, my grandmother, my great-grandmother? They're all crazy, and it runs in my family. But it stopped with me."

Eva paused. "No one knows about my life before New York. You showing up like this...It's a trigger."

"I understand," conceded Shane. "And I'll go. But can you tell me one thing?"

Eva shrugged vaguely.

"You happy?"

She looked dismayed. It was like no one had ever asked her that, or it was something she'd never thought about. Or both.

"I'm fine."

"How's your head?"

"I said I'm fine," she spat, her eyes welling up. She dug her knuckles into a temple again, the pain obvious.

"That bad? Still?"

Eva's silence was answer enough. And her tears, threatening to spill.

"Fuck." Shane's face was a mask of worry. "Do you have good doctors? Do you have a...a...man or someone who helps? Does anyone take care of you?"

"Does anyone take care of *you*?" she exploded.

"I mean, no."

"Then why are you assuming that *I* need help?"

Eva began snapping a rubber band encircling her wrist. It was sharp enough to redden her skin. He'd noticed her doing this before, at the Brooklyn Museum. Watching the compulsive way she pulsed the band against her skin, a flash of unease coursed through him. He wanted to ask her what she was doing.

But I already know, don't I?

"I didn't mean to upset you," said Shane. "I just hoped you had some support."

"Well, I don't. God, why did you come here?"

Overwhelmed by her reaction, he said, "To apologize."

"Please don't," she whispered. "I can't talk about that night..."

And then a tear fell. Shane shot up straight in his seat. Reaching across the table, he gently held her wrist.

"Genevieve," he said. And she began to sob.

"Don't follow me." She grabbed her bag and fled the diner.

It took willpower Shane hadn't known he had not to run after her.

Instead, he watched her from the window as she stormed down the sidewalk lining Eastern Parkway, getting smaller and smaller, until she turned a corner and disappeared. With every step she took, the years melted away. Shane was hurtling backward into his teenage self, before the books, the success, the travel. Back in the dark ages, when his loneliness was like quicksand, when he'd ruin himself to make it stop—and the only bright spot in all of this was loving a beautiful girl with demons ferocious enough to slay his own.

For seven days, a million Junes ago.

Chapter 10

THE WOMEN

"*PARDON ME?*" GASPED CECE, HER LAVENDER ICED LATTE CLASPED TO HER chest. The condensation created a massive wet spot on her silk Gucci blouse.

No loss, the blouse was off-season. Besides, nothing mattered more than Eva's unbelievable story.

Eva, Cece, and Belinda were crammed on a rustic love seat at Maman Soho, a café noted for its South of France vibe—that is, blue tiled floors, string lights, and quirkily pretty baristas in bangs and last night's lip stain. Eva wasn't up for an emergency lunch with the girls this morning, especially after Shane. But there was no arguing with those two.

"Shane was your teenage sweetheart?" gasped Belinda.

Eva slumped in the rustic love seat. Her two best friends had witnessed the exposing banter with Shane on stage at last night's panel—there was no hiding from them. So she'd told them an abridged version of the truth. Which was that she and Shane had gone on a few dates in high school. Nothing major.

"Shane was nobody's sweetheart," she said. "He was trouble."

"So, Shane was Shane," said Cece. "And you were?"

"Not thinking clearly," mumbled Eva. "Look, we just had this instant... thing. And then it burned out. No biggie."

"Nope." Belinda wagged her index finger at Eva, her Reiki-infused bracelets clinking. "That ain't it. Details, please."

"I barely remember any!" Eva hoped she sounded convincing. "It's probably a blur for Shane, too."

"It's not a blur for him, ma'am," said Belinda. "The way he was looking at you? *My* panties disintegrated."

Eva sighed. She needed a hug, a nap, and a sleeve of Thin Mints. Not this.

"Eva, honey," said Cece, with exaggerated calm. "Are you Eight?"

"I can neither confirm nor deny," she said.

Cece raised a weaponized eyebrow.

"Fine. I'm Eight," admitted Eva.

"And he's Sebastian?"

After taking an extended sip of her latte, she said, "Sort of?"

Belinda yelped, fanning herself with her straw fedora.

"What I'm hearing you say," started Cece grandly, "is that you and Shane Hall...*my* Shane Hall...who's come up in countless of our book-world conversations over the years, conversations in which you've *pretended not to know him*...You two were teen lovers? Secret soul mates who were so inspired by each other that you've been communicating through your art across miles, decades, and years of impassioned memories?" She slammed her floral teacup down on the whitewashed table. "My heavenly *word*, how could you keep this telenovela a secret?"

A doe-eyed barista glanced over at them sharply. Eva tossed her a bright smile, then lowered her voice to a whisper.

"Because I barely survived Shane Hall. I barely survived myself. It was a dark time. My home life was traumatic. I was a chaotic, angry kid. Why reminisce?"

"Actually, this explains a lot about who you were when we met," noted Cece. "Totally feral. Remember when that bartender called you 'baby'? You stubbed your cigarette out on his hand! And said, 'Take my order or kiss my ass, your choice.'"

"No, it was 'Take my order or suck my dick,'" corrected Eva.

Belinda snorted. "So, why did you break up?"

"Doesn't matter." Eva waved her hand dismissively. "I've lived entire lifetimes since then."

"This is a word." Belinda crossed her legs, her gauzy palazzo pants billowing. "Men don't define our journey. It's about honoring our queendom. Vibrating at our divine plane."

Cece rolled her eyes. "Relax, Badu."

"When I think about it, *which I never do*," started Eva, "I'm just shocked we got so intense so fast."

"I felt passion like that once," Belinda mused. "Remember Kai, the bouncer from that Bushwick hookah spot? He fucked the soul out of me one evening, and I turned over and wrote a sonnet called 'Skyscrapers Penetrating the Night Sky.'"

"It ran in the *Paris Review*!" said Eva. "I admire your ability to write about penises so lyrically. It's a tricky body part to describe. One wrong adjective, and it's a tumor."

Belinda nudged Cece. "You ever experienced wild love?"

"Hmm." She swirled her straw in her latte. "I'd die for my hairdresser. We've all seen what Lionel does with 4C hair."

"You'd die for Lionel," said Eva, "but not your husband of twenty years?"

Cece had known her terminally reserved plastic-surgeon husband, Ken, since preschool. His appearance suggested that God had struggled to remember what Billy Dee Williams looked like in *Mahogany*, and had almost gotten it right. They were a perfect match. Spelman. Morehouse. AKA. Alpha. Their grandfathers had been best friends at Howard, class of '46. What they lacked in passion, they made up for in obviousness.

"I adore Ken, but I'm not built for romantic passion. Men are such children. I just read an article about mainland China's female shortage. Grown men are living alone in filthy houses and dying prematurely because there's no women to make their doctor's appointments."

"Speaking of doctors," said Belinda, "my gyno just performed a goddess ritual on my vagina. She steamed it, saged it, and then spoke wisdom into my crotch."

"I wonder if my vagina's wise," mused Cece.

"Mine's dumb as fuck, judging from her choices," said Belinda.

Am I really laying my burdens at the feet of these Muppets? Eva wondered.

"I should go," she said. But she just sat there, her face cloudy.

Belinda and Cece exchanged glances. There was more to Eva's story. And they knew they'd never hear it.

These three knew each other's pizza order at Roberta's, shoe sizes, and favorite Spotify playlists. But Cece and Belinda knew nothing about Eva's pre-Brooklyn life. She'd alluded to a nomadic childhood. But actual details? Throwback Thursday content? Forget it. She never traveled home for holidays. Where *was* home, even? Belinda and Cece didn't know, but they respected Eva's privacy. Mysterious pasts weren't unusual for transplanted New Yorkers. Moving to New York was about reinvention. If you didn't want that, you stayed in Kenosha, Wisconsin.

Once you crossed the Verrazzano Bridge, you were free to shed skin. The Dallas trust fundie became a Red Hook hipster. The Tennessee hillbilly became a well-married tastemaker. In New York, you were who you said you were.

Eva was private. But she was clearly struggling.

Cece pulled Eva into an embrace. Belinda hugged them both. Nearby, a PhD student glanced up from her laptop and snapped a pic for Instagram Stories (#Heartwarming #GirlPower #NeverthelessShePersisted).

"Back then, I felt defective," she said, gently disentangling herself. "Like an alien. I was in so much pain, it burned through everything—my thoughts, my personality, my emotions, everything. Until Shane."

"You met another alien," surmised Cece.

"And the magic's still there! What's his sign?" Belinda googled his birthday on her phone.

"We never had magic," lied Eva, swallowing a pain pill dry. "Just hormones. Honestly, you shouldn't be allowed to have orgasms like that before you're twenty-one. It gives you brain damage."

"March thirtieth." Belinda grimaced. "Damn, he's an Aries. The thots of the zodiac."

"Run," advised Cece.

"Actually, you might need exposure therapy," mused Belinda, nibbling on Eva's untouched scone. "Spend a lot of time with him, until you've demystified his memory. Like when you eat fifteen doughnuts in one sitting to cure your sugar addiction."

"But I don't have time to eat Shane!" moaned Eva. "Today alone, I have a meeting with a potential director and a parent-teacher conference..."

"*And* a book due to my inbox on Monday," reminded Cece.

"Oh. Well, prose before bros," cosigned Belinda.

With that, Eva reached for her bag. She was feeling floaty and tingly from the painkillers, her brain-throb ebbing to a gentle wave. "Love y'all. If I survive this day, I'll text later."

Eva soon found herself stationed between two dynamic women in a Soho landmark again. But this time, it was at Crosby Street Hotel, and with Sidney Grace, *Cursed* producer, and Dani Acosta, the buzzy director interested in filming it.

Set back on a quiet cobbled street, the hotel lobby was like a surreal secret garden—where kooky dog sculptures and rococo chairs coexisted with lavish greenery. What better place to discuss bringing Eva's adult fairy tale to life?

And it was going shockingly well, considering that Eva was mid-crisis. In the eight months since Sidney had bought the film rights, a stream of big-name directors had rejected her proposal. Dani Acosta was Eva's final hope. Her most recent indie, *The Lady Came to Play*, was a Toronto International Film Festival smash about a violinist haunted by a ghost who makes invisible love to her during perfor-mances. Dani was wearing navy lipstick and a sequined tank—and the only thing surpassing her enthusiasm for *Cursed* was Eva's enthusiasm for *her*.

"…and I see lushly ominous visuals with erotic undertones—you get me?" Dani had been raised in East Harlem, and her voice had sumptuous Nuyorican flavor.

"Like *Bram Stoker's Dracula*!" gasped Eva.

Drunk on creative synergy, Dani raised her hands to the roof, where a human-head-shaped chandelier hovered. "We're kindred, you and me."

"Literally." Sidney delivered "literally" the same way she would've said, *Sorry for your loss*. She'd attended LA schools populated by Ritchies and Joneses, and now she had a deadpan vocal-fry pitch that never varied. The biracial daughter of an Earth, Wind & Fire guitarist and a sitcom actress, she was quite connected—and a lot savvier than she let on. At twenty-seven, she'd already produced two Netflix documentaries.

Sidney was desperate to produce a feature film. Dani was desperate to prove she wasn't a one-hit wonder. And Eva was just desperate.

"Dani, I saw *The Lady Came to Play* twice," said Eva. "What inspired the invisible lover?"

"I made love to a ghost," whispered Dani. "I was vacationing at this bizarre ancient hotel in Istanbul. One night, a spirit whooshed under my blankets, and we had mystical intercourse. Ghostly hands all over me."

"Werk." Sidney had no patience for this budding girl-crush. What about production details? Budgets, locations, talent.

"Who was the ghost?" Eva was wide-eyed.

"Turns out, I was hallucinating from an intense Turkish flu," laughed Dani. "*My* own hands were ravishing me!"

Eva giggled. "I've lost my touch. Pardon the pun."

"I like you." Dani leaned forward, coffee-brown eyes boring into Eva's. "And I like your ballsy witch. Let's make magic."

Eva glanced at Sidney, who gave a deadpan nod.

"Dani Acosta," announced Eva, "I think you're the perfect director for *Cursed*."

"Saaame," drawled Sidney, who'd made the decision forty minutes ago. "Let's talk casting. Newbies? Zendaya? Those *Dear White People* cuties?"

"I'm thinking actual white people," said Dani.

"Actual what now?" asked Eva.

"To get real distribution and financing, this film needs white characters."

"But . . . they're Black," sputtered Eva, suspended between disbelief and confusion.

"They're a fantasy," retorted Dani.

"Wakanda's a fantasy, but it's in Africa!"

"Wakanda has Marvel power behind it," Dani reminded her. "Two Black leads will handicap *Cursed*'s potential. You don't want a Black film; you want a *big* film. I see Sebastian as the *Spider-Man* kid, Tom Holland? And Kendall Jenner playing Gia."

Eva was aghast. "She can barely play *herself*. Have you seen her on a runway? It's like she's walking the plank!"

She was in a cold-sweat panic. Black people existed and thrived in all spaces, realms, worlds. And Eva wrote Gia and Sebastian so well that readers of all races took them at face value. A triumph in any genre.

Cursed was Eva's version of protest lit. Whitewashing her characters would erase her career.

"Vampires and witches are already 'other,'" reasoned Dani. "If they're also Black, they're too niche. Imagine finding an audience for a film about a Taiwanese werewolf and fairy."

"But I'd watch that!" Eva's phone buzzed on her lap, cutting off her next thought. It was a text from Sidney.

BE SMART. Dani's our last non-D-list option. We'll work out kinks later. Say yes.

"Yes," said Eva, heart sinking. "Kendall. Spider-Man. Genius."

Minutes later, she was on the subway, bound for Audre's parent-teacher conference in Brooklyn. Her heart was throbbing in her temples. How had she allowed that meeting to career so far out of her control? Where was her integrity? Maybe she didn't have any. Only a sellout would bleach and brighten her fictional babies for a paycheck. No. The very idea was a searing humiliation. Out of self-preservation, Eva banished it to the back of her mind—she couldn't break down now; there was no time.

At least Audre was at the top of her class. Nothing to worry about there.

And so she walked into Cheshire Prep all easy breezy. Here, if nowhere else, she knew everything was right with the world. She strode the hallways of the sprawling Victorian mansion with the smugness of a woman whose daughter was the queen of seventh grade.

Eva was secretly proud of Audre's popularity. Audre was a leader in a school full of overachieving, hypercompetitive alphas from two-parent homes with old family money. It took confidence to own that crowd. And Audre did it by being friendly and empathetic and not an asshole.

My golden child, thought Eva, sweeping into Head of School Bridget O'Brien's office. With a bright smile, she kissed her daughter's cheek and sat next to her at Bridget's desk. The office was a nod to Cheshire Prep's 150-year history, with accents like 1920s club chairs and Edwardian gas lamps.

Bridget herself was also a bit of a throwback. Tall and svelte, the fifty-five-year-old gave off Hitchcock-blonde vibes, with her back-combed platinum bob and belted Burberry dresses. She had two interests: lasering her crow's-feet and ensuring that Cheshire Prep became NYC's top private school before she retired in 2021. Thus, she favored students who won titles.

Audre had earned all-state gold medals from debate-team championships, plus first place at visual-arts regionals. She was so golden, Eva had a standing invite to Bridget's annual holiday dinner party at her Cobble Hill town house.

"Audre's suspended," said Bridget.

"I'm sorry?"

"I'm suspended," whispered Audre.

"I heard her!" snapped Eva, who was only now noticing the swollen redness around Audre's eyes. *And Eva's cameo ring, on her left hand.* Shocked, she glanced down at her naked finger. That morning had been so hectic, she hadn't realized she wasn't wearing it.

Eva gaped at Audre. "What did you do?"

Audre's eyes rolled up to the gold filigree ceiling. As if Eva's question, rather than getting herself kicked out of school, was the true indignity.

"Earlier in the year, we spoke to you about Audre's peer-counseling Snapchat sessions." Bridget's airy voice only *just* disguised her blue-collar Boston-Irish roots. Until her freshman year at Vassar, she'd spoken like the entire cast of *The Departed.*

"But she stopped making them," Eva inserted hurriedly.

"She did, and Snapchat videos disappear after twenty-four hours. *But a screenshot lasts forever.*" Bridget unearthed a file from her desk drawer. "A few weeks ago, Audre posted a video of her session with Clementine Logan."

"Clementine Logan." Eva feared where this was going. "Her mom's Carrie Logan, the dean of students?"

"Bingo," sighed Bridget. She slid a printout across her desk to Audre. "Clementine made an alarming confession about her mother on the video. A student took a screenshot, created a meme, and it's been circulating all week."

Eva glanced at the printout of the meme. In it, Clementine was mid-wail with tear-streaked cheeks. The image was blurry, but the caption wasn't:

TFW YOUR MOM'S GETTING HER BACK BLOWN OUT BY YOUR ENGLISH TEACHER.

Eva's jaw dropped open. Audre sniffled.

Bridget's Botox-frozen brows struggled to furrow. "TFW means—"

"That feeling when," said Eva. "I know."

"Mom has 24K Instagram followers." Audre's voice was shaky but proud. "She's familiar with social-media linguistics."

Bridget looked relieved that she wouldn't need to translate "back blown out."

"So, the English teacher isn't her husband?" asked Eva haltingly. "Jesus, Audre."

"I posted it *way* before you made me stop!" she wailed, her buns quivering. "And I had no idea Clementine Logan's mom was a cheater!"

"Mr. Galbraith, the English teacher, has been let go," announced Bridget.

"Bridget, I apologize. But Audre never meant to hurt anyone."

"Perhaps, but she has detention for the rest of the week." Bridget smoothed her bulletproof do with French-manicured fingertips. "And the honors board is undecided about inviting her back next year."

A miserable groan escaped Audre's throat. Eva looked over at her beloved baby, the spawn of her loins, and wanted to choke her within an inch of her life.

"Audre, can you wait outside for a moment?" managed Eva.

Thrilled to be dismissed, Audre escaped to the hallway.

Bridget waited three seconds before locking the door. Then she grabbed a pack of Parliaments from her purse, opened a massive window, and lit up. After a lung-expanding drag, her posture relaxed.

Only in front of select parents did Bridget drop her classy veneer and get raw.

"Swear to Christ, Eva," she muttered on an exhale, "I don't need this psychosexual melodrama right before I retire."

Eva met her at the window. "This was a youthful error. How can I fix it?"

She grabbed her forearm, *willing* Bridget to remember how delightful she'd been at her holiday dinner.

Bridget peered down at Eva with her Windex-colored eyes. When she spoke, she sounded exactly like who she was: the daughter of a man who, every evening of her childhood, ran numbers in their basement with a crew of local heavies while wearing a T-shirt proclaiming, I CAME HERE TO FIGHT OR FUCK & I DON'T SEE YOUR SISTER.

"You tell me."

Bridget's skin was flawless thanks to free Restylane injections from Dr. Reece Nguyen—offered as collateral to keep his ninth grader in school after her Forever 21 shoplifting scandal. And Bridget's enormous hair was freshly styled thanks to free visits to Owen Blandi Salon— offered in exchange for Bridget allowing Owen's permanently vaped-out son to graduate.

Bridget O'Brien could be bought. But what did Eva have to sell?

"What do you need?" asked Eva.

"Know any English-lit teachers?" she asked, taking a drag.

"I don't think so, but…"

"Eva, this scandal can't be my legacy. I need to bury it with a new-teacher announcement. Fast. Find a suitable replacement for Mr. Galbraith, and Audre has a spot in eighth grade."

Eva loathed being strong-armed. Bridget was a crook, but Eva had been hustling her whole life. But this was about her baby. Audre couldn't get expelled. It took great restraint not to slip into Genevieve mode, telling this bitch to fuck completely off.

"Give me a couple days," spat Eva, spinning on her heel. With her hand on the doorknob, she said, "You really are so corrupt, Bridget."

"This is your daughter's academic career," Bridget said, stubbing out her cigarette on the windowsill. "I've done worse for less."

"But enough about your helmet hair," Eva clapped back. Then she slammed the door so hard the hinges shook.

Eva found Audre leaning against a wall, eyes squeezed shut. Her Vans were placed shoulder-width apart, and she was breathing steadily in and out. Meditating. Eva knew it.

"Audre Zora Toni Mercy-Moore."

Audre's eyes flew open, and then she crashed into Eva, enveloping her in a one-sided embrace. "Mommy, I'm so sorry."

"I try to be the best mom I can be." Eva was speaking more to herself than to Audre. "How is my daughter facing suspension? How?"

"I'm sorry!" stage-whispered Audre.

Sorry don't fix the lamp, bé, she heard her mother say.

Get out of my head!

Eva grabbed Audre's forearm and marched her to a private alcove by the girls' bathroom. She spun her around so they faced each other. "I'm pretty sure you broke up a marriage. Do you get the ramifications of that?"

"Yes!" she exclaimed. "But husbands cheat all the time with no repercussions. In a way, it's like I'm dismantling the patriarchy?"

"Oh, *grow up*. This isn't about the patriarchy."

"You say everything's about the patriarchy!" Audre began to weep. Her tears left blotchy streaks in her cotton-candy-pink blush (the only makeup she was allowed to wear). She looked so young, like when she was a first grader playing in Eva's makeup.

"Do you realize that I'll have to sell my fucking soul to keep you enrolled?"

Nodding and sobbing, Audre saw a classmate walk down the hall—and quickly shielded her eyes with her hand.

"All I ask," reasoned Eva, "is that you kill it in school, excel in art, stay kind, and cuddle with me during *Stranger Things*. Ruining your academic career does not fit into this scenario."

Audre's tear-shiny eyes narrowed into slits. With head-spinning quickness, she went from sad to seething.

"Maybe I want more than good grades and *Stranger Things*," she blurted out. "I want to be a butterfly! Fly around, following my heart. Guess what? I don't even love art. I do it 'cause I'm awesome at it and it's *your* dream for me. My dream is to be a celebrity therapist. Possibly with a nail-salon franchise. Which you've never supported, BTW."

"You've never mentioned a nail franchise!"

"Well, I've thought about it." Audre took a step away from Eva, her fists on her hips. "Look, I messed up. Noted. I'm not perfect, like you."

Eva threw her hands up. "You know I'm not perfect."

"You are! Because you don't *live*. You just write books you hate, and obsess over me. You don't have boyfriends or travel or do fun stuff or want anything more than you've got." She took a breath. "You write about love, but you won't go get it. *You don't want anything.*"

Eva's hurt was instant and excruciating. "How...dare you psycho-analyze me?"

Emboldened by her speech, she went further. "Quick question. Why did Daddy leave? Was he not perfect enough for you?"

"Excuse me?"

"You're not a person," said Audre, with disdain. "You're a robot."

And then the only thing between them was endless, temple-throbbing silence. Another kid came barreling down the hallway. This time Audre turned away from her mom, waved, and smiled. But when she faced Eva and saw her stunned expression, she wilted. Her bravado gone.

"You done?"

Audre nodded, instantly sorry.

"You're right," said Eva, voice trembling. "I'm a robot. A robot who's set up your life so you have the freedom to try new things and make messes and still have a life to come back to. *I'm* the reason you get to be a butterfly, you ungrateful...*tween.*"

Hot tears stung her eyes. No. She had to keep her cool.

"And another thing!" yelped Eva, decidedly not keeping her cool. "When would I date? With what time, energy? I give it all to *you*, kid. There's nothing left over for anyone else! Think about that the next time *you* fuck up and then have the *unbelievably* reckless audacity to critique *my* life choices."

"Mommy, I'm—"

"Sorry. I know," Eva spat. "I'm on deadline. I gotta go," she said, storming off. Abruptly, she paused. "And gimme my ring," she said, slipping it off Audre's finger.

With that, she left her precious child standing alone in the storied hallways of Cheshire Prep.

Once she was outside on the blazing-hot, brownstone-lined Park Slope street, she sank down onto the school steps. She was in too much pain to walk home. So she swallowed a pain pill and brooded.

Eva did want things. She wanted the world for her daughter. She wanted to see her characters on the big screen, racially intact. And deep down—fathoms deep, where she buried her weightiest wants—she wanted to go to Louisiana and research her dream book. The one that might turn her and Audre's life upside down. The one uncovering the truth about her bloodline, the incorrigibly untamed, dangerously wild Mercier women.

Eva wanted things. She'd just forgotten how to get them.

She used to be brazen. Where was that girl who'd run away from her mother, to Shane, to Princeton, and then to New York? Who was that girl?

There was only one person who remembered. And he'd been texting her since she'd fled the diner.

With trembling hands, she pulled her phone out of her purse.

Today, 11:15 AM
S.H.
Call me.

Today, 11:49 AM
S.H.
Please, Genevieve.

Today, 12:40 PM
S.H.

Just wanna make sure you're okay. Please.

Today, 2:10 PM
S.H.

Okay, I have no right to know anything about you anymore.

Today, 2:33 PM
S.H.

Fuck it, yes I do.

Today, 2:35 PM
S.H.

I'm staying in the West Village. 81 Horatio Street. I'll be here till Sunday. Please come, if you want to talk. Any day, any time. But if you don't, I get it. And I'll leave and never bother you again. Just know that I wish you the most brilliant, weird, and wonderful things, every day of the world.

Eva stared at her phone. Like if she looked hard enough at it, it would burst into flames. And she'd be rid of him forever.

Brilliant, weird, and wonderful. When was the last time she'd experienced any of those things? She didn't know.

But she did know she'd do anything for Audre.

She also knew that Genevieve had always lurked on the outskirts of her personality—muted by motherhood, career, self-preservation, and common sense, but *there.* Eva was older, but the same bones were under her skin. The same flame, dulled to an ember, waiting for a spark to set her ablaze again.

And most importantly? She knew an English teacher.

Chapter 11

AN AGGRESSIVE ACT OF PERSONAL REINVENTION

SHANE HALL WAS RUNNING FOR HIS LIFE.

The diner disaster had scrambled his brain. His heart was shredded. His stomach was in knots. In a former life, he would've dealt with this in dangerous ways. But due to his recent aggressive act of personal reinvention, he was no longer a drinker. He was a runner. A capital-*R* runner, and you knew he was serious, because he bought Nike Vaporflys, the sneakers the Olympics almost banned for giving runners an advantage. And he was wearing the Garmin Forerunner 945 GPS watch to monitor his pace in pro-marathoner style. Most notable, though, were his elite-grade compression socks, which were recommended by Usain Bolt in an old *Esquire* he'd dog-eared in some midwestern JetBlue VIP lounge. His gear was fire.

Shane didn't half-ass anything. He ran as hard as he drank.

Never mind that in AA, he was warned of the dangers of cross-addiction—when you put down a drink and pick up a new obsession, like evangelism or multilevel-marketing schemes or rescuing pit bulls. And fine, Shane knew that his running habit bordered on extreme. But what new addictions could possibly scare him? Not having a drink was excruciating, and he beat that. Not having anything else would be easy.

So Shane ran and ran, until the steady, hypnotic rhythm of his footfalls and his modulated, focused breathing coaxed him into calm.

Because he'd had a day.

The sun was just about to set beyond the Upper Manhattan skyline, and Shane was trying to outrun it. He'd already run the six miles from his rental in the West Village, down the West Side Highway and around South Street Seaport. Now he was looping his way back up. At first, his pace was too aggressive, too swift—but for the past ten minutes or so, he'd started slowing a bit. He was right on the cusp of exhaustion. But that was what kept Shane going, that flicker of uncertainty, the threat of burning out.

And he had to keep going, because he wanted to be home before nightfall. He couldn't be away from the apartment for longer than an hour. He'd told Eva to come by if she needed him. And ever since she'd fled, crying, from the diner that morning, he'd been waiting for her. He probably wouldn't hear from her—but on the off chance that she wanted to talk, he had to be there.

He'd been the one to make her cry. It was what he always did, destroying the people he loved the most, the things that made him happiest. Seeing her that upset again, knowing he was the cause of it—it had triggered an old panic that was too deep-seated to shake. He had to fix it. He couldn't let that be the last time they saw each other.

Chin down, eyes trained ahead of him, he blazed his way down the West Side Highway running path—the glittering Hudson River winding lazily to his left, with the New Jersey skyline stretching beyond it. It was thickly hot, the kind of heat that makes you listless and lethargic. Visibly drained tourists draped themselves over benches, while the path was crowded with barely moving senior joggers and mommy groups ambling by with designer strollers. Everyone but Shane was on chill mode.

Was it selfish to hope for even a second more of Eva's time when *he* was the reason she wasn't okay? Probably. Was it reckless and childish to have sent her all those texts? Fuck yes. But he'd analyzed the situation too many times since this morning, and he didn't know what else to do.

I shouldn't have come at all, thought Shane, almost colliding with a twenty-something couple who were somehow successfully jogging while sharing EarPods.

But he had come. He'd started another fire. This time, he'd stay and put it out.

Slowing his pace, Shane glanced up at the horizon to check the sunset. The predusk sky was vivid with waves of fuchsia and lavender, and not for the first time since getting clean, he was struck by how alive the world looked. He was suddenly so alert. It was how he'd been as a little kid, before he'd started anesthetizing himself. Back then, he'd felt things too deeply for his own good.

One time, while waiting in a Kmart checkout line, five-year-old Shane had seen some guy steal a waffle iron from a woman's cart while she wasn't looking. His mind had quietly spiraled over it. What if waffles were all she had to feed her thirteen badass kids because their dad squandered her modest bank-teller salary on fantasy-football bets and scratch cards? *What if her life depended on that waffle iron?* He'd obsessed about it for days.

And snakes used to ruin him. Just the idea of them. Shane couldn't bear the thought of those delicate-looking reptiles trying their hardest to travel around their patch of forest while legless and footless. It broke his heart! They were so unfairly handicapped. He used to obsessively sketch pictures of snakes with four legs, until it occurred to him that he was, in fact, drawing lizards.

The world was too loud for little-boy Shane. What he didn't know was that he was training himself to be a deeply empathetic writer—understanding nuanced emotion, spying humanity in unexpected places, seeing past the obvious. He was taking notes for his future self, who would write it all down. Every fucking thing he saw. And thank God he was good at it. If nothing else, writing helped organize the chaos in his brain—even if it had only come in four intense bursts over the past fifteen years.

I'm already thinking of my career in past tense, he realized, speeding up a bit.

Shane wrote his books hoping to smooth out the jagged edges of his life. Which didn't exactly work. If reviewers were to be believed, his novels could rearrange the way a reader thought, sparking existential epiphanies. But he could never reach himself. In fact, his biggest triumphs were followed by his biggest benders. No matter how dizzying his professional highs, Shane just couldn't resist the pull of the tide sweeping him out. Self-destruction was always imminent.

No, if writing had been the cure, the past fifteen years would've looked very different. He wouldn't have taken so long to get sober. He might've picked a permanent place to live, put down actual roots. Invested in Seamless or Spotify. He'd have gotten serious about the business of living.

And he would've found Eva long ago.

Stretching ahead of Shane was Pier 25. Families swarmed the turf overlooking the water, taking pics or waiting to hop in rented kayaks. Shane glanced over at the dads with toddlers on their shoulders, while moms juggled cell phones, snacks, stuffed animals, and juice boxes in two hands. It was all so exotic. He'd always appreciated families from a distance, looked at them like they were a fascinating experiment: all that intimacy and domesticity couldn't have been more foreign.

Maybe it was the disjointed way Shane grew up, but he didn't know how to cultivate that sense of home. So he rejected it. He always lived alone, far from crowds and populated cities—especially ones that reminded him of DC—preferably near the ocean, and rarely longer than six months. Rentals only. There was a freedom in staying at places that weren't his. Shane reveled in that vaguely disorienting vibe of bed-and-breakfasts, Airbnbs, somebody's seaside shack—just-passing-through places where things were a little bit off. Lamps instead of overhead lighting. Sheets aggressively scented with some foreign fabric softener. Jumpy ceiling fans and dusty bookshelves with eclectic '80s paperbacks (often historical westerns featuring covers with chesty women and sometimes a horse). It was impossible to get too comfortable in a place that kept reminding you it wasn't yours.

And it was impossible for anyone to know him, either. Which was perfect. During his lost years, he hadn't wanted people to see how unstable he was. Of course, sobriety had shown him that everyone was a little bit off. His shit was just closer to the surface.

What's wrong with you? Eva had asked that first day. Shane had been fielding this question for years. But when Eva said it, it was the first time he'd actually given it any real thought. She'd asked with curiosity, not judgment.

Shane was a complete stranger and confessed to breaking his arm on purpose—but she didn't write him off or condemn him or, worse, laugh. She didn't try to convince him to stop. Eva's generosity was stunning—she just wanted to know why.

And he would've told her. But back then, he couldn't articulate the reasons why he did that to himself.

Keeping a steady pace, Shane powered past City Vineyard, the riverfront restaurant with its dazzling downtown skyline views and digital nomads sipping rosé in plastic glasses. The sweet, fermented scent of *bar* wafted over him on the dry, hot breeze, driving him to run faster. With every heavy footfall, every forward swing of his upper body, the bones in his left forearm reverberated—a low thrum, just enough so he could never forget his old habit. And what, exactly, was wrong with him.

The first time it happened was when Shane was seven, the terrible event that had sent him hurtling from foster home to foster home, where he learned new crimes, new dysfunctions, new ways to be unloved. That was one piece of it. The other was every time he broke his arm, it *hurt*, but when it dulled, he'd be shot through with this remarkable insight about himself. It was the only time he saw who he was, crystal clear.

The second time, he was a third grader in a DC juvenile detention center, and a guard was mercilessly kicking his ass for sleeping through lunch. Shane kept fighting back, a mad-as-hell Mighty Mouse with rapid-fire fists. Finally, the guard knocked him off his feet with a quick, decimating blow to the jaw—and Shane purposely used his arm to break his fall. Bone, broken.

Oh, he realized. *I'm a person who doesn't know when to stop.*

Another time, he was a twelve-year-old in the schoolyard. In a school full of rowdy, troubled misfits, Shane already had a reputation for being the craziest. In front of a crowd, some girl dared an older kid to crack him over the head with a Snapple bottle. Just to see what Shane would do. In a flash, Shane had the older dude in a headlock and then flung them both against a brick wall—elbow first. Bone, broken.

Oh, he realized. *I'm a person people watch for entertainment.*

Later, at seventeen, a loudmouth knucklehead was bullying the new kid. And to save her, Shane whacked him in the face with his casted arm. Bone, broken.

Oh, he realized. *I'm a person who'll do anything for this girl.*

Before Eva had so dramatically collided with him on the bleachers, Shane had felt like he was slipping away. And there was certainly no school counselor, no parent, no concerned social worker grounding him to the earth. Then he met Eva, and she breathed the same air. She stuck to his bones, imprinted herself on his brain—and thoroughly rearranged his world, in the best way.

Stop thinking about the past. Start thinking about how you're going to explain yourself to this woman.

Shane was mired in these thoughts when his phone vibrated on his arm (where it was slotted in his Nathan iPhone armband, rated Best Accessory of 2019 by RunnersWorld.com). He froze abruptly on the path. A few paces behind Shane, a group of baroquely mustachioed and muscle-bound Bushwick dudes skidded to a halt seconds before they would have body-slammed into him.

"The fuck, bro?"

The near collision didn't register, because Shane was too busy praying this was *it*. The moment. Eva finally wanted to talk. He issued a silent plea to the universe that he was right, and snatched the phone out of his armband.

It was Marisol, Datuan, Reginald, and Ty. Four of his favorite students had texted him, one after the other.

Wiping sweat from his forehead and drooping with disappointment, Shane zigzagged through the joggers to a small stretch of Emerald City–green grass to the left of the path. Finding an empty spot, he collapsed on his back, exhausted and winded.

So Eva still wasn't speaking to him. But hearing from his kids was second best.

Like he did with Ty, Shane promised all the students he mentored that he'd always be available. These were at-risk kids. None of them had real parental figures, and he'd happily stepped into the position.

Shane strongly doubted he'd have his own children. He didn't trust his DNA. And the question of who his birth parents were—well, he had a feeling it was better not knowing. But for a misanthropic nomad with no professional training in mentoring teenagers—and whose own teenage years could've inspired a chilling docuseries on Vice TV—he owned the role. It fit him almost too comfortably. Shane's life as a teacher hit harder and was more rewarding than making it onto a bestsellers list.

He was probably too attached to surrogate-parenting other people's kids. There'd been a few moments, like when Bree, his favorite student in Houston, was strong-armed by a cop after a neighbor called the police on her loud-but-innocent sweet-sixteen party, when his investment spilled over into something unhealthy. His reaction was thunderous, and it was the first (and only) time he felt unsteady in sobriety. But he loved those kids. They needed him. And Shane never actually slipped, so it was worth the risk.

Today, 7:57 PM
Marisol
MR. HALL!! Is cat food poisonous when people eat it? Mistakes were made.

Today, 7:59 PM
Datuan
Wuts good. Funny shit. Principal Parker thought WTF meant Well That's Fantastic.

Today, 8:02 PM
Reginald
Sup broke up wit Tazjha shes a bad GF told her actions speak louder than wombats
*wombs
*WORDS *WORDS *WORDS
Fucken autocorrect

Today, 8:06 PM
Ty
Wyd
I like the planetarium

Shane's brows crinkled in surprise. Ty didn't like anything! And if he did, he certainly never articulated it. He barely articulated anything at all. Shane's entire goal in setting up the internship at the planetarium was to get him invested in something, show him what it was like to pursue a passion. Shane glanced up at the sky. He wanted to be home before night fell, in case Eva stopped by. He had time for a call.

"Ty! What's good, dog? I got your text."

"Yeah."

"You like the planetarium internship?"

"It's aight."

"Tell me about it. Why do you like it?"

Silence.

"Ty?"

"I'm shrugging."

Shane sighed. He really needed to work with Ty on his communication skills.

"You just said, 'I like the planetarium.' That's a powerful declarative statement. When you express an opinion, you should be prepared to support it with viable evidence. You enjoy it, based on what?"

"I don't know. It's just chill. Like, I don't know why." Ty paused for a moment. "I mean, in the sky theater..."

"Sky theater!"

"That's what Mr. James calls it. In the sky theater, it's like I'm a real astronomer. Like, *for real* for real. I can see the sun's path from east to west. Look up close at the moon."

"That's incredible, Ty. I know the moon's your shit."

"Yeah, and today we learned about bizarre stellar objects. Like neutron stars, pulsars, black holes. And there's...there's...a girl."

Shane smiled. "Oh, word?"

"Yeah. She be in there sometimes. She draws or whatever. Today she drew a white dwarf."

Shane stared blankly into the sky. "But why?"

"A white dwarf's a star that's exhausted its nuclear fuel."

"*Ohhh.* What's her name? You talk to her?"

"Nah. I can't talk to her."

"She bad, huh?"

More silence.

"Ty, are you shrugging?"

"Yeah."

"Listen. You're smart. You're loyal. You're one of the most interesting kids I've ever met. You never know, this girl might go to the planetarium every day, hoping that you'll speak to her. Just try."

"Can I ask you something." As usual, Ty's questions sounded like statements. "How you know when you're really feeling a girl."

Shane sat up a bit, leaning back on his elbows. Liking the planetarium girl was monumental for a deeply insecure kid like Ty and must be dealt with gently.

"When it's real," declared Shane, "you won't even have to ask the question. It just hits you. Kind of like being shot."

"Shot," repeated Ty, sounding doubtful.

So much for gently, thought Shane.

"Hear me out," said Shane. "It's like you know something dramatic happened. But you don't know your insides have been ripped open until after the fact. That's what falling in love is like. When it's real, you don't fall in love with any awareness. You don't get a say. You get hit fucking hard and then process it later. You know?"

More silence.

"I ain't tryna get *shot*, fam."

"Ty, it was a metaphor."

"Yeah, but like, I just wanna ask her if she wants to go with me to Cold Stone or whatever. Get some ice cream," grumbled Ty. "You're doing too much."

"See, you don't even need my help! You got a plan," said Shane encouragingly. "Just ask her out tomorrow. And be confident with it. If you believe you're that dude, she will, too."

"Maybe I should ask her if she's lactose intolerant first."

"Under no circumstances should you do that."

"Nah, you right."

"Listen, you got this," said Shane. "Hit me back, let me know how it goes."

"I'll get at you. Good lookin' out," said Ty, and then he clicked off.

Shane slipped his phone back in his armband, buzzing with hope for that kid. Ty would be fine.

The sun had just set, and there was still a chance—an off chance, a slim-to-none chance—that Eva would come. He set off jogging through the bendy West Village streets, back to Horatio Street.

There was a strong possibility that the diner was the last time he'd ever see Eva. But he couldn't help wanting more. Seeing her again was stressful and world tilting—but underneath, it was good. Too good. On the flight to New York, Shane had imagined a million scenarios of how their meetup would go. He'd hoped he wouldn't feel anything.

But like he'd just told Ty, he didn't really have a say in it, did he?

Chapter 12

TWENTY QUESTIONS

2004

IT WAS AFTER DARK WHEN SHANE BROUGHT GENEVIEVE TO AN IMMENSE, uninhabited mansion on Wisconsin Avenue. As always, he felt nothing but derision for people who'd own a place like this and not even bother to live there. If it were his, he'd have to be forcibly removed.

The decor looked like a museum. There were gold-filigree accents and animal-skin rugs everywhere. Twinkling chandeliers. A dizzyingly abstract, primary-color-splashed painting hung over a horsehair couch in the foyer. That couch was a prickly horror, never meant to be sat on.

Genevieve plonked herself down on it immediately.

She didn't ask how Shane knew the alarm passcode. Or why, despite the house being bathed in darkness, he knew his way around. Tomorrow, he'd explain that it was his friend's childhood home. She lived on campus at Georgetown Law. Her dad was the Korean ambassador, and since her parents more or less lived in Seoul, the house was usually empty. She'd extended an open invitation for Shane to stay whenever he wanted to escape.

He hoped Genevieve wouldn't ask what he did in return for her generosity. Not that he was ashamed. He just didn't want her to know how desperate he was.

But then Shane remembered her expression in the ER when he asked her to run away. The look on her face had been wild, a flash of despair mixed with thrill. An automatic yes, because the alternative was unthinkable.

This was a girl who understood desperation.

Shane led her through the Mexican-tiled kitchen, to a servant's stairwell, and up to a suite on the third floor. Once a fancy teenage girl's bedroom, today it doubled as attic storage. Photo albums, dolls, ancient magazines, snow globes, and flutes were stacked in neat piles. There were two massive French doors leading out to a terrace overlooking a rolling green backyard with a kidney-shaped pool. Holding Genevieve's hand, Shane led her slowly to a canopied four-poster bed, plush with pale-pink bedding.

Then he reached under the bed and pulled out a tray with gallon-sized baggies holding endless amounts of weed, pills, syringes, powders. They were labeled by feeling: COMA (Valium), CHILL (weed), PARTY (cocaine), LSATS (Adderall), WHORE (ecstasy), NUMB (Percocet), and so on.

The Georgetown girl was a whimsical drug addict. And he was her dealer.

Shane peeled off his tee and collapsed on top of the covers next to Genevieve. They smoked a roach till it was gone. At some point, they curled into each other, Genevieve's face nestled into Shane's neck, his fingers tangling themselves in her curls. It was a hazy, blissful thing, holding her so close in this innocent way.

He slept harder than he had in his life.

Around 10:00 p.m., Annabelle Park strode into her parents' home. She was wearing a baby-pink Juicy Couture minidress and diamond studs. Nestled inside her Louis Vuitton dog carrier was her Chihuahua, Nicole Richie.

Annabelle knew Shane was there. He'd called. Of course, he and his beautiful dick were always welcome. Plus, he was *fabulous* company, because he never spoke. She'd gossip to him about DC elites, and he'd lie there, looking deceptively attentive. Grinning, she trotted up both flights of stairs.

Annabelle flung open her old bedroom door. Instantly, she was assaulted by the decadent scent of expensive weed—and the sight of Shane, in her bed, all cuddled up with some chick. *That messy motherfucker!* Her first instinct was to kick him out, but…well, she wasn't a monster. Where would he go?

In ten months, she'd learned only three things about Shane. The first was that he lived in some Miss Hannigan–ass "children's shelter." The internet said it was an asylum where minors were sent after failing more than twenty trial runs with foster families. The "good" kids took brain-dulling antipsychotic meds with no argument, while "bad" ones were put in solitary, tied to radiators, twisted Victorian shit. She couldn't send him back there.

(By the way, yes, Annabelle was feeling mildly jealous. But it would pass. After all, she was in the middle of planning a $125,000 fall wedding to Dr. Jonathon Kim at the Four Seasons in Georgetown.)

Whenever it was vacant, Annabelle's parents' house was a crash pad for her assorted strung-out friends and their strung-out friends. There were few things she respected less than her parents' house. Shane and the waif with the tragic hair could stay. The staff would be back next Monday to clean up, anyway.

Annabelle crept in to get a closer look. Shane and the girl sported matching black eyes. She was clasping Shane's arm as if she were adrift in a biblical-level seastorm and he were her only anchor.

Annabelle felt sad for her. Shane couldn't be anyone's anchor. He'd never love anything more than getting obliterated.

The second thing she knew about Shane was that despite being chased by some powerful demons, he always survived unscathed. But Annabelle suspected that the girl who fell for him wouldn't have the same luck. When it was over, she'd stagger away, scarred for life.

Annabelle tiptoed downstairs to the servants' kitchen. She grabbed two bags of frozen peas and a chilled bottle of Polugar vodka. Back upstairs, she carefully laid the frozen bags on their faces (for the bruises). Then she placed the vodka on the nightstand. Shane couldn't wake up without it. That was the third thing she knew about him.

With a smug hair flip, she picked up Nicole Richie, spun on her Choos, and left. Annabelle's haters thought she was a mean coke whore with fake cheekbones—and yes, she *did* have fake cheekbones, but she also had a very real heart.

Annabelle Park, soon to be Annabelle Kim, was twenty-two and was grateful to be an adult. Grown women knew better than to attach themselves to time bombs. Teenage girls couldn't wait to be ruined.

When Shane woke up, he didn't know what time it was, what day it was, or where he was. All he knew was that he awoke *gently*. Floating. Peaceful.

And as he did, Shane gradually came to the awareness that he was caressing the preternaturally soft, sweet skin of a girl. And that he was big-spooning this girl, and it was Genevieve. And then he remembered everything. School, the hospital, the frantic dash to the house, and then smoking and smoking before drifting off together.

Hazy flashes from the night came rushing back. He remembered jolting awake from a dream, realizing she was too far away, and pulling her against him, with an unthinking neediness he'd never allowed himself to feel before. At one point, during a brief glimmer of consciousness, he'd realized they were clinging to each other ferociously, smothering each other so that it was almost too hard to breathe, but it felt so good that before drifting off again, he thought, *Fuck it, dying like this would be worth it.*

Shane opened his eyes. Genevieve's head was lying on his good arm (which was 100 percent numb), and his casted one was resting on her hip. He took in the spacious, girly room with the canopy over the king-sized bed shading them from the sun streaming through the glass terrace doors. The clock on the wall read 2:00 p.m. They'd slept for thirteen hours.

Groaning a little, he felt his usual morning tremors, the uncontrollable shaking that alerted him he'd need a drink. Soon. But not right now. Right now, he needed to bury his entire face in the coconut-scented warmth of Genevieve's hair. The way she had become so important to him in just a day was inexplicable.

But inexplicable things happened to him, and Shane accepted life's oddities. He didn't know if this made him an adventurer or an idiot, but one thing was true—nothing interesting ever came from a clear path of rationality.

On the bleachers, all he'd wanted to do was enjoy his vodka-and-ketamine buzz while reading a book he'd already read fourteen times. It was comforting to Shane, knowing what words were coming next. And *that* was what was inexplicable about Genevieve. It felt like she was supposed to come next. Like the chapter had already been written, and they were just taking their places. Like he already knew her by heart.

Shane inhaled her scent again, savoring her. *Nothing's better than this*, he thought sleepily. That was when he noticed the vodka on the nightstand.

Suddenly wide awake, Shane gazed from the bottle to Genevieve's perfect almond-brown shoulder and then back to the bottle. With clarity, he decided that the two most urgent things in the universe were (a) keeping her in his arms and (b) procuring the vodka. How he would get from here to there without waking her up was a question of logistics.

Carefully, his good arm still trapped under Genevieve, he reached over her with his casted arm, fingers still inches from the bottle. He scooted her forward a bit and, with Herculean effort, lunged across her and grabbed at it. Shane twisted off the cap with his teeth and downed three huge gulps.

As he took a breath and another swig, the shaking slowed, and he started to feel normal.

Shane reached over Genevieve and placed it back on the nightstand. He stared at the ceiling. Then he rolled her over and reached for it again.

"How many times we gonna do this?" asked Genevieve, her voice muffled by the pillow.

"Whoa!" he exclaimed. "You're awake?"

"I am now." She grabbed the bottle and handed it to him, turning so they were face-to-face. God, she looked adorable in his T-shirt, with her wild hair and sleep-creased cheeks.

"Hi," he said, with a face-splitting smile.

Genevieve smiled back—but then her expression grew dark.

"What's wrong?"

"No, I'm just…I'm confused," she stammered, looking lost. "What happened? Where am I? And…who are you?"

Shane's eyes widened. Had Genevieve's head hit the floor after she got punched? Did she have concussion-related memory loss? No. *No.* He wouldn't panic.

"What's the last thing you remember?" he asked.

Genevieve squeezed her eyes shut. "Cincinnati."

"Cincinnati?"

"It's in Ohio," she said.

"You serious?" Shane sat up, propping himself against the velvet headboard. He dropped his head into his hands. "No, no, no, no…"

Genevieve's mouth trembled and then her eyes crinkled, and she burst out laughing. "You're so shook!"

"Fuck *me*," he breathed. Despite himself, his mouth curved into a grin, and then he chuckled shakily. "I really thought you had amnesia."

Looking proud, Genevieve sat up next to him, shoulder to shoulder. "Convincing, right? I grew up watching *Days of Our Lives*."

"You're a very strange person," he said worshipfully.

Nodding in agreement, she leaned her head on his shoulder.

"No, but for real. You remember how we got here, right? You're not scared?"

"Nothing scares me," said Genevieve with confidence. Shane didn't quite believe her, though, because just then, the phone in her backpack buzzed. And she tensed against him. It buzzed and buzzed, but she made no move to answer it. He wondered who was calling her. Slipping his arm around her shoulders, he pulled her closer, wanting to obliterate her worry (or at least cuddle it out of her). Genevieve let out a small, contented sigh that ended in a slight moan. And it took all he had not to kiss her.

Shane couldn't. He couldn't make it about that. With everything that had happened in the past twenty-four hours, kissing should've been nothing. But with Genevieve, it'd be something. With her, it'd be a promise.

"I don't even know you," murmured Genevieve, tracing an old scar on his chest with her index finger. "Why don't we feel like strangers?"

"Don't ask," said Shane. "You pull a loose thread and the whole shit unravels."

Her phone buzzed again. This time she looked over at her backpack, which was flung across a wicker chair. Her face was cloudy with worry and dread, but she continued to ignore it.

She bit her bottom lip. "Hey. Wanna go somewhere and be bad?"

"Youthful-indiscretion bad? Or arrested bad?"

"I can't get arrested. My face is all bruised up. How would my mug shot look?"

"Authentic." Stretching a little, his leg hit something cold. Shane dug underneath the sheets and unearthed a bag of defrosted peas. "We slept with peas? These yours?"

"No. Everyone hates peas."

"Huh." Shane took an indulgent swig from the bottle. Something oxidized in his brain, and he was starting to feel properly drunk. "This is good vodka." He studied the bottle with a quizzical expression. "Whose is this?"

"Do *you* have amnesia?" Genevieve said, smirking.

"Yo," he said, "my short-term memory is so fucked."

"Ketamine is a terrible habit."

"Life is a terrible habit," he said, a reckless glint in his eye. "Wanna go down to the pool and get fucked up?"

Before she could answer, Genevieve's phone buzzed again.

"Yes, let's go swimming!" she said quickly. "But what about your cast?"

"Saran Wrap," he said with a shrug. "Will swimming hurt your head, though? I don't wanna make it worse."

Genevieve rested her chin on his arm. She gazed up at him with a soft expression, a trace of a smile playing on her lips.

"No one ever asks," she said quietly. "I'll be fine. But how fucked up are we getting? What if we drown?"

Shane couldn't respond. He was tangled up in her face. He lost track of the conversation completely, hopelessly captivated by her onyx eyes, her languid energy, the buzzing warmth of her skin against his.

What if we drown?

He already had.

Genevieve's phone buzzed again. This time, she shot Shane an apologetic look and yanked the phone from her backpack. From the bed, Shane saw the name LIZETTE flash across the screen. She muted the phone and tossed it on the chair. And stood there, rubbing her temples with her knuckles. Her mood had changed. She was radiating anxiety.

"Does your friend have anything for pain?" She sounded vague and far away. "I don't have my pills."

Shane reached under the bed for Annabelle's stash and crawled out of the bed, handing Genevieve the baggie labeled NUMB. "Yeah, I sold her most of this shit. I'll just restock later."

"Thanks." With downcast eyes, she grabbed a switchblade-sized pouch from her backpack, shifting her weight from one foot to the other. Preoccupied, she started scratching her inner arm, the skin blazing an angry red.

"Genevieve. You good?" he asked, moving closer.

"No!" She raised her hand, stopping him. "I mean, yes. I just...need to...use the bathroom. Give me a minute."

Nodding, he said, "Whatever you need to do."

Genevieve walked across the buffed-to-perfection wood floors to the adjoining bathroom, the interior of which was outfitted in Burberry-plaid wallpaper and gold fixtures. She shut the door behind her.

He knew what she was doing in there. He wanted to stop her, but it was none of his business. On the one hand, they *were* currently sharing a space. But on the other, it would be hypocritical of him to dictate which destructive behaviors were or weren't appropriate.

Clutching the vodka, Shane knocked on the bathroom door. "Can I just stand here? On the other side of the door?"

The silence lasted too long. Shane wondered if he could break down the door if he had to.

"Why?" Genevieve's voice sounded weak.

"So you're not alone."

"Really?" She paused. When she spoke again, her voice was closer. "Yeah, I guess."

Shane leaned his back against the door. Scratching his jawline, plucking at his bottom lip, cracking his knuckles. "You wanna talk, or..."

Just then, he felt a Genevieve-sized pressure on the other side of the door.

"Okay." She sounded close enough to touch. "Let's talk."

"Twenty questions," he said, clearing his throat. "I'll go first. What kind of French are you? Haitian? Algerian?"

"Louisiana."

"Your dad's from Louisiana?"

"My dad's unknown."

"So's mine."

"Ever wonder who yours is?"

"Nah, I'm good. The concept of 'father' just feels made up, like Santa or the Easter Bunny." Shane tapped the bottle against his leg. "Never believed in those niggas, either."

"When I was little," said Genevieve, "I wished he was Mufasa."

Shane paused. "I'm gonna say something controversial."

"Don't tell me you haven't seen *The Lion King*."

"It's just...victors write history, right? What if Mufasa was the bad guy? And we don't know, 'cause he's the star of the story? 'Circle of Life' feels like propaganda to put working-class animals in their place. Like, shut the fuck up, you're meant to be eaten. Maybe I'm buggin'."

"You're not buggin'; you're a *psychopath*," she said, but he could hear a smile in her voice. "My turn. Do you know your mom?"

"Nah. Orphan. You got a mom?"

Her silence felt heavy. "Sometimes."

"Better than nothing, right?"

"Debatable," she sighed. "My turn. Any hidden talents?"

Shane tapped his bottom lip, wondering if he was going to admit this to her.

"I can sing," he confessed haltingly. "Really sing. On some smooth R&B shit. Like, no matter the song—it could be 'Happy Birthday'—my voice comes out sounding like Ginuwine. It's fucking embarrassing."

Genevieve wailed with laughter. "Sing something! A big song, like 'End of the Road.' The 'Thong Song.' 'Beautiful' by Aguilera."

He half grinned. "You want me to humiliate myself for you?"

"No, I want you to *want* to humiliate yourself for me."

They laughed, and soon they were quiet. Shane taking measured sips and Genevieve silent.

Shane was seeing double. He closed one eye, and his vision rebalanced.

"Hey," he started. "Why do you do it?"

"Don't know. I go into a daze." She sounded far away again. "There's a relief after."

"Does it hurt?"

"That's the point."

"Same with my arm," he admitted. "Hurts, but I need it. Like it's the glue holding me together."

She said something inaudible. And then "Gonna sit now."

Shane felt her weight slide down the door. He sat down, too. He didn't know how long they were like that. Time was elastic. After a while, Shane passed out. He must've slept hard, because when Genevieve finally opened the door, he fell flat on his back with a dull thunk.

"Let's go to the pool!" She sounded strong, cheerful.

Shane peered up at her from the floor. Genevieve was wearing a brilliant smile, like the pills had kicked in and what had been hurting her no longer did. She was soaking wet, hair dripping. Had she taken a shower with her clothes on?

The only sign that she'd cut herself was the discreet Band-Aid on her inner forearm.

Stupefied, Shane stared at his drenched T-shirt gripping her skin, her bra, her panties—and he was caught between a helpless surge of arousal and uneasy fascination. *It's like nothing's happened.* She didn't seem hurt. She seemed triumphant. A force of nature.

For a heated, drunken moment, Shane thought he'd hallucinated the whole thing.

But then, confidently, she stepped over him, dripping everywhere and striding out of the room. "Get up!" she called out over her shoulder.

Without thought, he did.

WEDNESDAY

Chapter 13

PRETTY SENTIMENTAL

THE NEXT MORNING, THINGS WERE STILL UNBEARABLY AWKWARD BETWEEN EVA and Audre. Eva's stomach was twisted in knots. It was less about the fight, really, and more about the way they'd spoken to each other. They never said purposefully hurtful things to each other. Other moms and daughters did. But not them.

In silence, Audre slipped out of the house with no breakfast.

Eva was destroyed—she really was. But she knew she had to get this done. The second Audre left, she threw on a short but casual tank dress, tousled her curls to hair-vlogger lusciousness, and speed-walked to the F train. In the three blocks to the subway, her tiny migraine escalated from dull to abusive (June humidity!) and threatened to puncture her fearlessness. She ducked into a bodega bathroom and shot herself in the thigh with her injectable painkiller. By the time she showed up in the West Village, she had a numb thigh, a woozy brain, and limp hair—but she remained focused. After grabbing two iced coffees at a beat-up Eighth Avenue café, she rushed through the labyrinthine cobblestone streets till she found the address.

Horatio Street oozed with designer charm and old New York splendor. Shaded by lush, overgrown trees, No. 81 was the second to last on the block, a nineteenth-century redbrick town house. It loomed one story taller than the rest, with a majestic stoop leading up to a dramatic cerulean-blue front door.

Eva climbed the majestic stoop of the town house, pausing at the top stair—breathing hard, her hands frozen, the iced coffees dripping onto her Adidas.

With no free hand to knock on the door, she gently kicked it with her foot. Nothing happened. She kicked it again. Still nothing. And then it opened.

Shane stood in the doorway, frustratingly broad-shouldered, bright-eyed, and exquisite—all rumpled white tee and gray joggers (*pornographic*)—his expression reading pure, unabashed shock.

"You're here," breathed Eva.

"*You're* here," he said on an exhale. "You came."

Eva nodded. "I did."

He thumbed his bottom lip, trying not to smile. "Why?"

"To bring you coffee," she said, because she didn't know how to tell him the truth. She thrust the cup into his hand.

"Thanks?" he said, confused. "Um. So. I went too hard with the texting. I'm sorry. It was the way you left. I was worried."

"No need. I'm fine." She caught her exceedingly nervous, fidgety reflection in the window. She didn't look fine. She looked like she was on her fifth grande latte.

"Wanna come in?"

"I shouldn't."

"Oh." Shane hesitated a beat before adding, "Want me to come out?"

Eva swayed a little, suddenly knocked off-kilter. Here she was, standing before him, in front of this big, beautiful old house, and she hadn't fully worked out her opener.

"You owe me," she blurted out.

"I owe you," he repeated.

"Yeah."

Shifting a tad, he thrust a hand in his pocket. "For the coffee?"

This was so hard. "No, I mean…look, I'm not here to talk about the past. But after the way we ended? Back then? You know you owe me."

"Oh," he exhaled, getting it. "Hell yes, I owe you."

"I need a favor."

"Anything."

"Really?"

Nodding slowly, he caught her gaze. "What do you need?"

Focus.

"Will you teach English at my daughter's..."

"Yes," he interrupted.

"...school? I don't know how long you're staying. But the head of school is desperate for an English-lit teacher for next school year. It's sort of an emergency."

"Yes."

"Don't you want to know why?"

With twinkly eyes, he said, "Tell me later."

"Bold of you to assume there'll be a later."

"Bold of you to assume there won't be."

Eva's eyebrows shot up to her hairline. "Excuse me?"

"A platonic later." Shane gestured at her, with his coffee. "You're saying the past is truly behind us, right?"

"Right."

"So let's start over. Be friends. You got somewhere to be?"

Frowning, she glanced at her watch. "Yeah. My life is...Well, it's falling apart."

"Wanna talk about it?"

She shook her head. "No. I better go."

"Okay." Shane's expression gave away nothing. "Bye."

Surprised, Eva let out an involuntary huff. "Bye?"

Leaning into the doorframe, Shane said, "You want me to convince you to play hooky? If you want to do it, do it. You're grown."

"Fine." She cocked her head, sizing him up. "Are you still dangerous?"

He chuckled. "Are you?"

"I'm a mom. I write letters to principals, demanding energy-efficient classrooms."

"And I was researching a silent Zen retreat five minutes before you showed up. We're so boring now. What trouble could we get into?"

Biting his bottom lip, he raised his coffee cup toward her.

"One hour," she said, clicking her cup against his. "Tops."

She took in his satisfied, sure smile. She'd never been sturdy enough to withstand that.

First things first, Eva had to tell Bridget O'Brien the good news. As she quickly emailed Bridget, her fingers flying excitedly over her phone, a sense of exhilarated relief flooded her. Audre's place at Cheshire Prep—and everything they'd worked for—was safe. Her baby's academic career, saved! Thank God for Shane.

And then as quickly as it came, her relief began to dissolve into something else—the slowly dawning realization that Shane was staying. Shane, in her city. Infiltrating her world.

It was a small price to pay for Audre's academic career. She wouldn't stress about this now. Instead, all she felt was gratefulness.

The sun shone amber and hot, but there was a gorgeous breeze—a perfect day for aimless wandering. So when Shane suggested they walk along the High Line, she cautiously agreed. It'd be a chill outing for a couple of old...friends? Whatever they were, Shane and Eva hit the hidden stairwell up to the High Line, just behind the tourist-packed Whitney Museum. The elevated promenade connecting the West Village to Chelsea was filled with food carts, fountains, and shaded gardens overlooking the city. After a short walk, they found the mini-amphitheater fronted by a glass wall looking over Tenth Avenue.

Eva was a bundle of nerves, but she felt surprisingly calm in Shane's presence. The sparse crowd on the steps radiated an infectious lazy-day calm: a nursing mom, a dog walker sunbathing with four Yorkies, an older couple sipping lemonade. Eva and Shane picked a spot and carefully launched into hesitant small talk. About the weather. Book sales. The second season of *Atlanta*.

Soon, after slipping into an easy silence, Eva dropped the circular chitchat and dove in.

"Soooo," she started. "Eighty-One Horatio Street."

"My address. What about it?" He shook his coffee, melting the ice.

"That was James Baldwin's house."

"As stated," he noted, "by the plaque on the door."

"No, I'm a Baldwin obsessive. I know he lived there, from 1958 to 1961." She raised her brows pointedly. "He wrote *Another Country* in that house."

"He did, didn't he?"

Crossing her arms, Eva hit him with a squinty-eyed look. "That's the novel you were reading on the bleachers. When we met."

He folded his arms and met her eyes. "Poetic coincidence."

"*Shane.*"

He beamed.

"You're pretty sentimental, bruh," she said.

"And you remembered it. So you are, too." With his smile splitting his face, Shane leaned back on his forearms, crossing his legs in front of him. The sun bounced off the planes of his skin. She found him stupidly irresistible.

"If you have the opportunity to make a moment meaningful, why not take it?" he continued. "I could've stayed at a Ramada Inn with sad salesmen dying slowly of cliché and ennui. Or I could rent my favorite author's house and hopefully get inspired to write. If not, I'd at least enjoy a week of full-circle symbolism."

"How's that working for you?"

"The full-circle symbolism? Well, we're sitting on bleachers again, fifteen Junes later, so I'd say it's going pretty well."

They shared a quiet look. Eva turned away first.

"I meant the writing," she emphasized.

"I can't make words do what I want them to do anymore." He sounded resigned.

Eva set her coffee down. "It's like those cases where people suffer major head trauma, slip into a coma, and wake up speaking a different language. I'd imagine that's what it's like. Writing sober for the first time."

"Yeah," said Shane, mulling this over. Then he let out a small, mirthless chuckle. "It's exactly like that. Like I woke up one day and didn't know English. I'm trying to write in a language I no longer speak." Then he said, "I can't write sober. I haven't said that out loud till now."

Eva leaned back, and they were almost shoulder to shoulder. "Not that I ever watched any footage of you over the years"—she smiled at him—"but you never seemed messy drunk. Just sleepy."

"God, is this about the NAACP Awards?"

"I'm just saying, you hid it well."

"Acting sober is an art," he explained. "The trick is to say *very* little and be *very* still. And if you do that too well, sleep inevitably happens."

"I read somewhere," started Eva, "that on movie sets, actors spin around in circles before shooting drunk scenes. So they're dizzy and off-balance."

"Smart," he said, swirling the ice in his coffee again—a twinkly, soothing sound. "You know what extras in crowd scenes do to look like they're mid-conversation? They repeat 'peas and carrots' over and over. But gesticulate, like they're really saying shit."

"Is that true?" She nudged him with her shoulder. "Act mad."

Scrunching up his handsome features into a menacing scowl, he mouthed, *Peas and carrots, peas and carrots.* He looked like a furious golden retriever.

Eva burst out laughing.

"What's funny?"

"Shane Hall, you're not scary anymore."

"I know. I put the 'hug' in 'thug.'"

They both giggled, until they'd forgotten what was funny. Eventually, they lapsed into comfortable silence, enjoying the sun. When Shane's phone dinged, he lazily glanced down and saw it was from Ty. A selfie of his round, smiling face next to a cute girl with braids, both holding ice-cream cones.

Today is perfect, he thought, damn near giddily. *Everything's perfect.*

"I can't get over how much lighter you are now," said Eva, taking in his expression. "Can I ask you how you stopped? Was it AA?"

Shane thought about this, folding his straw wrapper into a tiny square.

"Nah, I hated AA. The endless sharing and group therapy. All to figure out why you drink. I've always known why, and it never stopped me. I got sober 'cause I wanted to. It was stop or die." He turned to look at her. "I'm too narcissistic to die."

"Huh. You sure therapy didn't work?"

Shane was on the verge of a retort, and then he got distracted by the sun glinting off her bare arms. His eyes traveled across her skin—no longer scarred, but scattered with delicate black tattoos. A half-moon; the Louisiana state symbol; a feather; someone's birth date etched into a dreamy, flower-strewn vine encircling her wrist. Her art was a beautiful distraction.

You'd never know what was underneath.

"How'd you stop, Genevieve?"

"Eva," she said softly.

"I know," he said after a pause. "It's hard for me to say."

"It's okay," she said, and it was. "After...us, I went to a mandatory psychiatric center, for self-harm."

"Your mom sent you?"

"No, the police," she said, offering no more information. "At the center, I found out that cutting was a reaction to feeling helpless. The only time I felt control." She ran her hand up and down her left arm, as if protecting it from searing memories. "Before that I thought of it as a divine ritual. Mayans believed that at birth, the gods gift humans with blood—so you cut yourself to give it back. Like a spiritual cleansing."

"You ever miss it?" asked Shane.

"Sometimes," she admitted in a slight voice. "Usually in the shower. I miss the sting when the water hit my cuts. Pretty sick, huh?"

"Not to me," he said, with no judgment at all. Eva sank into this energy, relaxing a bit, thankful for it.

"I don't miss drinking," he continued. "But I do miss having a crutch. At first, I'd look at sober people like, damn, y'all really out here feeling everything?"

"Yeah. I miss having a way to mute it all."

"I miss vices."

In silence, they sat shoulder to shoulder, inches apart, bodies mirroring each other—but not touching.

"You're still wearing the ring," he said.

She didn't realize he'd been looking at her. Heart fluttering, Eva held up her hand, squinting at her old cameo ring in the sun. "It makes me feel protected—I don't know why. Do you have anything like that? Like, a security blanket?"

"No." Shane looked out into the street. "No, not anymore."

Eva tucked a curl behind her ear, watching hipsters leave Artichoke Basille's Pizza down on Tenth Avenue. And then, offering Shane a shy smile, she stood up, heading down the bleachers to the glass wall.

Standing there, she leaned forward until her forehead rested against the cool glass. The feeling was incredible, like she was suspended in the air, over the street below. Like the world stopped and started here. Her eyes fluttered shut, and she felt Shane stand next to her.

"I did this with Audre once," she told him. "Feels like you're floating, right? Close your eyes."

They stood there for a beat, or two or three, before she glanced at Shane.

Shane's eyes weren't closed at all. He was drinking her in, his expression wide open and mesmerized. In the sun, his eyes shone paler than usual. Eva remembered this color, this gold-flecked honey. She remembered it all. How easy it was, falling into him. One minute she was fine; the next minute she was gone.

"Let's go," said Shane, breaking whatever spell they'd fallen under.

Eva blinked. "Where?"

"To find new vices. Undangerous ones."

"Are they worth it," asked Eva, "if they aren't dangerous?"

"Don't know." And then, with boyish delight, he said, "Let's find out."

Shane and Eva found their first safe vice—an artisanal gelato stand on Little West Twelfth. And they went hard, ordering three-scoop cones before heading back out to the shadow-dappled, mazelike West Village streets.

Shane's cone was brimming over with olive-oil ice cream, and Eva's was cinnamon-cappuccino gelato. It was delicious. The whole afternoon was delicious—so much so that Shane was already nostalgic for it before it had even ended.

It was like the space-time continuum had hiccupped, and they'd never not known each other. They were light as air, giddy with their rekindled friendship. Shane wouldn't dare tempt fate by asking for more than this. This moment was perfect enough. Just this. Just Eva. An Aphrodite in Adidas. His distractingly, dizzyingly sexy Eva, who had barely touched her gelato, because she'd spent the last seven blocks deconstructing the feminist subtext in *Guardians of the Galaxy Vol. 2.*

Shane, not even a superhero guy, was instantly converted. Eva's passion was contagious. Her laugh felt weightless. Her delivery was so . . . bossy. At one point, deep in discourse, she used her glasses as a headband, pulling back her hair—and Shane watched one spiral escape, bouncing onto her forehead. In agonizing slo-mo.

I'd risk it all for that single curl.

Shane was aware that he was going nuts. It was almost too much to walk, talk, and eat ice cream at the same time. Thankfully, Eva plopped down on a bench outside of a nineteenth century apothecary. As she finally dug into her melting gelato, he asked the question that had been on his mind since that morning.

"Subject change," he said clunkily. "Why'd you say your life's falling apart?"

After a dramatic groan, Eva explained Audre's Snapchat scandal.

"...and Audre's a dream. But she thinks she knows everything about the world. She's desperate to be grown. It's scary! Mothering her, I feel so lost sometimes. My only example is my mom, who was many things, but 'mother' wasn't quite one of them."

Before Shane could answer, he saw that across the street, on the corner, an olive-skinned twenty-something with a pink ponytail was gawking at them. She grinned, typed something into her phone, and then giggled. Thankfully, she wasn't in Eva's line of vision.

Motherfuck, he thought, ducking his head. The young fangirls were so wild. The kind with "Eight" inked on eight different body parts.

"You never really told me about your mom," he said, facing away from the girl.

"Hmm." Eva licked her gelato. "Let's see. She was from a tiny town, Belle Fleur. Growing up, people called her Mandy, a nickname for Mantis. 'Cause she was born with her hands in a prayer, like a praying mantis. On the bayou," she started in her mom's Louisiana drawl, "your given name is just a suggestion." She smiled. "Lizette suits her better."

"Sounds fragile and tragic."

"That's my mom," said Eva, nodding. "Anyway, she wasn't trained for anything beyond winning pageants. She got all the way to Miss Universe in 1987 but was disqualified."

"On some Vanessa Williams shit?" asked Shane.

"No, 'cause she couldn't enter the swimsuit competition with a second-trimester bump." She chuckled. "After I was born, we moved to LA, but she was too short to model, and her accent was too thick to act. Her saviors were rich men. She became a sort of... professional mistress. Which was lucrative, for a while. The homes, clothes, schools—all top-notch. You know, I don't remember the inside of any apartments I lived in as a kid? Just the view from my bedroom windows. A man-made lake with marble mermaid fountain in Vegas. The back of a ritzy Persian restaurant in Chicago. In Atlanta, it was a cul-de-sac with a heavy stray-cat population, all of which I named after Wu-Tang members."

"That's a lot of cats."

"After each break up, we'd move. By the time I was a teenager, the cities had gotten seedier, and the men she chose were nightmares. But she never saw trouble coming, you know? She was so childlike," said Eva. "She slept all day, went out at night, and I was left on my own." Eva paused, her brow low. "Lizette was a kook. But to be fair, *her* mom, my grandma Clotilde? Also a confirmed kook."

"She was a professional mistress, too?"

"No, a murderess."

"A…what?"

"Grandma Clotilde had 'fits.' Fainting spells, the blues, and…" She stopped abruptly.

"And what?"

"Violent headaches."

Shane stared at her, unblinking.

"The town thought she was possessed. Especially since she'd get excruciating headaches after she drank the 'blood of Christ' every Sunday at mass. Of course, the blood of Christ was just cheap red wine, a classic migraine trigger. But no one knew this in the '50s." Eva laughed a little. "Everyone thought she was a—"

"A witch," interrupted Shane, looking incredulous. "A witch with migraines."

Eva's dimple popped.

"One day my grandfather was singing in the shed, in this loud baritone. Legend has it, she was having a month-long spell and couldn't *bear* the noise, so she went crazy and shot him. The sheriff was too scared of her to prosecute, but she was run out of town. She left Lizette with an aunt and started over in Shreveport. Oh! And she became an entrepreneur. Apparently, she made a mean jambalaya. She cashed in on the witch thing, selling her recipe at county fairs. CLO'S WITCH'S BREW: SPICES KISSED BY SATAN HISSELF. Her handcrafted labels show up on southern-aesthetic Pinterest boards. My mom told me all of this. She was one hell of a storyteller. It's the only thing we have in common."

Shane slumped back against the bench.

"*This* is your lineage? That's some remarkably dark, fantastic shit!"

"It gets darker." Eva had been holding on to these stories her entire life and was ecstatic to let them go. "When Clo was an infant, *her* mom, Delphine, took off in the dead of night. No warning, just fled to New Orleans and passed as a Sicilian. Changed Mercier to Micelli, became a showgirl, married the attorney general, had a "white" son, conquered 1930s society—and when her husband died a few years later, she inherited his house. A secretly Black woman owned the finest mansion in the very, very racist Garden District."

"Imagine living with the fear of being found out," said Shane.

"I guess she couldn't. At forty, she drowned herself in the tub during her annual Christmas party, with a house full of New Orleans aristo-crats. She wrote '*Passant blanc*' on the tiles, in lipstick. Outed herself." Eva shrugged vaguely. "The story was buried, apparently. I have white cousins who don't know who they are. I found them on Facebook. They're extremely white, too. Republican white."

"*You have Fauxtalian family members?*"

Shane wanted more. As Eva talked, she transformed—her hands floating in the air, as if grabbing pieces of the story, her voice fluid, shape-shifting. Like she'd lived the stories herself.

Eva was all of these women.

"This is a book," said Shane. "*Please* write it."

"Right, and what would the title be? *Unstable Mothers and Unattended Daughters?*" Eva sounded like she'd thought about this. A lot. "Plus, I have to write book fifteen before I start anything else."

"This is the book you brought up at the diner," said Shane, remem-bering. "The one you said no one would read? You're wrong! This is Black American history told through some fascinating matriarchal badasses."

"Look, Audre doesn't know about any of this. She thinks Lizette's a hero. I've...tweaked history a bit, 'cause I want her to be proud of who she is," insisted Eva. "I've never even been to Belle Fleur."

"Go." Abuzz with energy, Shane turned his whole body to face her. "Go."

"Can't." Eva shook her head. "It'd require breaking myself open."

"Why don't you want to?"

"It's a mess in there," she said hollowly.

He wondered when the last time she'd fallen apart in front of someone was.

"But that's the good stuff," he insisted. "It's you."

"I can't afford to fall apart," she said.

Eva met his eyes then. And Shane saw that she looked starved. Something potent and protective hit him. He wanted to grab her and run. Which, historically speaking, probably wouldn't end well.

"Shane," she said quietly. "Why haven't you said my name?"

Shane flinched, caught off guard. It was disorienting, being caught between what he felt then versus his feelings now. If Shane spoke her new name, then she stopped being a memory. She became tangible. And he'd have to confront what was real. Which was that Eva Mercy was unspooling him, as slowly and surely as if she'd tugged a thread.

Shane was here to come clean and go. Falling for her wasn't the plan.

"I can't say your new name."

"Why?"

Hesitantly, he said, "I can't afford to fall apart, either."

Shane heard Eva's tiny huff of breath and saw her lips part, but he never got to hear her answer—because there was the pink-ponytailed chick standing in front of them. Blocking the sun. Waving maniacally, as if she were a great distance away.

Jolted out of a big moment, they peered up at her with confused (Eva) and annoyed (Shane) expressions.

"Hiii!" she shouted. "I'm Charlii. With two *i*'s."

"We all have two eyes," Shane muttered.

"I saw that you guys had, like, an intense vibe? I thought you might need to relax, so I'm inviting you in! But hurry, we close at 3:00 p.m."

"In where?" asked Eva.

"The Dream House. I'm the door girl." Pink Ponytail gestured at a nondescript town house across the street. It had a black door with a sign reading THE DREAM HOUSE in white block letters. A Midtown-corporate woman in Ann Taylor separates stumbled out, yawning contentedly.

"Ohhh," breathed Eva, facing Shane. "I read about this on Refinery29. It's an art installation that's like preschool naptime, but for adults. You drop by, meditate, sleep, chill. And then go back to work, refreshed."

Shane was skeptical. Twenty years ago, he would've robbed every sleeping idiot in that house.

"Is napping around strangers safe?" asked Eva, damn near reading his mind.

"We have *thorough* rules," insisted Pink Ponytail. "So, Dream House is a sound- and light-immersive experience. The rooms are dark except for soft lilac lights, and there's incense and hypnotic music—but you'll hear different tones whether you're standing, sitting, or lying down," she pitched. "Out here it's chaos, global warming, Mike Pence. In there, it's peace, art, freedom. It's like a safe acid trip!"

A drugless high? Eva looked at Shane. Shane looked at Eva.

Ten minutes later, Shane and Eva were enveloped in a womb-like room, floating away.

By then, Charlii-with-Two-Eyes Sanchez had already uploaded her iPhone X pic of Shane and Eva onto the *Cursed* Facebook group—with a detailed description of the sighting. As backup events coordinator of the quite niche Latinx Bruja Association at Queens College, she was a massive fan of Eva's girl-power witch—but as a lifelong New Yorker, she was far too cool to let Eva know.

Chapter 14

GIRLING ABOUT

"Sparrow always does this," wailed Parsley Katzen, who was ten minutes into a diatribe. "She's so thirsty. Such a try-hard."

Audre was in no mood for this drama. All Parsley ever talked about was Sparrow Shapiro. And *Riverdale*. And now Audre was stuck sitting next to her for the next hour. As if detention could get much worse.

"I wore my new platform booties yesterday," started Parsley, "and Sparrow goes, 'Oh, I ordered the same ones from Urban Outfitters last weekend.' Bitch, no you did not. You just need an alibi for when you come to school wearing my shit."

Fighting off an eye roll, Audre gave the mildest response she could muster. "Maybe she did buy them. We all buy the same stuff. Look, we're both wearing the Keith Haring Vans."

"Vans are ubiquitous," scoffed Parsley, who Audre suspected didn't know how to spell "ubiquitous."

This isn't about Sparrow stealing your booties, thought Audre. *This is about Sparrow stealing your bat mitzvah entrance song. As if anyone had the monopoly on "Old Town Road."*

Audre didn't want to discuss this anymore. The good news was, distracting Parsley was easy. "Your brows are *the cutest*. Did you get them microbladed?"

"Yes! At Bling Brows. They're good, right?"

"Iconic." Audre stifled a yawn.

Parsley squealed and then checked her reflection in her iPhone. She stuck out her tongue, threw up a peace sign, and snapped a selfie. "I'm so cute, *ugh.*"

Perfect. Now Audre could mope in peace.

All day, she'd been holding back tears. But since her brand was Consistently Composed, none of the four other kids in Cheshire Prep's strikingly low-stakes detention would've noticed.

Audre could count on one hand the number of times she'd been outwardly bummed at school. Or said a really inflammatory cuss word, like fuckshit. Or trashed a friend behind her back. No one ever knew how she really felt.

Audre Zora Toni Mercy-Moore was a leader, after all! And in the wrong hands, this social power could inspire cliquey shenanigans. Thusly, Audre always tried to seem positive, chill, sane. If her day sucked, she'd just go home, sketch something, read *You Are a Badass: How to Stop Doubting Your Greatness and Start Living an Awesome Life*, and cuddle in bed with her mom.

Audre's emotions were hers to deal with. Other kids really just wanted to talk about themselves, anyway. If you let them, unobstructed, they trusted you. Besides, therapists should never introduce their feelings into a session. (She'd learned this in third grade while reading Freud's *A General Introduction to Psychoanalysis.*)

So despite being stuck in detention and devastated, she was cool. Never mind that the day before, her mom had implied that Audre was the reason she had no life, no love. No real happiness.

I'm a robot, so you can be a butterfly.

Had she always felt like Audre was holding her back? Had her birth been a mistake?

Audre and her mom had never had an all-out brawl before. They were bickerers, not fighters. But yesterday, in Cheshire Prep's main hallway, her mom had glared at her like she was the catalyst for all the stress, strife, and strain in the world.

I'm ruining her life, thought Audre. *I can fix everyone I know but her.*

And it stung, because Eva was her best friend. Of course, Audre adored her dad and his big, bustling extended family in California. On Sunday, she was flying out to spend the summer in Dadifornia—and she already knew it'd be a blast. Her dad was vacation, though. Eva was home.

It had been only the two of them forever. Girling about, creating inane rituals for the hell of it. Taking adventure walks every Saturday. Watching midcentury musicals on Wednesday nights. Collaging vision boards to manifest Oscar wins. Attending drag-queen bingo every Easter. Ordering the entire menu at their June brunch at Ladurée (steak au poivre, macarons, chocolate éclairs, lavender tea, and a Pepto Bismol chaser!) each year before Audre's flight to California.

Tweens were supposed to hate their moms, because most mothers had forgotten how confusing it was to be twelve, thirteen, fourteen. How pointless and powerless you felt. But Eva *got* her. She validated her thoughts, her opinions. Besides, she wasn't like other moms. She was like the young, quirky aunt on a network sitcom. The one you ran to when your actual mom was too uptight to discuss Plan B.

Audre idolized her.

When Audre was four, she'd tried to hop into the shadow that Eva cast on the walls. What she wouldn't have given to try her on.

On her sixth Christmas, she'd asked Santa to make Eva the same age as her so they could be BFFs.

In second grade, she'd snuck up on a napping Eva and colored her entire forearm with a highlighter. Because she was "important."

On days when Eva was too busy to notice, she snuck her special ring out of her room and wore it. To be like her and to feel protected by mommy magic.

And to this day, insomniac Audre still crawled into bed with her, every night around 3:00 a.m. And Eva, usually balancing an ice pack on her head, big-spooned her back to sleep, her warm hand cupping her cheek. Her sheets always smelled of the peppermint and lavender oils she rubbed on her head at night. Audre loved sinking into this scent. And if Eva wasn't in too much pain, she'd sing her an old lullaby.

Dors, dors, p'tit bébé
'Coutes le rivière
'Coutes le riviere couler

Eva didn't speak Creole, so she sang it in a bastardized, phonetic way. *Dough-dough, tee-bay-bay.* Neither one of them knew what the song meant, but it didn't matter. This was when the good sleep started. The peppermint-and-lavender, dough-dough sleep.

Audre's thoughts slowly ratcheted up from miserable to indignant. *She thinks I'm a burden.*

As if it were so easy being Eva's daughter. A babysitter for a twelve-year-old? Constant check-ins, even if she was just walking to a friend's house? And then there was the whole *Cursed* thing. When Atticus Seidman texted the entire class a gross scene from book six of *Cursed*, Audre had to play along, when all the while her soul was cringing.

The sex itself didn't freak her out. Audre was raised by a mom who used the correct words for private parts, was consistently honest about where babies came from, and championed masturbation ("Self-love is paramount!"). Sex was natural, but her mom writing about it wasn't. Gross. She was so asexual! She was just…Mommy. Cuddly and cute. It was like imagining Pikachu writing porn.

Earlier that year, Ophelia Grey's mom had forbidden her to attend Audre's birthday party, because Eva was a "smut peddler." Audre, despite her embarrassment, would defend Eva to the death. She told Ophelia that her mom was repressed, and suggested she try a dildo called the Quarterback, which she'd read about on BitchMedia.org. Eva had been furious with her. But after bedtime, Audre had heard her repeating the story to Auntie Cece and giggling till she cried.

Audre was proud of her mom, unconditionally. But because of one mistake, Eva was no longer proud of Audre.

What else could she do to please that woman? She was a model student. She'd never kissed a boy. Yes, she'd tried a Juul at Brooklyn Bowl's teen night, but she'd barely even felt anything—until she went home and ate her entire bag of Halloween candy during the span of a six-minute YouTube cheek-contouring tutorial.

Eva didn't know how lucky she was, having a daughter like her. If Audre couldn't make her happy, nothing would. If living a dry, dateless life was good enough for her, then fine. But it wasn't Audre's fault. She hadn't asked to be born. She'd learned this lesson from a powerful codependency-themed episode of *Iyanla: Fix My Life*.

Plus, the threat of being expelled wasn't the end of the world. Audre was having second thoughts about her private school anyway. It just wasn't real. She was secretly dying to go to public school, to experience true oppression. There, she could effect the most change.

How can I say I'm a plugged-in cultural force, when I'm surrounded by so much useless affluence? she thought. *Private school is a dated, classist concept.*

She was stifled at Cheshire Prep. And maybe that was the difference between Eva and Audre. Eva accepted being stifled. But Audre wanted to taste life, feel it, do stuff, go places. Be an adventurous woman. Like Auntie Cece! Or Grandma Lizette.

Audre wished she knew Grandma Lizette better. They FaceTimed on birthdays and holidays, but she'd visited Brooklyn only a couple of times. Eva said Lizette had a fear of flying—plus, they were always too busy with school and work to travel much—but Audre always wondered why Grandma Lizette wasn't in their lives more.

In Eva's stories, Lizette sounded divine. Too beautiful, too unique, too powerful for the world. When Audre's Contemporary Art teacher assigned their final project, to paint a feminist icon—she knew she'd paint her grandmother. Lizette, who'd won a zillion titles in the notoriously racist, misogynist pageant industry and, with no education or resources, launched a career as a model and traveled the globe with her daughter. Eva was always talking about the years she'd spent in Switzerland. All that, and then Grandma Lizette had managed to send her daughter to Princeton, too! What *couldn't* she do?

Grandma Lizette was a true American success story.

She would've loved me, Audre mused, her thoughts drowning out Parsley's tirade about whatever.

As Audre continued to plummet, the supervising TA, Mr. Josh, was quietly freaking out. His blond pompadour was sweaty at the hairline, and his peaches-and-cream complexion had flushed a ruddy red. All session, he'd been glued to Book Twitter on his phone, following gossipy tweets with links from Lit Hub, LiteraryGossipBlog, BookBiz, et cetera.

Now he was pacing back and forth in front of the whiteboard, waiting for an opportunity to interrupt the girls. Parsley finally paused for breath. And then, summoning all the prep-school charm that kept him afloat at Vanderbilt while he really wanted to grow his hair to his knees, climb Mount Kilimanjaro, and write about the journey like a male Cheryl Strayed, he approached Audre's chair.

"Hello, girls. How are you holding up?"

"We're good, Mr. Josh," said Audre. "Are we talking too much?"

"No, no, you're fine! Audre, could I speak with you for a moment?"

Her heart sank. God, what did she do now? Pasting on a smile, she said, "Sure. Is everything okay?"

"No, no! You're great. It's just...*ugh*, sorry, I'm nervous." He shook his whole body like a wet dog and started over. "Audre, your mom knows Shane Hall?"

Frowning, she asked, "Who?"

"Shane Hall, the novelist? He wrote *Eight* and *See Saw*."

"Oh, him." She wrinkled her nose. Shane Hall wrote what she called "F-train books": the hardcovers grown-ups toted on the subway to flex that they were reading An Important and Culturally Relevant Book. Audre was a compulsive reader but wasn't into F-train books. She knew about him, though.

"Didn't he have a DUI or something?" asked Audre. "It was on TMZ, I think. My mom wouldn't know someone like that."

"Shane Hall," mused Parsley. "His name sounds like a dorm."

"I think your mom definitely knows him," said Mr. Josh, thrusting his iPhone in Audre's face.

There was Audre's mom, snuggling up to Shane Hall on a bench. Eating ice cream. Looking happier than Audre had ever seen her look. A different kind of happy. The kind of happy that is, in fact, reflective of a person living their best life. The kind of happy that isn't at all held back by a bothersome daughter.

Is Mommy dating this man? she wondered, her mind a swirl of confusion and hurt. *Is she in love? What was that "who has time to date" speech about, then? Why did she lie to me? She's out there, happy AF, while I'm feeling guilty?*

"Anyway," continued Mr. Josh, who Audre had forgotten was in the room, "Shane Hall is my favorite author. And I have a manuscript that I'd kill to get in his hands. I have it on a thumb drive. Do you think if I gave it to you, you could pass it to your mom?"

And then, for the first time in her school career, Audre let go.

"Quick question, Mr. Josh," she said.

"Yes?"

"*WHAT IN THE ACTUAL FUCKSHIT IS MY LIFE?*" she wailed. Then she apologized. And burst into tears.

Chapter 15

DREAM HOUSE

For two cynical skeptics like Eva and Shane, the Dream House, upon entrance, was a bit too earnest.

DREAM HOUSE RULES

Welcome to the DREAM HOUSE. No smoking, vaping, eating, drinking, cell phone use, picture-taking, talking above a whisper, touching, or exchanging of bodily fluids permitted. This is a safe space, don't make it weird. Please store valuables in a locker. If you're in a PRIVATE room, feel free to close the door— but there are no locks. Each person is assigned a freshly washed pillow and blanket (via our eco-friendly laundry service!), please toss in the linen basket when you're done. When your hour is up, your Sleep Guide will give you a gentle nudge. Please do not strike the Sleep Guide, he/she/they is/are simply doing his/her/their job.

And what's your job, you ask? To do three things: Relax! Restore! Recharge!

"And flights of angels sing thee to thy rest." —*Hamlet*

Upon entry, a gazelle-like Sleep Guide handed them freshly laundered plush pillows and blankets. Assuming that they were a couple, she led them toward a private room. Tucked in the first two floors of a classic Edwardian brownstone, the warren of rooms was, indeed, a soporific sleep chamber. Silence was optional, so some light whispers could be heard above the soft, ambient, hard-to-place tonal soundtrack. The smoky-sweet scent of incense wafted unobtrusively through the halls, each room bathed in darkness except for the drowsiness-inducing images projected on the walls. One room seethed with gently pulsing blue dots. Another room glowed burnt sienna, thanks to a crackling bonfire projected on the wall; it was so realistic, Eva almost felt the toasty warmth as she walked by.

People dozed on the floor, lying on massive body pillows, their skin glowing in different colors. In one room, a woman snored softly. A guy in an ill-fitting suit lay next to her, lips murmuring a soundless chant. Or prayer. Maybe he was reciting the lyrics to Lizzo's "Truth Hurts." Who knew? The point was, he was relaxed.

Eva couldn't imagine dozing off within the next hour. Sleep called for five milligrams of Ambien, an ice pack, a painkiller shot, and her white-noise app. But the trippy-hippie vibe *was* soothing. Damn near sublime. The best part was that it was an unexpected twist. Like Alice toppling down the rabbit hole or Dorothy nodding out in Oz's poppy fields. When she set out to see Shane this morning, she definitely hadn't imagined ending up in a hazy, hypnotic fun house. At 2:50 p.m.

With her daughter, her career, and her life in tatters, Eva had no business wasting an hour in this place. But here she was, lost to the world. It felt like what happened here didn't count in real life.

And then there was Shane.

She wasn't ready to say goodbye again. She was aching to make their afternoon last. There was no way to pretend that her day with Shane, though platonic, wasn't the biggest thrill she'd had in forever. It was so easy. Scarily so.

Eva felt a jolt in her personality around him. Shane was pulling her back to her real self; all the goofy, random, raw, dark moments she usually hid were on full display. And he drank it all in. The give-and-take of luring him in and allowing herself to be lured: God, it was exhilarating. She'd forgotten the way they existed in each other's space. That old current was still there, buzzing in the air between them.

Eva was dizzy with it, wanted to suck it into her veins. She felt daring and flirty—jolted awake after too many years of being afraid to feel anything. And if she never saw Shane again after today, she'd be fine. Today was enough.

Stay tuned for this and other lies on Fox News at eight, she thought.

When they arrived at their room, Eva spread their blankets on the matted floor, Shane fluffed the pillows, and they lay down. And that was when two cynical skeptics became very, very sleepy.

Eyes feeling heavy, Eva glanced around the cozy (if borderline-claustrophobic) room. It was the size of a modest walk-in closet. Neon lights reading NIGHT NIGHT decorated the ceiling, pulsing a low, hazy violet-blue glow. Four beats on, four beats off, like a heartbeat. The color turned their skin a surreal, soothing violet.

Eva turned to face Shane, fluffing the pillow under her cheek. He lay flat on his back, one hand tucked behind his head. She watched him watching the flashing words—soon his lids shuttered, his lashes resting on his cheekbones.

"I need a room like this in my house," he murmured.

"Where's your house?"

"Well, yeah, I need to get one first." He opened his eyes, turning his head toward her. "I could never decide where I wanted to stay. Before I started teaching, I'd move twice a year. Nairobi, Siargao, Copenhagen, anyplace near water. Laos. I went on a motorcycle trek there once. Vietnam has the most dramatic terrain. Jungles and mountains and waterfalls. Technicolor-green grass. You feel like the topography's happening *to* you. Did you know over there they call the Vietnam War the American War?"

"As well they should," said Eva, cozying her cheek into the pillow. "What's your favorite place?"

"Taghazout, a shipping village in Morocco," he said, no hesitation. "A nine-year-old kid taught me how to surf there."

"Your life sounds made up, I swear."

"It's true!" he insisted. "And I was good. I ripped my stomach open on coral, though. Probably should've gotten stitches, but I had to act cool in front of this little dude, who was fearless. He was surfing before he could talk. Missing a pinky finger. Tatted up. A fucking pirate. Anyway, I duct-taped it together and it healed crazy."

"There wasn't any Neosporin in this town? Let me see the scar."

It was almost pitch black, but Eva could feel Shane's smirk.

"You're asking me to take off my shirt?"

"God, no." She bit her lip. "Just pull it up."

"You asking or telling?"

"Telling."

He looked at her for a moment with an air-crackling gaze, then reached behind his back and pulled his shirt off completely. In the dark, she made out a puffy, jagged scar snaking across his stomach. More vividly, she saw his strong arms and chest. And his lightly muscled abs, and all that smooth deep-sienna skin stretching down, down, to the barest happy trail disappearing into his jeans. Jesus.

Eva wanted to suck the skin there so badly. Just above his jeans.

"Why are you such a thirst trap?"

"You forced me to do this!" Shane whispered into the dark, pulling his shirt back over his head. "Go to sleep."

"Can't sleep," she murmured. "I'm distracted."

"Why?" He turned his head to face her. And then their eyes locked in silent conversation. It was all so dreamlike. Minutes were melting into each other. Their blinks became slower, the two of them wearing syrupy, satisfied smiles.

Finally, Eva delivered an answer that neither of them believed. "I'm trying to memorize this room. It's good material; maybe it'll show up in a book," she said, yawning faux drowsily. "Honestly, as stressful as writing is, I can't imagine not doing it."

"It's heady, right?" he muttered, eyes focused on her mouth.

"Yeah, the power's so good. Making complete strangers laugh, cry, get turned on. It's better than sex."

"Is it, though?"

"I wouldn't remember, actually," she admitted. "I'm at the sexual equivalent of rock bottom. It's been ages."

"You? But you're such a filthy writer."

"I have a filthy imagination," she corrected.

And sometimes it's enough, she thought. *Mostly, it's lonely.*

Cece had once diagnosed Eva as touch-starved. (One of her authors wrote a self-help book about it.) When someone went too long without touch, they became hypersensitive to the slightest graze. There was truth to it. Last weekend, Eva had almost had an orgasm when her hairstylist shampooed her. And her hairstylist was a grandmother of six.

Eva had been consciously avoiding Shane's touch all day. If he so much as brushed up against her, she might explode.

"I'm at rock bottom, too," said Shane. "I've never had sober sex."

Eva gasped. "That long? Why?"

Shane didn't know how to answer this. He'd had a lot of sex, with too many women, in increasingly depraved ways, a lot of it good, most of it a blur—and it was a relief to stop. Normal, healthy people didn't use sex as a post-vodka chaser.

"Never got around to it," he said.

"I don't miss it," Eva said, with a dismissive flick of her wrist. "Honestly, I'm practically a virgin again. It'd probably hurt."

"I'm so backed up, it'd be over in two seconds."

"Good thing we're not having sex."

"I, for one, am relieved," said Shane, with a wolfish smile.

Eva giggled into her palm, despite herself. "Why is it still so easy to talk to you?"

Shane gazed at her until the glint in his eye faded a bit. "Always was. It's just who we are."

"Do you remember everything?" she whispered. "About us?"

It took him a while to answer. "It's funny. The past decade is a blur, but I remember every detail of that week."

"I was hoping I'd romanticized it over the years. That we weren't real." Her words sounded delicate, breakable.

There was the quietly hypnotic, faint sound of a piano, and the incense swirled softly. And then Eva felt a familiar pull. Just like when they were seventeen, there was no space between them. There was an overwhelming need to get closer, always.

Unthinking, Eva slipped her hand into his. Shane squeezed it and then brought her hand to his mouth, pressing a lingering kiss into her palm. She gasped, electricity tearing through her. It was the slightest touch, but she felt it everywhere.

Eva had been imprisoned in pain for so long, she'd forgotten how *good* feeling good was. Her entire body roused. Suddenly, she was aware of everything—her skin, her cells, the bones under her skin. Heart fluttering, core throbbing.

Touch-starved.

Shane watched her reaction with lidded eyes. Then he lightly ran his lips along the inside of her wrist. She let out the tiniest whimper, her back arching. It was electric.

Breathless and embarrassed by her reaction, she sat up, burying her face in her hands. *No.* They were in a public space. Behind an unlocked door. She was a mother! And Shane was a Bold-Faced Name. Were they really fated to get caught dry-humping at an art-world pop-up? The welcome sign said NO TOUCHING! If they got caught, Book Twitter would implode. Audre would fling herself into the East River.

But then she opened her eyes. There was Shane, gazing up at her, looking for all the world like the reckless, irresistible boy he'd once been—but now with experience and grown-man gravitas and a rugged North African surfing scar and the most fuckable crinkles around his eyes—and nothing mattered.

There was no hell she wouldn't risk for this man. And he knew it.

"Come here," he said.

Eva straddled him, her hair falling in his face. Shane ran his hands up the backs of her thighs and over her ass, and then, not gently, he gripped her hips and pulled her down against him. Their lips were inches away from each other.

"Twenty questions," he whispered.

"Go."

"Why'd you really come to see me?"

"To ask for the favor."

"Liar." Shane tossed her over onto her back, pinning her wrists above her head with one hand. Instinctively, her legs drew up, wrapping around his waist. "Why'd you come?"

"For you." Her hips stuttered against his, desperate for friction. "Wanted you."

"You got me," he rasped, leaving hot, sucking kisses down her throat. "Your turn."

Eva trembled beneath him, his mouth scrambling her brain. She couldn't ask Shane the obvious questions (*Where'd you go? Why'd you leave? How could you?*). Over the years, she'd trained herself not to care about these answers. Besides, this moment wasn't about him; it was about her. So she went for something easier.

"Do you ever think of me?"

Lightly, he ran his tongue along her neck, up to her ear, nibbling on her lobe. "I never learned how to stop."

"Oh," she said. And then shakily added, "Your turn."

"So did you? Romanticize us?" asked Shane, eyes catching hers. "Or were we real?"

"We were real," she whispered, almost inaudibly.

"Then?" He ground himself against her and she moaned.

"*Y-yes,*" she gasped. "Then. And now."

Abruptly, Shane freed her wrists and cradled her face. She slid her hands up his back, gripping his shoulders. Slowly, he lowered his face toward hers, then stopped. He dipped down, then paused. He'd been waiting a lifetime to have her like this, buzzing for him, craving him, desperate—and he wanted to savor it.

But she let out an impatient groan, digging her nails into his shoulders, and Shane caved. He crashed his mouth into hers, drawing her into a luscious, searing kiss. The delicious shock of it was enough to make Eva freeze, but then she melted into him, lost in the heat of his mouth, the slide of his tongue, the teasing nip of his teeth, until she was unable to form a coherent thought beyond *yes* and *want* and *ShaneShaneShane.* He kept at it, kissing her senseless. It went backward in intensity, slowing down to a soft, searing smolder—almost too hot to take.

They stopped only to catch their breath.

"One more question," he said.

"We're still playing?" She wet her lips with her tongue.

"Yeah." Shane glanced toward the door, then back down at her. Eyes glinting in the dark wickedly. "Are you still bad?"

"Yes," she said without thinking, reaching down to palm his dick, huge and hard in his jeans. She rubbed along the length of him, teasing out a low groan. "Are you?"

"Yeah," he said, pushing her dress up and slipping off her strapless bra. Dipping down, he ran his soft, hot mouth along the swell of her breast, his teeth catching on her nipple. He swirled his tongue around it, sucking deliciously—and then, his stubble scraping her skin, he dragged his mouth to the other. Her helpless, shuddery gasps were making him so hard, he wondered how he'd survive this.

"Yeah," he growled against her breast. "I'm still bad."

"Why? T-tell me."

Shane lifted his head, taking her in. Eva looked radiant, so slutty, with her dress pulled up under her arms, showing off sheer panties, curls everywhere, panting, trembling, lips raw and swollen from kissing. She had a bruise blossoming on her hip, where he'd gripped her.

"'Cause I'm old enough to know better," said Shane, drawing her into a quick, dirty tongue kiss. "But I'm gonna do it anyway."

"Do what?"

"Fuck you. Here."

And then they tore into each other. Frantically, Shane managed to get her soaked panties off one leg, and Eva pushed down his jeans and boxers—but there was no time to get all the way naked. He dug into his wallet for an ancient condom (offering a silent prayer to several deities that it still worked) and slipped it on. Then, covering her with his tall, strong body, Shane sank into Eva with excruciating slowness, careful not to hurt her.

It did hurt, but the burn was *exquisite*. Wanting more, Eva cupped his ass and pushed him deeper. She gasped, and Shane kissed her quiet—driving into her with steady, deep strokes, and all she could do was take it, wave after wave of pleasure. When he felt her whole body begin to shudder against his, he slid his hand down between their sweat-slick, half-clothed bodies and dipped his middle finger over her clit. He rubbed her slowly but fucked her hard—and it was so good, so intense, that it sent her over the edge, shattering her to stillness.

And when Shane followed seconds later, he put his mouth to her ear and finally said it.

"Eva," he rasped, voice wrecked. "Eva. Eva."

He uttered it like an incantation, the only name that ever mattered and Eva, heart slamming into her ribs, clung to him in the violet-tinged darkness. Feeling both lost and found.

Later, Eva regretted it. Not the sex. She regretted leaving Shane there, alone, in that room. Getting up, throwing on her clothes, grabbing her bag, and rushing out. Not saying goodbye. But really, what did he expect?

Eva had trained herself not to care *why* Shane had abandoned her. Instead, she took it as a lesson. Ever since that day fifteen years ago, she'd never allowed herself to be left again. Husband, hookup, long-lost lover. It didn't matter.

Eva always left first.

Chapter 16

NO SAFE THRILL

Over the years, Eva had tried to forget her teenage week with Shane. And honestly, much of it was lost, due to her vodka-drenched, pill-obliterated, weed-smoked state.

This was what she remembered.

She remembered standing in front of the bathroom mirror, gingerly touching her darkened eye. Fingering her hacked-off hair. With a mournful sigh, she'd tried to pull it into a pony, but it wouldn't reach. And then Shane had appeared behind her in the mirror.

"I look like an electrocuted poodle," she sighed.

He fought off a smile.

"Go ahead, laugh," she said. "I look funny."

"No, *you're* funny," he said. "Look, you could have hair down to the floor. You could be bald. I could be blind. You'd still be pretty, Genevieve."

He said it like his opinion was fact. Her skin flushed fever-hot, and her palms went humid.

Shane backed up and leaned against the doorway. Genevieve turned around to face him.

"You pronounced my name right," she said.

"Been practicing."

"Say it again."

"*John-vee-ev*," he said with a smile. "It sounds like it tastes good."

"How can a word taste good?"

"Synesthesia. It's when you're overstimulated and your senses get confused. You see music. Hear colors. Taste words."

"Oh." Her mouth went dry. She blinked, and he was in front of her. The sink pressed against the small of her back. She held her breath. Gently, Shane cupped his good hand behind her neck, his gaze traveling from her eyes to her mouth. Then, for the first time, he kissed her— a lingering, pillowy peck. Innocent. He deepened it then, slanting his casted arm across her back and pinning her to him.

"You do taste good," he said, drawing back a little.

"So much…thank you." Flustered, she said the words out of order.

Shane's eyes flickered, and he seemed both smug and charmed. Then he dipped down to kiss her some more.

She remembered her mom calling on and off for a good two days. She never answered, but she kept the bulky Nokia phone on the charger, just in case (in case of what, she wasn't sure). On the third day, she moved it into the kitchen downstairs so she wouldn't hear the buzzing.

She remembered her first non-self-administered orgasm. They were lying out in the grass by the pool in their underwear, roasting in the swampy DC heat. Shane was listening to her ramble about how *Carrie* and *The Exorcist* represented the male fear of female puberty.

"I secretly wanna get a period. Just once," he said as he popped a WHORE pill on his tongue and tenderly kissed it into her mouth. "What's up with you and horror?"

"It's an escape."

He trailed kisses along her jawline, down her neck. Pausing at her jugular, he murmured against her skin, "Keep talking."

"It's a safe way to…to feel…"

"Feel what?"

"Intensity," she breathed. "A thrill, without being in actual danger."

He sucked the skin above her collarbone into his mouth. Then he bit her. Hot, wet, hard. Electricity bolted through her, and she let out a quivery cry. Shane's eyes flickered. Lightly, he cupped her throat with his hand. Ghosting his lips over hers, he said, "There is no safe thrill."

He squeezed her throat, and she went boneless. *Christ.* She didn't know this was something to need. His mouth traveled, restless, over her skin, down to where she was drenched. Then he sucked her till she shattered, tearing fistfuls of grass from the earth.

She remembered walking in Adams Morgan at sunset. When it started to rain, Shane broke into a parked Chevy Nova (using that mysterious ATM card) to wait it out. He was behind the wheel, Genevieve was shotgun, and they snorted lines of PARTY powder off Shane's paperback copy of Paul Beatty's *White Boy Shuffle*.

Something had been weighing on her mind, and she didn't know how to bring it up. She'd tried and failed several times. But now, feeling electric with coke confidence, she dove right in.

"Gotta ask you something," she started.

"Yeah, what's up?"

"You a virgin?"

"Virginity is a social construct," he said proudly.

"Seriously," she said, rubbing her burning nose. "Are you?"

"Um...no." He looked vaguely uncomfortable. "Are you?"

"No," she said.

What she had meant was *No, Shane, I'm not a virgin, because I was closing my register at Marshalls last summer and the tall, dead-eyed stock guy who never acknowledged me in public asked me to chill, so we smoked a bowl in his mom's basement and I asked him not to put it in, but he did, and afterward he high-fived me for not crying. No, Shane, I'm not a virgin. I'm the kind of girl who went back for more, 'cause I told myself he thought I was special. I'm not a virgin. I'm the queen of delusion, and boys lie but I believe, so please, oh please, be careful with me . . .*

". . . ask?" Shane was saying something.

"Sorry, what?"

"I said, why do you ask?"

Instead of answering, she bit her lip, shrugging coquettishly. And then she grabbed his face, kissing him until it escalated into a desperate make-out session. A Tipper Gore look-alike pounded on the window, shouting, "Go home!" Genevieve peered at her over Shane's shoulder, clicked open the blade of her pocketknife, and grinned. Bra strap in his teeth, Shane gave Tipper the finger. The woman clutched her purse and hurried away.

They hated everyone who wasn't them.

She remembered that sometimes, Shane would wake up fighting. He'd punch at the air, sweating, tangled up in the sheets. Instinctively, she'd run the tips of her fingers over his chest, arms, back, any skin she could reach—tracing the infinity sign over and over, little figure eights, till he slept.

It was the only thing that calmed him.

This memory was the faintest. It wasn't until years later, when Shane published *Eight*, that it came rushing back.

She remembered lying in the fetal position on the bed, her brain shrieking, waiting for her cocktail of narcotics to kick in. Sunset bathed the room in a warm strawberry-amber glow. Shane was lying facedown in a dusty corner, playing Scrabble with himself. Brow furrowed, lips pouting, he mumbled, "*Fuck.* I'm just so hard to beat."

She stared until he glanced up, face aglow with violet bruises.

"You're beautiful," she purred.

With a drowsy smirk, he began to croon the Christina Aguilera power ballad. She gasped and then burst into delighted laughter because, goddammit, he *did* sound like Ginuwine!

Groaning, Shane folded in on himself with boyish self-consciousness, tucking his face into his tee. Like it was a new thing, letting his guard down. Like his goofy side (and absurd vocal range) was for her only.

She drifted off, helplessly endeared, forgetting that she was a stolen girl stealing moments in a stolen house—and sooner or later, she'd have to pay.

She remembered going on a 7-Eleven run around 2:00 a.m. and sneaking off with a zillion Hostess treats. Together, they took the bus to the Barry Farm area of Southeast DC, the site of Shane's court-ordered home. The Wilson Children's Shelter was a county-owned, one-story building on a broken-down block. She couldn't believe people lived there. It looked like an abandoned Staples.

Under the gauze of night, they snuck in through a janitor's entrance. While Eva waited in a hallway that smelled of bleach and piss, Shane slipped into the crowded bedrooms, leaving a Twinkie under each kid's pillow. Then they slipped out.

Afterward, they sat on a bus-stop bench a couple of blocks away. One cracked streetlamp lit the block. A siren went off endlessly.

"I wish I could protect them. They're innocent, you know? Actually, Mike and Junior are fucking menaces. But in a pure way."

"You're pure."

Chewing the inside of his cheek, he looked at her. "If you knew about me, you wouldn't like me anymore."

Resting her chin on his shoulder, she slipped her arms around him. "How do you know I like you?"

His smile flickered, then faded. "I had parents once," he continued quietly. "Foster parents, from when I was a baby to about seven. I really loved them. They loved me back, too. One day, I was doing dumb shit, wearing my Superman cape and jumping off the counter. I broke my arm. My foster mom drove me to the ER. She was scared, 'cause you could see the bone and I was losing a lot of blood. She ran a red light and crashed into an intersection. She died. I didn't.

"After that, my foster dad acted like I didn't exist. Then he sent me away. Who wants to live with the kid who killed their wife?"

Genevieve, too struck to answer, gently curled her arm through his and held his hand. She squeezed, offering absolution the only way she could.

"Anyway. The kids in there? I don't want them to get locked up, like me. The more times you go, the harder it is to tell yourself you don't belong there. Prison is the school of the unlearned lesson." He paused. "I'll probably go back a third time."

"I won't let it happen," she promised. "What do you like to do? Besides fight?"

"Write."

"Don't fight. Write." She cuddled closer. "There. A mantra, to keep you out of trouble."

"Don't fight. Write."

"Right." She kissed him to bless it.

She remembered that they were never sober. Shane drank to seek oblivion; she stayed high to outrun pain. They did it together—but she cut herself in private. In the bathroom, daily, she'd sterilize her blade with alcohol pads and then carve a few lines on her upper thigh or upper arm, mostly, just deep enough for beads of bright crimson to bubble up in a perfect row. She went into a dissociative trance when she did it, the world slowing, the burn slicing through her pain. A blessed relief each time.

Shane saw her cuts. *I don't judge*, he'd said. But soon, his eyes started to linger over her tortured skin, clouding with concern. They both had their twisted compulsions, different corners of the same hell.

Once, though, she woke up in face-melting migraine pain and begged him to press her slashes. He didn't want to, but he did. She doubled over, gritting her teeth—and when Shane crushed her into his arms, she felt his chest quicken. And his tears dampened her cheeks.

★   ★   ★

She remembered lying under a shady tree in Rock Creek Park, toward the end. Their cycle of highs and comedowns was beginning to fray her nerves. And her pain was getting worse. She'd just vomited behind a tree. Now her head was in Shane's lap, and he was rubbing her temples with her lavender oil.

"Do you miss your mom?" he asked.

Yes.

"No," she said. "It's a relief being away from her. She tries to be good, but she...doesn't take care of me. And she has shit taste in men."

"Does she know how sick you are, G? If my kid was—"

"Don't talk bad about her!" She slapped her hands over her face and burst into tears so violently it shocked them both.

"Hey. I won't. I'm sorry—she sounds dope. Don't cry." Gently, he pulled her into his lap and cradled her against his chest. "Fuck it, cry."

Eventually, the steady thrumming of his heartbeat lulled her quiet.

A few hours and Percocets later, she felt good enough to walk back to the house.

"Why do you hate your mom's dudes?"

"They hurt her," she said plainly.

The world was buzzing and popping. A flock of pigeons passed above them, squawking, but they sounded miles away.

"Do they hurt you?"

She shrugged. "Some of them do. The current one, her boss at the bar? He tried. I pushed him off me and he fell out, drunk. I can handle myself."

"What's his name?"

She told him.

"What's the name of the bar?"

She stopped on the sidewalk. Shane did, too, peering down at her with an expression that could melt a rock. She told him.

She remembered waking up that night and seeing that Shane was gone. He didn't come back that night or the next day. She waited for him—

dusting shelves, scrubbing bathrooms, taking showers, torturing her arms, sleeping. Was he gone forever? Had he hurt himself? Jesus Christ, was he in jail again? If he was, *she'd sent him there.*

That night, she woke up to a thunderstorm raging outside. She'd left the terrace door open, and that side of the room was soaked. So was Shane, who was leaning against the bedroom door. He was all bone and lean muscle and sopping-wet T-shirt and soggy, broken cast, with a fresh cut across the side of his neck. She sat up in bed, and he didn't move, just looked at her with hooded, dilated eyes, his chest rising and falling in a violent staccato.

"He won't bother you anymore."

And this was how she knew she was as crazy as he was. Her fear evaporated, and all she felt was a perverse, potent throb, making her squeeze her thighs together. He slayed dragons she couldn't. He was a fucking outlaw. And she wanted that power inside her.

Good girls were supposed to want a prom kiss from the quarterback, not a face fuck from the hot psycho. But she supposed she wasn't good, 'cause she was on Shane in seconds, ripping down his soaked jeans and boxers—draining him till he was weak, and she was full.

She remembered standing on the terrace at dusk, gazing three stories down into the pool. She knew she'd taken too much of…something, 'cause she was in a state of both syrupy wonder and creeping hysteria. Plus, her pain was so vivid that she could barely follow her own thoughts.

But the thoughts were loud.

Everything felt so out of control. Her dependency on Shane suddenly terrified her. When he'd disappeared, she'd felt herself dissolving. What if he hadn't come back? And what about after this? This house, this adventure? What was the plan? Would he want her when it was over?

She lost things. She'd lost her health. She'd lost Princeton. She'd surely lose her mom, after this. She'd lose Shane, too. Boys left after they slept with you. It was why she hadn't slept with Shane yet.

Shane was her lighthouse. If he went dark, she'd be lost, treading black water forever.

I won't survive this, she thought, stroking the smooth plastic encasing her pocketknife. *This pain. It's too much.*

Maybe she'd just let go, then.

She climbed up on the middle horizontal bar of the railing and leaned far over, waiting for gravity to take her.

But then she felt Shane's hard, casted arm encircle her chest, knocking the wind out of her and yanking her back into the room. He dropped her on the bed and then climbed next to her, grabbing her jaw with his good hand.

"The fuck you doing?" He shook her.

She blinked hazily. Her eye sockets hurt from knuckling them in her sleep, trying to relieve the insistent stabbing in her temples. She wondered why she bothered.

"Don't die, baby."

"Gimme a reason."

"Me," he rasped. "Stay for me."

"Selfish."

"I am." He slipped his arm under her shoulders, pressing her to him. "I need you, so you can't die."

"Just...just let me."

With a desperate groan, he dropped his face into the hollow of her shoulder and begged.

"Stay. I'll make it worth it. I'll make it so fucking good, Genevieve. You'll be so happy, I swear. Just gimme your pain; I'll take it all. Promise to stay, and I'll never leave. Me and you, forever. Promise me."

Her eyes fluttered open.

She didn't want to promise with words.

She somehow untangled herself from Shane's arms, pushing him backward and straddling him. She reached for her knife, flipped it open and grabbed a lighter off the nightstand. With unsteady hands, she dipped the blade in the flame.

Shane's chest rose sharply, then froze.

Carefully, she carved a jagged, sloppy *S* on her forearm, right below her elbow crease. It was just deep enough to spill droplets of blood on his chest.

Shane reached for the fifth of vodka on the nightstand, downed it, then offered her his good arm. She dipped the blade in the fire again and scratched out a crooked *G* in the same place on his arm.

The hurt was intense, but they were so wasted, it *buzzed*. Just another thing to feel. With a feral growl, he flipped her over, and the rest was chaos—ravenous kissing, sucking, biting, clawing, and then Shane sinking into her, fucking her like he was giving her a reason to live. He didn't stop till she fell apart beneath him, soaring, shaking, sobbing, and utterly, wholly his.

She remembered waking up in an airtight embrace. A familiar scent enveloped her, and she nuzzled deeper into it. As the fog of unconsciousness lifted, she recognized the scent. White Diamonds. And Black drama.

It was her mom, mascaraed tears streaming from her movie-star eyes.

In the light of day, the room looked like a crime scene. The sheets were a mess; empty bottles cluttered the floor; pills and powder dusted the nightstand. She was covered in love bites, scratches, and cuts, her *S* hidden behind gauze. A furious Korean American chick with a Dior saddlebag was shrieking into a cell phone. Medics and cops swarmed around the bed, and an IV needle jutted from her inner elbow, attached to a saline bag. She heard someone say she'd overdosed.

"You're lucky to be alive," said the disembodied voice.

Alive, yes. Lucky, no.

"Wh-where's Shane?"

"Who is Shane?" drawled Lizette distractedly. "Oh, bé. If I can't make them stay, you can't. Mercier women are cursed. *Cursed*."

THURSDAY

Chapter 17

AN UNANSWERED QUESTION

"I'M TELLING YOU, THAT THING UPSTAIRS ISN'T MY DAUGHTER. SHE'S ALREADY seen every fucking psychiatrist in the world, and they sent me to you, Father. She needs a priest. You can't tell me that an exorcism wouldn't do her any good! You can't tell me that!"

It was 9:00 a.m., and Eva was watching *The Exorcist* on her phone, in bed. She'd woken up an hour earlier, intending to write. But when the alarm blared (her ringtone was Cece singing "Write your, write your book" in the key of Rihanna's "Work work work work work"), she'd elected to watch her comfort movie instead. This scene always killed her. This woman's twelve-year-old daughter was up in her bedroom, gruesomely possessed by the devil—while a priest wrote it off as depression. Never mind that the girl was humping crucifixes and levitating. It was an old story, really. Women telling the truth, and no one believing them.

Depression, my ass, thought Eva. *In the words of Grandma Clo, it's Satan hisself.*

Eva knew every word of *The Exorcist*, and the familiarity always lulled her into calm. After the Dream House, she made the walk of shame home, relieved the babysitter, ordered La Villa pizza for dinner, and ate in silence with Audre, and then they both escaped to their bedrooms. She couldn't face her daughter. How could she go through the motions—making homework inquiries, checking in on the status of Audre's art project—when she'd just recklessly thotted throughout the West Village?

Cringing, Eva curled herself into a ball under her pristine white duvet. What if they'd been caught? She'd already searched DREAM HOUSE + SHANE HALL + EVA MERCY several times, and nothing had come up. Just in case, she preemptively booked an appointment with a Google-search cleanup agency.

She was shocked at the recklessness of her behavior.

And then there was her silent standoff with Audre. They'd never fought like this. In a few days, Audre would fly off to Dadifornia for the summer, and Eva couldn't bear it if she left angry.

Before Audre woke up for school, Eva put her breakfast out on the table, with a note saying, "I love you, baby. Let's talk when you get home." Then she snuck back to her bedroom. Even mid-awkwardness, she wanted her daughter to know that she was there. But Eva needed her space, too. She was still tingling from Shane's touch, his mouth, his everything—and she wanted to indulge in it for as long as she could.

Eva bit her lip, trying to keep her guilty, thrilled smile from spreading. Shane. She'd divulged all to him. He'd cracked her open, and she'd come spilling out, slow and sweet as honey. She wanted to hate letting him get inside again. She'd been so willing to give it all up.

Over the years, during lazy daydreams, she'd sometimes allowed herself to fantasize about running into him. But in her thoughts, they'd still been kids. She couldn't imagine them relating to each other as adults. Whatever Shane sparked in her, she'd thought she'd outgrown. But they weren't who they used to be. They were better.

She pulled the duvet closer to her chin, her cheeks blazing, and she had an epiphany. Shane wasn't a thing to outgrow. He'd always fit. No matter how old or young or sophisticated or raw she was. No matter how much time had passed.

Shane was inevitable.

I need to be careful, she thought. But careful didn't exist with Shane. It was like entering a burning building. You could wear sunglasses and lather yourself in sunscreen, but you'd still go up in flames.

With a groan, she rubbed a temple and sat up, propped against three pillows. All of this was moot, because she'd fled from the scene. She had to apologize. But there was no cute meme to send after you had semipublic ex sex, came so hard that tears sprang to your eyes, and then bolted with your unhooked bra hanging out of your armhole.

Eva thought she'd feel powerful, leaving before she was left. But all she felt was emptiness. She'd wanted to stay locked in his arms forever. Or at least until their Sleep Guide issued them a fornication fine for breaking the rules.

Running away wasn't empowering. An empowered woman would've indulged.

Focus, she told herself. *Step one, text him. Step two, own up to it. Step three, tell him you had a great time. Step four, explain why it can't go any further.*

She picked up the phone.

Today, 9:30 AM

EVA: Lol?

SHANE: Lol? Seriously?

EVA: I'm sorry.

SHANE: No, don't apologize. I more than deserved it.

EVA: You did, but I'm still sorry. It was ridiculous the way I left.

SHANE: No, ridiculous was me, lying on the floor, alone, with my dick out.

EVA: Actually, that was a beautiful sight.

SHANE: . . . thank you?

EVA: Np.

SHANE: Can I see you? I need to see you.

EVA: I don't think it's a good idea.

SHANE: But we had a perfect day.

EVA: We did! But...let's leave it at that. We finally have closure. An ending.

SHANE: That felt like an ending to you?

EVA: *panicked silence

SHANE: Don't panic. I'm fucking shook, too. Please, can we meet somewhere?

EVA: Texting is safer.

SHANE: Why, tho?

EVA: Seeing you in person makes me forget the things I should remember.

SHANE: Was that a haiku?

EVA: Shane.

SHANE: I wanna SEE you. You home? I'm coming over.

EVA: You don't have my address.

SHANE: It's easy to get. I have Cece's number, and you know she loves drama.

SHANE: *hopeful silence

EVA: Fuck. 45 7th Avenue. Ground floor.

SHANE: You sure? If you really don't want me to...

EVA: Get over here, before I change my mind.

Eva threw back her covers and bounded out of bed as her phone went flying, landing in her plush shag carpet. She'd deal with that later. Instead, she started pacing in boxers and a Bad Boy Family Reunion Tour concert tee, knuckles thrust into her pounding temples, her mind zipping from thought to thought.

It's 9:45 a.m.! Did he mean he was coming now, or later in the afternoon? I need to put on blush, clean up the living room—fuck, we have zero food except Five Guys takeout and Pirate's Booty. Should I get wine? No, no, no, OF COURSE Shane can't have wine. Calm. Down. Start with a shower. Do I have time to book a quick highlights appointment? Shit. Shit. Shit. Is this crazy?

She flung open her bedroom door and bounded down the hallway to the kitchen. Coffee first. Then painkillers. Then she'd figure out the rest.

Slightly skidding in her fuzzy winter socks (her feet were permanently frozen, despite the almost-summer temps), she ran into the kitchen.

"AH!"

Eva jumped half a foot in the air and let out a proper slasher-flick scream. There was Audre, sitting cross-legged on the kitchen floor. Bent over her portrait of Lizette. She was surrounded by a flurry of feathers, paints, strips of fabric, and sequins. The second she heard Eva's scream, she shrieked, too, hopping to her feet and brandishing her paintbrush like a sword.

Then they were standing there on opposite sides of the kitchen, breathing heavily, staring at each other. Audre had a burgundy feather stuck to her cheek.

"What are you *doing* here?" yelped Eva, clutching her head. That scream had rattled her brain.

"Um, I live here?" said Audre, with utter calm. She was wearing over-sized Princeton sweatpants and the Hogwarts Sorting Hat she always wore when she was working on her art. "The *hell*, Mommy."

"Language!"

"Oh, my eternal bad. What's the proper response when your MERE PRESENCE sends your mother into ACUTE HYSTERIA?"

"Audre," said Eva, trying to modulate her breathing, her head and heart thumping wildly. "My love. Why aren't you at school? Please don't tell me Bridget O'Brien expelled you. Do. Not. Tell. Me. That. 'Cause I will absolutely sue Cheshire Prep. She promised me—"

"I'm not expelled! *Goddd-uh*. It's the second-to-last day of school. We have today off. Like we do every year, for teachers to finish report cards. Didn't you, like, get an email?"

Eva couldn't keep up with Cheshire's administrative emails. They sent one for everything, from notices about lice epidemics to parent-led Zumba classes.

Keeping her head very still, Eva gingerly slid onto the bench in her breakfast nook. Audre watched her, knowing all the signs. Huffing, she grabbed a fresh ice pack from the freezer and tossed it to her mom, who caught it with one hand.

"Thanks," breathed Eva, pressing the frosty ice pack to her left temple. "I forgot about today. I think I'm losing my mind."

"No comment," Audre said, pouting. She plopped onto the bench, across from Eva—a not-yet-graceful girl with noodly limbs and an endless neck who, one day, would be elegant in the extreme. But today, she was a newborn giraffe.

In an effort to be casual, Eva asked, "How's the portrait going?"

"Fine."

"It's lovely. You really captured your grandmother's essence, even though it's an abstract piece. Your dad's gonna be so proud."

"Dad co-designed the characters in *Monsters, Inc.* and *Brave*," she mumbled. "This is nothing."

"Okay, Audre," she said, letting it go. "So. Did you see my note this morning?"

"Yeah."

"Any response to it?"

Audre shrugged, slipping off her wizard hat. Underneath, her hair was a riot of ringlets, identical to Eva's. "No. I mean, yeah. Like, I guess we should talk."

Audre's lower lip was poked out, and she wasn't blinking, because if she did, tears would fall. Eva shouldn't have been so nervous to launch a difficult conversation with her own kid, but so much of Eva's self-worth depended on how her daughter thought of her. She knew it was unhealthy and over the top, but it was also true.

"We can't tiptoe around each other like this, babe. You're my girl. You're my person. I love you bigger than—"

"I know, bigger than Ursula in the dramatic finale of *Little Mermaid*."

Eva had been saying this to Audre her entire life. It was one of their things. But Audre wasn't moved.

"I'll go first," sighed Eva. "I'm sorry that I yelled at you at school. It wasn't the place or time. I was just shocked, you know? You're always so consistently on point. The last thing I was expecting was to walk into that meeting and find out that you're facing *expulsion*."

"You act like I'm the worst daughter, though," she said. "Do you know why Parsley was in detention? Tequila!"

"She brought tequila to school?"

"No. She snuck a tequila-soaked tampon to school *in her actual vagina*, let it absorb into her bloodstream, and was blackout drunk by fourth period."

Eva stared at her daughter, thunderstruck.

"Point taken," she said. "Look, I don't think you're terrible. My expectations of you are high, because I want you to have every option in the world. Options I didn't have."

Her daughter sat in stony silence. Eventually, she plucked the burgundy feather off her cheek and started slowly shredding it on the table.

"Audre. Say something."

Finally, she glanced up, meeting her mom's eyes.

"Are you sorry you had me? Do I make your life harder?"

"No! Where is this coming from?"

"You said I was a burden, Mom. You said you don't have any space for a real life, because I soak up all your time and energy."

"I didn't say that!"

Audre's brows rose to the ceiling.

"Yes, I said that," admitted Eva. "And it's true. It's hard for me to date and do spontaneous stuff other single women do. But I'm also not interested in dating. I love my life the way it is! Just me and you, kid."

"Just me and you, huh?"

Eva cocked her head. "Yeah. Who else?"

Audre shrugged insolently. She was acting strange. This was more than just the fight. She was holding something back.

"By the way," Eva continued, grasping at straws, "when you called me perfect? I'm far from it. And when I was around your age, I had a really tough time."

"You went to an Ivy League school! And wrote a bestseller when you were barely legal."

"Honey, I was also sick. Even sicker than I am now. Wanna know how I got to Princeton? My grades dropped so dramatically my senior year that they rescinded their offer. I had to write an essay from a hospital bed"—*psych ward, just tell her*—"begging the university to take me back. Explaining that I had a debilitating illness."

"Really? Can I read it?" Audre asked shyly, her mood shifting a bit. She was always hungry to hear more about her mom's childhood. When Audre was little, she'd ask Eva relentless questions. *What's your funniest memory? Did you ever have a crush that liked you back? What was the scariest movie you saw in the theater?* Eva could always answer those. The deeper questions, she couldn't.

"Yes, baby, you can read it," said Eva, getting up to move to Audre's side of the bench, scooting in next to her. Audre hooked her arm through Eva's and leaned her head on her shoulder.

"So, you fought to get back into Princeton."

"I did," said Eva.

"You fought to keep me in school, too," started Audre. "How? I mean, what did you say to Mrs. O'Brien to change her mind?"

Audre peered up at her, with her massive doe eyes, and Eva froze a little. She wasn't prepared to explain Shane.

"I did her a favor. I found an English teacher to replace Mr. Galbraith. Shane Hall. Heard of him?"

"Ohhh, I've heard of him," responded Audre cryptically. "How do *you* know him?"

"Well, he's a Black author," said Eva, kissing Audre's forehead. "We more or less all know each other."

"Huh. How well do you know him?"

"I mean…"

"Do you, like, *like* him?"

"Why would you ask that?"

"Because I saw pics of you two. Outside, yesterday. And it was clearly a date."

Eva disentangled herself from Audre and stared at her—mouth agape, heart pounding, temples exploding.

"Audre," she started, forcing a casual little laugh. "I don't know what you saw. But if I was seeing someone, you'd know it. Honestly, does Shane Hall even seem like my type?"

"You don't date, Mommy. What even is your type, the Invisible Man?"

This was too much. In seconds, her migraine went from annoying to obliterating. Vision starting to blur, she grabbed her purse off the table and fished for her bottle of pain pills. She swallowed two dry and reminded herself to breathe. The numbing effect rolled across the pain like the tide, sweeping it away, where it was unreachable—at least until three hours from now, when the effect would wear off and the pain would come crashing back to shore.

Eva would take any respite, however meager. It wasn't until her mid-twenties that she found a doctor to prescribe effective pain treatment, and she was eternally grateful. Especially today. She had to be in fighting shape for this conversation.

"I met with Shane to ask for his help. That's all! So not a date! In fact, it was low-key humiliating to ask a favor of someone I hadn't spoken to in ages. But I'd do anything for you."

Audre thought about the pics of her mom with that dude. They looked like the poster for a syrupy rom-com. And her mom looked flirty—in a way that Audre had never seen. *She was literally throwing herself at that guy.*

Eva claimed that she had no time for men. And then, out of nowhere, she was caught canoodling with an actual man? Sharing ice cream on a romantic day date? Audre had done a deep dive into *Cursed* Twitter and uncovered more fan pics of them looking googly-eyed all over the West Village. Eva had been with Shane for hours. Either her mom was whipped as hell, or she was an A-plus actress.

Audre yelped. Suddenly, it all made sense. Audre flung her arms around her mom's shoulders and started to weep and wail.

"Noooooooo, Mommy! Tell me you didn't! Oh, I feel terrible! You're right, I'm the worst daughter."

"What are you talking about?" Eva was flabbergasted by Audre's sudden hysteria.

"I know there are no bounds to maternal love. I mean, hello? I read *Mommy Burnout!*"

"Who hasn't?" said Eva, who hadn't. "Audre, what do you think I did?"

"You...you...seduced that man, to keep me in school, didn't you? You had sex with him for me. *And I'll never forgive myself!*"

Eva was too astounded to formulate a response. And she didn't have time, anyway—because the buzzer rang.

She'd forgotten. An hour ago she'd been embroiled in heavy text banter with Shane Hall, but the second she'd seen her daughter's face, everything else had vanished from her mind.

Including the fact that Shane was on his way. And now he was here.

Chapter 18

A SERIES OF RASH DECISIONS

CECE SINCLAIR HAD GREAT TASTE. EVERYONE KNEW IT. SHE WAS THE MOST powerful book editor at the most powerful publishing house. Everyone knew that, too. She was also an impeccable hostess, a terrifyingly focused doubles tennis player, and probably the most important advocate of Black and brown authors of her time.

She was many things (some might argue too many), but there was only one thing that kept her pulse racing, her complexion glowing, and her juices flowing. It was being a connector of dots. You needed the best tailor this side of the Hudson? She'd have you covered. You needed a last-minute plus-one to the Studio Museum in Harlem Gala? She'd have a dashing, out-of-work telenovela actor delivered to your doorstep in a tux by 5:30 p.m. Looking for a trainer? A donor egg? A direct route to Valerie Jarrett? Cece Sinclair was your woman.

Cece didn't have all the answers. But she *believed* that she did. And it was of vital importance to Cece that her friends and associates, the greater literary community, and the finest Black families up and down the Eastern Seaboard believed it, too.

Right now, she was deep in thought in her Clinton Hill brownstone, sitting in her home office—which was beautifully furnished in a mid-century-lite aesthetic (funded mostly by her husband Ken's salary as CEO and chief surgeon at Sinclair Reconstructive Surgery Arts). Sporting her casual-Saturday finest—a Proenza Schouler cinch-waist dress and Essie Ballet Slippers–painted toes—she was dead glamorous but also agitated. Because there were two dots she couldn't connect.

There were several beats missing from this Eva and Shane story. Gaping holes. It was her job to know a fully fleshed-out, no-stone-left-unturned narrative when she saw it—and, ma'am, this wasn't it. Cece knew good and goddamn well that Shane wasn't just some sepia-tinted, nostalgic fling. No one was so undone by a fling that they were moved to write about it for their entire adult life.

Eva was withholding information. And it was driving Cece nuts. Shane wouldn't talk, because Shane was an enigma. Eva wouldn't talk, either, because she was an enigma wrapped in a mystery wrapped in blackout curtains.

BANG! The sound reverberated through the apartment.

My nerves, she thought. *How much longer will Ken subject me to this incessant clatter?*

For the past five weekends, Cece's husband, Ken, had devoted all his time to refurbishing their dining table. Hammering away. The banging set her teeth on edge, but she tried not to show it. He worked so tirelessly at his practice. Household projects were his happy place. Fine. She just wished Ken could find a quieter hobby.

Sucking her teeth, Cece abruptly stood up and began pacing. Ken always called her nosy, and while she pretended to be offended by it, she *was* nosy. And nosy women bristled at being left out of gossip. It made them irritable and prone to risky decisions made out of sheer desperation.

And, as desperation dictated, she'd throw a party. Tomorrow. A pre-awards party, to kick off Sunday's Black Literary Excellence Awards. Everyone was already in town for the Litties and looking for trouble to get into. She was due to host one of her exclusive, membership-only soirees, anyway.

Yes, Eva claimed she'd "sooner die" than be trapped at the same party with Shane. But she was also the queen of standing in her own way.

Cece had known Eva since she was a lost nineteen-year-old. She'd more or less helped her grow up, and she felt responsible for her. Cece knew, better than anyone, that Eva was stuck in a rut—a book rut, a life rut, an everything rut—and death of inspiration was *ruinous* for a writer. Maybe she just needed a little push, to get out of her head. To break free! Cece would gift her with a gorgeous backdrop to properly reunite with her old flame—and hopefully get book inspiration out of it. And wasn't her job as a book midwife to create a nurturing atmosphere to help her authors to create magic?

Shane would be the special guest. The literary blogs were buzzing; everyone wanted to catch a glimpse of him in real life. There wasn't a lot of time to party-plan, but conveniently for Cece, her guests never expected her invites to be timely. The spontaneity was part of the fun. And the best part was that Cece could finally get answers. Shane and Eva were her writer children. And as their mama, she had a right to get to the bottom of their situationship.

BANG!

Ken's been a wonderful husband. But five more minutes of this and I poison his LaCroix.

Cece perched atop her desk, her hostess brain whirring. She'd invite the usual suspects. She'd have to allow kids to come, to make it impossible for Eva to use the "no babysitter" excuse. It'd be fine; she'd corral them in a guest room with Shake Shack sliders, a babysitter, and the Disney Channel.

She'd call her girlfriend Jenna Jones to find her something fabulous to wear. Jenna was a former fashion editor who now hosted a ubiquitous YouTube style show called *The Perfect Find*. By virtue of her fashion-royalty status, she knew all the PR folks at all the fashion houses (even the small, indie-cool ones that Cece herself couldn't get to). Jenna was Cece's secret style weapon.

Yes, she'd call Jenna! If only she could remember where she'd put her phone. She couldn't hear herself *think* over Ken's incessant banging.

Cece swept out of the office and across the floor to the dining room. The room was chaotic. The table was upside down on the floor, and Ken was crouched next to it, hammering a leg back into its socket.

"Ken. You. Are. Killing. Me."

Dashing Ken, a.k.a. Billy Dee Williams Lite, pushed his glasses up his nose and asked, "Do the legs look even to you?"

With an extravagant exhale, she smoothed her dress and crouched down next to him. "Almost there."

"Good," he said, and continued to hammer away.

"Sweetheart, I'm going to hear that banging in hell."

"You're not going to hell," Ken muttered, a screw jutting out from between his lips.

"Oh please. I own real estate down there," she said breezily. Giving his shoulder a squeeze, she stood back up and resumed pacing. There was so much to do between now and tomorrow's party.

When Cece hostessed, she did it from her *soul*—with, she supposed, the energy most women her age poured into their children. But she'd never wanted kids. Books were her kids. They cuddled up with her at night, kept her warm, quieted her thoughts when her marriage seemed thin, her life choices felt pointless, or her job seemed stagnant. At brunch, Belinda had asked if she'd ever felt wild, deep love. What Cece didn't know how to say was that she didn't need it. She was happy not to feel *anything* super deeply. The top level of life was enough for her. The beginning of the night, when there was the buzzing possibility of intrigue and drama—instead of the end, when everyone was wasted and weird and dark. Long ago, she'd learned that life could be bitterly disappointing if allowed. There were blows and stumbles, but your job was to stay *interested* in the world.

It was why Cece was so adept at sniffing out bestsellers. She'd read a manuscript once, and without giving it intense thought, without letting the words marinate, she'd know if it worked. Cece barely took a breath between reading the last page of a novel and convincing Parker + Rowe to buy it. And after forty bestsellers, no one doubted her instincts.

Not even Michelle, of the Chicago Robinsons (whom Cece had met at the Farm Neck Golf Club in the Vineyard when Sasha and Malia were just toddlers). At the 2017 National Congressional Black Caucus Conference, when Michelle divulged that she was conceptualizing a memoir, Cece didn't need to hear the pitch. She knew the hook at first blush.

"South Side, darling," she whispered into Michelle's diamond-studded ear. "Make sure you give us South Side."

"Really? You think people want to know about my childhood?"

"I don't think, Shelly," said Cece wisely. "I know."

She also knew, instinctively, that there was delicious potential in Eva and Shane. They just needed…a push. Cece couldn't wait to see what lusty magic her party would inspire—and she prayed that Eva would pour it into the pages of her new manuscript. She may be over *Cursed*, but her fans weren't, and their publishing house wasn't. Eva had to deliver.

Just then, Ken chuckled at her from where he was sitting on their pristine amber-wood-paneled floor.

"What's funny?" she asked.

"You're plotting, Celia. I can tell."

"I'm not plotting; I'm planning."

He snickered to himself, the same screw sticking out of his mouth. "My nosy girl."

Cece grinned. She was nosy, and she was his girl. Both were true, for better or for worse.

"Work on the left leg a bit more," she said, then blew him a kiss and swept out of the room.

On the other side of Brooklyn, Shane was leaning into the doorway of Eva's brownstone. He rang the doorbell twice—and nothing. Maybe she'd changed her mind. Now he was rethinking every life choice he'd made until this moment.

The sensible thing to do would be to leave. But what if she hadn't heard the buzzer? No. He'd wait a while longer. He couldn't go yet.

Yesterday was both too much and not enough. The day had left him in knots, and now Shane had a restless, bone-deep itch to be in her vicinity. He wanted to watch her do things, say things. Hold her hand, make her laugh. Fuck her senseless. Give her everything she hadn't had in so long. Give her the best of him.

According to AA guidelines, relationships were forbidden until you were two years sober. This rule made sense, but Shane couldn't have anticipated this happening.

High school relationships aren't supposed to be meaningful, he reasoned. *Our frontal lobes weren't even developed. How did we know it was real?*

Teenagers didn't know how to distinguish between a crush and something deeper—let alone be right about it. At seventeen, Shane hadn't been right about anything. But her.

His mind flashed back to one small moment at the Dream House. Eva was under him, breathless and blissed out, her mouth plush from kissing and her cheeks on fire from climaxing. And Shane was deeply, existentially happy. He buried his face in her neck and gathered her up in his arms, clinging to her so tightly, he couldn't fathom ever letting her go.

The embrace felt monumental, like they were melding together all the people they'd ever been over the years. Closing the loop. Eva nuzzled her face against Shane's throat, lips skimming just under his jaw.

"Missing you never ends," she said on an exhale.

But before he had a chance to say the same thing back to her, she slipped out from under him. And was gone.

Shane understood why she'd left. But it had crushed him. He'd gotten her back, only to lose her again.

Shane had always felt tortured by his memory of that week. He saw it all, so clearly. Every detail, in vivid technicolor. No drink could make him forget. But what he hadn't banked on was the seemingly insignificant but monumentally important details he'd forgotten about Eva coming back to him.

Like when Spotify plays a song you haven't heard since childhood, and it reminds you who you are. Like "Oh yeah, I'm a person who knows all the words to Will Smith's 'Wild Wild West.'"

When Eva left yesterday, Shane had been resigned to leaving her alone. It hurt like hell, but he deserved it. So he kept himself busy for the rest of the day. He went for a six-mile run, chilled, didn't drink, ate something, didn't drink, tried to write, didn't drink, and then slept. But then Eva sent that text. And somehow, he'd found himself sitting on her stoop, waiting for her to open the door.

His phone buzzed, and he yanked it out of his jeans so fast, his pocket went inside out.

It was Ty.

"WYD," said the teen.

"It remains to be seen," said Shane, peering up into Eva's window.

Shane had talked to Ty yesterday. And two days before that. He committed to twice-weekly check-ins with all his mentees. Sometimes, just hearing the voice of someone who believed in you could turn a shit day into something a bit brighter.

"Ty, why aren't you in school?"

"It's the second-to-last day of the year," he said, offering no further explanation.

"How's your girl?"

"Good."

And then Shane launched into the rapid-fire questions he asked all his kids.

"You turning in completed homework?"

"Yeah."

"You engaging in any illegal or nefarious activity?"

"What 'nefarious' means."

"Criminal."

Ty paused, thinking. "Nah?"

"You fighting?"

"Not since you was here."

"You staying hydrated? Sleeping eight hours?"

"Sleeping be mad hard sometimes. My brain don't turn off. But a nigga trying. My mantra helps."

"Proud of you, my dude."

Shane could feel Ty's smile, thousands of miles away.

"Mr. Hall? Can I... Could you lemme hold two hundred?"

"Two hundred US dollars? What for?"

"My sister's nigga rents out studio time or whatever, and I thought... I just been trying to get on this rap shit for a minute. Get on SoundCloud, get a deal."

Shane burst out laughing. When Ty didn't join him, he shut up, quick.

"Oh. Okay, but since when are you an emcee? You've never mentioned rap."

"My shit's flames."

"Interesting. Ty, what's your rap name?"

"Undecided."

"Undecided is your name?"

"Nah, my name's *undecided*."

"Don't take this the wrong way," started Shane, with caution. "But the fact that you don't even have a rap name makes me question your sincerity. Every Black male invents a fake rap name by third grade."

The teen was silent.

"Your sister introduced you to this dude? Princess?"

"Yeah."

"Princess lives in a hollowed-out Chrysler parked inside of a condemned

Tastee Freez. Does it check out to you that she'd date a dude with a legit studio rental space? Or is it more probable that they're hustling you?"

Cornered, Ty let out an exasperated sigh.

"I gotta get out of here," begged Ty. "I lied. I haven't eaten in two days. Niggas think I eat, 'cause I'm big-boneded, but I don't. Princess and Mom take all my money. Maybe rap will get me out. This dude knows managers and producers and what have you."

"Ty, I'm not giving you money for this. I don't trust it. I gotta go, but we'll talk about it later."

"I thought you was a real one," Ty said, and his voice was barely audible. He sounded destroyed. "Peace."

The phone clicked, and Shane slumped against the front door. He fucking *knew* Ty wouldn't be able to stay on the straight and narrow. Maybe Shane was too hard on him. Maybe he should send him money. Besieged by conflicting emotions, he took a massive chug out of his water bottle just as a tall redhead strolled by with a full-grown toddler strapped to her chest and did a double take.

"My God. You're Ta-Nehisi Coates!"

"Nah. But he'd appreciate that you pronounced his name right," he said, downing the last of his water. "I learned the hard way."

And then finally, *finally*, he heard the buzz. Before Shane could pick an emotion to focus on, he flew through the heavy mahogany door.

Chapter 19

HETEROSEXUAL MEN LOVE ME

Eva took forever to buzz Shane up.

She'd been locked in a debate with the most overimaginative, stubborn, dramatic girl that Brooklyn had ever produced. (Outside of Barbra Streisand, maybe.)

Audre was convinced that Eva had whored herself out for her. And with Shane waiting downstairs, Eva had no time to convince her otherwise. She was throwing on random clothes from her bedroom floor, rushing to get cute, while trying to talk Audre off the ledge. Not to mention that she was unprepared for Shane to meet Audre and had no idea what to say to him after their Dream House tryst.

When they heard the knock on the door, both Audre and Eva raced down the hallway, but Audre got there first. She threw open the door and stood there, fists on her hips, squinting up at Shane with a thunderous frown.

He jumped at least six inches off the ground. "Jesus *fuck!*"

"Shane! Language!" Eva skidded into the doorway in her fuzzy house socks and knocked Audre out of the way with her hip.

"But that's...She's..."

"Unexpectedly home, yes," Eva blurted out, breathless. She couldn't imagine how absurd they both looked. Eva in her Bad Boy Family

202

Reunion tee and hastily thrown-on denim short overalls, with her hair piled atop her head like a perky pineapple—and Audre in her sweats and Hogwarts Sorting Hat. They were both breathing hard, unfinished business shimmering in the air between them.

"Shane, this is Audre. Audre, this is Shane. Um, we need a sec alone." Grabbing a stunned Shane by the biceps, she used all her strength to push him back out into the hallway, shutting the door behind her.

"I'm giving you five minutes!" hollered Audre, her voice muffled behind the door.

Gesturing for Shane to follow her, Eva scurried up the stairs to the second-floor landing, outside of the apartment above her. She needed to be out of earshot.

With a dramatic exhale, Eva collapsed against the two-hundred-year-old wall as Shane did the same. She wondered how many other illicit lovers these walls had seen.

Panting, she said, "I haven't breathed since you buzzed."

"You didn't tell me your daughter was here!" Shane was caught between panic and excitement. "Jesus, she's the cutest person I've ever seen. You gave *birth* to her. A whole human. And you're letting me meet her?"

"Only 'cause I forgot she had today off from school!" Eva was reeling, in flustered disbelief that Shane was here, in her building, right now.

"Oh. *Ohhh.*" His heart sank. "Listen, I'll go. I don't want to make anything weird for you. Or her."

"Don't go."

"Really?" He beamed.

"You need to help with my alibi."

"Oh." His heart dropped again. "What alibi?"

"Audre saw fan pics of us online—ice cream, cuddling on a stoop— and I guess we looked...you know." She made a dreamy face at him. "Like this."

"What, goofy?"

"Smitten."

Shane nodded, his fingers slowly plucking his bottom lip. Lazily, his gaze drifted down from her eyes to her mouth to her bralessness and back up again.

Eva's mouth parted. He smirked at her, all cocky swagger.

"I can imagine," he said.

"Anyway," she continued, cheeks blazing, "she has decided that I seduced you into saving her academic career."

"Seduced me? She used those words?" Shane put his face in his hands, muffling a chuckle. "Oh no."

"I've never met anyone more dramatic." Eva threw up her hands and rolled her eyes theatrically.

"I have," he said, grinning.

"This week is too much for me." Eva's head felt too heavy for her body, and she dropped her forehead on Shane's chest. She let it stay there, rubbing her head into him, relieving the pressure, just wanting to be soothed.

Shane froze momentarily, taken aback by the intimacy. Even after yesterday, he didn't want to jump to any conclusions about where they stood.

"It's okay," he said softly, not touching her. "Can I hug you?"

"Please," she breathed into his shirt.

Bending down slightly, he slid his arms around her waist and scooped her up, pulling her against him. On tippy-toes, she clung to his shirt and buried her face in his neck.

"Tighter," she moaned, and he squeezed her. He wanted to live there. Pressing his fingers into her hair, he gently massaged her scalp.

"You're here," whispered Eva, feeling dizzy, "'cause I want you here."

Shane made a small noise in the back of his throat that would embarrass him later. "Are we gonna talk about what we did?"

"There's no time—my daughter thinks I'm a hooker. I have to fix this."

"I'll help." He ran the backs of his fingers along her cheek tenderly, needing to feel her skin. She let out the faintest sigh. "Audre has a healthy imagination, which isn't a stretch, considering who her mom is. I'm great with kids."

"But she's *my* kid." Eva lifted up her face to look at him. "And this isn't how I wanted you to meet her. I mean...not that I even thought about you meeting her."

"No, I get it," he said, pressing his face into her curls. Coconut and vanilla. So heady.

"We'll just tell her we're reunited old friends. Which isn't a lie," she whispered, sliding her arms around his neck, pulling him even tighter. He groaned at this and, without breaking their embrace, walked her backward, till she was up against the wall.

"Just friends," he repeated.

"Yeah," she breathed.

Leaning in close, Shane pressed his lips to hers and softly sucked her tongue into his mouth, drawing her into a slow, deep kiss. Lightly, he nipped her bottom lip with his teeth—and the jolt was so intense, her legs buckled.

"Okay," he whispered against her mouth before abruptly letting her go and stepping away. She blinked, a bit unsteady on her feet.

Pleased, he stuck his finger into her cheek dimple. "Boop! Let's go, friend."

Shortly thereafter, Eva, Shane, and Audre were sitting at the Mercy-Moore kitchen table. There was fresh light coming through the garden-facing window, and daisies sprouted from a ceramic vase Eva and Audre had picked up on their summer vacation to Barcelona two years ago. The table was a vintage number Eva had found in a Williamsburg shop that was going out of business. This was about five minutes before Williamsburg became a thing. It was a delicate, thin slab of raw redwood sitting upon iron legs. Over the years, it had acquired weird grooves and nicks, nail-polish smears, paint smudges, ancient Sharpie scribbles. It was a living Eva-Audre timeline. No man had ever sat there.

And judging by the way this is going, this'll be the last time.

Shane had thought that reasoning with Audre would be a breeze. After all, he successfully managed an average of twenty-five kids most days of the week. But this one was different.

"I want to start by reminding you that I'm your mother," said Eva. "I don't have to defend anything I do. But because I don't want you to ever breathe a word of this insane story to anyone at Cheshire Prep, we're gonna clear this up. Right, Shane?"

Shane swallowed. He'd never been so intimidated. "Right. Right."

"Mr. Hall here is an old friend from high school," continued Eva. "He's in town for the week, and we met for an iced coffee. I didn't use my feminine wiles to get him to teach at your school next year. I don't even know if I *have* feminine wiles. Maybe I did once and misplaced them. In any event, there were no wiles."

"I see." Audre adjusted her wizard hat and gestured at Shane. In her most official debate-team-captain voice, she said, "You may speak, sir."

In his most official prep-school-English-lit-teacher voice, Shane said, "I know this is our first time meeting. And you have no reason to trust me. But all I did with your mom was platonically chill. Really."

"Really? Really, *Shane Hall?*" Audre spat his name like she'd recently found unsavory trivia about him on Google. Which she had.

"I can assure you, I'm too gentlemanly to...agree to...what you're suggesting."

"Do you or do you not have several DUIs?" Audre folded her arms across her chest.

"Audre Zora Toni Mercy-Moore! You apologize to Mr. Hall right now."

"Shane," said Shane.

"Mr. Hall, I'm sorry. That was rude," Audre allowed. "But, Mom, you're being a hypocrite! You went crazy on Coco-Jean's brother when you thought we were being inappropriate. As if I'd crush on a client."

"A client?" asked Shane, surprised. "What services do you provide?"

"And now *I* can't react when *you're* inappropriate?"

"I'm. Your. Mother." Eva clapped with each word, for emphasis. "I'm *supposed* to interrogate sixteen-year-olds consorting with my twelve-year-old. It's my *business*. But even if I did trade sexual favors to keep you in school, it's none of yours."

"But you didn't," said Shane.

"Of course I didn't." Eva grabbed Audre's hand. "How'd you even dream up such a tacky idea? Is this 'cause I let you watch *Empire*? Honestly, sweetie. Can you see me doing this?"

Audre glanced at Shane and then back at her mom.

"I guess not," she said, with weary acceptance. "No. I guess I'm doing the most. But imagine my confusion! You tell me you're not dating. And the next day, you're booed up with some guy—a guy whose help you need. It didn't add up. Until you said you'd do *anything* to keep me in school."

Shane nodded. "Reasonable conclusion."

"The only thing happening in those photos," said Eva, "was two old friends catching up."

"Good friends," added Shane, who had thought he'd be far more articulate and helpful during this conversation but was tongue-tied in the presence of Eva and her dynamo baby, who had the energy of a great auntie judging neighborhood antics from her front porch. It was fascinating, seeing his Eva this way. A mother!

It had been decades since he'd spent time with a family. He was dazzled.

Meanwhile, Audre had propped her chin in her hand, eyes darting from Shane to her mom and back again. Her indignation was slowly turning into curiosity.

"So how come you've never mentioned Shane before?" asked Audre. "And in which city did you go to high school together? I know you moved a lot for Grandma's modeling jobs."

Grandma's modeling jobs. Eva cringed, hearing Audre saying this in front of Shane. He knew better.

"It was a school in DC. I lived there my senior year. It was a long time ago, sweetie." Eva got up and went to the counter, grabbing a banana. "Whew. I'm glad we settled that! Is anyone hungry? I have Toaster Strudel!"

"Mr. Hall, I'm sorry for jumping to conclusions," said Audre. "This was a lot for me. Mommy never hangs out with heterosexual men."

"Not true," said Eva, her mouth full of banana. "Heterosexual men love me."

Audre spun around to face her. "Why haven't you spoken since high school?"

"I've been busy with you, Audre. And Shane is always on the road."

"But you've never mentioned knowing him."

Audre said "him" like Shane didn't have an actual name and wasn't sitting right in front of her. Shane was being back-burnered, but he didn't mind. He was just thrilled to be in Eva and Audre's orbit.

"I just...Like I said, we moved a lot," sputtered Eva. "My memories are a blur."

HELP ME, she mouthed to Shane, behind Audre's head.

He cleared his throat, and without really thinking, he called upon his only superpower. He told a story.

"You know what, Audre? Me and your mom's friendship is hard to quantify in linear terms."

Linear terms, thought Eva, impressed. *I'm fascinated to see where this goes.*

"This isn't going to seem relevant, but years ago, I had a pet turtle. I was living in this little shack in Popoyo, a surfing town in Nicaragua. No one locks doors or anything. One morning, I woke up and there was a massive turtle in my bed."

"How is that sanitary?" asked Eva.

"Shhh, Mom," said Audre.

"Anyway, he chose me, and that was fucking that. I loved him instantly. And I took great care of him. I did all this research on what turtles like to eat, and twice a day, I'd make him tiny fruit salads with live crickets as garnish."

"Gross!" Audre looked at Eva, delighted.

"Crickets were extremely his shit," said Shane. "Anyway, he liked to follow me around, and since he moved so slowly, I walked really slowly so he could keep up. We would just shuffle around the house together, like geriatrics."

"Hmm. Codependency," said Audre. "Continue."

"He was my little man, you know? I spoke to him in Spanish exclusively."

"Why?" asked Audre.

"He was Nicaraguan," he said simply.

"Hold on," said Eva. "You speak Spanish?"

"*Suficiente para hablar con una tortuga,*" he said.

"You're actually insane," said Eva, chuckling.

Shane grinned, visibly proud of himself. "Anyway, one day I came home from surfing, and he was gone."

"Where'd he go?" asked Audre.

"Off to chill with some other drunk writer, I guess. I was gutted. But then one day he came back. I dropped everything. This time he stayed for a good six months before he wandered off again."

"Very slowly, I assume," said Eva.

"In the back of my mind, I'm always low-key hoping I'll run into him again."

"Well. All will be revealed in the fullness of time," mused Audre. "Mr. Hall, did it ever seem weird to you that you were so attached to a turtle?"

"It *was* weird. And, like you said, codependent." Shane shrugged. "But I accepted it. He showed up one day, and we had an immediate friendship. We drifted in and out of each other's lives, but we were attached, no matter what. Me and your mom are like that. We'll always be friends, no matter how much time goes by."

"I see. One second." Without saying a word, Audre got up from the table and walked out of the room.

"What did I do?" he whispered to Eva.

"Wait for it," Eva whispered back.

Thirty seconds later, Audre entered the kitchen in a new look. A sensible black sleeveless jumpsuit and horn-rimmed glasses with no prescription.

"Honey," started Eva, "what is this outfit?"

"Doctorate in Psychology Realness," she announced, and then slid back into her seat. "Mr. Hall, it's clear from the turtle thing that you need therapy. Here's my card. I can help you, if it's okay with my mom."

"It's not okay," said Eva. "Shane, whatever you do, don't give her any money."

"Can I at least ask a couple more questions?" Audre leaned over the table toward Shane, conspiratorially. "What was Mommy like in high school? Did she sign your yearbook? What clubs were you guys in?"

Shane folded his arms across his chest, thinking. "Honestly? She was the smartest girl I'd ever met. And fearless. She'd say anything that came to her head, like you."

Audre brightened. "You think we're alike?"

Shane glanced at Eva where she stood at the counter, watching them. Then he smiled at Audre. "Yeah, I do. A lot."

"No, I was a misfit." Eva settled back onto the bench, next to her daughter. She slid a glass of lemonade in front of Shane.

"We both were," he said.

"In a way," said Eva, "you helped me. I realized that I wasn't the only hot mess in school."

"I never realized I was lonely," he said. "Until I met you and I wasn't anymore."

And then Shane and Eva slipped into a moment, and for a few prolonged, heightened beats, they forgot that Audre was there. Audre felt the temperature change in the room. She got up from her seat and slid onto her mom's lap.

Audre did this sometimes. While Eva helped her with homework.

While they marathoned *The Bachelor*. Despite being long and gawky, she still needed to cuddle. But this was a territorial move, catlike—as if she picked up something possessive in Shane's gaze and needed to claim Eva as hers.

Eva got it. She linked her arms around her daughter's waist and gave her hand three squeezes, their secret *I love you* code. Audre squeezed back and relaxed a little.

"Honey, should you get back to work on your piece?"

"Yep, going," said Audre, hopping off her lap and picking up her art from the floor.

Shane witnessed their entire wordless exchange with the awe and reverence of a city dweller's first visit to the Grand Canyon. He let out a gasp. "You did that? It's dope!"

"I like collaging," she said shyly.

"It reminds me of Man Ray," said Shane. "Or, no, what's his name, the dude out of Seattle who collages with vintage magazines? He has such a surreal perspective on ordinary life. What's his name?"

Audre gasped. "You know about Jesse Treece? Wow, thanks! But I could never be like him."

"Good," he said. "Be like you. Who is the woman in the piece?"

"My baby's a great artist," Eva blurted before Audre could answer. "Let's show him your gallery wall!"

"*Mom*. Noooo."

"Come on, let me be a proud mama, please."

Ushering them both out of the kitchen, Eva led them to the hallway near her master bedroom. The wall was covered in ten years' worth of framed portraits of Eva and Audre—drawn or sketched or painted with increasing sophistication, by Audre.

Shane went mute, studying Audre's work. No matter the medium, her pieces were bright, vivid, evocative. But also, he noticed that she'd littered the back- and foregrounds with melancholy, using withered florals and vintage mementos. Porcelain dolls and dusty books. Objects visiting from another time. It was almost a manifestation of Eva's vibe. Audre was happy and well adjusted, not prone to her mother's darkness—but she'd absorbed her edge anyway, through osmosis.

Eva watched Shane admiring her baby's art, and her heart stuttered. She couldn't help it. Shane was in her house, casually chatting with Audre the way a collector would speak to an artist at a showing. Eva tried to play down how delicious this felt. How domestic. Because hope was coiling up into her brain, like a snake piercing her with its fangs. Just like when she first met him, that day on the bleachers.

Grow up, she told herself. *You know how this ends.*

Of course she did. But it felt so delicious, she was starting not to care.

"...collage knocks you off-balance, a bit," explained Audre. "You know, seeing elements that don't belong together."

"Like your portrait, right? With the feathers and the corduroy hair. It almost feels like its rippling in the breeze."

"Exactly!" She beamed at Eva. "It's Grandma Lizette, by the way. She's a nonconformist, like you. You met her, right?"

"No, I never had the pleasure."

"We always hung out at Shane's house," Eva said quickly.

"Grandma Lizette has a real appreciation for art," said Audre, adjusting a crooked frame. "When Mom was little, she took her to the Georgia O'Keeffe Museum in Santa Fe. And the Picasso Museum in Paris."

Shane glanced quickly at Eva. Eva made a tight expression. And again, Audre got the distinct impression that she was on the outside of something.

"Well...," she said, backing out of the room, "I'm gonna go finish my piece."

Shane stuck out his hand to her. She shot him a confident smile and shook it.

"It was an honor to meet you," he said. "You're such an impressive person."

"Ask her to name the capital of Maine, though," Eva said with a smirk.

"Mom!" To Shane, Audre replied, "I'm really not that impressive. I'm just wildly verbal for my age. But thank you. And don't be a stranger."

With that, she shoved her artwork under her arm and headed off into her room. And then stopped abruptly.

"Oh," said Audre, turning around to face them. "Quick question."

"What?" asked Eva and Shane simultaneously.

"Which one of you is the turtle?"

"I'm sorry?" asked Eva.

"Which one of you is the turtle? You know, the one who leaves and comes back and leaves again, while the other waits?" she said, spinning on her heel. "It's a metaphor, writers. Think about it."

She left them alone as they stared straight ahead. Looking at each other might have started a fire.

Later, they loitered on the sidewalk in front of her brownstone. It was just after dinnertime, and the Park Slope sidewalks, overrun with out-of-school kids all day, were quieting down. The sun was setting in rosy lavender streaks. Audre was upstairs, collaging. Shane and Eva couldn't stop touching each other—a hand on a shoulder, fingers tracing cheek-bones, indulgent hugs—and they'd stopped trying. All was right with the world.

Eva had writing to do, so Shane had to go. They'd been in the process of saying goodbye for almost a full hour.

"Well," he said. "That was the highlight of my week. The second highlight."

"Audre liked you." Eva was trying to manage her giddiness. She felt as if she were going to explode all over Seventh Avenue.

"And y'all are just magical together," he gushed. "She's incredible."

"Thank you," said Eva, beaming. *"Friend."*

"Anytime. Friend."

She lightly knocked her shoulder against his. He knocked her back.

"Well," he said, cracking his knuckles, "I'm gonna go. Let you finish hexing me in book fifteen."

"Oh, that reminds me," started Eva hesitantly. "I need your opinion. How would you feel if Sebastian were white?"

"That's one hell of a hex."

"No, I'm serious. *Cursed* is going to be a movie. Which is so exciting. But the director wants to make Sebastian and Gia white. You know, mainstream appeal."

Shane couldn't help but laugh. "Me? White? Nah, stop playing."

"Believe me, it's not a joke," she said, tucking a few escaped tendrils back into her topknot.

Seeing her resigned expression, Shane knew she was serious. "You can't green-light that. Come on. You've got too much integrity for that bullshit."

"I really just need the movie to be made." With a little shrug, she leaned against the front gate. "Besides, the characters are mythological. They can be any race."

Shane stared at Eva for several beats, trying to discern if she believed what she was saying. Or if she was talking herself into it.

"You know you can't do that," he said, dismissing the idea.

"I need this movie. It'll afford me a break, so I can do other things."

"Your job as an artist, a *Black* artist, is to tell the truth."

"My job as a *single-mom* artist is to make money," she pointed out. "I already know the truth."

"Hmm," mumbled Shane, unconvinced. "It sounds like you're trying to talk yourself into the idea of whitewashing your characters. You can't really want that. *Cursed* is who you are."

"It's just a story," she said, with quiet finality.

Shane leaned against the gate next to her and took her hand in his. "Can I ask you something? Did you really go to Paris with your mom? And Santa Fe?"

"It was partly true," she said, comforted by the warmth of his skin.

"My mom dated an art buyer once. Way back when she had fancy boyfriends. He flew her around to auctions. They visited those museums together. Just not with me."

For a while, they stood there, silent. Holding hands. Lost in their own thoughts, they stroked each other's palms. Twisted their fingers together. It was the most natural thing. Then Shane made his bare arm parallel with Eva's—so his *G* and her *S* lined up.

"How," she started, "do you explain this to people?"

"I don't."

"That simple, huh?" Eva was awed.

"It's ours," he said simply. "Sacred."

"I wish it were that easy for me," she said. "I had to invent an *entire mythology* to explain it. If *S* was about a fictional character, I could live with it."

Shane nodded. "Is that like what you did with your mom? Rewriting her history for Audre's sake?"

Eva squeezed his hand and let go.

"There's more than what you see," she said softly. "Between me and Audre. We've been through a lot."

"Do you want to talk about it?"

She backed away from him, shoulders slumping a bit. "My head's worse when it rains. An intense rainstorm can land me in the hospital for a week. When Audre was little, these episodes really rattled her— and eventually, she developed a rain phobia. One drop, and she'd lose it. During Hurricane Sandy, she shrieked till she burst all the capillaries in her face. She'd become too hysterical to leave the house. I had to take her out of kindergarten for a while."

There's no way to explain this guilt, thought Eva. *Knowing that your child's tormented, and it's all your fault.*

"I went to a million doctors. Desperate to get better, to be normal. For her. Some kook even put me on methadone, which is illegal now. I mean, it's an opioid. I was zonked. Cece basically moved in with us for a year."

"God, Eva."

"The point is, I do a lot of mothering from the bed. Ordering dinner, checking homework, braiding her hair—all from the bed. Physically, I'm limited. But I *can* tell stories. Spin scary stuff into magic. Storms terrify my baby? I tell her she's sensitive to rain 'cause she's a weather fairy, like the impundulu in South African mythology. She's got a sociopath for a grandma? In our house, she's an eccentric feminist shero."

Feigning confidence she didn't feel, she turned to face Shane. The naked grief in his face eviscerated her.

"So yeah, I stretch the truth. But I'm weaving a world to protect her from the real one." She shrugged slightly. "Maybe it's not just for Audre. Maybe I tweak my memories of Lizette so I can sleep better at night. I can't help it. I know better, but a part of me still worships her."

Shane drew Eva into his arms. She went easily, settling into his chest.

"You're the strongest person I know," he said. "What you're teaching Audre about resilience, strength, creativity? She's lucky to have you. She's dynamic as hell, and it's all you."

Eva went still. And then she pulled away sharply.

"Stop," she said. "Just stop." And she turned on her heel, opened the gate, and flew up her stoop stairs. Stunned at this sudden shift, he followed her up the steps, taking them two by two.

"Stop what?" said Shane.

Eva ripped her keys from her pocket and tried to line the right one up with the lock, but she fumbled and dropped them. Shane picked them up—and with an exasperated exhale, she whipped around to face him, sticking her hand out.

"Gimme my keys."

He handed them over. "Stop what, Eva?"

"Stop making me fall for you again!"

Shane flinched. "How am I making you? It's happening to both of us."

"Really? I didn't show up to . . . wherever you live . . . and disturb your peaceful life, out of nowhere. You came here to do this. On purpose."

"I meaaan, I don't really do anything on purpose," he said, keeping his voice light with self-mockery, trying to calm her. "I had no plan, no ulterior motive, other than to apologize. On some AA shit. But I'm not sorry this happened."

"I can't do this," she said, brows pinched with stress. "I can't let you suck me in. You just met my *daughter*. I have too much to lose."

"Suck you in," he repeated.

"Yes!"

"It's easy to blame me, right?"

"Excuse me?"

In the near darkness, Shane's eyes blazed. "I showed up in Brooklyn, unannounced. Yeah. But let's tell facts. *You* came to Horatio Street. *You* convinced me to go to the Dream House. And *you* left me there. I know you twist history to make things easier for you, but I've never *made* you do anything. Do you ever think about your role in all of this?"

"My role?" Eva's voice rose five decibels. "Please, I'm not even a real person to you! Just a piece of fiction you made up."

"Nah. *You're* fiction that you made up."

She wanted to slap him. "Nice. Go home."

"I will. But first, this. Do you even remember that house? You scared the *fuck* out of me. I slept with one eye open, 'cause I was terrified you'd cut too deep. Or take one pill too many. *You* branded us. *You* did that. There isn't just one dangerous person here. There's two. We're the same."

Too infuriated to speak—seething, knowing that this was uncomfortably accurate—Eva turned her back to Shane and fumbled with the lock again. When she spun back around to face him, trembling, she unloaded all the bottled-up fury she'd been holding in for years.

"WHERE DID YOU GO?"

Stunned, he shook his head. "What?"

"Where did you go?" She stepped toward him, raging, keys digging into her palm. "Okay, we're both bad. But *you* disappeared. Not me." Angrily, she swiped tears from her eyes. Couples and families were breezing past,

oblivious to the weeping woman and her tormented-looking man at the top of the stoop.

"Yesterday was perfect," she continued, raging. "Today was perfect. We're so fucking good, *still*. Look at all the time we lost! *How could you leave me?* That morning, when I woke up and you...you weren't there. I had to teach myself how to breathe again, in a world without you in it. Do you get that?"

Eva gasped, pausing to catch her breath. "You begged me to stay, promised me you'd never leave. But it was all a lie. You never even tried to contact me. Not even to see if I'd made it out alive! Is it fun for you to ruin lives and escape unscathed? Are you sick, or just a liar? *I stayed alive for you.* But you killed me, anyway."

"Eva..."

"I told myself I didn't care." She was openly weeping now. "But I do. You broke your promise. Where did you go?"

This was what Shane had come to tell her. But everything had changed. Especially after he'd seen Audre's portrait of Lizette and witnessed how Eva had softened her mother's history.

I know better, but a part of me still worships her.

Shane didn't want to unthread Eva's emotional connection to her mother. But he owed her an explanation, and it was the only part of this trip he'd actually planned for.

"I didn't leave you," he said finally.

"What?"

"Your mom never said anything?"

"No," she said, her voice cracking, pleading. "What happened?"

"I didn't leave you."

Confusion flooded her face.

"I would never have left you. It was...your mom. She sent me away."

"You're blaming it on her?" Eva trembled with white rage, fisting her hands to steady them. "When I woke up, I asked for you. She didn't even know who you *were*, Shane."

"How do you think she got there?" Shane's voice was an unsteady mix of regret and pain. "I found her number in your phone, and I called her. When she got to the house, she called the paramedics. And the police. And sent me to prison."

The blood drained from Eva's face. "No."

"Ask her," he said gently. "Ask her."

FRIDAY

Chapter 20

IT WAS THAT BOY

GALVESTON, TEXAS, WAS BLAZING. IT ALWAYS WAS, BUT THE END OF JUNE WAS brutal. Especially up in Lizette Mercier's attic–cum–rehearsal studio. The AC in her rickety leased house refused to work, except (randomly) on Sundays, Mondays, and Wednesdays.

To combat the oppressive heat, Lizette scattered Home Depot fans around the periphery of the pink-painted attic—which caused papers, boas, gowns, bedazzled sashes, robes, and other sequined miscellanea to fly about as if caught in a windstorm. Lizette relished the drama. Sometimes, she even threw confetti directly into the fan, just to get her girls used to being distracted while performing. Something always threw you off on stage. Bright lights, a glimpse of your boyfriend, side-eye from the judges. Your competition doing terrible things to ruin your stage presence, like when Emmaline Hargrove flashed that hairy, nude Burt Reynolds centerfold from an old '70s *Cosmo* at her, from the wings.

When was that, 1983? No, '84. The Miss South Louisiana Mardi Gras pageant. Emmaline Hargrove was trash. Lizette got revenge, though. First by nailing the talent portion of the show ("Brick House" on clarinet) and then by nailing Emmaline's dad (Justice Peter Hargrove). Lizette won Miss Congeniality that year. It wasn't the big prize, but she was pleased, nonetheless.

Sometimes smaller victories count more, she thought. *That's quite the catch phrase, actually. I should get that printed on a banner for my girls.*

It was time to replace the banner draped across her back wall, anyway. TO THINE OWN SELF BE TRUE. After winning Junior Miss Crawfish, one of Lizette's girls had crafted the glittery sign for her. It was a decade old, and the sequins had fallen off the *e* in "thine." TO THIN OWN SELF BE TRUE didn't make sense, but she always encouraged her girls to remain as skinny as possible, so it still worked.

Lizette wasn't sentimental, but she did love gifts from her students—sweets, stuffed animals, bouquets. Her favorites were the thank-you notes. She was the most successful pageant coach in the greater Galveston Beach area. Which was a feat, considering she ran a strictly word-of-mouth operation. No marketing. And definitely no social media. She loathed the thirstiness of Instagram, and Facebook felt like a yearbook from the Twilight Zone. To Lizette, all the "conveniences" that were supposed to make your life easier were actually just the tech equivalent of mosquitoes buzzing in your ears. She hated mosquitoes. And she hated being bothered.

Plus, Lizette didn't want to be found. The internet wasn't a place for people with secrets.

Her first client had been her neighbor's daughter, whom she'd spied practicing for Little Miss Forever Beautiful in their shared backyard. The perky fifth grader had been working on a majorette routine but kept dropping her baton. "You need a longah wand, darling," she'd called out over the peeling, ticky-tacky iron gate dividing their lawns. "One to match ya wingspan!"

Lizette had continued with her unsolicited performance notes—and when Kaileigh swept every title in the competition, she knew her advice had value.

Right now, she was working with Mahckenzee Foster, a twerking, tap-dancing, death-dropping demon. Lizette leaned forward in her director's chair, lasering in on the little girl's form. Lizette wasn't a trained dancer, but she did understand presence. When she worked as a cocktail waitress, the mere cadence of her walk inspired *chaos*. Or, at least, it inspired drunken, red-faced white men to shout "Halle Berry" at her. Lizette looked nothing like Halle. It was that white-person phenomenon where they see a pretty brown face and declare that it looks like the first pretty brown face that springs to their minds. She'd been compared to Thelma from *Good Times*, Jasmine Guy from *A Different World*, and the Black girl from *Saved by the Bell* who went nuts—no resemblance.

Just another way they make you feel invisible, she thought. Lizette knew that the only person she looked like was herself. And Clo Mercier.

All told, her past didn't bother her. Nothing bothered her, really. She lived on a Xanax-assisted cloud, stubbornly impervious to bad feelings and dark days. When a depressive thought popped up, she swatted it away.

"One more time, sweet Mahckenzee," she purred, adjusting her kimono so it draped prettily around her legs. At fifty-five, with dreamy doe eyes and hot-rollered hair rippling to her shoulders, she looked like she ran an upscale 1940s brothel, not a kiddie-pageant consultancy.

When Lizette first heard her Samsung Galaxy ring, she ignored it. The phone sat on the director's chair next to hers, the one she reserved for helicopter moms who wanted to observe rehearsals. After it rang a good six times, Lizette caught a glimpse of the name lighting up her screen. She yelped and then accidentally crushed her Diet Coke can in her right hand.

"Holy shit," she said, grabbing the phone. "Whoa, whoa, whoa. Okay. Mahckenzee? Keep practicing, doll, I'ma step downstairs for a moment. Need to take a call."

"Okay... Miss... Miss Lizette!" panted Mahckenzee, who'd been dancing for forty minutes straight.

Lizette floated downstairs. She looked in her wall mirror, added a bit more CoverGirl Red Revenge lipstick to her bee-stung lips, and then draped herself over her white leather-look couch.

"Hello, Genevieve," she cooed, all honey-mellow tones and lilting accent.

"Hey, Mom. Hi." Her daughter sounded frantic. And close, as if she were yelling from the next room. It must've been an emergency if she was calling her on a random afternoon in June. They talked exactly four times a year: twice in April (on each of their birthdays), once in September (on Audre's birthday), and at Christmas. She couldn't imagine what had precipitated the call. But to her daughter, *everything* was a crisis.

Lizette had barely seen Genevieve since she'd moved away from home. When she came back from that psychiatric ward where the police sent her (she would never have had her flesh and blood committed, good *God*), Genevieve had told her in a long, teary midnight conversation that her therapists had said she needed space. From her mother. For her health.

Space!

Those were her words, in that kitchen, in their janky rented apartment in Washington, DC. That home had never felt like one, just an in-between purgatory riddled with bad luck. Everything fell apart in DC. Genevieve went missing. Lizette's lover went missing, too—and then, one night, he hobbled into his bar, where she was cocktail-waitressing. She yelped, seeing his chubby, square frame propped up on crutches and his face bruised to hell and back.

She sidled up to him, a vision in black lace.

"My condolences to the other guy," she chirped breathily into his hairy ear. An attempt to appeal to his (unearned) vanity—but he didn't react at all. He just looked right through her. It wasn't a look, actually; it was an *unlook*. The end.

It shouldn't have hurt so much. She'd been dumped before. But this one had such potential! Lizette had met him while waitressing in Vegas. Over Bloody Marys, he'd invited her to live in DC, promising to set her up nicely and teach her how to manage his bar. She'd hoped he'd be her forever guy. She was so tired of starting over with a new man every couple years, only to be abandoned for unspecified reasons. When bad things happened over and over, it was a sign. God was telling you to change. Your attitude, your hair, your address. Something.

So she knew why Genevieve had fled. Lizette also knew that no matter where or how far you went, you couldn't outrun *yourself*. But her daughter was grown. What could she do? She hugged her, kissed her, and helped her pack for the dorm. And "space" stretched across years. Until one night, Lizette picked up a *Glamour* in the dressing room where she was dancing, and saw a profile on Genevieve, in the Ones to Watch section. And discovered that she had a baby and an ex-husband, neither of whom she'd met.

Lizette didn't lay eyes on Audre till she was two. It was cruel. She hadn't raised her daughter to have such ghastly manners. But in the end, maybe Genevieve had been right to sever ties. Genevieve was *Eva* now, and she and Audre were both thriving.

Everything turns out the way it oughta, she thought.

"What's wrong, bé?" She plucked a cigarette from the Parliament pack under her couch cushion and lit up. On an exhale, she said, "Must be trouble."

"Are you smoking?"

Lizette took a deep drag and then blew smoke directly into the receiver. "No."

"You said you'd quit. I sent you those e-cigs. Did you get them?"

"Jayzee Mahdee Joseff!" *Jesus Mary Joseph.* "Why you tendin' to my business? Don't antagonize me—I'm in the middle of class." She glanced above, where Mahckenzee's rat-a-tat-tat-tat tapping pounded through the ceiling.

"I need to ask you something. It's important."

"You sound off," said Lizette. "You been crying?"

"What happened the morning you found me in the Wisconsin Avenue house?"

Slowly, as if moving through water, Lizette brought her fingers to the corner of her mouth. They'd never talked about this. Genevieve always insisted she didn't want to revisit that morning ever again. Long ago, she'd put her foot down. Why now?

"I don't like to think about that morning," she said. "I'm having a hard day, G. So many girls, so little time, and I'm *exhausted*. You should see little Mahckenzee up there." She gestured at the ceiling, with her cigarette. "No bigger than a minute, but she projects to the stars."

Upstairs, Mahckenzee's tapping was actually shaking the ceiling. Lizette's crystal chandelier, a long-ago gift for excellent services rendered, was swaying. That was probably dangerous. It could fall on her.

Ah well, she thought, her eyelids fluttering shut. *We all die of something.*

"I need you to tell me every detail, Mom."

"Well, why you ain't asked till now? When you came back from that insane asylum—"

"Insane asylum? It was Howard University Hospital's psychiatric ward, not *One Flew Over the Cuckoo's Nest*."

"Well, whatever. You *forbade* me to ever discuss it again. You made me promise."

"I was a kid!"

"Yes, a stubborn, hincty kid with volcanic emotions. I ain't wanna upset you, so I did what you asked. Besides," she said haughtily, "there are things we just don't talk about. That's our relationship."

"We have a relationship?"

"Lord, the theatrics."

"Tell me," Genevieve demanded. "Please."

"Oh, fine." Lizette propped herself up on her silk pillows. With an indulgent yawn, she sank into a feline, full-body stretch, her kimono fluttering and rippling around her killer legs. Then she crossed her feet at the ankles and lit up her eleventh cigarette of the day.

"Think. How . . ."

Lizette heard her daughter's voice crack a little.

"How what, Genevieve?"

"How did you get to the house?" she asked, in a flimsy, hesitant voice. And Lizette wasn't positive, but judging from the way she asked the question, it seemed that she already knew the answer. How she knew, Lizette had no idea. But her hunches were rarely wrong.

A chill knifed through her. Lizette knew she was on trial. But she had no idea where this interrogation was coming from.

"I don't want to talk about this," she whined petulantly.

"I really don't care."

What did she have to lose? Her daughter already hated her. And if God was judging her for her crimes, lying to her daughter to protect her would be the least of her sins.

"I'll try to remember," sighed Lizette. "I'd been calling you all week, and you never answered. Imagine if Audre ran away like that?"

"She wouldn't," said Genevieve, with devastating finality.

Lizette cleared her throat. "Um, finally, on Sunday morning, my phone rang. But it wasn't you."

"Who was it?"

"It was that boy."

"Shane?"

Shane. Lizette rolled her eyes to the ceiling at the mention of his name—and then realized that she could no longer hear Mahckenzee tapping upstairs. Unacceptable. She slipped off her violet stiletto and threw it at the ceiling, where it hit with a thud and then landed on an accent table, in a tray of pink-and-yellow macarons.

She eyed this pastel tableau from the couch. It looked like the cover of a '90s chick-lit novel.

"Mom, are you there? *Shane* called you?"

"Yes! How many times I gotta say it?" Lizette held a pillow to her chest. "He was all distressed. Said you were in trouble, and gave me the address. I drove there so fast I got a ticket. Got there, and you...you weren't breathing. He was crying, saying it was all his fault. Which it was. Because there were drugs everywhere. Pills, liquor, just depravity. A razor. And you had terrible cuts! I knew he'd done it all; you were my innocent little baby."

"Oh, Mom," she moaned. "Jesus, you got it so wrong."

"I called the paramedics," she said proudly. "And then I called the police. And then they called the Oriental girl whose daddy lived there."

"You can't say 'Oriental,'" she said flatly. "So you called the police. It was you."

"If I knew the cops would send you to the loony bin, I wouldn't have. But yes, I called the police! That boy kidnapped you. Hurt you. You were *bleeding*. Any mother would've done the same. Imagine if it were Audre. Besides, he knew he was guilty. You can't imagine…He…he wouldn't let you go. He was holding both of your hands in his and just wouldn't let go. And then he crawled in bed and held you. *Right in front of me.* So disrespectful. Imagine if it was your baby? He refused to move. When the cops got there, it took all three of them to drag him away from you."

Lizette hadn't thought about this in years, but the memory still infuriated her. How dare that boy, who was clearly to blame, be so upset? *She* was the mother. *She* got to be upset. Lizette's world was falling apart, her boyfriend had just dumped her, and here was this kid, so consumed by love for her daughter that he had to be *physically dragged away*.

Genevieve was a child. She hadn't even lived yet. Why did she get that kind of adoration, when Lizette had never experienced it? It wasn't the order of things. It wasn't fair.

"What happened then?" Genevieve asked, in a broken whisper.

"I had him arrested and put away. Good fucking riddance. I believe he went to juvenile detention. They told me it was his third time. Serial predator."

Silence.

"You're welcome," said Lizette, nervousness creeping through her.

Nothing.

"Hello?"

"All these years." Genevieve's voice sounded reedy. "All these years, I thought he was a coward. A liar. I hated him."

"Well, who's to hate if it ain't him?"

Her daughter had no response to this, apparently. Her silence was so complete, so lengthy, that for a moment, Lizette thought she'd hung up.

"You never noticed that I cut myself?" she asked hesitantly. "You must've known."

"*What?* You were so secretive. How would I know that?"

"I know when Audre gets a papercut."

"Well." Lizette took a deep drag. "You need to get you a life, bé."

"I cut myself. He didn't do it. And I'd been taking drugs—your drugs, or getting them from your boyfriends—*my whole life*. I wasn't your innocent little baby."

"How'd you get them from my boyfriends?" Lizette's voice went cold, sharp. She hated being reminded of her failed loves. And how hard her life had been. And that she was never able to fix what hurt her daughter. But Genevieve had always felt so unreachable. Her pain took her to a place where no one could follow.

"I'd been watching you my whole life, Mom."

"Careful your tone."

"I was in agony. I needed help."

"I know you suffered, my bè. But what could I do? I prayed for you; I still pray for you. But you can't fight a curse. I *been* tellin' you to get some houseplants."

The force of Genevieve's long-suffering exhale carried across nine states.

"My girls always ask me why I got so many dead plants. I tell 'em what Mama Clo told me. Deceased plants are good luck. When a houseplant dies, it's because it's absorbed bad energy and juju. Bad juju meant for *you*. They're protection." After dropping this gem, she took a deep drag off her cigarette. "Everybody's got an affliction, Genevieve. Whether it's mental or physical or spiritual. You just gotta remember what good you got."

"Please don't get philosophical, Mom. It doesn't look good on you."

"Everything looks good on me, except dolman sleeves," she said testily. "Look. I don't know what's got you ornery or why we're discussing ancient history. But a word of advice? Get over your childhood. I got over mine. You think *you* had it bad? I had to perform unspeakable acts for pageant judges just so I could win a little money to buy groceries and fake Jordache jeans from Family Dollar."

Genevieve's silence was deafening.

"They were called Gordache jeans," said Lizette sadly.

"You sent Shane away." Genevieve sounded like she was speaking more to herself than to Lizette. "He was terrified of going to prison again. I told him that I'd make sure he never went back."

"Oh, G," Lizette cooed. "That boy preyed on you. That's what they all do! They want the pretty girl but then get jealous of your youth and vitality. So they lure you down the path to ruin and break you."

"Jealous of youth? Shane and I were the same age!"

"Well, I know, but I was talking about me!" Lizette smoothed her kimono over her legs, exasperated.

After another extended silence, Genevieve finally spoke. "You were jealous."

"I've never been jealous in my life! But I'll tell you what. Mercier women *are* cursed. We are. And if I can't make a man stay, there's no way in hell you could." Lizette tightened the sash on her kimono. "I don't know why you're so determined to hate me. You get got by a cute li'l criminal, I rescue you, and *I'm* the villain? How's that work?"

"You really want me to explain this?"

"Go 'head and judge me, miss. I fear nothing but the pitiless gaze of the Almighty. You could be Mommie Dearest or Clair Huxtable—don't matter what kind of mother you are; daughters always blame moms for every mess they make." Lizette took one last drag and then stubbed her cigarette out in a crystal ashtray. Under her breath, she said, "In fifteen years, Audre'll give her therapist an earful."

"You don't understand one thing that's happened to you, do you?" Genevieve asked wearily.

"Stop being so morose, G. We had some really fun times when you were little! Remember those adorable lovebirds?"

"They died of lead poisoning."

"And that's my fault?"

"They died of lead poisoning because when they chirped at night, you'd throw pencils at their cage."

"Well, who knew pencils were edible? Did you?"

"Goodbye, Mom."

"Stop being so mad at me! You know, boys like Shane belong behind bars." Lizette was grasping at straws now, just trying to keep Genevieve on the phone. Genevieve had always confused her. When you're pregnant, you think you're gonna have a little you. A tiny person with your same thoughts, same feelings. But her daughter came out wholly herself. Self-sufficient, stubborn, too clever for the world, and an utter mystery. Lizette never really knew how to raise her, and Lord knows Genevieve never gave any clues.

"I saved you from a world of trouble. Look at who you've become! You're..." Lizette stopped talking then, because her line went dead.

Ah well. It wasn't the first time her daughter had hung up on her, and it wouldn't be the last. She dragged herself off the couch and swept back upstairs to Mahckenzee, one out of dozens of girls whom Lizette had made perfect, in her image. With each new student, Lizette had a chance to get it right. Season after season, show after show, again and again.

Chapter 21

WHAT A COINCIDENCE

Eva was way too frugal to have a habit of Ubering. Besides, she lived right by the Q train. But tonight, she didn't care. She didn't care about anything except getting to Shane.

Cece had agreed to watch Audre for the night. She was only too happy to spend the night with her favorite faux niece, but on one condition: Eva had to *vow* to attend her party tomorrow. "You know, just an insidery get-together to celebrate the Littie Awards." With a rushed "Anything you want, of course, yes, I'll be there," Eva agreed and zipped out the door.

Eva was barely cognizant of what she was agreeing to. She had only one thought in her brain.

I need him, she thought while ordering a thirty-seven-dollar Uber. *Need him,* she thought while racing over the Manhattan Bridge and through downtown. *Need, need, need,* she thought while flying up the stairs at 81 Horatio Street.

It was 9:45 on a warm, weirdly windy Friday night—far from yesterday's glaring heat and her fight with Shane. Horatio was quiet, but she could hear the distant revelry of rich recent grads cocktailing and carousing at the outdoor *Biergarten* on Washington.

But here, in front of James Baldwin's ostentatious peacock-blue door, the darkness was so complete she felt like it might swallow her whole. Heart thundering in her chest, she leaned against the door's smooth surface, forehead-first, palms flat. She allowed herself a few deep, cleansing breaths, just to dull the thudding in her head, which had been threatening to explode since she'd hung up on Lizette.

And then, for the second time in two days, Eva knocked on this door.

But this time, she pounded. And Shane opened it right away.

She could barely see beyond him. There wasn't a light on in the house. Just darkness upon darkness. But she saw him, breathtaking in front of her. Tall, strong, solid. Hers.

Eva met his eyes, and something jolted inside her.

"I know everything," she said, wanting to sound pulled-together, but the hitch in her voice betrayed her.

"Come in."

She didn't budge. She had to say what she'd come here to say. And it spilled out of her like a flood.

"My mom told me. And you were young and scared and trying to be tough—and I promised you that you'd never go back. I promised. And she sent you back." She gulped dryly. "Shane, I'm sorry. I'm so sorry for everything I said yesterday. I'm sorry for blaming you for all these years. For hating you. I hated you so much."

"I know," he said hoarsely. "Just come inside."

"No, listen. I hated you only because..." Eva paused. "It was because loving you wasn't an option."

Shane averted his eyes, his jaw clenched.

"Why didn't you tell me?" she asked. "Why?"

"I couldn't," he said. He looked years younger, vulnerable.

"There's so much I need to know."

"Later."

"But..."

Shane grabbed her by the front of her dress and pulled her inside the shadowy foyer. He slammed the door and pressed her back against it. The only light came from the moon, dimly shining through the open bay windows across the apartment.

Disoriented, Eva blinked. She was acutely aware of everything: his scent, his rugged scruff, his crumpled tee, the line of his biceps, his eyes. Shane overwhelmed her. She was dizzy with him.

With a groan, Shane smashed his mouth against hers, kissing her into the door.

He tangled his hand in her curls, pulling her head back to deepen the kiss. Over and over they savored each other, their kisses hot and hungry.

"Fuck," he said. "You're here."

"I'm here."

Mouth open on her neck, he slipped his hand beneath her short, gauzy slip dress and slid it up her inner thigh. Possessively, he squeezed the soft skin there. She went liquid.

"Tell me what you want," Shane rasped into her ear.

She wanted him all over her, his scent, his mouth, his tongue, his hands, *him*. She wanted him to mark her so she'd never remember anyone else. "Just want you. Everywhere."

Shane grabbed her hand and dragged her through the darkness to the bedroom. The wind picked up again, rattling the massive windows and howling against the building.

Between broken kisses, they stumbled blindly into the moon-dappled bedroom. There was a rumpled, rainy-day sexiness to the bed, a poufy duvet collapsed in Shane-shaped dents. They dropped onto it together, a tangle of limbs, pillows toppling to the floor.

Grabbing her jaw between his fingers, Shane drew Eva into a quick, filthy kiss. And then, without warning, he flipped her around.

Starting at her ankle, he ran his mouth up along the back of her calf, scratching her with his stubble, leaving a searing kiss behind her knee. She moaned, grabbing the sheets in her fists, but he kept going, planting a wet love bite just under her butt cheek and then *slowly* dragging his tongue up along her spine. Ravenous, Shane pushed her sweaty curls aside and sucked Eva's neck.

"Turn around," he directed lustily. Without thought, she did. Inching his way down her body, he slipped his hands under her ass, pulled her to his mouth, and went for it—no teasing, no buildup. The shock was delicious. She cried out. Arched her back. And then he stopped.

With a teasing smirk, he climbed up her body.

"Hi." He grinned.

"Wh-why'd you stop?"

"Needed to kiss you." He did, chastely, on her mouth.

"You're the worst. Fuck me. *Please*. Fuck me on James Baldwin's bed."

Shane laughed. "This isn't James Baldwin's bed. You think they had Sleep Number beds in 1961?"

"Oh." She grabbed at his arms. "Well, then fuck me on this Sleep Number bed."

"Cum first. Then I'll fuck you."

Before she could think, he was avidly tonguing her again. And she was coming apart.

"Eva."

"What?" she whimpered, riding wave after wave.

"Eva."

"*What?*"

"Look at me."

She peered down at Shane's face, his wicked mouth on her—and *oh*, it was an obscene, exquisite sight. Once her eyes locked with his, Shane sank two fingers deep inside her. Gently, he hooked them in a come-hither motion, and that was it. She came, riding out every jolt.

The spike of her orgasm subsided, but her high didn't. Despite Shane reducing her to Jell-O, Eva managed to climb on top of him. Gripping him, she carefully eased herself down. With a throaty groan, he grabbed her ass in one hand, her breast in the other, and gave up control.

"Go ahead," he rasped, catching his bottom lip in his teeth. "Take what's yours."

Eva did, grinding against him, winding her hips. Their breathing went choppy, their eyes squeezed shut, he moaned her name, she went incoherent, he squeezed her tighter, and finally, the electricity sent them both over the edge.

Dazed, Shane sat up, pulling Eva toward him, wrapping his arms around her. Eva crossed her legs behind his back. And they held each other there, for who knows how long. At some point, they toppled onto the bed together, still attached.

Hadn't they always been?

Later, she sat with Shane on the terrace floor, overlooking a hidden garden in the backyard. The night had turned cool, so they were wrapped in an oversized beach blanket.

"This week," she started. "Is it history repeating itself?"

"History doesn't repeat itself," said Shane. "But it rhymes."

"Who said that? Nas?"

"Mark Twain."

"Mmm," she said. "Great philosophers, both."

A few hours after that, they were lying horizontally across the bed. The wind had picked up again, rattling the windows. Cum-hazy after a drowsy fuck, they were tangled up together in the dark, her back sealed to his chest, his face buried in her hair. And finally, he told her what had happened that last morning in DC.

"You didn't wake up," Shane said in a solemn voice. "I couldn't bring myself to slap you, like in the movies. But I shook you hard and nothing happened. You were dying. And it was my fault. I'd given you all those drugs."

Eva pulled his hand from her breast up to her mouth and kissed it. She tucked it under her chin.

"I held you for a long time, just, you know, crying and trying to figure out what to do. Then I remembered your phone down in the kitchen.

When I got it, I saw, like, thirty missed calls from your mom. So I called her.

"And I knew how it'd look when she got there. *I* broke into that house. *I* brought you there. *I* had prior arrests. And over the previous eight hours, I'd emptied a bottle of vodka and snorted an indeterminate amount of heroin. So yeah, I knew it'd be bad for me."

"Why didn't you leave?" asked Eva. "You could've called her, hidden somewhere, and then found me later."

"I couldn't leave you," he said with finality. "And I couldn't deny it when your mom accused me of hurting you." He paused. "I was almost eighteen, so I was tried as an adult. But I was only locked up for two years. Good behavior."

"You?"

"Yeah. I was different than before. I kept my head down. Didn't start shit. Remember the mantra you gave me?"

"Yeah. Don't fight, write."

"It kept me safe. And I wrote *Eight* there."

Eva turned to face him. "I'm so sorry."

"No, I'm sorry. That's what I came to New York to say. I'm sorry I broke my promise. And I'm sorry I didn't find you the second I was released. But by then, you'd published your first book. You were a success, and I didn't want to ruin it. Back then, I was convinced that I ruined everything I touched."

Eva looked at him, remembering what he'd revealed to her long ago: losing his stable, happy life with his foster parents. Blaming himself.

"After I accidentally broke my arm, and my foster mom . . ." He paused, jaw working. "When I survived the crash on the way to the hospital and my foster mom didn't, I started breaking my arm on purpose. Drinking all day. And I decided that I didn't deserve good things."

Eva held him tight. It was all she could do. Hold him tight enough to smother that thought, for good.

★ ★ ★

Later, Shane and Eva lay in a tangle on the plush living room rug, staring up at the stained-glass window on the ceiling. Shane was on his side, tracing the planes of her face with his fingertips. Across her eyebrow, down the bridge of her nose. Cradling her face in his palms, he smooshed her cheeks together so her lips poked out. Then he stuck his finger in her dimple.

"Just say it," Eva said with a smile.

"I've never said it. To anyone."

"It won't hurt, I promise."

Shane grinned, a heart-stopping thing. Then laid his face on her breasts, closing his eyes.

"Ready?" he asked.

"Ready."

"I love you," said Shane. "Dramatically, violently, and forever."

She kissed the top of his head, smiling brighter than the sun.

"I've always loved you," he whispered.

"What a coincidence," she whispered back. "I've always loved you, too."

Some indeterminate time later, Eva and Shane were eating mint gelato out of the jar, in the brightly tiled kitchen. She was perched on the island. They were each wearing a pair of Shane's boxer briefs, and nothing else.

"...and I can't make this movie with white characters. I couldn't live with myself," she said. "But I don't know what to do. I can't even finish book fifteen."

"Isn't it due next week?"

"I've been distracted." She smiled, licking gelato off her spoon.

"I'm out," he said, pretending to walk away. "I can't be responsible for the downfall of your career."

"Stop, you're not," she said, grabbing him by the waistband. "Honestly, I just can't find the spark anymore. And all I wanna do is write my family's story. Go to Louisiana, like we said. Research those women and write."

"Do you realize how valuable you are?"

"Please," she scoffed, scooping up more gelato. "To the literary community?"

"To me."

She looked at him.

"Come with me to Belle Fleur," she blurted out. "Audre flies to her dad's for three months tomorrow. You don't start teaching till late August. We have time!"

"Let's go," he said with a grin. "I'll be your research assistant. Among other things."

"Yeah?" Lasciviously, Eva licked a dollop of gelato from her bottom lip. "What else do you wanna be?"

Shane watched her. Then he plucked her off the island and turned her around so her back was against him. He slipped his hand under the elastic of her boxer briefs and slowly massaged her clit. Her head fell back against his shoulder.

"I wanna be everything," he said, his mouth against her ear. "Wanna be the reason you light up. I wanna make you laugh, make you moan, make you safe."

He kept stroking her as she quivered helplessly.

"I want to be the thought that lulls you to sleep. The memory that gets you off. I wanna be where all your paths end." He nipped her earlobe. "I wanna do everything you do to me."

He pulsed his finger then, and she came with a shuddery cry.

"You're hired," she breathed.

Finally, Eva dozed off in Shane's arms just before dusk. They were on the couch, or perhaps the bed again. Later, she'd remember mumbling, "You know you're the turtle, right? The one who comes and goes as he pleases while I wait for you?"

She never heard his answer, because she slipped off into sleep. Deep, contented, trusting.

SATURDAY

Chapter 22

WORD TRAVELED FAST

Happy Saturday, gorgeous people! You're cordially invited to my abode today at 1pm. Bring nothing but your dazzling personalities and most scandalous industry gossip. As usual, this is a private affair. No phones. But! Since this is a day party—parents, feel free to bring your kiddos. I'm designating the downstairs guest bedroom a kiddie wonderland, catered by Dylan's Candy Bar and Shake Shack. (One thing: I do adore your children, but please discourage them from touching the chintz chinoiserie settee in the lounge. It was a wedding gift from my husband's godmother, Diahann Carroll.) See you shortly!

EXACTLY NONE OF THE INVITED AUTHORS, VISUAL ARTISTS, WEB WHIZZES, filmmakers, and fashion designers on Cece's list were surprised that the invite came a mere eight hours before the party started. That was her tradition—and it kept everyone on their toes. *"Stay* ready so you don't have to *get* ready" was one of her many mottoes.

Her penthouse was littered with modern art, sharp corners, and priceless objets d'art, but it was also a true indoor-outdoor space, with a massive terrace overrun with greenery, and bathroom windows looking out onto the Lower Manhattan skyline. Cece had worked hard with interior designer Lee Mindel to make the space function as no more than a chic backdrop. So when she entertained, the *people* were the decoration. In that setting, each of her guests turned into a star. They stood out as unique, special, colorful characters.

Oh, and they *were* characters. Milling about were some of Artsy Black Manhattan's loudest personalities. There was Janie, the Story-Topping Memoirist. Craig, the Rascally Gallerist. Tilly, the Giggly Graphic Novelist. Keisha, the Proudly Basic Jewelry Designer. Rasheed, the Intolerably Fine Book Agent. Cleo, the Fashion Photographer Obsessed with Her Blessings. Lenny, the Film Editor Who Pledged Q at Duke and Needs You to Know It.

Everyone was there. The sun shone bright and warm through Cece's windows. Champagne was flowing. Beautiful waiters served bacon-wrapped asparagus, tiny crab toasts, and parmesan tuiles. Vegans were offered petite Iittala glass cubes filled with fresh-cut fruit. A deejay (hidden in the kitchen) played chill but fun tracks à la Solange, Khalid, and SZA. Some guests were kiki-ing on the terrace, many were strewn across the couches, and the parents were *truly* kicking up their heels, because their little Chloes and Jadens were downstairs in their finest Zara Kids ensembles, blessedly out of sight and taken care of.

Eva wore her favorite "summertime sexy" look: a black romper with a strapless bustier top (it made her legs look endless, and her boobs luscious). She'd swept her curls to the side with a vintage pin and added smoky eyes. She was in full siren mode.

She was also loopy as hell after a night of no sleep and endless orgasms. Neither her brain nor her legs were working properly—and she kept dissolving into embarrassing, secret giggles.

Eva loved Shane and he loved her. Nothing else mattered. Certainly not what anyone else thought. But earlier, they'd tried to make a plan for how to approach the day.

Today, 10:28 AM

   SHANE: You going to Cece's?

   EVA: I have to, she tricked me.

   SHANE: Then I'm going, too. I fucking miss you.

   EVA: You saw me this morning. 😍

   SHANE: I'm in withdrawal.

   EVA: Same x1000.

   SHANE: How do we act, in public?

   EVA: Normal!

   SHANE: But what's our normal? Naked?

   EVA: Good point. This is weird.

   SHANE: We'll figure it out.

   EVA: You know she threw this party to get the tea on us, right?

   SHANE: Fucking Cece. You gonna tell her?

   EVA: I won't have to. She'll know.

And Cece did know, the second she laid eyes on Eva. She was dripping with sex; it was *obvious*. Eva couldn't remember the last time she'd felt so light. So unguarded! Shane had fucked away all her defenses. And now she was a mushball. Giddy. Aglow. Swooning from happiness in plain view of forty-five gossipy Blacks. But she didn't care. Around 3:30 a.m. (after the gelatogasm), she'd had an epiphany.

Something had been unlocked in her. For so long and in so many ways, Eva had been holding herself back. Now she wanted to figure out who she was—and then *be* her, *delight* in her. Delight in everything! Have an actual life and live it! She vowed to herself to be honest—with herself and with everyone. In pain? Admit it. In love? Claim it. Life was too short to be anything but herself.

Listen to me, she thought. *I get one slice of dick and turn into a wide-eyed Disney princess.*

She didn't realize that she'd laughed out loud until Belinda and Cece looked at her with eyebrows raised. They were struggling to maintain a conversation with Belinda's latest service-industry boy toy. She'd traded in her Trader Joe's dude for Cain, a copper-skinned snack she'd hired from TaskRabbit to build her IKEA dresser.

Cain was twenty-four, stocky, sexy—and he spoke only in one-word responses.

"So," started Cece, resplendent in a fitted fuchsia pantsuit and white teddy, "it's a fun party, right?"

"Vibes," Cain said, nodding.

"Cain, that's such a cool name," said Eva. "Is it biblical?"

"Facts," he said.

"Do you have a brother named Abel?" Eva giggled at her own joke. "I bet you hear that all the time."

"Word," said Cain.

"You know, I've never met a Cain *or* an Abel," mused Cece.

"The Weeknd's real name is Abel," said Belinda.

"Is your brother the Weeknd?" Eva asked Cain. "If so, I have some notes about his hair."

"Clownin'," said Cain, chuckling.

Belinda quickly steered the conversation toward something he could talk about.

"Babe," she said, "tell them about your blossoming deejay business!"

"Datshitfiyah," said Cain.

With that, he'd officially worn out his welcome.

"Babe, go get me another Aperol spritz." Belinda—who was slaying in a cropped white halter top, a floral maxiskirt, and long box braids—patted Cain's ass and sent him on his way.

"Wowwww," said Eva, stifling a giggle.

"Okay, but did you see how fine he is?" whispered Belinda. "And he's just level one of my summertime thot journey."

As if on cue, the deejay spun a Travis Scott track into "Hot Girl Summer." The crowd let out a collective "Ayyy" and champagne glasses went up.

These partygoers hadn't been the cool kids growing up. They'd spent their adolescence buried in art books, scrawling poems into steno pads during recess, living full stories in their heads. Distracted by their artistic micro-obsessions, many forgot to learn how to engage with the world. They were too busy studying life, storing up their notes to use later in a novel, a song, a script, a painting. They were observers, not joiners.

As adults, they made up for lost time. They were now a bunch of celebrated, critically acclaimed thirty-something artists who behaved like tenth graders. They gossiped like crazy, made out at house parties, and made awkward, drunken decisions. Exhibit A: across the room, Khalil, the inescapable mansplainer from the Brooklyn Museum panel, was dry-humping a potted plant.

Cece grabbed her husband, Ken, by the arm. He was midconversation with a famed art-world titan. "Honey! See that man over there dressed like Carlton Banks? Please cut him off."

Ken, who appeared to be completely asleep behind his pleasant expression, kissed the titan on the cheek and hurried off.

"Children are downstairs," huffed Cece. "What's *wrong* with Khalil?"

Belinda snorted. "How much time you got?"

"Actually, not much, because I have to make the hostess rounds," said Cece. "So, while I'm here, madam"—she pointed her martini glass at Eva—"I suggest you explain that luminous glow. Did I really need to orchestrate a whole-ass party to get an explanation?"

Eva bit her lip and shrugged.

"I will not stand for this mysterious shit," said Belinda. "Stop being *such* a Scorpio with an Aries moon. What happened this week? You go missing for days and then show up here looking like you got hit by the dick truck?"

"Who got hit by the dick truck?" asked a famed bookfluencer with two million Instagram followers and an ear for gossip. She was shimmying by on her way to pluck shrimp off a tray.

"She said *dump* truck," corrected Cece smoothly. "I know, the music is so loud."

The bookfluencer grimaced, offered her apologies, and floated off.

Eva crowded the girls closer to her. Audre was tucked away downstairs with a gaggle of toddlers watching *Paw Patrol*. This was a safe space.

"My plan was to ignore Shane," she whispered. "But we had a day together. And it was…it was fun. *Really* fun. He met Audre!" She gestured for Belinda and Cece to move in closer. "We had sex all over James Baldwin's house last night."

Her friends gawked at her.

"Where?" asked Cece.

"Nicely done!" Belinda approved. "I've always wanted to get naked and rub myself all over Langston Hughes's abode in Harlem. You know, to manifest his gifts."

"No, no, no," said Eva. "Shane's renting James Baldwin's place for the week."

"That's lovely," said Cece. "Two successful authors reuniting, having their first adult sex together while surrounded by the spirit of a literary legend…"

Eva took a sip of her seltzer. "*Wellll*, it wasn't the first time. That was three days ago. At a downtown art installation."

"The hell y'all doing out here?" said Belinda, pouting and jealous. "I'm supposed to be the kinky one!"

"It sounds crazy, but the whole thing feels so natural. As kids, we were too raw; we just weren't ready for each other. Now we are."

Cece radiated satisfaction. Eva had admitted to a relationship with Shane. At her party. The exorbitant price tag was worth it. "So do you really think you can pick up where you left off, after fifteen years?"

Eva didn't answer her. Because she'd stopped listening. Instead, she was beaming in the direction of the front door.

There was Shane. Exasperatingly handsome in a dark tee, dark jeans, and three-day stubble—and gazing at Eva like she hung the goddamned moon. Eva smiled even wider, if it were even possible. And then, flashing the smirk of the century, Shane stuck his finger into his cheek, in the exact spot where Eva's dimple was flashing at him across the room. Eva winked at him, shooting him finger guns.

Belinda fell out laughing. "Y'all are the *corniest* dorks. I'm in *violent* support of this."

"Look at everyone's faces," gasped Cece, delighted by the revelers' breathless reaction to having a Mysterious Author within their midst. A members-only party wasn't a party without a surprise guest. Thrusting her drink into Belinda's free hand, Cece rushed off to greet her famed protégé.

She wasn't the only one. It took only a few minutes for Shane to become swarmed by fawning peers. Between sweet glances her way, she could read on his face that he was uncomfortable. He was trapped, forced to be social when he just wanted to be with her.

It was all Eva wanted, too. She was seconds away from taking a flying leap into his arms. Instead, she stood there, radiating big love energy in Shane's direction. And slowly, one by one, the partygoers picked up on it.

Word traveled fast.

Overheard near the terrace:

"Wow. I've never seen Shane Hall smile," said a busty memoirist.

"I've never seen Shane Hall, period," remarked a bespectacled *New Yorker* essayist.

"Who's he making eyes at? *Eva Mercy?*"

"They're dating," said the essayist. "I saw fan pics yesterday. Black Book Twitter."

"Stop," exclaimed an agent. "I always assumed she was a super-femme lesbian. Aren't vampires a lesbian thing?"

"She does have that Zoë Kravitz energy."

"Zoë Kravitz isn't a lesbian."

"Neither is Eva Mercy, apparently. She's looking at Shane like he's a sizzling steak fajita."

Overheard near the bar:

"I fucked Shane Hall at BookExpo America in 2007," whispered a gazelle-like novelist. "He was so sweet!"

"Then it wasn't him, girl," said her agent.

Overheard near the cheese smorgasbord:

"Eva's hella chill," said a sneaker designer who spoke in a '90s-slam-poetry voice. "It doesn't sit well with my spirit, her falling for the dangerous type."

"He's fine as fuck, though," said an Alvin Ailey choreographer with a multicolored manicure.

"Name me a fine man who isn't problematic."

"True. Pretty women are normal, but pretty men are nightmares."

"On the low-low," started the designer, "ever since I started dating unattractive men, I've been thriving."

"Where do you find them?"

"Atlantic Center on a weeknight. Between the DMV, Applebee's, and Home Depot? Bitch, you'll leave with a main *and* a side."

Overheard on a couch:

"I can't believe Shane Hall's here. He's so intimidating," whispered a wide-eyed young author who'd just dropped a smash debut novel, *I Sing of Rainbow Children.*

"We're just as talented," lied her friend, a celeb ghostwriter. "And we're not hot messes."

"Somebody said he's sober now."

"I don't believe it. I was at a garden party at the 2010 Frankfurt Book Fair, and I saw this man sniff a rose bush, accidentally inhale a bee, punch himself in the nose, and knock himself out."

"You a whole liar."

"On God. I was like, how'd this wreck write *Eight*?"

"It happens. Look at Mariah. She can't walk across a stage without assistance from sixteen Puerto Rican male dancers. But she's the voice of a generation."

Overheard near the bookcase:

"Khalil. Why're you wearing a green shirt with pink pants?" asked his ex, a snarky screenwriter. "You an AKA? A tube of Maybelline Great Lash?"

"How dare you? You're wearing a wide-brimmed straw hat with a lace blouse. You look like Ida B. Wells."

"You gon' respect my Great Migration realness."

"Somebody told me Eva's dating Shane," grumbled Khalil. "You think it's true? Why him? Jerk-off."

"I'd like to jerk him off," she muttered. "They *must* be dating—look at how close they're standing! Damn, Eva's glowing. That skin."

"Yeah," Khalil reluctantly agreed. "She has the complexion of a wealthy infant."

"And I heard she just got hit by a dump truck," she whispered, in awe.

Meanwhile, by Cece and Ken's Kehinde Wiley portrait...

Shane, after doing the social equivalent of rowing across the Atlantic, was finally standing in front of her. They gazed goofily at each other, the air crackling between them.

"Hi, baby," said Shane.

Eva's stomach dropped. She wasn't ready for "baby."

"Hi," she cooed.

Stuffing his hands in his pockets, Shane leaned toward her and said, "Everybody's talking about us."

Eva took a cursory glance around the room. "I know. Is it weird? Do you care?"

He absentmindedly tapped his bottom lip, his expression rascally. "Not in the least."

With that, Shane wrapped an arm around her shoulders and kissed her temple. Preening, she linked her hand in his. They slotted together perfectly, like two puzzle pieces.

Cece's gasp was heard round the world. *Et voilà*, the Black book world's new prom king and queen were crowned. She'd gotten her moment!

She almost burst into applause.

Downstairs, Audre was bored. She was stuck in a big, AC-frigid bedroom with eight children—all of whom were under six years old. They were watching *The Lego Movie* as if it were actually compelling. As if it were something *good*, like *Midsommar*.

Audre couldn't relate to small children (not even when she was one). Plus, a casual study of the demo showed that they all had mental illnesses. Audre had already diagnosed a handful of kids with OCD, ADD, and attachment disorder. The worst was a five-year-old named Otis. Total menace. Dressed like a tiny rapper in skinny jeans and Jordans, he had put a trash bin up on the dresser and was repeatedly dunking with a kiddie basketball. After every couple of dunks, he'd bust out in an aggressive Milly Rock. And then he'd moon the room.

If these little psychos are inheriting the world, thought Audre, *the future does not look promising.*

The au pair, Lumusi, had fallen asleep in an uncomfortable-looking accent chair twenty minutes ago—leaving Audre effectively in charge of this preschool. *Rude.* She hadn't come to this party to be an unpaid babysitter. In fact, she'd been under the impression that she'd get to be a real party guest! Sipping mocktails on Auntie Cece and Uncle Ken's terrace while chatting with the cultural elite about politics, art, and world events!

Auntie Cece's penthouse was Audre's second home. She shouldn't have to stay hidden downstairs. She could hear the twinkly, forbidden sounds of grown-up mirth and merriment coming from upstairs—and she'd never experienced such FOMO.

She huffed as Otis ran around in circles, bare-assed. She refused to waste her brain cells and an adorable outfit (a Free People knit minidress) on this upscale Gymboree.

I'm outta here, Audre thought, and headed upstairs.

Chapter 23

THAT FAMILY FEELING

"EVA MERCY!"

Cece rushed over to her wall-to-wall bookcase, where her dear friend was canoodling with her unofficial guest of honor. "There you are," she trilled. "There's someone I'd love you to meet."

"Right now? Why so urgent?" Eva didn't feel like meeting anyone. Really, she didn't feel like doing anything not involving this man and his pheromones.

"Networking is always urgent." Cece linked her arm with Shane's and fixed him with a faux cold stare. "Shane."

"Cece."

"I'm so mad at you."

"You're always mad at me." Shane's expression was pure mischief. "What'd I do now?"

"I discovered you. *I gave you life.* And never once did you reveal that you knew my Eva in high school."

Eva barely heard this. She was squinting at a cater waitress with a coppery-red bob, who was offering a tray of crab cakes to a nearby couple. The waitress was gawking at her and Shane. Confused, Eva gave her a vague wave. Did she know that woman? She couldn't place her.

"...and yes, you do have Sebastian's eyes," rambled Cece. "Or he has yours, rather. But why would I ever think she'd based him on *you*? It's so far-fetched. Besides, Black men with hazel eyes aren't that uncommon." She paused. "Actually, I can't think of a man. But Regina King has them."

The waitress was hovering. Cece tapped her shoulder and cleared her throat loudly. With a little jump, the waitress scurried off. Eva squinted, trying to get a good glimpse of her face.

"My bad, Cece—it just never came up."

"Spare me!"

"No, it's true," he laughed, and it was a pure, easy sound. Cece had never seen him so...unencumbered. What had Eva done to him? "High school was hell. Why talk about it?"

"Now is so much better," said Eva.

"Yeah," he said.

"Yeah." She smiled.

Shane kissed her on the mouth with a loud smack. Because he could.

"Aw," sighed Cece. "Friends, if this lasts, do let me know if I'll have to prepare for a wedding. I'll need to get my thighs in order."

"Jesus, a wedding?" Eva cocked her chin in Shane's direction. "Are you even the marrying type?"

"I *am* a little jealous of your first husband."

"Shane Hall, are you asking me to be your ex-wife?"

"I'd be honored."

"I hate to interrupt this flirt-off," said Cece, "but, Eva, you *must* meet Jenna. Shane, I'm gonna steal her for a sec."

"Do you have to?" He grimaced. "I'm too socially awkward to be left to my own devices. What do I do?"

Without a drink, he thought. *What do I do at a party without a drink?*

"You're fine," Eva assured him. "Just look broody and enigmatic."

"Or lead with a relatable personal story," suggested Cece.

Shane chewed his bottom lip. "Like the time I saw a dead dude come back to life? I used to drive a hearse to funerals, and one time, this corpse sat straight up. Burst his coffin wide open. Yo, I hollered till I was hoarse. I found out later he had a degenerative spine disease that made him fold up. The undertaker had forgotten to tie him to a splint. You know, to keep his spine straight."

Eva and Cece looked stricken.

"Don't talk," advised Eva. "Just pretend you're on a call."

Cece dragged her away. And Shane was alone.

Across the party, Audre was giddy with the thrill of escape. She traipsed over to the bar and confidently asked for a Sprite spiked with grenadine. This sounded more sophisticated than ordering a Shirley Temple.

She scoped out the place. As long as she avoided her mom, Auntie Cece, and Auntie Belinda, all three of whom would send her back downstairs, she figured she'd be fine. The second she stepped into the crowd, the non-radio-friendly version of Khalid's "Talk" started playing, and it felt like her very own theme music. It was a sincere challenge to refrain from dancing. But she had to seem mature. Her space buns weren't helping her case, but oh well.

As Audre snuck through the crowd, she enthusiastically eavesdropped (an underrated pastime, she thought).

This party really wasn't that different from the bar and bat mitzvahs she'd attended all year. Clocking the crowd, she could suss out the cool girls, the posers, the thirsty guys, the hot boys, the newbies. She wondered which person her mom was. She also wondered *where* her mom was.

Behind her, Audre caught a snippet of a conversation.

"Ugh, why do I let him get me in my feelings?" wailed a high-pitched voice.

"Because you're a Cancer, my good sis. You're a sensitive giver. But you need to harness *your* radiance. Activate *your* divine. And budget the fucks you give." There was a pause for emphasis. "Now, if you'll excuse me, I need to go home and feed my two kittens, Growth and Metamorphosis."

Without even turning around, Audre knew that was Auntie Belinda. Ducking her head, she scooted along the perimeter of the party and ended up at the sliding doors opening out to the terrace. It was Audre's favorite place in the apartment. With its modern, tropical feel—white furniture, sleek firepit, lush greenery—it looked like the backyard of an Argentinian villa. When Audre was little, she used to hang out on the terrace in Cece's plush terry bathrobe for hours. She'd pretend to be an international pop star on holiday in a ritzy hotel after having just completed a grueling world tour. It was quite an involved game. She'd sip invisible peppermint tea to soothe her overworked vocal chords. Cuddle with her invisible lapdog, Tiana. And repeatedly ask her invisible assistant, Bathsheba, if she'd picked up her dry cleaning yet and booked her brow wax. Now that she thought about it, she must've been a handful.

Lost in first-grade memories, Audre turned the corner at a massive arrangement of peace lilies. Startled, she let out a little yelp. Because she was not, in fact, alone as she'd thought. There was Shane, chilling on an overstuffed white chaise.

"Hi, Mr. Hall!" Then she saw the phone pressed to his ear. "Oh! Sorry."

"No, no, I'm faking a phone call," he admitted with an embarrassed chuckle. Beaming, he stood up and gave her a one-armed hug.

"Why?"

"Antisocial," he said apologetically.

"Ah. Should I go, then?" Before he could answer, she plopped down on the chaise, tucking an ankle under her thigh.

"No, stay!" Shane slipped his phone into his pocket. As he did, it buzzed. He ignored it. "I love talking to you."

"What should we talk about?"

"I don't know. I'm not good at normal-people small talk. I always want to get weird. Start a conversation about wildly unfounded conspiracy theories. Liminal spaces. Dermoids."

"Shoulder muscles?"

"No, that's deltoids," said Shane, taking a gulp of seltzer. "A dermoid is a medical phenomenon. Sometimes an embryo'll eat its twin in the first trimester. After it's born, it grows dermoids, or pieces of the other baby, in inconvenient places. Fingernails, eyebrows. Teeth."

Horrified, Audre clapped her palm over her mouth.

"Imagine living your whole life with a blinking eyeball in your liver," he said, delighted at this captive audience.

"Do you have a dermoid, Mr. Hall?"

"Nah," he said sadly.

"In social situations, my impulse isn't to get weird. It's to get deep. Like, hi, I'm Audre, and I'd like to pick your brain on religion, the trans military ban, homelessness, taking a knee during the anthem…"

Shane was blown away. "Okay. Let's do it."

"Yes!" She punched the air. "Religion?"

"Religion. Hmm. I guess it's like fire. In good hands, fire can be used to do positive things, like keep you warm. Make s'mores. In bad hands, it can burn a witch at the stake. Lynch a Black body." He shrugged. "When used for good, religion's cool."

"Well put. Trans ban?"

"Barbaric."

"Homelessness?"

"Been there. No clue how to fix it."

"Fair. Do you recognize the national anthem?"

"As what, a marketing scam?" Shane shook his head. "Miles Davis said there are two categories of thinking: the truth and white bullshit. The national anthem is white bullshit."

"Wow, okay. *Retweet.* You passed."

Shane's phone buzzed in his pocket for the fifth time. With a quick apology to Audre, he checked the call log. It was Ty, phoning him to death—which was a little much, given that they'd just talked that morning (yet another frustrating, lengthy debate about Ty's hypothetical rap career).

I'll hit you back, Shane texted.

"Mr. Hall, what's the source of your social anxiety? This party is full of writers. These are your people."

"You'd think so, right? Here's the thing. They all know me, but I don't know *them*. Or I've met them but don't remember. A long time ago, I used to..." Shane stopped here, knowing he couldn't tell Audre that he'd spent most of the past fifteen years blackout drunk. "My memory is not the greatest. So I never know who I have a past with. It's disorienting."

"Fascinating. I need an example."

Shane thought about this, squinting and stroking his chin.

"There's a dude out there named Khalil who hates me. No idea why."

"You don't remember even a small detail?"

"Truthfully, I can't imagine ever speaking to that guy. He's the human equivalent of a spam email," he said with distaste. "I must've done something, though. Who knows? I used to be an ass."

"Listen, I navigate the choppy waters of Cheshire Prep every day," said Audre. "Adult social stuff can't be harder than seventh grade. It's not hard to make friends. Just be an active listener. If you listen hard enough, you can tell what a person needs from you. And if you give them what they need, you've got a friend for life."

Shane couldn't help but chuckle at this tiny wise woman. "You're terrifyingly astute."

"I know." Audre grinned, her dimple popping like Eva's. With an indulgent sigh, she lay back into the pillows, gazing off into the greenery-packed backyard beyond the terrace. "It's a burden, if I'm honest."

"You've got all of us figured out, huh? It's like you're the emotional-support buddy of the world."

"I should trademark that."

"But do you have an emotional-support buddy? Are your friends good listeners, like you?"

She thought of Parsley with her self-obsession and almost cackled. "Nooo. I love my girls—don't get me wrong. But middle school is so tragic. FaceTiming boys at sleepovers, vaping at Governors Ball—it's silly. My friends are silly. But I'm not silly. I'm pretty sure I'm supposed to be an adult."

"Adulthood is a lie, Audre. We're all just tall toddlers."

"Oh, I'm aware. I'm excited to do it *right*. Better than y'all."

He eyed Audre, a slight girl, all limbs and eyes and brain, and nodded. "You know what? I believe you will."

Shane held up his glass of seltzer, and Audre clicked it with her Shirley Temple. And then they sat for a minute, enjoying the balmy air and peaceful backyard views from Cece's balcony. She would've been able to see the skyline of downtown Manhattan way off in the distance if not for the two small, intertwined magnolia trees sprouting from Cece's Brooklyn-jungle backyard, their branches stretching to the terrace.

"Mom is my emotional-support buddy," admitted Audre. "She's my person."

Shane smiled softly. "Soul mates."

Abruptly, Audre turned her whole body to face Shane. "You and my mom aren't just friends, Mr. Hall."

"What? But we are."

"Please, I'm not a child."

"You are a child, though."

"Only chronologically." Insulted, she folded her arms across her chest. "Are you gonna be nice to her?"

"Nice?"

Audre peered around the corner, in the direction of the sliding doors. Shane followed her gaze. No sign of Eva, so they were clear.

"Be nice to her," she said, low and fast. "My mom keeps a lot of stuff inside, but her thoughts are really loud. I know she's been scared and lonely. She has a disability, but you probably know that. It's a barometric-pressure thing. When it rains or snows or gets really hot or really cold too fast, she hurts. But alcohol, stress, loud noises, and weird smells do it, too. You have to learn her triggers. And please, just be patient with her.

Sometimes she has to lie down for a long time. You might feel bored or lonely or even rejected, but she can't help being sick." Audre rested her hand on Shane's shoulder. "Mom feels guilty about who she is. Make her feel happy about herself."

Shane nodded but kept his mouth shut. Words escaped him.

"She can't put on lipstick, 'cause her hands shake too much from pain," revealed Audre. "But she put it on today. For you."

"I hear you," Shane managed, his words a broken croak. "I get it."

"Are you crying, Mr. Hall?"

"No," he said, squeezing his eyes shut. He hadn't shed a tear since that morning in DC a thousand Junes ago. He'd thought he'd forgotten how. "No, I'm not crying. I'm fucking bawling."

"Ugh, I have this effect on people. But it's okay to cry," she said, handing him a cocktail napkin. "Destigmatizing male vulnerability is the first step toward rebuilding the absolute ruin that straight men have left the world in."

"This is so inappropriate. I'm sorry." With a mighty exhale, Shane ran his hand over his face. Christ, this girl was a feelings ninja. "Don't worry—I'll be nice to her."

"You have to promise."

In theory, he knew that making promises to children was a dangerous thing. You fall short, you shatter their safety net. But he did it anyway, because he *knew* that he'd keep his word. What was the point of doing the grueling work of staying sober if he didn't also become trustworthy? Shane was a surrogate dad/uncle/mentor figure to dozens of lost kids, and he'd vowed to them all that he'd be a FaceTime call, a text, or even a flight away. Which he was.

It wasn't easy. Being permanently on call for a cross-country crew of delinquents was stressful as hell. And time consuming. Ty called him every time he hit a high score on Roblox. Shane had no idea what Roblox was, but if it kept Ty off the block, then cool. Shane was responsible for him. He'd made a vow, and he staked everything on it.

"I promise," he said definitively. "Real talk? I waited a long time to make your mom happy. Fifteen years felt like thirty."

"Well, *duh*, why didn't you find her before?"

"Scared."

"And now?"

"Still scared. Just don't care."

"Have you had a lot of girlfriends?"

"A few, yeah. No one is your mom," he said. "Turns out, that's a huge problem for me."

"Mr. Hall, I'm extending an invitation to you," Audre announced grandly. She sounded a lot like Cece. "Tomorrow, I'm getting on a plane to Dadifornia."

He looked at her blankly.

"My dad's house. In California. Me and Mom always go to brunch at Ladurée before my flight. Wanna come? We make it really fancy. You have to dress up."

Shane drew back a little in surprise.

"Yeah? But that sounds like a special thing for just you and your mom."

"It is. But you are, too."

"You think I'm special?" Shane's face got hot, a tingling rush of warmth spreading all over him. His hands trembled. What the hell was happening?

This is that family feeling, he thought. Of total acceptance, belonging to people. A connection that eclipsed everything. Shane hadn't experienced this since his foster parents—for so long that he'd decided he didn't deserve it.

So he'd expected to never feel it again.

"Yeah, you're special. You can quote me on that." Audre gave him a fist bump. "BTW, you're not antisocial. You talked to me."

"I said I couldn't talk to normal people. You're not normal."

"Team abnormal," she giggled.

Shane remembered how he'd said that to Eva once. *You're not normal.*

Now, like then, it was given and received as a compliment. Mother and daughter mirrored each other in the most striking of ways.

— —

One hundred and ninety-five miles away, in Providence, Rhode Island, thirteen-year-old Ty Boyle was scared. He was a big dude, so this feeling wasn't usually part of his emotional language. But it was right now, and the only person he would've admitted this to was ignoring his calls. Maybe he wasn't ignoring him. Mr. Hall wouldn't do that. Maybe he was just busy.

Ty was standing outside an old, abandoned clapboard house in Elm-wood. Despite Mr. Hall forbidding him to do this, he'd agreed to meet with his sister Princess's boyfriend, largely known as Other Mike, a.k.a. O-Mike, at his recording-studio rental. This didn't look like a studio. It looked like the haunted house on Neibolt Street from *It*.

For a usually rowdy neighborhood, especially at the start of summer, the block was eerily quiet. Why wasn't anyone outside? Ty checked his phone. It was 2:30 p.m., and O-Mike was supposed to meet him at 2:00. Ty had come up with $200 to rent the space, so O-Mike was going to let him record a track. Mr. Hall wouldn't give him the money, so his new almost girlfriend had lent it to him. She worked the register at Old Navy after school and could make the money back in a week.

Ty had been writing rhymes for two days and had felt confident enough to run some by her. She liked them. She liked him.

He leaned against the filthy porch and shoved his hand deep in his jeans pocket, where his composition notebook was rolled up. He ran his fingers along the cover to calm his nerves.

Mr. Hall had said this wasn't a good idea. He'd reminded Ty that Princess was both a junkie and a liar—and so O-Mike probably was, too. But Ty wasn't an idiot. On the off chance O-Mike was trying to hustle him, Ty had brought a Colt .38. That was in his other jeans pocket.

O-Mike didn't show up until 3:00. But he came out the front door. Followed by a billowing cloud of smoke.

"Where you been?" O-Mike was a very short, very thin dude. He was about ten years older than Ty, but he looked forty. A *hard* forty. Black lips, ashy knuckles, bloodshot eyes, and jeans with unintentional holes.

"I been right here," said Ty. "I was waiting for you."

"Nigga, I been here the whole time." O-Mike burst out in a wild cackle. And then he looked over his shoulder, into the house. Ty thought he heard a voice coming from the darkness inside.

That's probably his producer, Ty thought.

O-Mike scratched under his arm and gestured at Ty. "You got my paper?"

"Yeah, I got it." Ty shifted from one foot to the other. The cash was stuffed in the pocket with his notebook. But this didn't seem right. O-Mike seemed jittery and desperate.

Ty had to stay focused. Rap would get him out of Providence. Rap was the plan. *Focus.*

"Where the studio at?" asked Ty.

"Gimme my paper," he said, sniffing, "and I'll show you."

"Princess in there?"

"Nah." He stepped closer to Ty. He smelled like weed, cigarettes, and something sour.

This felt wrong. And he was alone. For a small, breathless moment, Ty considered running. O-Mike had a dude with him. At least one, maybe more in the house.

Hand in his pocket, Ty pushed the emergency contact number on his phone.

Mr. Hall, he thought wildly. *Pick up.*

Chapter 24

FABULOUS HISTORY

BACK AT CECE'S PARTY, IN A RELATIVELY QUIET AREA BY KEN'S GRANDFATHER'S grand piano, Eva was meeting new people.

"I'm so *thrilled* to get you two in the same room," gushed Cece, clasping her hands under her chin. "Jenna Jones, meet Eva Mercy, esteemed author of *Cursed*. Eva Mercy, meet Jenna Jones, fashion editor and host of *The Perfect Find*."

Eva reached out to shake Jenna's hand, but the scarlet-lipsticked stunner said "I'm a hugger!" and crushed her to her boobs. She smelled fantastic, like expensive perfume and coconut oil.

Draped in a long-sleeve paisley maxidress plunging to her navel (vintage Dior) and shoulder-skimming beaded earrings (Nairobi street market), Jenna radiated strong Fashion Eccentric energy.

"Oh! I've seen your web series!" Eva gasped with recognition. "The one where guests make their dream fashion piece, and you partner with retailers to sell it?"

"That's me," she beamed with charm. "Sorry, can I ask where you got that cameo ring? I've been staring from across the room. Such opulence."

Eva held up her hand, and all three women peered down at her rusted, nicked—but striking—oval ring. "It's an old vintage ring of my mom's. Feels like it was made for me, though."

"It's vintage, all right." Jenna turned Eva's hand left and right. "Judging from the casing, it's over a century old. I bet there's fabulous history tied up in that ring."

Cece grabbed a glass of wine from a cater waiter's tray, the wheels turning in her brain.

"Eva, how's the film going?" she asked smoothly. "If you haven't hired a wardrobe stylist yet, you two should make it happen."

Eva and Jenna gasped at each other. Cece was floating on air. *Connection, made.*

"What movie?" asked a young, cute guy who'd materialized next to Jenna. He looked so much like Michael B. Jordan, it was criminal.

He reached out to shake Eva's hand. "I'm Jenna's husband, Eric."

"Eva, tell him about your movie!" Cece's expression was so sneaky, she might as well have rubbed her palms together and cackled. "Eric's a Golden Globe–nominated director and Sundance darling. I, uh, heard you're in the market for a new director?"

Eva's jaw dropped.

"Dump Dani Acosta," Cece whispered in her ear. "He's your guy."

With that, her work was done. Cece rushed away to make sure the kitchen cut off the hors d'oeuvres soon. It was past 5:00 p.m., and everyone had been day-drinking for hours. If she didn't get these Negroes out of her house soon, they'd start tearing shit up.

Both Jenna and Eric were looking at Eva expectantly.

"My movie! Okay." She cleared her throat, weirdly nervous. "Well, I write a series about a witch and a vampire. A producer, Sidney Grace, bought the film rights. And she's fantastic. But our director wants to make the characters white, to be more mainstream. It's crushing, actually. But hey, that's showbiz." Eva wiggled jazz hands, trying to make her career setback a little joke.

"Awful!" exclaimed Jenna.

Eric shook his head vehemently. "Nah. Nope. Unacceptable. Did you write the script?"

"Yeah, about a year ago."

"Good. That gives you more power than you think you have." Eric pulled out his phone and started scrolling through his contacts. "Me and Sidney go way back. I'm about to text her right now."

"Wait, why?"

"Because I'm directing your *blockbuster*, son," he said with a sunny grin. "I'm between projects. House-husbanding is hard; I need to get back to work."

"Our son is an adorable menace," said Jenna, by way of explanation.

"And I'm a sci-fi geek," he said. "Let's do it. Let's make some Black fantasy shit."

"Let's. Do. It." Eva clapped on each word, bursting with creative excitement.

Just then, Jenna grabbed Eric's arm and pointed across the room. "Honey, am I hallucinating, or did I just see Otis running around up here? Aren't all the kids downstairs?"

"They have a babysitter," said Eva, trying to sound assuring. "My daughter's helping, too. She's twelve and really responsible."

"Oh shit," said Eric. "No, that's him. Unpacking some woman's purse. Gotta run, more later..." And then he hurried off.

Jenna rested a hand over her eyes, in full-blown maternal exhaustion. "I knew bringing Otis wouldn't end well. My son's over there pickpocketing a Tony winner."

Actually, thought Eva, adjusting her glasses, *now he's mooning her.*

"Did you say your daughter's twelve? Is that her out on the terrace with...Wait, is that Shane Hall? As in *Eight*?"

Eva stood on her tiptoes, and over the crowd, she spotted Audre and Shane leaning against the railing, with their backs to the party—clearly deep in conversation. She whispered something to him, and he dissolved into shoulder-shaking, eye-crinkling laughter.

And for the third time that week, she said, "Jesus, Audre."

"Well, well, well," said Eva, tapping Audre and Shane on the shoulder. They both spun around, wearing identical *oh shit* faces.

"Hey!" said Shane.

"Hi!" said Audre.

"Audre, what are you doing here? You're supposed to be downstairs, helping to watch the kids. Now there's a little boy up here running around naked. This is an adult party. You had one job!"

"Yeah, that's Otis," said Shane. "Audre told me about him. What a terror."

Audre shot her mom a brilliant, braces-laden smile.

Eva wanted to be annoyed. But she couldn't help being tickled—and touched—seeing Shane and Audre bond. And without her, no less. What could they possibly have been talking about?

Maybe it was better that she didn't know.

"Mom, guess what? I invited Shane to our brunch tomorrow."

Now, this, she never would've guessed. Their annual pilgrimage to Ladurée was a sacred ritual. Eva actually took the time to carefully plait Audre's hair into a majestic braided crown. And she put on Fenty bronzer!

This was an astonishing break in tradition.

No friend had ever attended. No auntie. No man. Audre looked forward to this fancy, private moment with her mom all year. Eva never thought she'd see the day when Audre would extend an invite to anyone—especially a guy she'd known for two days. A guy whom she'd brutally cross-examined in her kitchen.

"You're okay with that, honey?" asked Eva hesitantly.

"I want him there," said Audre with a mysterious twinkle in her eye. "And I *know* you do."

Eva had never thought about what it would be like, inviting him into their world in a real way. The logistics of actually merging their lives. But yeah. Yeah, she did want him there. Suddenly slammed by a wave of shyness, she caught Shane's eye, bit her lip, and then looked down at her feet. Shane was a fidgety mess—cracking his knuckles, jaw clenching.

Audre watched their awkward little dance with exasperation. If she hadn't known they were in like, or whatever, she would have assumed they were demented.

"Shane?"

"Eva?"

"Do you really want to come? You don't have to, you know." Eva was giving him an out. Maybe it was too fast. On the surface, it was just brunch—but it wasn't, really. It was commitment. And she didn't want to pressure him into a role he wasn't ready for.

Over the years, Eva had trained herself not to expect anything from anyone, especially men. To not even ask or want. This, though? This she wanted.

Not want, she thought. *Need.*

"You can say no," she said.

"You serious? I wouldn't even know how to say no to you two."

"Really?"

Shane's face split into an irresistibly sunny smile. "Ladurée, on me."

And Eva looked so elated that Audre did what every Generation Z kid was acculturated to do during memorable moments. She snapped a pic. (In portrait mode.) Without warning, she pushed them both together so they were side by side. Then she backed up and aimed her phone.

"This is a big deal, you reuniting like this. Does your high school class have a Facebook group? You gotta upload this pic."

"No," shouted Eva and Shane simultaneously.

"Wait, those two trees behind you are making a weird shadow. Their branches are all tangled up." Audre gestured for them to move to the right.

They did. And then Shane flung an arm across Eva's shoulders, Eva reached around his waist, and they cheesed.

"You know what I read?" asked Eva through her pasted-on smile. "A tree grows its branches out until it touches the tips of the next closest tree. And they're linked forever. Because if they're really close, their roots grow together. They're so intertwined underneath that no matter what happens above ground, they stay connected."

Shane pressed her a little closer to him. Under his breath, he asked, "Do you think our roots are connected?"

"More than," she said.

Audre, witnessing their whispering, actually gagged. "*Gross.* Sorry. No, it's cool. I'll get used to this—it's fine."

Shane felt both grounded and light as air.

Feels like family.

Deep in his pocket, his phone continued to buzz, ignored. He was way too happy to deal with it.

SUNDAY

Chapter 25

DNA AIN'T NO JOKE

Ladurée on West Broadway was the Soho outpost of one of Paris's oldest, most raised-pinky-finger tearooms. And it was an *experience*. Known for its patisseries and macarons, the restaurant was a silk-trimmed succession of adorable salons, each one more girly-cozy than the next. Eva and Audre always made a reservation in the curtained-off Pompadour Salon, an airy, bright sitting room with louche banquettes and twinkly golden chandeliers dangling from a blue-sky ceiling.

It felt like they were visiting Versailles. And in their carefully chosen ensembles, they looked like Parisian princesses, too. Tomboy princesses. Audre was rocking her lofty crown braid and a marigold off-the-shoulder sundress (with Doc Martens). And Eva felt impossibly romantic in a backless black crepe halter dress (with Comme des Garçons Converse).

There was something so decadent about stuffing your face with tarts and bacon while dressed like an influencer. Their brunch was always an event. But today, having a special guest star cast a shimmering quality over the day.

Eva felt so light and heady, she was almost levitating. Because of Shane, of course, but also because of the emergency pain shot she'd administered that morning. It had rained all night, and she'd gasped awake in agony. Pain did not go with her dress. Praise be for gummies and prefilled syringes.

Eva and Audre had shown up slightly early. Shane wasn't there yet, which was perfect. Using her calligraphy skills, Audre had carefully created dainty little place cards and prix-fixe menus for each of them. It was a surprise, the perfect touch for what would be a perfect brunch.

They chatted while they waited.

"...and Ophelia keeps begging me to go to sleepaway camp with her, but I really don't want to. Why do people camp? On principle, I don't believe in sleeping outside."

"You know I don't get it, either." Eva loathed camping and suspected that Audre had picked up that line from her. For a second, she was hit with vague guilt for discouraging her kid from trying new experiences.

Fuck it, she thought.

"Camping is arrogant," said Eva. "The forest is filled with undomesticated wildlife out there living happy, peaceful lives. How dare we assume that we're welcome in their home? It's like if a bear broke into our apartment like, 'It'd be a fun experience to live here for a week.'"

"Ophelia said I was being bougie," said Audre, perusing the ornately designed menu. "Should I get truffled dauphine potatoes?"

"Bougie? Ophelia's parents are multimillionaires!" She nibbled on a madeleine. "Wealthy Brooklynites always want you to think they're struggling. Ophelia's family drives a 2001 Ford Focus."

"To their Bridgehampton mansion! I know, the *irony!*" Audre giggled, loving the grown-up gossip sesh with her mom.

"And yes, get the truffled potatoes," Eva announced with supreme decadence. "You deserve it after coming in first place in your art competition."

Eva was fiercely proud of her baby. Out of the entire upper school, seventh through twelfth grade, Audre's portrait of Lizette had won the top prize of the year. Which meant she had landed an internship at the Brooklyn Museum the following school year.

"Did you really think it was that good?" Audre looked uncharacteristically bashful.

"It was breathtaking, my bé," said Eva, eyes softening. "I know we've had a tough time this week. But you know I love you more than anything, right? I'll always be proud of you. You're my best thing."

"Mommy! I can't get mushy on an empty stomach." Audre hid her face behind a linen napkin. "But I love you, too. Now, what are you ordering?"

"The crab cakes, to start. When Shane comes, we'll get entrées."

Actually, crab cakes are a no, she thought. *I have to fit into a leather minidress for the Litties.* The awards ceremony was later that evening, at 9 p.m.—and her dress was unforgiving.

Eva would never say this out loud to Audre. Bad self-image modeling.

Blowing on her lavender-lilac tea, Eva perused the menu again. And then she heard the bell over the front door twinkle through the space. Shane!

She jerked her head up so fast, her glasses bounced on her nose. It wasn't him, but rather a touristy-looking senior couple.

Ridiculous. She had to calm down; she was *perspiring*. And she kept checking her hair in her spoon (she'd piled her curls atop her head, in a dreamy upsweep). This was ridiculous. Shane had seen her in various states of undress several times over the past week. Why was she acting like a nervous spinster before her first date?

She needed to chill. And she would, when she saw Shane. It was only five minutes past their 10:00 a.m. reservation time; he'd be there soon.

Meanwhile, Audre was scrolling through her phone, looking at gossip accounts on Instagram.

"Mom, if you could date any man in Hollywood, who would it be?"

"From today or previous eras?" Eva grabbed another madeleine from their basket and nibbled away.

"Today," said Audre.

"Hmm. Lakeith Stanfield. And honestly, I'd take either Hemsworth."

With a gust of warm air, the front door flung open again. Eva glanced up in anticipation. It wasn't Shane. A model and her lapdog. And her stomach sank, just a tad.

"How about you?" Nonchalantly, Eva checked the time on her phone—10:13.

"Nick Jonas," divulged Audre. "But he's taken."

"And short. How would he reach you?"

A lanky, heavily perfumed waitress came by to take their appetizer orders. Unable to help it, Eva checked her phone. But she hadn't heard from Shane. This was definitely odd. For the past three days, they'd been in a near-constant textversation. But today, nothing.

She shot him a text anyway.

EVA: We're saving a seat with your name on it. Literally! Can't wait to see you.

By 10:40, she still hadn't heard from him. And she couldn't imagine why. There was no way he could've forgotten—not after promising Audre. And her. Rubbing a temple, she mentally reminded herself to regulate her breathing. It would be fine. He'd come.

"I'll be right back, honey," she told Audre, scooting back from the table. "Just running to the ladies'."

Once she was out of Audre's line of vision, she speed-walked over to the hostess's table.

"Hi, have you gotten a message from Shane Hall?" she asked the hostess, a beautiful, elfin girl with a pixie haircut and high-waisted capris. "He's meeting me here. We had a reservation at ten. Did he come too early? Maybe he got the time wrong."

The pixie pulled out her pencil-scrawled ledger and scrolled through, line by line. "No, we haven't had a Shane Hall this morning."

"Oh," she said, her heart sinking.

"Give him a call, though. This happens all the time. You know, we have three establishments in Manhattan. One on Madison and one on Fifty-Ninth. Maybe he mixed up the location?"

Eva all but smacked her forehead. She felt so dumb. Of course, that was it. No wonder! Born-and-bred New Yorkers mixed up restaurant locations all the time, and he was a newbie.

If I'm honest, the Madison Avenue Ladurée is better, she thought to herself, with intense relief. *He's probably there. We should've gone there.*

Eva thanked the hostess and texted Shane the correct address to make sure he had it. After waiting exactly forty seconds with no response, she called him—but it went straight to voicemail. Feeling increasingly pathetic by the minute, Eva called up every Ladurée location on the island, attempting to find him.

Nothing.

With a thumping heart and clammy palms, Eva headed back to the Pompadour Salon and sat down. It was eleven.

"Where's Mr. Hall?"

"Shane?" Eva smiled brightly. And made up a lie on the spot. "You know what? I forgot to tell you. This morning, he said he was so excited about our invitation but that he forgot that he scheduled an IKEA delivery today. You know they give you an insane window, like six a.m. to three p.m. There's a chance he'll be late."

"Oh no! That sucks. But we did ask him last minute. I hope he can come; I really like him."

Eva swallowed down the lump in her throat. "Me too."

"He likes you, too," said Audre in hushed tones. "Why am I whispering? This is weird. You, with a boyfriend!"

"Audre, you're so dramatic. He's not my boyfriend."

"Okay, cool. By the way, you're sweating off your eyeliner."

Eva tossed her napkin at Audre, and she giggled.

"You excited to see Daddy?" asked Eva, changing the subject.

"Yeah, I miss him! It's refreshing to be around someone one thousand percent un-snarky."

"He gets such a kick out of getting a kick out of things."

"And I heard from Daddy that Athena's started a woke wellness spa. She actually got her massage-therapist certificate. The spa's called And Still I Rise. Auntie Belinda would love that."

"Huh. What happens at a woke wellness spa?"

"Exfoliation, by any means necessary?"

Eva laughed at Audre's joke, but it was a hollow sound. It was 11:17 a.m. He was more than an hour late, with no word. She texted him once more but, deep down, knew that he wouldn't answer. And then she started to panic.

Dear God, she thought. *Please let him be okay. What if he started drinking again? What if he's lying in a ditch somewhere? Does New York have ditches? What if he's hurt and I can't reach him? I'm his only real friend! What do I do?*

She briefly considered calling local hospitals and then nixed the thought. She was being dramatic. And she didn't want to freak Audre out.

So, with a trembly voice, Eva called a waitress over to put in their entrée orders.

By the time their fancy, complicated egg dishes came, Eva had no appetite. She couldn't taste the food.

It was time to land the cover-up. Scrolling through her phone, Eva faked a gasp. "I'm so silly," she said. "I've been so caught up in our conversation, I missed his text ages ago. IKEA's late, so he can't make it. He says he's devastated he missed you."

"Yeah?"

"I don't know what you two talked about at Cece's, but you definitely have a fan."

"We bonded," she said with a mysterious smile. "Tell him it's cool, and we'll hang out after Dadifornia."

Eva nodded, too fast. "Of course, baby."

"Mom, why are you so wiggly? You're doing that thing where you shake your right leg at triple speed."

"No reason," she said dryly, stuffing roughly fourteen fries into her mouth. "I think I just have to pee."

"Before you go to the ladies', I have something to tell you. I think I like a boy."

Eva almost choked to death on her fries. "What? *Who?* Dash Moretti from algebra?"

"Ew, no. I'd never date a Cheshire Prep boy. Yeah, he looks like Shawn Mendes, but he has no soul. No, this guy, Zion? He's Athena's godson."

"Oh, isn't he your stepmom's third or fourth cousin? You played together when you were little."

"Yeah, and now he's *cute*. Look at his Insta."

Audre slid her phone across the table, and Eva checked him out. His latest post was a pic of him, mid-soccer tournament, rocking a retro high-top fade. Cute, he definitely was.

"If you don't tell me every detail of this developing crush, I'll die."

"Of course I'll tell you!" Audre smiled, eyes shining. "And you, same. You better give me Shane updates while I'm gone. He promised me he'd be nice to you."

"He did?" Eva's hands were trembling, so she sat on them.

"If he doesn't, he's dead," Audre said, taking a healthy bite of her egg dish. "I can be savage if necessary."

Eva could barely force a smile. She'd moved past panic and settled into hurt and humiliation. It was 12:00 p.m., and she'd been stood up. It was mortifying, watching the clock and having to come up with a lie to protect Audre's feelings. Standing Eva up was bad enough, but standing Audre up was another thing altogether.

She wouldn't let him hurt Audre with his carelessness the same way he'd hurt her before. Why would he take the time to bond with Audre and, *Jesus*, promise to be nice to Eva—if he wasn't going to come through? Eva was furious that she'd let her guard down, allowing herself to trust. Have hope.

Once the check was paid and they were headed for JFK Airport in a Lyft with Audre's luggage—and she still hadn't heard from Shane— Eva's bewilderment had blossomed into a tumult of feelings. Blind rage at Shane, and the urge to soak up every last moment with Audre before she left.

While Audre headed into a Hudson News for a magazine, Eva called him twice. A last-ditch effort. But it was pointless, because Eva already knew what had happened: brunch had been too much pressure, and he'd bounced. It wasn't a far-fetched thought. Even *she* felt it was a little soon to welcome Shane into a special date with her daughter. But she'd believed that their connection was deeper, their roots were connected. Right?

She supposed she was wrong. And then Eva spiraled.

Shane had changed his mind. About them. About *her*. Eva was too much for him. He didn't want her after all. It was immense pressure, taking on a woman and her daughter. Yesterday was fun and games, but when he'd gotten home and put some distance between them, he'd realized that an instant family wasn't for him.

It made sense.

Shane was able to live a lusty, unencumbered life, because he answered to no one. His books read the way they did—airy, untethered, all *vibe*— because that was who he was. Defiantly ungrounded and not accountable to anyone. He didn't have to check in or be present or keep his promises.

What they had was inarguable, and Eva couldn't fault him for falling back in love with her. But she did fault him for making her believe that he was ready for it.

And making Audre believe it.

She made place cards. She was so excited to see me excited.

Caught somewhere between her feelings of humiliation, rage, and sadness, Eva excused herself and headed to the ladies'. She felt tears coming and couldn't let Audre see. Once she was in the bathroom, not a tear fell—staring in the mirror, she screwed her face up twelve different ways to no avail.

You colossal idiot, she told herself, her expression ice cold. *How many times do you need to be taught this lesson?*

Standing in line at the Delta check-in, Eva felt a pang of desperation at how much she'd miss her daughter. The past week had been a flurry of emergencies, but Audre, as always, would be all right. She had a place at Cheshire Prep next year. She'd have a ball with her dad all summer and maybe get (even more) radicalized at her stepmom's woke spa. Maybe she'd have her first taste of puppy love. Without Eva by her side. But it was okay, because she knew that she was raising a strong, smart, self-possessed daughter who could fend for herself. Her baby was growing up.

Holding hands, Eva and Audre walked to the line at security. It was time for her baby's summer to start. Eva swept Audre into a mighty, bone-crushing hug.

"Goodbye, my honey," she said, letting go. "Have the best time, okay? And be safe."

"I will—don't worry," Audre said with a smile. "And Mom?"

"Yes?"

"I know you made up the IKEA excuse for Shane. I know you're sad he didn't come. But give him a chance. He's a good person. I *know* he is, and I'm an *incredible* judge of character. You push stuff away that isn't safe and obvious, Mom, but love isn't safe and obvious. Love is risky. Take the risk, woman."

Flabbergasted, Eva didn't even know which part of this speech to address. So instead, she dissolved into nervous, breathy laughter. "How on earth would you know that love's risky?"

Audre rolled her eyes. "Hello? I know *Lemonade* by heart."

With that, her very wise little girl was gone. And then Eva took a Lyft directly from LaGuardia Airport to 81 Horatio Street. She rang the doorbell twice. He didn't answer.

Eva felt it in her bones. He was long gone.

Shane *was* long gone. That morning, around 7:00 a.m., he'd awoken to relentless ringing. He'd sprung up, feeling around in the dark for his phone, instantly thinking something had happened to Eva.

"Eva? You good?"

"Hi, Mr. Hall. This is Officer Reid, from the Providence Police Department."

"Who?"

"Providence, Rhode Island," the gruff male voice said by way of explanation.

"Okay." He ran his hand over his face and sank back into the pillows. "Why are you calling so early?"

Why are you calling me at all? he thought, with a sudden rush of dread.

"Well, I have some unfortunate news."

In seconds, he was wide awake.

"Ty."

"Yes."

"What happened to Ty?"

"I'm calling from RI Hospital. Ty was in an accident earlier yesterday afternoon. A scuffle with another teen out on parole. He was shot several times, and . . . and it's not looking good."

"Jesus. *Jesus.* What? Where? Is he . . ."

"All we know is that the shooter stole two hundred dollars from him. And he might be an associate of Ty's sister, Princess. They were at an abandoned house in Elmwood. Ty mentioned something about a music studio."

Shane stared at the wall. He could barely breathe.

"Mr. Hall?"

"He's gonna make it, though. Right? He'll be okay?"

"The doctors don't know. Are you nearby? The boy asked for you, and I can't locate his guardians."

"I'm coming."

"Appreciate it. Like I said, he asked for you. And he's in intensive care alone."

Shane knew how it felt to be so vulnerable and frightened—and stuck in a hospital with no trustworthy adult who cared whether you lived or died. No parent to swoop in and rescue you. To do what the fuck grown-ups are supposed to do.

He had to do what he'd promised.

"Yeah. Okay, yeah, I'm coming."

In a fever, he booked the only outgoing flight to Providence that morning, at 9:30 a.m. His return flight was at 4:00 p.m., so he'd be back in time for the Littie Awards that night.

And because he couldn't help it, because it was naturally where his mind went, Shane decided, with clear-eyed finality, that this was his fault. Ty had called him, and he hadn't answered. Ty had tried to reach him, and he'd been too busy being happier than he had any right to be.

And it wasn't until that moment—midflight, leveled to near paralysis by the worry and self-hatred he was feeling over Ty—that he remembered. He froze in his seat, taking in a slow, deep gasp, and was immediately overtaken by a clammy, prickly sweat.

Eva. Eva and Audre.

He'd forgotten. He'd forgotten, because he had no experience with being needed. As a beloved author, he was a lot of people's favorite person. But no one had ever *really* loved him. At least not since he was little.

Shane was loved now. And Shane was happy. And he knew, without a doubt in his mind, that he'd made a mess of that, too. He'd been naïve enough to think that it could have lasted.

But Shane wasn't made for these things.

By the time Eva got home that afternoon, she'd stopped waiting for Shane to call. Instead, still wearing her fancy brunch dress, Eva carefully lay atop her duvet, balanced an ice pack on her forehead, and phoned her ex-husband.

"Eva!" Troy's voice was as crystal clear and enthusiastic as always.

"Hey! Just dropped Audre off; she's on her way."

"Fantastic. Athena's been making comfort food for her all day. Gluten-free, of course. And vegan everything. Chia-seed ice cream. Athena's a marvel."

"Sounds delicious," she said politely. "How are you, Troy?"

"Great! But not as great as you, apparently. I heard you're seeing someone."

"That girl *cannot* keep a secret."

"Is it a secret?"

"No. No, I guess not." Eva slipped her ice pack down over her eyes, where her sockets were *pounding, pounding, pounding*. Unconsciously, she fingered her cameo ring. "Can I ask you something? Was I hard to live with?"

"Nooo," said Troy, without taking a moment to think about it. "I just wasn't ready. You're complicated, you know? I thought you were a problem that needed solving. But you don't need solving. You need understanding. I was too young and too scared to figure that out."

After a lengthy silence, she curled up into a ball. "Thank you for that, Troy."

"So. Does he make you laugh? Really laugh?"

"He does, actually."

"I've always wondered if there was someone who'd do that for you. When we were together, I felt like someone else had stolen all your smiles before me."

He had, she thought, clutching her stomach.

"I hope you're happy together."

"Thank you," she said, so grateful to have Troy as a co-parent. "Take care of my baby, okay? She's so tough, but fragile. Don't let her sink too deep into herself, with the books and the art. Make sure she goes outside. And make sure an adult is present when she hangs out with Athena's godson."

"Why?"

"And remember she doesn't like cheese or condiments."

"I know. She's mine, too, remember?" he laughed. "Audre's always fine. She'll FaceTime you when she gets here. You take care. Bye, Eva."

"Bye, Troy."

Eva lay there for two hours as waves of ruthless, savage melancholy crashed into her. Last time, it'd taken years to get over Shane. Maybe this time it'd be easier.

When she finally pulled herself up, she stepped out of her dress, sat down at her desk, and cracked open her laptop.

She wasn't good at love. But at spinning a narrative? She was.

Cece was convinced that she'd be winning a Littie for Best Erotic Romance in a few hours. Eva didn't think so, but it *would* give the movie a boost. Energized, she googled that director, Eric Combs. Judging from his robust IMDb page, he knew what he was doing. With his vision, Sidney's production prowess, and her words, her movie would happen, the way she'd always wanted. They'd *will* it to happen.

With her face smeared with mascara tears, naked except for boy shorts, she pulled up her *Cursed, Book Fifteen* draft. Her deadline was tomorrow, but she could do this. She would turn heartache to triumph and *knock this shit out*.

Several minutes later, nothing had come to her. So she crawled into the back of her closet and yanked out a small plastic bin filled with three overstuffed notebooks. Sitting on the floor, she pulled out her journals. They were ages old, dusty, and worn. These notebooks had traveled with her from her mom's various apartments to the dorm and, finally, to her Brooklyn home. Each one had a name scrawled on the cover in Sharpie, in Eva's looped, rounded teenage handwriting.

One for her mom, Lizette; one for her grandma Clotilde; and one for her great-grandma Delphine.

The yellowing lined pages were filled with notes compiled from late-night family stories her mom would tell her, drowsy on downers, after her dates. Online research. Anonymous poking in Belle Fleur Facebook groups. Calls with Louisiana records departments. Since she was a kid, she'd done everything but physically go down to Belle Fleur to research. It was a lifelong obsession, trying to glue together the broken pieces she'd inherited. These stories were her life's blood.

On a whim, she called Lizette.

"Mom?"

"Clay?"

"Who?"

"What?"

"Are you dating a man named Clay? And do I sound like him?"

"Your voice is so *loud*, Genevieve. I was napping! Having the sweetest dream about Clay. Who isn't my lover."

"Who is he, then?"

"A professional Easter Bunny, lives up the street." Submitted without explanation.

"Great. Well, I hate to bother you, but I need you."

"Twice in one week? I'm flattered. You've never needed me for anything."

Lizette would never get it. Eva needed her for everything. She'd just never had her.

"Mom, you used to have an old scrapbook. Really old. The one with the photo corners framing black-and-white pics? I need to see photos of grandma and great-grandma. I don't care how faded they are." Lizette had let her look at the album only a couple of times. "Just...can you email anything you have? Like, now?"

Lizette fell quiet for a moment. Eva wondered what she was doing right then. What her house looked like. What she was wearing. "You always loved hearing stories about Clo and co."

"I loved hearing *you* tell stories. You're good at it."

"Well, where do you think you get it from?" Eva could hear the smile in her voice. "You ain't the only one's colorful."

"Believe me, I know."

"DNA ain't no joke, I'll tell you what." Lizette yawned. "I'll email you now. Say thank you."

"Thank you, Mom."

"You're eternally welcome, bè."

Within minutes, five scans popped into Eva's inbox. She opened them, fast—and then stopped breathing for a moment. What she saw leveled her.

The first pic was her great-grandmother Delphine. It *must've* been Delphine, because she looked to be in her early twenties, *1922* was scrawled on the corner of the photo, and she was olive-skinned enough to pass for Fauxtalian. She was perched on the hood of an ancient Ford, her bee-stung lips and flapper cloche hat signifying wealth. But the car and the fancy getup receded into the background as Eva immediately zeroed in on her delicate hands crossed on her lap.

Her delicate hands and her cameo ring.

The second photo was Grandma Clo. A bright-eyed beauty wearing a 1940s-era victory-rolled hairstyle and a wise-beyond-her-years expression. And the cameo ring on her fuck-you finger.

The third photo was Marie-Therese "Lizette" Mercier herself. It was a pageant shot—probably from the late seventies, considering the Sister Sledge hair. Her mom was wearing a winner's cape, a triumphant smile, and the cameo ring.

Eva's ring wasn't some suitor's gift to her mom. It had been passed down for generations, infused with the love, fury, and passion of these women. Her women. Her people. And their stories, like the ring, were now hers.

And finally, she knew what to write.

Chapter 26

SEVEN DAYS IN JUNE

THE LITTIE AWARDS WERE, IN A WORD, EXTRA. IT WAS THE BLACK BOOK world's big chance to celebrate itself. And since people born of the African diaspora tended to turn "celebrating themselves" into an art form, the festivities were lavish.

Also, it was open to the public for the first time *and* being streamed live on BET.com. The sponsors included Target, Cîroc, *Essence*, Nike, and Carol's Daughter. An exciting professional moment, to be sure, but Eva was adrift in a sea of conflicting feelings. Every feeling, it seemed. After writing (and sobbing and writing and sobbing) for hours, she was more than a bit delirious. Dizzy from pain. Loopy from meds. Fiercely proud of what she'd written. Desperate for waffles. Itchy from Spanx. And then, of course, there was her heart.

Eva was heartsick. She'd written through it, because she was a fucking pro. But the helpless, searing ache in her heart was too big. Ignoring it was useless. She refused to let it take over.

Because even bigger than her sadness was her determination. She was at the Litties, not just as a nominated author but as a woman on a mission. With every word she'd written, her purpose had become clearer than ever. Eva Mercy was focused on the future, her next step, and no one (not Shane, not even herself) was going to rattle her.

This new Eva, the *free* Eva, was tired of being rattled by life. How long had she lived being too terrified to show her real self? There was power in showing the messiness of her life and what it took to hold it together. This week had liberated her. And whether she liked it or not, Shane had a lot to do with it.

She felt free with him.

Goddamn him, she thought to herself, squeezing her eyes shut, wishing she could banish his ridiculously lovely face from her brain.

This isn't about him. It's about me. Occupying all the space I need to. Standing tall in exactly who the hell I am. A damned good mom and writer with a terrible disability who overcomes it every day and whose best work is ahead of her and whose ass is perched for the gawds in her dress.

Eva was wearing a vintage Alexander McQueen number she'd borrowed from Cece. The long-sleeve, sharp-shouldered leather minidress was a badass goth purple ("very Rihanna circa 'Disturbia'!" said Cece). And because she *truly* was committed to being her authentic self, she wore it with platinum door-knocker earrings and Stan Smith sneakers.

The outfit was symbolic. Gia's signature color was purple. Sebastian's fangs were platinum. And tonight, she was saying goodbye to them both.

But for now, she was sitting at a round table in the dazzling ballroom of Cipriani Wall Street. The space was already dramatic, with its grand, cathedral-like interior and mile-high ceilings—and tonight, it was all gussied up in Harlem Renaissance drag. The forty author tables were decked out with sumptuous silver-and-black linens and Jazz Age–inspired centerpieces—massive crystal champagne glasses overflowing with chunky strings of pearls. Lights were low, and a spotlight shone "Black Literary Excellence Awards 2019" on the dance floor. The all-female R&B band was clad in flapper gowns (the look slightly clashed with its "upscale Black barbecue" set list, which included uptempo hits by Frankie Beverly and Maze, Mary J. Blige, Teena Marie, Kool and the Gang, and several artists produced by Teddy Riley). In the middle of it all was a small stage with an art deco podium.

It was like a *Gatsby*-themed wedding. But with awards and no cake.

At the moment, Eva was applauding the weepy woman who'd just won Best Historical Fiction. Through grateful tears, she thanked her energy healer and LeVar Burton's *Reading Rainbow*—and then the emcee, OG actress and *Black-ish* star Jenifer Lewis, who had titled her recent memoir *The Mother of Black Hollywood*, announced that the ceremony was taking a short break so everyone could eat. Resplendent in a belted teal caftan and matching turban, Jenifer looked like a wildly chic fortune-teller.

As waiters served an already-congealed chicken paillard dinner, the band played a strikingly faithful cover of "Gin and Juice"—and the tipsiest folks hit the dance floor. (Including Belinda, who was celebrating her Best Poetry Collection win.) In the far back of the room, the people in the standing-room section—mostly fans, readers, and bookfluencer bloggers—were getting autographs and frantically updating their social-media accounts, while most of the nominees, besieged by nerves, stayed in their seats and picked at their chicken.

The tables were assigned by award category, and each had its own distinct vibe.

The authors at the Best Chick Lit table were *glam*—on the smoky-eyes-and-sequins level of Bravo reality stars on a reunion episode. The Best Biography table boasted scholarly fifty-something women with Kamala Harris hair and adoring second husbands. Each of the six HBCU alums at the Best Political/Current Affairs Book table sat there with weaponized Twitter fingers flying over their iPhones, smelling faintly of beard oil and weed. Meanwhile, the podcast bros from Best Sports Book were hotly debating the NBA draft to impress their one female co-nominee—a bored, pretty WNBA star turned writer who could've dunked on every last one of them.

Eva's table was the Best Erotic Romance nominees—an unlikely-looking bunch. Far from sex-crazed floozies, erotica writers were mostly mild-mannered moms wearing their church-function finest. Eva had known her competition for ages: Ebony Brannigan (*Thug Pa$$ion*),

Bonnie Saint James (*So Dark Her Desire*), Georgia Hinton (*Lust and Found*), and Tika Carter (*The Sinful CEO Part 7: Sluttily Yours*). Every year, they were nominated together. And every year, grande dame Bonnie Saint James won for her series about a raging nymphomaniac working as a female spy in World War II Paris.

Bonnie would probably win again, and this certainty made the evening relatively stress-free for Eva's group. While the rest of the ballroom was alight with nerves and halfway to wasted, the civilized erotica writers talked shop.

All except Eva. She was half listening to the gals, half keeping an eye on the door across the ballroom. Shane wasn't here. Surely, he wouldn't dare come? What would she do if he did?

It doesn't matter, she thought, force-feeding herself rice pilaf.

"Ebony, how *do* you type with those acrylics?" asked Georgia.

"The click-clack sound is so satisfying." She wiggled her fingers. "ASMR! Tika, what have you been up to?"

"I just started leading a collaborative e-course on romance writing."

"Wowww," said Eva, who didn't know what a collaborative e-course was.

"My latest workshop was about incorporating condoms in sex scenes," said Tika in her faux-lofty voice. She was from Gadsden, Alabama, but spoke like she starred in *The Crown*. "It's our responsibility to promote safe sex."

"Oh please," scoffed Georgia. "As Zane, the queen of erotic fiction, once said, if a reader chooses not to protect themselves because my protagonist rawed her sister's baby daddy during a conjugal visit, then her problems are bigger than condoms."

Tika cocked a brow. "Zane said that?"

"Well, I'm paraphrasing," huffed Georgia, and then she changed the subject. "Eva, what have you been up to, ma'am?"

"Me?" Lost in thought, Eva was not prepared to jump into this conversation. "Nothing, just listening to murder podcasts, mostly."

Tika gestured at her with her fork. "Aren't we due for book fifteen?"

"*Oh*," she said with a faraway smile. "You know I'm superstitious. I never talk about what I'm working on."

"Always so mysterious, Eva," Tika said with a smirk, sipping prosecco.

"*Very* mysterious," agreed Ebony. "We heard who you're dating! When, what time, and upon what hour did this happen?"

"Leave that child alone," said Bonnie, finally speaking up. She was a no-nonsense sixty-something woman who, no matter what she was doing, always looked like she'd rather be binge-watching *227*. "This isn't a high school cafeteria."

Isn't it, though? thought Eva, who saw a flurry of texts come from Cece, who was seated across the ballroom. Earlier in the evening, Eva had told her about Shane's brunch no-show—and was now regretting it.

Today, 9:23 PM

Queen Cece

Darling, are you hanging in?

Today, 9:25 PM

Queen Cece

Heard from him yet?

Today, 9:29 PM

Queen Cece

If he doesn't show up, I'll kill him. No, I'll let you kill him first.

Today, 9:33 PM

Queen Cece

EVA! You might want to check your FB fan group. I take full responsibility. I'm already drafting a letter to the catering agency, but I think one of the waiters at my party was spying on you and Shane. The redhead. How was I to know she was a CURSED stan? She looked so sophisticated!

Eva couldn't deal with Cece's texts right now, and she *definitely* didn't want to check her fan group. Her category was next. She just wanted to get through this with her head held high and then go home. Lamely, she tried to join the conversation but couldn't find an opening in Georgia's rapid-fire shop talk. She always spoke in romance-writer jargon, which was maddening.

"...and in my new novel, I can't decide if I should give my female lead a HEA or HFN." (Happily Ever After or Happily for Now.)

"Is her man worthy of a happy ending?" asked Ebony.

"Hard to say. He's somewhere between an alpha male and an alpha-hole."

"I love writing alpha-holes," sighed Tika. "Who doesn't enjoy a sexy jerk?"

"Sexy jerks are overrated," muttered Eva.

"Your vampire Sebastian's an alpha-hole, and he's fabulous," enthused Ebony.

"Is he?" countered Eva. "Every time he sleeps with Gia, he wakes up on the opposite side of the earth from her. He knows it'll happen, because of their curse. But he does it anyway. That's not sexy," she said with a pointed hair toss. "That's pathological."

"Gia's just as much to blame," Georgia pointed out. "She's not quite a TSTL heroine"—Too Stupid to Live—"but almost. No offense."

"None taken. Gia's definitely TSTL," agreed Eva, her eye sockets starting to thump.

Not now, she thought to herself. *I can't deal with an episode right now. Just let me get through this night.*

"She's a witch with magic powers," Eva continued, fishing for a gummy in her purse. "But in every book, she uses them to fight her way back to a depressed vampire. Or to hex the vampire hunters stalking her man. Never once did she consider saving herself. Figuring out how to break the curse. Or at least putting a love spell on some regular dude who she could have a functional relationship with."

"But then it'd be over," said Tika.

Eva smiled weakly, knives stabbing into her temples. "It would be, wouldn't it?"

She barely got out the words before she broke out in a cold sweat. Between the loud dinner chat, the uproarious laughter from the dance floor, the booming bass from the band (now tearing it up to "Where My Girls At?" by 702), and this conversation, the low-grade migraine she'd woken up with had surged to "possibly vomitous."

She needed a painkiller injection, quickly.

"You okay, honey?" whispered grande dame Bonnie, seated right next to her. The rest of the table had returned to their alpha-hole convo.

Nodding, Eva swallowed the gummy whole and fanned herself with the menu. She was on fire.

"I know what to do." Bonnie rolled up the sleeves of her Chico's blazer and grabbed Eva's wrists. Without warning, she held them against her ice-cold Sprite glass. Eva yelped at the shock. But then, in mere seconds, she started to cool down. Her rapid-fire heartbeat even settled a bit.

"Menopause trick," Bonnie said with a wink, ever efficient. "Listen, whatever's the matter, you'll overcome it. We're made of guts and gumption, honey. Guts and gumption."

"Great title for your next book." Eva managed a shaky, grateful smile. She scooted her chair back, saying, "Excuse me. Just need to call my daught—"

And then stopped herself. This was her go-to pain-emergency excuse when she needed an injection. She was sick of relying on it. So instead, she did something she'd never done before.

"You know what? I'm not stepping away to call Audre." Eva threw her shoulders back. "The truth is I . . . I have an invisible disability."

"A what?" asked Ebony.

"A disability. My head is fucking exploding, and it's so bad that, Ebony, your nose is melting into your face and I'm concerned that I might vomit on my borrowed Alexander McQueen. The edges of my vision are starting to fray and curl, like paper on fire. Can you imagine? When I was little, I thought it happened to everyone. I described it to my second-grade teacher once, and she thought my mom was giving me LSD. Wouldn't have been a reach, actually."

Bonnie grabbed her clutch. "My word, honey. Do you want an aspirin?"

Eva outright giggled.

"Thank you, Bonnie, but no. If aspirin worked, I'd be a totally different person. I'd be breezing through life like Chrissy Teigen! I'd be married to a pleasant pop star and hosting game shows. I, too, would be the funniest person on Twitter. I'd out-Teigen Teigen."

Eva was on such a roll, she didn't even notice that the women were looking at her like she was losing it.

"Actually, I just took an edible. And now I'm gonna find a ladies' room and shoot myself with a Toradol injection." She made a stabbing motion at her thigh. "No, it's fine, I do it all the time. Feel free to eat my chicken paillard. No reason to let free protein go to waste. See y'all in ten!"

Eva's words were slurring; her vision was blurring—but my God, was she *exhilarated*. Just by that one small (huge) admission! She felt unburdened, unshackled. With a triumphant grin, she confidently strode from the table and across the dance floor. Holding a temple, she pinballed through the maze of people—until she was sideswiped by Khalil. He grabbed her by the waist and dipped her dramatically. Without hesitation, she elbowed him in the ribs, and ignoring his wail ("SENSELESS VIOLENCE, SIS?"), she headed toward the back of the room.

The only thing standing between her and the exit doors to the lobby was the standing-room-only crowd of fans, book-club members, and Goodreads contest winners, just there to support their favorite authors. They were a lively bunch, rocking tees and totes repping their favorite books. One woman was dressed up like the cover of Tiffany Haddish's *The Last Black Unicorn*. Another was convincing Tayari Jones to sign her iPhone case.

Scanning the crowd for an opening, Eva lasered in on a group in the back. Wow, they were *especially* loud. And loudly dressed.

And familiar. They were...Wait...

Wait.

Barely five foot three in her sneakers, she rose to her tippy-toes and saw the witch hats, the brooms, the platinum *S* rings.

One woman held a sign with the pic of Eva and Shane eating ice cream. In Sharpie, she'd written, BEST OF LUCK TO EVA AND HER REAL-LIFE SEBASTIAN, TONIGHT! A dude had silk-screened Shane's photo on his tee, accompanied with a quote from *Cursed, Book One*: HIS EYES WERE A CURIOUS BRONZE. LIKE A TUMBLER OF BRANDY ILLUMINATED BY THE SUN.

Another woman, with a *very* familiar-looking coppery bob, brandished a poster reading HIGH SCHOOL SWEETHEARTS → BESTSELLING BAES! #SEBASTIANANDGIAAREREAL.

High school sweethearts? But...no one knew...

Eva squinted at the woman. *The red bob.* She slapped her palm over her mouth. It was the hovering waitress from Cece's party! Quickly, she checked the latest post on her Facebook fan group.

The *Cursed* Crew Group

Major fandom news...

I spotted Eva and Shane Hall at a Brooklyn party. VERY together. AND I overheard that they dated in high school. AND I overheard that Sebastian is based on him. We've found our Sebastian, kids. #staycursed

Eva's migraine was face-meltingly, unreasonably awful. And now she was being hit with the fact that her best friend would accidentally hire a *Cursed* fan to pass out shrimp.

Eva was horrified. She wanted to clean it up—to march up to that spying waitress and demand that she stop spreading lies.

But...they weren't lies. Shane *was* Sebastian. And they *were* high school sweethearts. Every author got inspiration from somewhere, and her muse just happened to be a real person. It was the truth, and it was hers, and she had nothing to hide.

A week ago, being exposed in this way would've killed her. But tonight, Eva accepted it. *She'd* done this. *She'd* whipped her fans into this frenzy over the years. She could finally see that their devotion was a testament to her work. To her, Sebastian and Gia were a burden. But to her readers, they were live-or-die love. Something to root for.

And then, despite her pounding head and rising nausea, clarity hit her. This was exactly what she didn't want. She wanted steady love. A love that was too ordinary to inspire fiction. A collection of sacred, small, everyday moments—not high-stakes drama. She wanted a relationship that was a choice, every minute of every day.

Fighting back tears, she wove her way to the group. Before anyone could react to her presence, Eva abruptly and enthusiastically embraced a fan wearing platinum fangs.

The group gasped.

"Eva Mercy, as I live and breathe!" exclaimed the fanged fan. "What's that for?"

"For staying with me all these years. In a ballroom of great writers, you picked me. Thank you."

With that, she made her way to the exit. Unburdened, unshackled.

Shane was pacing in the lobby, the muted sounds of music and applause floating through the doors. He'd been pacing for so long, he was beginning to worry that he'd never have the nerve to enter the ballroom.

The lobby was empty, except for a few photographers and junior publicists hanging around the step-and-repeat. Every so often, the doors would open, and people would rush through to the lounges. But no one bothered him, which was no accident. His expression strongly discouraged people from wanting to chat.

Shane had left the airport bathroom so quickly he hadn't gotten a chance to check his appearance. He was a bleary-eyed, unshaven wreck in the cobalt-blue Tom Ford suit he didn't remember buying or packing. Sore from head to toe, he'd been clenching every muscle in his body all day. He hadn't eaten. He was still reeling. He'd lost Ty.

By the time Shane had gotten to the hospital, Ty was on a ventilator and unresponsive. Shane held his large, soft hand, willing him to wake up. He bargained with him, promising Ty that he'd do everything to keep him safe, that he'd visit Providence once a month—no, twice a month. He'd buy an apartment in town, where Ty could stay. Shane told him that he'd never have to do anything dangerous for money again, that he'd give Ty whatever he needed. Finally, he recited the planets over and over, until his voice cracked and the futility of it made continuing too painful.

It was no use. Ty was gone. So Shane said goodbye.

His loss felt too great, too raw, to process. But despite how hollowed-out he felt, he willed himself forward. He could think of only one thing now: what he was going to say to Eva.

This time, he would be prepared. It wouldn't be like when he showed up a week ago, winging it. She deserved more than that.

He wrote an entire speech on the plane.

He practiced in the rental car he drove to the Litties.

And now he was rehearsing as he was pacing.

Shane was ready. Until Eva burst through the doors of the lobby, shocking the hell out of him.

She breathed in a dramatic gasp and then cringed, pressing a knuckle into her temple. He saw a flurry of emotions mar her expression, and then...nothing. An ice-cold, terrifying calm settled over her face.

Shane forgot everything he'd planned to say.

"Hello," she said.

"Hey," he rasped, and didn't recognize his voice. He hadn't spoken in hours. Clearing his throat, he walked in her direction. She crossed her arms over her chest, and, message received, he stopped in his tracks just a few feet away from her.

God, Eva was breathtaking, even in her remoteness. Shane's chest clenched.

"I'm sorry," he managed.

"Don't apologize."

"I can explain."

"So can I," she said crisply, and closed the space between them so they were a few feet apart. "I'm sure you have a good reason for standing us up. Maybe you forgot. Maybe it was too much, too fast. And fair enough. But you didn't just stand me up; you stood up my daughter. You don't promise things to kids and then disappear."

For reasons Eva couldn't know, this seemed to hit him like a punch to the jaw.

"Believe me," said Shane. "I know."

"It was just a silly brunch, but I thought…" Eva stopped, swallowed, and started over. "I know it's only been a week, but it felt…"

"Bigger," he said, his voice breaking on the word.

Just then, a group of women swept through the doors, on their way to the ladies' lounge, and the ballroom noise roared into the lobby. The women rushed by, ignoring them.

"I'm sorry. I'm sorry for letting you two down. Audre…She's incredible. You're both more than I thought I'd ever get, and I…I've never been held accountable to anyone before. This is new. I don't know how to do it yet."

Eva moved closer to him, searching his face. He couldn't meet her eyes, but he imagined what she must be seeing. His eyes rimmed dark, his two-day stubble, his features etched in grief.

"Look at me," she said.

When Shane's eyes met Eva's, his heart flared and burst, flickering out like a spent light bulb—and he wondered why the sweetest things in his life had to be poisoned with tragedy.

"What happened to you?"

Scratching the side of his jaw, he thrust his hands into his pockets.

The women passed back through the doors to the ballroom. Eva and Shane heard Jenifer Lewis order everyone to their seats, to get ready for the next category.

They didn't move.

"Tell me what happened," she whispered.

"One of my students was shot." *Say his name.* "Ty. And he...he didn't have anyone. He was all alone in a hospital, and he was hurt, with no parents who cared. Just like us. Remember?"

Eyes widening, Eva nodded.

"He'd been trying to call me. But I was too busy—I was happy, so I ignored him. I was so fucking happy." Shane shook his head. "He died today. He's gone. Thirteen years old. *Thirteen.* I promised him I'd be there, and I wasn't."

"Shane."

"I guess that's what I do to people. I don't deserve a family. I can't..."

His words were cut off, because Eva gathered him into her arms—and her grip was so tight, she almost knocked the wind out of him. "Stop. You deserve a family. It wasn't your fault."

Shane was almost too numb to react. But then, after a few moments, he slid his arms around her waist, pulling her flush against him. And finally his muscles released. He slumped against her, face nestled in the crook of her neck, giving in to the grief.

"It wasn't your fault," she repeated, pressing her lips against his temple.

Shane nodded, but it felt like nonsense—just the words people have to say when someone's hurting. He squeezed her tighter anyway, grasping the leather of her dress in his fists.

At some point, from inside the ballroom, they heard Jenifer Lewis's muffled voice announce Eva's category.

"Back to your seats, cullids! Time for the Best Erotic Romance award! Where my sex writers at? Chiiiile, good thing I don't write what goes on in my dirty-ass

mind, *y'all'd be filing for unemployment. I see you, Bonnie. You know I'm dirtier than you!*"

"That's you," Shane said.

"I know."

Neither moved, still holding on to each other. From far away, they heard Jenifer's booming voice over the mic, ordering the Littie president to hand her the envelope. She began reading off the nominees.

"It's not your fault," Eva repeated, louder this time.

Shane wondered if perhaps she was right. Maybe it was true, and none of this was his fault. And maybe there were people out there who could really let themselves off the hook. Maybe he could have been that person if he hadn't caused his foster mom's death or disappeared on Eva, or if he'd been there for Ty when he needed him. Until he learned how to absolve himself, *forgive* himself, he had no business escaping into a relationship with Eva. He'd just bring those demons with him.

And then, for the first time ever, Shane ignored what he desperately wanted and made his first truly responsible decision.

"I can't do this," he said. "Us."

Eva let out a tiny sigh and pulled out of the hug. Palming his cheeks, she rested his forehead against hers.

"No, you can't."

"And Louisiana..."

"I'm going without you," she said definitively. "It's fine."

"I don't want to hurt you or Audre," he said, his voice tinged with resigned sadness. "I'm not good enough for you yet. But I want to be, and I'll work on it. I promise."

Shane couldn't believe it was over, that they were dissipating like wispy plumes of smoke. It was impossible to tell what Eva was thinking. She seemed sturdy with resolve.

"Don't make promises," she whispered. "Our promises don't stick."

"Eva..."

"Just be kind to yourself."

"I'll try."

"Are you going to drink?"

"No."

"Are you going to hurt yourself?"

His eyes flashed with such pain that Eva dropped her hands from his face.

"Shane?"

"Nothing hurts worse than this."

Eva's breathing went choppy, and she shut her eyes, wanting to unsee the crushing vulnerability in his face. She'd never imagined that losing Shane a second time would tear at her like this, in new, adult places.

It was unbearable. So then, almost imperceptibly, she slid on a tough veneer, an old affectation that was pure Genevieve. Crossing her arms in front of her, she tilted up her chin with faux bravery.

"Here's a thought. Maybe we work better as a flashback." She shrugged broadly. "You know, meet once every fifteen years, for seven days in June. Make some memories. Move on."

"Maybe." He looked at her.

From the ballroom, Jenifer Lewis's voice boomed. *"And the winner is . . ."*

Eva and Shane stood there, unmoving.

"Eva Mercy! For Cursed, Book Fourteen*!"*

Shane immediately swept her into an embrace, his face aglow. And helplessly, she let go of the old armor and allowed herself to luxuriate in his arms, to breathe him in. One last time.

"You won," he whispered. "You won!"

She turned her face up to his. And because he couldn't imagine not doing it, he kissed her. A soft, bittersweet, lingering kiss that radiated through her, everywhere.

In a voice so low that Shane may have imagined it, Eva whispered, "And lost."

At the podium, Eva gripped the cool, heavy glass award in her palms. The lights were too blinding, driving daggers into her temples, so she couldn't make out faces in the crowd—which was good. Lord knows she hadn't prepared anything.

"Thank you. Really, just, *thank you*. You can't imagine what this award means to me. I grew up with these characters. They're in my DNA. And I'm so proud that my readers love them as much as I did. Which is why it hurts me to tell them this: there isn't going to be a book fifteen."

A guy brandishing a witch's broom at the back of the room let out a piercing shriek.

"I'm so sorry, sir." She swallowed. "For half my life, I've hidden behind these characters. I've hidden in general. I've spent so much time being scared. Scared of digging too deep into who I really am, for fear of what I might find. What ghosts I might confront, secrets I might uncover. Better to bury it all. I thought I couldn't be a successful person if I had demons. But what fully realized person *doesn't*? No one expects men to be flaw-free. Women are expected to absorb traumas both subtle and loud and move on. Shoulder the weight of the world. But when the world fucks with us, the worst thing we can do is bury it. Embracing it makes us strong enough to fuck the world right back.

"So instead of writing about Gia, a witch who uses her powers to fight for a man, I'm fighting for myself. I'm not even sure who I am, because I've been in hiding for so long. But I do know that I'm Delphine's great-granddaughter, Clotilde's granddaughter, and Lizette's daughter. I come from a long line of weirdos, outsiders, and misfits. *I'm* a misfit. And my purpose is to give us all a voice. I'm going to write their story, which is mine, too.

"But I'll always appreciate *Cursed*, and my readers, too. I wish I could've tied up the series for you, in a bow. But I couldn't. How do you finish a love story that you...you never wanted to end?"

She could barely eke out that last sentence.

"Anyway," she continued. "Thank you. For letting me write for you, for so long."

An hour later, Shane accepted his Langston Hughes Lifetime Achievement Award. At the podium, he stood in silence for five seconds, then ten. Twenty. His expression was unreadable to everyone.

Everyone except Eva.

Finally, Shane angled the microphone up and spoke five words.

"This is for the misfit."

And with that brief speech, which was tweeted and retweeted so relentlessly that both *Cursed* and *Eight* fans began calling themselves #MisfitHive, the 2019 Litties were a wrap.

Epilogue

It was midnight on July 4 in Belle Fleur. Genevieve Mercier, long-lost child of the bayou, sat gazing out the window of her aunt Da's guest bedroom. It was velvety black outside, save for the occasional firecracker illuminating the sky, the prismatic colors reflecting off the lake just beyond the house.

The horizon was eternal, endless, complete. All that existed was the swampy lake and a dramatic sky. America was celebrating itself—and Eva was feeling brave.

So she picked up her phone.

Today, 12:47 AM

    EVA: Hope this isn't weird. Just checking in to see how you're doing.

    SHANE: Oh! Hi! I'm good!

    EVA: Great! You are?

    SHANE: No. I'm sad, but trying not to be. Been trying to stay busy. Running 8 miles a day. Researching clean eating, again.

    EVA: Yeah? What are you eating?

    SHANE: Well...I get choice paralysis at Whole Foods, and end up going to the bodega for dinner. Have you tried Entenmann's

Lemon Iced Cake? Fucking triumph of unnatural ingredients. Idk. I guess I'm flailing. I don't really know how to mourn properly.

EVA: No one does. But maybe grief counseling could help?

SHANE: Maybe. But enough about me. Tell me about Belle Fleur. Everything.

EVA: It's heaven. Hot, humid, haunted heaven. It's such a vivid place. It's like, people settled here three centuries ago, and no one left. Everyone's related. The supermarket checkout lady asked me "who my people was," and when I told her I was a Mercier, she listed, like, nine ways we were cousins. I feel like I'm HOME on this bayou full of short people who inherited generations of farms and fields and stories and terror and rage and brilliance and resilience and gumbo and culture. And everyone looks like me!

SHANE: Everyone looks like you? The fucking promised land.

EVA: :)

SHANE: Eva, it sounds revelatory. Can we talk? I just wanna hear your voice.

EVA: I can't talk to you yet.

SHANE: Okay. I understand. Reading your words was almost as good.

TWO DAYS LATER...

Shane collapsed on the grass in the middle of Washington Square Park after running his usual eight miles around Lower Manhattan. He was bathed in sweat, sticky, and pissed off. Running was supposed to make him feel good. And it did, while it was happening. But after, when his heart was thundering, his chest was burning, and his darkest, most buried thoughts were suddenly excavated, crystal clear and loud—there was only one thing he wanted to do. And he couldn't. Shane couldn't risk hurting her, so he had to find a way to fix himself *by* himself.

He wanted to talk to her.

That was where Shane was—flat on his back, a mere six feet from a fleet of meditating Hare Krishnas—when he got a text from her.

A voice note. Just her voice.

"Shane? Hi. I said I couldn't talk to you yet. And I can't. I'm not ready to hear your voice, but I know you're in pain. So it might help you to hear mine. I'm just gonna talk, okay? Um. Where do I start? So, I'm staying with my aunt Da. She found me on Facebook's 'Belle Fleur Creoles' page after I posted that I was looking for a room to rent. Da is short for Ida. Two syllables takes too long down here. Also, she's not really my aunt; she's my grandma's second husband's niece, but no one keeps score. You'd love her, 'cause..."

Eyes shut, grinning, Shane folded his hands on his chest and drifted.

LATER THAT DAY...

Today, 3:23 PM

    SHANE: Wyd?

    EVA: Cowering in a corner.

    SHANE: WHY? You okay? What's wrong?

    EVA: I'm in mortal terror. Aunt Da's house is so charming. But it's been in her family since the 1880s. It's OLD, with water bugs, and there's a huge one on my bed.

    SHANE: Huge, like what?

    EVA: LIKE CHRIS CHRISTIE OKAY? LIKE UNCLE PHIL. HUGE.

    SHANE: Lol. You're in the South, right? Lean into it. Lure him into a mason jar, deposit him under the shade of a mighty magnolia tree, pour him a mint julep, and skedaddle.

EVA: I saw Aunt Da smush one with her thumb. Right on her kitchen counter. It crunched like it had BONES, Shane. And I crumbled. You know, feel such a kinship with Aunt Da. But when she did that, it hit me...like, wowww lady, we're from different worlds. SORRY, GOTTA GO, IT'S MOVING!!!

A DAY LATER...

Today, 2:40 PM

SHANE: Did the water bug eat you?

EVA: Yes, I'm texting from his larynx. What are you doing?

SHANE: Wondering how your head's doing in that humidity.

EVA: Truthfully? I'm in ferocious pain, rn. Still in bed.

SHANE: Fuck. Is there anything I can do to help from here? They got Seamless on the bayou?

EVA: Too nauseous to eat. You know what'd help? If you told me a story. An original one. Actually, no, I want a poem.

SHANE: You're v. demanding. Hmm. I'm a terrible poet, but I got you. Hold on.

SHANE: .....

SHANE: ....

SHANE: There once was a girl named Eva
I liked her the moment I see'd her
Wish I could live in her dimple
If only life were that simple
I was a fool to ever leave her
There once was a boy named Shane
Who'd kill to ease her pain
If only he could change the past

If only this poem didn't suck ass
But Eva has only herself to blame
EVA: This is my favorite poem of all time.
SHANE: It could've been better, but nothing rhymes with Genevieve.

THE NEXT DAY...

Mrs. Fabianne Dupre—or Mama Fay, as she was affectionately called—was one hundred and one years old, with a silver braid wound around her head, cheekbones that screamed Shoshone Nation, and no teeth. The whole town knew her because she'd taught math to four generations of Belle Fleur children—in the tiny schoolhouse behind Saint Frances Church, which happened to be the oldest American church built by Black people and the epicenter of Belle Fleur. Mama Fay knew Delphine, Clothilde, Lizette, and everyone else in the Mercier bloodline—so Eva made a call to the farmhouse that Mama Fay's granddaddy had built, where she lived with her widowed niece.

After the niece served Eva a light snack (meat pies, pralines, two slices of pecan pie, tea cakes, and sassafras tea), Eva settled in on Mama Fay's rickety, whitewashed porch. And Mama Fay, who was laid out on a wicker recliner, began regaling Eva with tales of the past. With dazzling precision. Mama Fay couldn't recall what she ate for breakfast, but she did remember leading the protest against Clotilde's teenage exorcism back in 1939.

"Your grandma'd be out there working in the hot sun, getting fits and head pains and all matter a vexins. She had a sickness, but it wasn't witchery. Her fool daddy was scared a her, that's what. His back went bad round fall '39, and he reasoned Clo put roots on him. Jay-zee Ma-dee Jo-seff." *Jesus Mary Joseph.* "His back went bad 'cause a fast women and slow horses, *not his own daughter*. Why women gotta be the cause a evilness in man? Now, I never got married. No, no, no, I ain't one of those *funny ladies*. I just won't fold myself up tiny so as not to put off no man. Anyway, Clo grew up and married a man same like her daddy. Scared. One spring they crops turnt dry, and the husband *and* the daddy *and* the same priest, Father Augustin, sprung a *second* exorcism on her. She let 'em. And went quiet for months. And then shot that husband in the shed. Let folks tell it, she shot him 'cause he was sanging a spiritual in there, and the holy noise poked the demon in her. Which I always took issha with. Won't no evil in your grandma. She couldn't long-divide for nothing, but she was a good girl. An *excellent* cook. And an *even bettah* shot."

Eva was listening but was soon lost in her own thoughts. For the first time, she could identify the striking difference between herself and her ancestors (aside from successfully mothering a child). She was the first to *almost* get love right.

Delphine, Clotilde, and Lizette had never been able to depend on their men. Because their men had never allowed them to be who they were—they'd crushed their true spirits, at every turn. But for Eva, Shane had done the opposite.

Mama Fay was "fittintuh" divulge even more details, but that's when Eva's phone rang. Apologizing profusely, Eva hurried down the porch steps and perched on an old tire swing hanging from the thick, gnarled branch of an ancient fig tree.

"Hi, Mommy," said Audre, her voice clear as a bell and giddy sounding.

"Sweetie! I miss you so much," she said breathlessly. She hadn't talked to Audre in three days.

"I got your package! With your cameo ring," she enthused. "I was shocked; you're legit giving it to me?"

"I legit am. I think it's supposed to be yours now."

"Why?"

"Long story. I'll tell you when I see you."

"Okay. Mom? I'm having an emergency." Audre's voice dropped to a whisper. "I'm at the mall with my Dadifornia friends, and we ran into The Boy."

"STOP."

"Swear. The four of us got ice cream and talked…and *ugh*, he's so cute, but I don't know if he likes me back. I don't know how to flirt."

Flirt! Eva wasn't going to survive the next five years. "Well," she started calmly, "what have you been doing?"

"For the past hour? Ignoring him. I can't even *look* at him. This is hard; I'd almost rather go back to being friends."

"But…isn't that all you are?"

"OMIGOD MOM YOU DON'T UNDERSTAND ANYTHING."

"Sweetie, don't raise your voice in public." Eva glanced over at the porch and saw that Mama Fay was asleep, her silver hair going glinty in the brilliant sun.

"How's Mr. Hall, Mommy?"

"I'm sure he's fine. But I want to hear more about The Boy."

Ignoring this, Audre said, "Do you think it's weird that he's gonna be teaching at my school? Like, are you guys cool?"

"We're adults, Audre. It's fine. We're friends."

"Yeah, that's what *he* said. Oh, when you talk to him, tell him that my stepmom, Athena, had a dermoid. When the doctors removed the cyst, it had a fingernail in it."

"What the whole *hell* are you talking about?"

"Just tell him. Love you, bye!"

And that was when it happened. As she tried to get up, Eva's foot tangled in the rope dangling from the tire swing. She tripped and fell, and the ancient branch snapped off the tree, toppling on top of her. Its jagged end landed just a few inches from her jugular. She easily could've died.

Of course, Eva had lived through near-death experiences twice before. That time in the house on Wisconsin Avenue. Then again at the hands of a dildo. And now this.

Eva believed in signs. She knew something dramatic was coming her way. She just didn't know what.

When she finally untangled herself from the swing, brushing dirt off her cutoffs and cursing to herself, she saw that Mama Fay had woken up.

The old woman laughed a little, a twinkly, tickled sound. "Mercier women. Y'all *do* get yourselves tangled up in it, don't you?"

THREE DAYS LATER...

Today, 3:14 PM

SHANE: I'm leaving 81 Horatio forever.

EVA: You didn't rent it for the whole summer?

SHANE: I didn't think that far. Yeah, so now I gotta find a new place. I'm in Crown Heights, right now, about to see an apartment. The fuck's Kennedy Fried Chicken?

EVA: Stay at my house.

SHANE: Absolutely not. That's crossing every line.

EVA: No, it's not! It's empty, for the rest of the summer. You'd be keeping an eye on the place. Really, you're doing me a favor.

SHANE: THIS FEELS WEIRD.

EVA: It shouldn't.

SHANE: YOU SURE?

EVA: YES, STOP YELLING. And what's a dermoid?

SHANE: You and Audre been talking about me, I see.

EVA: No, we were talking about her stepmom, Athena. Who had a dermoid.

SHANE: Ask Audre if Athena has pictures.

LATER THAT EVENING...

Today, 5:35 PM

EVA: Hey. I just arrived in New Orleans. I found the house that my great-grandma Delphine owned. The one who mysteriously left grandma Clo at birth, and moved to New Orleans to pass as a Fauxtalian? I met the granddaughter of her housemaid for coffee. She said Clo didn't abandon the baby at all. When Delphine's husband saw that Baby Clo was much browner than he and Delphine, he accused her of cheating—in the middle of mass at St. Frances! Then he ran her out of town. She wasn't cheating, of course. You and I know that Black folks come out all different shades and colors. But Delphine never forgave herself for abandoning her baby. Remember I told you she wrote a message in lipstick on her bathroom tiles, before drowning herself in the tub? *Passant Blanc*, the term for Blacks passing for white. She didn't just write it on the wall. She scrawled it all over her body, apparently. Her white son paid a fortune to the NOLA police to keep the scandal out of the papers and off record, to maintain the lie of his "racial purity."

SHANE: That's...chilling. The cruelties of colorism. And imagine what we don't know. What's her side of the story?

EVA: It's all pretty intense.

EVA: .....

EVA: ....

SHANE: You okay?

EVA: Sometimes I wish you were here. Experiencing this with me.

SHANE: It's all I think about.

THE NEXT DAY...

Today, 2:15 PM

EVA: Since I've spent the last twenty-four hours as a go-between, I've decided to start a thread with all three of us. Talk amongst yourselves.

AUDRE: Mr. Hall!

SHANE: Ms. Mercy-Moore! What's good? How's Dadifornia?

AUDRE: It's fun, but this year is different. I'm noticing things in a more...anthropological way. The differences between people, depending on where they're from. There's a North Cali accent! And people dress differently than Brooklyn kids. Like, they wear Fila instead of Adidas. You know, the older I get, the more my awareness of what is cool is heightened.

SHANE: I like that. There's a difference between being cool and being cool-aware.

AUDRE: Mr. Hall, you get me. Do you like our place?

SHANE: I do! But I miss you guys. It's hard being around your stuff, and not getting to chill with you two.

AUDRE: Are you lonely?

SHANE: A little. So. Your mom doesn't want me to ask you for therapy advice, butttt.....

EVA: SHANE.

SHANE: ...I lost someone I was close to, and it's hard. Therapy doesn't work for me. (No offense.) Any suggestions?

AUDRE: Mr. Hall, you should really go to therapy. Black men don't go, and it's an epidemic.

THE NEXT DAY...

"Hi. My name is Shane, and I'm an alcoholic—and a drug addict sometimes. I don't want to be here, but a little girl told me I needed to talk about my problems, and honestly, she's only twelve but she's really fucking...astute. So. I guess I'm here now. Or whatever. Yeah, so th-thanks for having me." He paused. "You're a great-looking crowd."

In unison, the Greenwood Baptist Church chapter of Park Slope Alcoholics Anonymous said, "Hello, Shane."

"He writes a lot better than he talks," whispered a bleary-eyed redhead in the back.

THE FOLLOWING MONDAY...

The day he'd moved in, Eva had sent Shane five huge dracaena plants from IKEA.

"For your protection," the note said.

Shane had no idea what this meant, but he watered those plants religiously. He even faced them toward the sun, to optimize the photo-synthesis. But one by one, like clockwork, they died. Shane didn't have the heart to throw them out, though. They were from her.

He did notice a funny thing, though. He was surrounded by deceased flora—but he felt better than ever.

VERY LATE THAT NIGHT...

Eva had written all day, and now her eyes were crossing. She curled up in Aunt Da's guest bed to take a break. She scrolled through her contacts until she reached Shane. After a beat, she called.

"Is this . . . you?"

"Hi," she said softly. "I just wanted to hear your voice. I wrote three chapters today, in Grandma Clo's house. In my mom's childhood bedroom."

"What was it like?"

"Surreal," she said. "I never had one bedroom, you know? There were so many, it's a blur." She grabbed the pillow under her head and held it to her chest, curling herself around it. "Can I ask you a question?"

"Depends."

"On what?"

"Nothing, just wanted to say it."

"I'm serious," said Eva. "Do you think this thing between us will ever wear off? Because I'm starting to feel like it won't. And fighting it seems . . ."

"Pointless."

Then there was silence, and Eva heard rustling on the other end of the line.

"The truth? I see you everywhere in your house. Everything smells like you. I hate walking out the door. Just wanna stay here, be surrounded by you." Shane paused for a bit. When he spoke again, his voice was low. Slow. Like he was delivering a truth he was hesitant to admit.

"I've been roaming around forever, and I've never been anywhere I wasn't itching to leave."

When Eva hung up, she stared at the ceiling for what felt like forever. If given another opportunity, could she trust Shane not to leave?

THREE DAYS LATER . . .
9:10 A.M.

"Hi," said Eva. They spoke first thing in the morning every day now. "What are you doing?"

"Nothing, just on my way to coach basketball at the Brownsville YMCA."

"Brownsville? Since when do you play basketball?"

"I don't; I'm trash. But I came to a realization. I need to mentor kids. I was doing it wrong before, getting way too close. Trying to save them because I couldn't save my foster family. Or you. It was unhealthy. With this, I just shout motivational shit from the sidelines, build some self-esteem, and go home. I mean...your home."

"Sounds perfect for you," she said. "Hey. Quick question. Would you come here if I asked?"

"You asking?"

Eva paused. This wasn't healthy. No, they weren't supposed to see each other. Wasn't the whole point of breaking up to focus on themselves? Work through past trauma? Separately? But Eva couldn't ignore the dissenting voice in her head wondering if maybe there was a chance they'd be stronger together.

Whatever curse had befallen her foremothers, Eva had broken it. She was in love with a man who embraced everything about her. She just didn't know if she had enough faith to accept it.

"Well, if you needed me," said Shane, "I'd come."

THAT AFTERNOON...

Audre was at a bonfire on Venice Beach, with her Summer Friends and The Boy. So fun, but the bonfire thing made no sense. It was almost ninety degrees. She had on a crop top, high-waisted cutoffs, and flip-flops. It was high summer. Why were they creating more heat? She loved California, but she'd never understand the way the natives thought.

Also, she missed her mom. They'd just chatted on the phone, and she'd sounded so *serious*. And distracted, as if she were speaking to Audre from galaxies away. Audre knew her mother, so she knew what was wrong. What was missing. And there was only one person who could help.

Audre scrolled through her phone and called the sneakiest person she knew.

LATER THAT AFTERNOON...

Today, 4:17 PM

CECE: Can you do me a favor?

SHANE: No.

CECE: I know it's last minute, but I need a panelist for the Peachtree Book Festival in Atlanta.

SHANE: No.

CECE: Please? One of my authors got sick and I have no one to replace her. The organizers called me, specifically, and asked for a recommendation. It'd be SUCH a feather in my cap.

SHANE: But I'm not even an author anymore. I've given it up. I'm a full-time teacher and part-time basketball coach who can't shoot free throws. Also, I'm house-sitting for Eva.

CECE: Come on. They're paying for everything! It's just a weekend. I won't mention that you owe me your life.

THAT FRIDAY NIGHT...

Eva was a fan of Atlanta. At least, the Atlanta she'd seen. She'd visited only for book conferences and signings—and the trips were quick, so she'd never had any non-touristy, off-the-beaten-path experiences. But it seemed to be a vibrant city with delectable food and fine men who spoke like André 3000. Also, it was the city that had produced Cece, so it had to be colorful.

When Cece invited her to Ken's "top-secret super-surprise" fiftieth birthday party in their hometown, Eva didn't need convincing. Especially since Cece was flying all her guests there.

Belle Fleur had become Eva's home away from home. So much so that she'd almost declined the invite in favor of the *cochon de lait* happening the same weekend. It was a Creole tradition, an outdoor feast featuring the roasting of whole pigs, zydeco dancing, games, and gossip. Apparently, Eva's great uncle T'Jaques won the pig-roasting contest every year, and this year the competition was fierce, because her seventh cousin Baby Bubba (who was eighty-three), had been seasoning his pig for *three whole months*. Plus, Eva's fourth cousin Babette-Adele was manning the craft tables, and she'd been spotted at Saint Frances Church's pancake breakfast, feeding maple-syrup-dipped bacon to a strapping young foreman who was not her fiancé, and Eva was dying to get the details.

Small-town life was delicious. And Eva had immersed herself in it, "from the roota to the toota," as Aunt Da said. She'd discovered her people. There was no denying it.

But there was also no denying that there was no cake fair, no *cochon de lait*, no Friday-night dance at Tibette Bros. Meeting House (established 1909) powerful enough to make her forget him.

Shane was the memory she couldn't escape. The bridge she'd never burn. The shiver she couldn't shake. Maybe this was just her burden, to carry the weight of missing him forever. Because who knew when he'd feel stable enough to be with her in a complete way? The reality was he might never get there.

But honestly—did that matter? He might never be fully emotionally stable. And Eva certainly wasn't the picture of glowing mental health herself. Maybe they'd always be disasters—but couldn't they support each other and grow together? No one was perfect! And maybe that was what real, adult love was. Being fearless enough to hold each other close no matter how catastrophic the world became. Loving each other with enough ferocity to quell the fears of the past. Just fucking *being* there.

Eva sighed, utterly grateful to be taking this quick weekend trip. This constant internal debate was exhausting. Hopefully, the change of scenery would clear her mind.

It was the first time she'd gotten dressed up since she'd left Brooklyn, and she really went for it. Smoky eyes; loose, side-swept curls; and a long-sleeve black floral minidress. Eva showed up at Floataway Café, a buzzy Mediterranean restaurant, feeling cute—and very proud of herself, because she was fifteen minutes early, so as not to spoil the surprise. The restaurant was breathtaking. A renovated warehouse, the space was intimate and rustic, with low lights, soft twinkly music, and open windows ushering in the balmy night air. And not a soul was there.

Eva knew Belinda couldn't make it, because she was on tour. And she wasn't sure who else was invited, but they certainly hadn't arrived yet, because except for the incredible-looking, slightly rockabilly waitstaff, the restaurant was empty.

A red-lipsticked hostess tapped her shoulder.

"Ma'am?" Her accent was honey. "Are you Eva Mercy?"

"Yes, I'm here for Cece Sinclair's surprise party?"

"Got it," she drawled. "Right this way, to the courtyard."

"Thank you," breathed Eva, fluffing her hair and following the woman across the empty restaurant. "Do you know if Cece rented out the whole place for the…"

Eva's words dissolved into a gasp. The courtyard was bathed in almost darkness, set up to be a romantic, garden-style café with the starry sky as a canopy. Clusters of gardenias nestled in painted pots, wafting their heady, sultry fragrance into the night air.

The hostess led her to a tiny table impeccably set with crisp white table linens and charmingly mismatched plates.

"You're a bit early," said the hostess, pulling out Eva's chair, "but the rest of the party's on their way. Our manager just said he heard there was a fender bender on I-85. Everyone's stuck in traffic, I bet. You must've just missed it!"

"Oh, makes sense."

The hostess nodded and sauntered off. Eva took a sip of water, pulled out her phone. She thought about texting Cece but figured she'd be caught up in pre-party stress. It was always chaotic, those moments before a surprise.

Instead, she indulged in her guilty pleasure. In her weaker moments, she scrolled through her and Shane's texts, reliving their relationship. It comforted her, remembering that it was real.

Listless, she plucked a gardenia from the vase on her table, sinking her nose into the velvety petals as she read.

It was real. She could almost hear him through the texts. Hear his slow, DC-inflected rasp, the way his voice dipped and slowed when it was late, too late to do anything except sleep, but they couldn't stop learning and relearning everything about each other...

God. His voice.

"Eva."

Eva whipped around. Shane. Standing at the entrance to the courtyard with the hostess, who winked at Eva, smiled, and raced back inside.

She had to be dreaming. Eva squeezed her eyes shut. When she opened them, he was there in front of her (looking like breezy, sexy perfection in a short-sleeve chambray button-down and black jeans). Before her brain could order her mouth to speak, he grabbed her by her shoulders, pulling her to her feet and into his strong arms.

"Shane!" she gasped, crushing the gardenia in her hand. "What... Why...are you..."

"Cece didn't tell me you were going to be here!"

"Of course I'm here—it's Ken's birthday! How could she invite you and not tell me?"

"Ken's birthday? I'm here for the Peachtree Book Festival."

"I've never heard of a Peachtree Book Festival."

"Me either! But what do I know? I never do any of that shit, so Cece asked me…"

"Cece asked you to come to Atlanta? To this restaurant? At eight p.m. tonight?"

Slowly, they released their grip and stood there, lightly embracing.

Hesitantly, Shane said, "She said it was for a panelist dinner."

"But you don't like people! How were you going to get through dinner?"

"My AA sponsor told me to push my limits socially. This is me growing!"

They looked at each other and at the romantic table for two and realized that Cece had once again used her infinite powers to orchestrate this entire thing. Inside the restaurant, they overheard the hostess saying to a server, "Skip the drinks menu, Paul. Just seltzer. Neither one of them drink."

Shane scratched the side of his jaw, chuckling. With a tickled sigh, Eva cast her eyes upward at the starry sky.

They'd been had.

The night stilled around them as they settled into the realization that they were alone together. After wanting it so badly. Eva took the gardenia still in her hand and waved it under her nose. She wanted to have a scent to accompany this memory.

"Would you have asked me to come to Louisiana?" asked Shane.

"Yes." Eva's gaze caught his. "Would you have come?"

"I had a bag packed. I was just waiting for the word."

"I think we were wrong to end this." Eva clutched the flower to her chest, where her heart was thundering.

Shane cupped her face in his hands. "It never ends, does it? Loving you never ends. Whether you're Genevieve or Eva. Whether I lose you for years or wake up to your face every morning. I love you. You're my home. And I want you forever."

Eva blinked up at him, eyes dancing. "Forever?"

Shane nodded, his mouth curving upward, slow and assured.

"Oh, *fine*," she whispered. "You can have me."

Shane beamed and ran his hand up the back of her neck, into her hair. Gently, he fisted a handful and tilted her head back.

Crickets chirped in that lazy midsummer way, gardenias scented the air, and the delighted waitstaff hung back, giving the lovers their moment.

They kissed, and they restarted, right where they stood.

Acknowledgments

I'm thankful to my entire family, but especially my mom, Andrea Chevalier Williams, and our extended Creole clan near and far, whose history is endlessly fascinating (but *far* less scandalous and dramatic than the Merciers', it's worth noting).

Huge thanks to my father, Aldred Williams. When I couldn't think of a title, I described the plot to him and he proclaimed, "Seven Days in June!" No hesitation. Honestly, I was both relieved and jealous.

I'm also thankful for the genius of my migraine doctor, Lisa Yablon, without whom I wouldn't have been lucid enough to write one word.

I'm grateful for the sense of humor and razor-sharp instincts of my literary agent, Cherise Fisher, who always gets it—and for the storytelling prowess of my impossibly clever editor, Seema Mahanian, who knew exactly how to make this story sing.

Huge thanks to my dazzling and wise daughter, Lina, for her patience in dealing with a constantly writing mom—and for giving me the best "Audre" advice. I took it all!

Finally, I'm eternally grateful to my Francesco, who inspired me in the most profound ways, and gave me the space (literally and figuratively) to write this thing when it felt impossible. With him, nothing is.

About the Author

Tia Williams had a fifteen-year career as a beauty editor for magazines including *Elle*, *Glamour*, *Lucky*, *Teen People*, and *Essence*. In 2004, she pioneered the beauty-blog industry with her award-winning site, Shake Your Beauty. She wrote the bestselling debut novel *The Accidental Diva* and penned two young adult novels, *It Chicks* and *Sixteen Candles*. Her most recent novel, the award-winning *The Perfect Find*, is being adapted by Netflix for a film starring Gabrielle Union.

Tia is currently an editorial director at Estée Lauder Companies and lives with her daughter and her husband in Brooklyn.